ELIDAD

EVA HULETT

Nikki,
Keep faith & justice
in your heart.

[signature]

Winter Goose
PUBLISHING
where words take flight

Winter Goose Publishing
45 Lafayette Road #114
North Hampton, NH 03862

www.wintergoosepublishing.com
Contact Information: info@wintergoosepublishing.com

Elidad

COPYRIGHT © 2017 by Eva Hulett

First Edition, January 2017

Cover Design by Winter Goose Publishing
Typesetting by Odyssey Books

ISBN: 978-1-941058-59-6

Published in the United States of America

To Mom

For never paying attention to the eyerolls or
"This is lame, Mom" comments when we didn't want to read

CHAPTER ONE

He banged again, louder this time. Then he paused, listening to the silence on the other side of the door. He hoped his desperation would reverberate through its hard exterior. Forcefully, he slowed his breath, straining his ear while waiting for some response—any sound of movement from within—but there was no answer to his unspoken plea.

His anxiety grew. Desperate for help, he reached for the handle, which he found unlocked. Turning it as quietly as he could, he cracked the door. Pressing his ear into the slight opening, again hoping to hear some movement, a sign to signify there was someone inside. Even if she had no intention of answering him.

His heart raced as he hesitated only a moment with the idea of trespassing. A feeling of hopelessness overwhelmed him, pushing forward through the barrier between him and his destination. The hopelessness evaporated as he entered and quietly closed the door behind him. His palms began to perspire. Being here was wrong, but he knew his purpose was more important than his feeling of unease.

The room was dark and musty, like the air itself was choked of life in the absence of the sun's rays. As he pressed deeper into the darkness, his eyes slowly began to adjust. The living room had been turned into a study. Every wall was lined with bookshelves appearing to have no beginning and no end, most of them cascading into the middle of the room. Every inch of the room was littered with composition notebooks and handwritten notes, some of which were crumpled and thrown around carelessly, others stacked in piles with spiral-bound notepads. The darkness didn't hide that these walls were the sanctuary of a recluse, desperately looking for something amongst the rubble of information.

Is this where she'd been for the last year, closed away in this room? He wondered if she was finding what she was looking for in this mess. Abraham bought the two-bedroom apartment in Alexandria for her after graduation. She preferred the small town feel to New York. Virginia was close enough to work in the city if she was needed, but spend most of her time in DC.

In the dim light that was trying to peek through large, heavy curtains on the far wall, he could see maps spread over a large wooden desk. One of them in particular looked very old and worn, marked with scribbles and calculations. A triangle outlined in red had a dagger driven through the middle of it, pinning it to the desk. He leaned in closer to see what was written under the blade.

"Do you always help yourself to other people's homes, Priest? Or are you starting your career as a cat burglar?"

The sound of her voice behind him made him jump.

"Good heavens! You nearly gave me a heart attack!" He brought his hand to his chest to make sure. "Have you heard of lights or answering your door?"

"Have you heard of trespassing?"

He shrugged. "You didn't answer the door because you knew it was me. What else did you expect me to do?"

She folded her arms stubbornly. "Yes, you're right. I have your knock memorized."

He could make out her figure in the darkness. She was much thinner than he remembered. Dark, untamed curls carelessly hanging over the shoulder of her wrinkled t-shirt gave him the feeling she hadn't been out of the house for a while.

"Do you think your life will be better if you stop answering your door?" His voice was accusing. "I suppose you stopped working, too?"

"Why should I work? Apparently, I'm not very good at what I do."

"That's not true, Elidad, and you know it."

She paused at hearing her name; she couldn't remember the last time someone used it.

She leaned against the doorjamb, crossed her arms. "Really, Aiden? If I'm so good at what I do, then why am I out of a job?" *Had* she been good at her job? She spent the last year wondering exactly that. If she was, as she had been told for so many years, then why did the leaders of the Catholic Church decide to let her go?

Aiden's silence lingered in the air as his response to her question. Remembering the last time he came to her house gave him pause. *He* had been sent by the leaders of the Church to inform her of their decision. Apparently she hadn't forgiven him yet. She spent most of her life studying the word of God, serving him, often risking her life protecting the Church and the people who worshiped within it. Without warning, the leaders decided her services were no longer needed. And without question, Aiden delivered that message. He felt his embarrassment rise in his cheeks. Pulling at the white tab in his collar he attempted to let the heat escape. He moved away from Elidad so she couldn't detect his weakness. "I regret hurting you like that," he confessed.

"You didn't hurt me," she assured, a little too quickly.

"It all did," he said sorrowfully, "you know, though, it wasn't my decision." He threw his hands up. "Don't shoot the messenger."

It was a lame attempt to lighten the conversation.

Her eyes narrowed, "Aiden, I've heard you say that a thousand times. You're stupid if you think you can hide behind that. When are you going to stop acting like a church drone?"

"A church drone?"

"Yes, you don't know what to think or feel unless they tell you what and how. You can't even tie your shoes without permission. You are their number one kiss-ass. I'm sure they are cloning you as we speak."

"The Church doesn't believe in cloning," he snapped. But he couldn't afford to fight with her; he needed her help. The reality that he might not be able to gain her cooperation began to sink in.

"Yeah, I know. There are a lot of things they don't believe in, aren't there?" she asked sharply.

The conversation was going in the wrong direction. She clearly didn't want to be in the same room as he, let alone help him. Maybe he'd been wrong. Maybe coming here was a mistake. To create more space between them, Aiden walked toward the curtains on the far side of the room. He hoped the distance would relieve the tension that had been steadily rising. It was too easy for him to make her angry. When he was near enough to the heavy material that hung drearily on heavy rods, he threw them open, allowing the sun to burst through the room like a tidal wave hitting the shore. He squinted at the stark contrast of light.

"That's better," he said as he turned, pausing a moment to take in the surroundings again as if they were new. "It's a lot less tomblike in the light," he observed with a half-smile, waving his hands over the mess.

Still standing in the doorway of an adjacent room with her arms crossed, she wasn't as amused as he. The light revealed how cruel the last year had been. When she came back from a stint in the Amazon as a missionary, she came back thin, but somehow looked healthier than she did now. Maybe she just looked happier then, content. The dark rings under her eyes were more than a subtle hint she hadn't been sleeping. Aiden wondered if she left the townhouse at all.

She'd always been a beautiful girl, full lips with high cheek bones made her look foreign. Her green eyes were striking; he could feel them searing into him with distain. She was muscular—apparently she was still working out—but looked like she lacked the ambition to take care of herself any more than that. Her hair was practically matted, her clothes in disarray. She had every right to look terrible, he felt guilty for judging her. What would *he* do with his life if the Church leaders decided one day that they were done with *him*? What would he do if they sent a man to his door to tell him he could no longer be a priest? What would he have then? His life would be over.

The last thing she needed right now was more stress.

Aiden remembered sitting here with her in this room after he told her the news. She had asked him over and over again, "Why?" But he didn't have the answer. They only gave him the message to deliver. He didn't ask, and they didn't bother to explain. It was here, in this room, that he shattered her whole existence. She had every right to be angry with him. In an attempt to avoid her eyes, he made his way to a large sofa that lined a wall facing her.

"Sure! I would love to have a seat, thanks for the invite," he said sarcastically as he plopped down on a dusty cushion. "Love what you've done with the place." He gestured, slightly chuckling, to a stack of books and littered papers.

"Are you going to get on with it, or continue to waste my time with your mindless small talk?" Her voice was cool.

Aiden knew she was hurting but she was still talking; she hadn't yet kicked him out of her house. Perhaps there was still hope for him.

"Get on with what?"

Her snort was one of disgust. "Come on, Aiden, the Church doesn't send you for nothing. I think we've established that. I know they want something from me. This isn't a social call."

"How do you know?" he said, feeling like a child.

She hiked her right eyebrow. "Because, I hear little boys are the *new* preference for social calls these days." A smile crossed her face as she caught the rage in his.

"Abraham is missing," he said, wishing his words would be an equal blow. He'd have to ask for forgiveness for that later.

"What do you mean *missing?*"

Aiden cleared his throat, ran a hand through his shaggy blond hair. "Did I say missing? I'm sorry; I misspoke. There really isn't any proof that he's missing, or that he's gone by any other means than his own."

She glared. "That's a load of crap. You wouldn't be here if you believed that. *They* wouldn't let you come if *they* believed that." She gestured to an imaginary entity outside the window. Aiden knew she meant the leaders of the Church.

"How long has he been missing?"

"Maybe six months," he said.

"Six months! How does a priest go missing so long with no one noticing?"

"Well, he was given a commission and was expected to be gone for some time . . ." Aiden was choosing his words carefully to ensure he wouldn't anger her further.

"What was he working on?"

Aiden shrugged. "I'm not sure. I don't think anyone knows."

"That's not the way it works, Aiden. He works on what they ask him to work on, or what is *approved* for him to work on, that's it. Someone knows what he was doing."

"No one told me."

"And I'm sure you didn't ask," she said, her eyes narrowing with disapproval.

"If it mattered, they would've told me." Defending himself against her felt like trying to stay afloat in an ocean during a storm.

"No, they wouldn't! That's exactly what I'm telling you! You're so afraid of making waves; you're blind to the obvious. What he was working on could be the reason he's missing. Of course it matters."

"I do know he was in Mexico. He's probably still there," Aiden said, hoping to appease her.

"I thought you said no one knew anything." Her voice was calm again, clearly agitated.

"No one knows why I'm here," he told her proudly.

She shook her head. "I highly doubt that."

Aiden sighed. It would be impossible to win her over. "They only *think* they know why I'm here. They don't know what I'm really going to tell you. Do you know Remiel?" he asked, trying to get her back on track.

"I met him a few times, briefly. But I know Abraham works with him frequently."

"Yes," Aiden agreed. "They became good friends and have been traveling together over the last couple years studying and teaching."

Her words overrode him. "Did he tell you where Abraham was?"

"He sent a letter, but no one talked to him. His letter told us Abraham went missing in Mexico." Aiden sighed. "His letter said a lot, but it left us with more questions than answers."

"Like what?"

"It was filled with pages of warnings, quoting the Bible, about the end of the world and the Antichrist. The Church thinks he's gone insane."

"Do they think *Remiel* is responsible for Abraham's disappearance?" Elidad appeared to be increasingly worried.

"It was discussed, but doubtful."

"How did they come to that conclusion? Did they make an educated guess?" Elidad asked mockingly. "Did they even bother to send someone to look for them?"

"Yes, they sent DelFlur," Aiden said proudly.

She rolled her eyes. "He's an arrogant ass."

"Yes, but he's the best." Aiden stopped abruptly, adding, "Besides you."

An audible sigh. "So, what did DelFlur find?"

"We'd like to know that ourselves." Aiden looked down at his hands to avoid her stare.

"What do you mean, you would *like* to know?"

Aiden continued to look at his hands.

"He didn't come back?" Elidad couldn't hide the shock in her voice. Aiden shook his head.

"There are *three* priests missing?"

He shifted on the sofa uncomfortably, clearing his throat. "They sent two more priests to look for them, and when they didn't stay in contact with the bishop, we started to worry."

"You *started* to worry." Her voice was condescending at best. "After five priests went missing, that's when you *started* to worry? What if

Remiel is psychotic? What if he killed everyone you sent, and you just kept sending them to slaughter?"

"There's no proof that any of them are in danger, I told you. We haven't even confirmed they're missing."

"Really, Aiden, and when will you confirm that? When you find them to ask?" Her body language made him feel smaller than he already did. She took a hair tie off her wrist, nervously pulled her hair back into a bun, and began pacing the floor.

He knew she was right, and wanted to crawl in a hole. "We just don't know for a fact yet, that's all. They aren't in contact with the Church. We're worried, but it doesn't mean they are missing or have come to any harm."

"Sure, Aiden. I'm sure you're right. I'm sure all five priests decided to take a trip together and not tell anyone. Now that you put it that way, it makes perfect sense."

As her voice elevated, his desire to leave did too. Aiden opened his mouth to speak.

"Are you an idiot?" she shouted before he could say anything. "This should've been handled better."

"They did the best they could," he protested, lowering his voice in an attempt to calm hers.

"No, they didn't. No one came to ask me for help. Why didn't you come to me?" she demanded.

Her eyes turned wild. If she could hurt him with a look, he'd be black and blue. Aiden looked away, afraid to make eye contact.

"Why? Why didn't you come tell me? No matter what they said, you should have come here first. You waited too long, Aiden. Abraham could be dead." The reality of her words was enough to stop her mid-thought. He *could* be dead. That thought brought a sickening feeling to her stomach.

Aiden hung his head. "I love Abraham too, you know. That's why I'm here now." With a surge of bravery, he looked up at her. "You will find him."

"I hope you're right." She took a deep breath, and looked out the open window to avoid Aiden's eyes. She always felt a sense of security, knowing Abraham was out there, knowing she could go to him any time she needed him. Now that security was dissipating.

"Where's the letter Remiel sent?" she asked, with dark thoughts flooding her mind.

Aiden smirked. "It seems to have come up missing."

She caught a flash of rebellion in his blue eyes. "What do you mean missing?"

"You know, lost." A grin widened his bold lips.

Elidad took a step toward him. "Where is it, Aiden?"

He took a self-satisfying breath as he reached into an inside pocket on his coat. "I told you, it's missing," he said as he withdrew an envelope. "And that's what I'll go to my grave saying, God forgive me."

A smile came across her lips. "There might be hope for you yet," she said, taking the envelope from him.

Turning it over in her hands, she examined the rustic exterior. The paper appeared to be handmade; the mill was coarse with thick fibers that were rough on her fingertips. Someone took the time to press this paper as thin as possible and square the edges precisely. Though it was not perfect, the paper had been folded nicely to form the envelope.

When she flipped it over, she could see the color of the paper was inconsistent from edge to edge with a teak yellow hue. A black wax seal was on the back with the face of a gargoyle pressed into it.

"Whose seal is this?" Elidad said.

"No one knows."

She looked over her hands at him. "You sure are helpful," she said sarcastically. "This paper is old," she observed as she began to open the envelope and withdraw its pages. Her hands moved delicately as she unfolded the small stack of paper. Bringing them to her face, she lightly sniffed them. To her surprise, they weren't musty-smelling as she'd anticipated. Their aroma was light and perfumey with a distinct oil scent.

"Very old," Aiden confirmed as he watched her peculiar investigation of the pages. "We can't be sure to the day, but around three hundred years," he said, watching her for a reaction.

"It looks that old."

Nothing seemed to surprise her, he thought. Either she was good at hiding her surprise, or she was always expecting the impossible. It made him wonder what she had seen in her life that made her this way. There were rumors of what she had seen and done, but they were so farfetched, he doubted half of them were true.

"Where does a priest get three-hundred-year-old blank paper?"

"All we know is that they might have been headed to the Metropolitan Cathedral. Remiel speaks about it in the letter."

"In Mexico City?" she asked.

He smirked. "I guess you paid attention in world studies."

"Abraham hates Mexico," she informed him.

"Who hates Mexico?"

She shrugged. "Nothing against the country. It's beautiful, but he gets sick every time he goes. He would be miserable for weeks, if he drank the water or not."

"That's where the postmark is from: Mexico City."

She turned the envelope in her hands. He was right. She hadn't noticed at first, but it was clearly stamped. Each page of the letter was handwritten in flawless calligraphy with what appeared to be a fountain pen, each line was crisp and straight.

"This is not the insane rant of a madman." She held the pages out for Aiden to view.

"How do you know?"

"Look at it, it's beautiful. It wasn't written by someone who was rushed or panicked; it's too methodical. Maybe he was under duress. Maybe someone was dictating it to him, but it doesn't look like the wild scribbles of a crazy man."

"Elidad," Aiden whispered, "I brought you the letter; no one was supposed to see it. They wanted it to be destroyed. If they knew I brought it here, I could be discharged."

"You'd probably be better off if they *did* discharge you."

"Yes, I'm sure. It's done wonders for you." He gestured around the room.

With nothing to say, for once, she glared in response.

Aiden rose to his feet and closed the space between them. "I regret that I'm always the one to bring you the worst news. I am sorry we never quite got along, but I'm here to help you now. I will help you find Abraham." He placed his hand on her shoulder to emphasize his sincerity.

"I don't need your help. I don't need anything from you."

"Actually, you're wrong. The bishop said that if you choose to help with the investigation, I am to be with you during your travels."

"No, thank you." She shrugged his hand from her shoulder. "I don't need help. You'll just slow me down."

"You don't have a choice, Elidad." His words were stern with conviction as their eyes locked. This was the first time he had stood up to her, face to face. "They won't give you their blessing unless I'm with you,"

She could see his jaw flex with his internal struggle. He was not about to give up any ground on the subject.

"I don't need their blessing." The anger in her began to flare as she mimicked his authoritativeness.

"Don't be a fool. Yes, you do. They won't correspond with you. They'll deny you access to all their information, and they won't give you safe haven abroad. Think about it. It would probably be nice to have some help with the traveling expenses. Like it or not, you need their blessing. You *know* you need it."

Feeling slightly defeated, she exhaled a sharp breath, shaking her head in frustration. He *was* right, though she hated to admit it. Without their blessing, life would be more challenging. Priests wouldn't talk to her, and travel would be more difficult. It would be hard enough to find Abraham. Without a blessing from the Church, she would lose precious time, and she had already lost so much. Looking him up and down, her eyes cut through him. "Why do they want you to go with me? You don't know anything that would be helpful. You are not an investigator. If their prize possession—DelFlur—didn't make it back, what makes them think you will?"

"They didn't have much of a choice," he admitted, "I was the only one who would go with you. No one else wanted any part of this. They're too afraid. And if I didn't go, you wouldn't either. I want Abraham home just as much as you do."

She considered his words for a moment, then straightened her shoulders. "We leave tomorrow."

"Okay." He was relieved she made her decision without much of a fight.

"We don't have time to waste. If you're not here, I'll leave without you." She forcefully pressed her index finger into his chest. "You know I can find my own way, Aiden, blessing or no."

He shrugged. "Yes, but this way will make it much easier."

"Not on you." She laughed as she dropped her hand back to her side. She was still holding the letter. "You aren't ready for this kind of assignment."

"I can handle it."

Shaking her head, she turned to walk back into the familiar darkness from which she had come. "No one is . . . *ever*. I trust you can find your way to the door."

Aiden watched as she once again became part of the shadows.

Could he handle it? Could he work with Elidad? She had despised him for years and even now she clearly couldn't stand to be in the same room with him. How could they hope to travel and work together? The reality is, he wanted to help Abraham, despite her hard feelings. He couldn't imagine someone holding the frail old man against his will.

Aiden was equally fearful for Elidad. Her life had been difficult, and he felt she might be losing hope in mankind. He wanted to reach out to her before her hatred won her over. Before she lost faith, Abraham was the only family Elidad had. He was the stability in her life. Without him, Aiden feared what she might do. He wasn't sure why he felt an obligation to be there for Elidad. They spent their childhood as adversaries, but now he wanted to show her she could count on people, and count on the Church.

He began to realize as he stood there alone, that the task he had chosen was much greater than he had originally thought. The important thing was he'd been successful in his agenda. All he needed when he came to her door was to convince her to help him, and agree to be helped by the Church. If she'd gone out on her own, they would've tried to make her travels more difficult. She didn't know it, but this was the best way. If he could find the strength to work with her, they might be successful in finding Abraham.

Aiden made his way back across the room, splitting the dust particles that floated in the sunlight. As they danced in his wake, he showed himself out.

CHAPTER TWO

Their plane lurched into the air. Elidad had called her priest in DC and requested the jet to be ready the night before. It made her feel like she was working again, though this wasn't the kind of case she imagined when she thought of going back to work. Headed to New York, the Church's jet was the fastest, low stress way to get to the city.

Elidad watched as raindrops streamed across the small window beside her. She was exhausted, having never really fallen asleep the night before. She tossed and turned all night with thoughts on where Abraham might be. What was he doing? Why wouldn't he be in contact with the Church? Was someone holding him against his will? Was he hurt? Or did he become so wrapped up in his mission that he simply had been too busy to contact anyone?

She closed her eyes for a moment, and tried to rub away the dryness.

Abraham wouldn't get so wrapped up that he would forget to make contact with his superiors. He wasn't like her. He followed protocol to the T. He would never disappear or work on his own without telling them what he was doing. He had served the Church for forty years. There was no other life for him. He stood by their every decision, backed every move, and followed all their rules. The reality this left was; he was somewhere stranded, injured, or imprisoned. It was common for missionaries to become martyrs or become imprisoned for their work, but not in Mexico. It was unlikely he was being held for ransom; kidnappers would've contacted the Church by now.

Elidad felt ill, thinking he may be injured somewhere, but it was better than being locked away. Who would imprison an old priest? In Mexico, they respected men of the cloth. And Abraham would never brake protocol and would report bi-weekly. There would have to be an amazing force keeping him from fulfilling his duties. His loyalty to the Church was the reason she hadn't talked with him over the last year. Through her pain of being let go, he sympathized with her, but ultimately he felt they had made the right decision. How could he? He knew her skills were unmatched by her peers. How could he feel that the Church was better off without her?

Abraham told her he felt they made the decision in her best interest, but how could that be? The only thing she'd been interested in her whole life was helping people. The pain she had felt at being discharged was bad enough, but to hear her father agree with them was unbearable. He taught her everything she knew. He trained her to be the person she was today, a soldier of God, and yet in the blink of an eye, he changed his mind. Did he regret raising her? Did he regret all those hours of work teaching her what he knew? Was she not able to become the warrior for whom he had hoped? Ashamed, she couldn't bear to face him.

The time had crept by over the last year. Many times she thought of calling, but never did. Getting lost in her studies, locked away from the pain of the outside world, a whole year passed and she didn't even know he'd been missing. She felt like she failed him.

The plane shuddered rhythmically in the storm, lulling her into a calm state. She closed her tired eyes, allowing her mind to drift to a place tucked deep in her memory—a place where green grass surrounded a tall, old building and a warm breeze washed over her like a security blanket, back to a time when life was less complicated.

The church bell rang out the twelve o'clock hour as children her own age were laughing in the surrounding yard, playing tag on a hot spring day. Elidad watched them from her hiding place behind a hedge. A smile came across her face at the sound their voices brought to her ears. She looked on, longingly, wishing she could play along, but knowing it was never as fun as it looked. The other kids tried hard not to include her in their games. Playing around her, they made sure she knew she didn't fit in.

From behind her, a cool breeze swept a voice across the grass. Looking over her shoulder, she expected to find someone standing close behind her. No one was there. She looked back at her classmates squealing with pleasure as they dashed over the freshly cut lawn.

Again, a voice whispered behind her. She swiveled around to inspect her surroundings. Had some of her classmates found her hiding spot? Were they trying to sneak up on her? She didn't see anyone. The only thing behind her was a large stained-glass window on the side of the brick building. In the center pane an angel stood, gallantly displayed with his hands outstretched, appearing to reach out to her.

Elidad stared at him as though *he* were the one hiding a secret. She stood still, holding her breath, daring him to speak again. It was he, wasn't it? Instantly, as if an answer to her challenge, the wind blew again, and she heard his voice, a whisper of a language she couldn't understand. His lips never moved, nor did his hands quaver from their certainty, and yet she knew it was he. She looked side to side, to make sure no one was there to witness her episode. She could hear what the other children would say if they knew she thought an angel spoke to her, an angel of any kind, especially one that had been soldered together. The wind swirled around again and the voice brought her eyes up to lock with his; looking into them, she knew he had something to tell her. Elidad knew where he stood, this angel of glass. She knew what door would lead her into the office where he stood watch.

Feeling the pull of curiosity, she swallowed hard, and in an instant of courage, she snuck out of the yard on a quest to find out what it was he wanted her to know. As Elidad neared the school hall, the severity of her task began to sink in. She wasn't sure if her classmates had seen her; if they had, they were sure to tell on her. But if she was lucky enough to go unseen, she was sure none of them would notice her absence.

Her heart pounded as she peeked down the long corridor that led to the office. She tried to move silently, sneaking past each door on the way. She paused at every little sound, fearing one of the sisters might find her. The punishment would be grave—she could see herself scrubbing toilets for a month. That thought slowed her steps, and her motivation began to dwindle. Suddenly panic-stricken, Elidad pressed her back against the wall, considering going back to the yard. She looked left to right. What was he trying to tell her? What was so important?

Elidad heard a noise. She quieted her breath, in hopes it would make her less noticeable. There it was again, the whisper, the same voice. Still, she didn't know what he was saying. Elidad turned and ran down the hall; she had to know what he wanted.

When she reached the door to the room where the angel in the stained-glass window was hovering, she pressed her ear to its hard surface. She'd seen the older children in school do this to listen to their teachers' conversations. It wasn't as simple as it looked. It was difficult to hear over her own breath. After a moment, she was sure there was no noise coming from inside the office. She pushed hard against the heavy wood with her small hands; the door opened slowly with a creak, and she slipped inside. Amazed at her accomplishment, she stood in awe for a moment.

She loved this office. It was warm and comfortable and smelled like oak and musty leather-bound books. It smelled like home. This was Abraham's office, and it had the only window in the building that displayed an angel. Elidad looked at him, confused. If he wanted to tell her a secret when she was in the yard, his lips were sealed now. No whispers came from him. She frowned, looking up at the angel with his hands outreached. *Why did you make me come all this way?* she wondered, still afraid to talk to him out loud.

The sky outside changed, as if a cloud was passing, and the window became brighter. The sunlight danced through the glass, and the angel's face glowed with light, much like she imagined a real angel's would. She never noticed before, but the light that came in the window shown through the angel's face and beamed down like a spot-light radiating on the surface of Abraham's desk.

In the light, Elidad found her prize, a large rough-edged book lying open on the desk. It was the book Abraham had been reading in class that morning. He was unable to finish the story, and she'd been upset when the bell rang, not wanting to wait till Monday to hear the end. Elidad planned all afternoon how she would beg him to finish the story at home. Even so, she knew he would make her wait to hear it with the rest of the children.

Her fingers touched the pages; they were warm from the sunlight. The book looked like it had been placed there, waiting for her. Was this what the angel wanted, for her to know the end to the story? Her excitement began to well up inside her as she slid the book closer. It didn't matter why she was here. What mattered was she wouldn't have to ask Abraham to finish the story; she could find out how it ended for herself.

"Elidad, I should have known it would be you." Abraham's voice made her jump. She turned quickly to face him. He was seated in a dark corner of the room in a large high-backed chair where he spent many afternoons reading and napping. She should've thought to look there.

Her lips instantly trembled, desperate to explain. "I only wanted to hear the end. I wasn't going to take it."

"Curiosity is not a sin, child. Perhaps though, asking would have been the better choice." Though he never raised his voice, he had a way of talking that made her feel terrible when she was in trouble.

She hung her head in shame. "I only wanted to hear the end. Next time I'll ask, I promise."

Elidad already made the decision not to tell Abraham about the whispers she heard, leading her to his office. It was easier for her to pretend it was the wind than to admit she thought she heard a voice. She was afraid that if she admitted it, the other children would eventually find out. They didn't need something else to tease her about.

Abraham smiled at Elidad as he came to stand beside her at the desk. "I believe you will, Elidad. I believe you will ask next time." He gently brushed the hair out of her face. "But might I ask, how did you plan on reading the rest of the story?"

She shrugged answering him matter-of-factly, "By looking at the pages."

He laughed at her honesty. "I realize that, little one. What I meant was, the book is written in Latin. How will you understand what it says without someone translating it for you?"

Elidad looked back at the large pages where she left them, under the spotlight of the window.

"Your Latin teacher says you are doing well, Elidad, but you have just begun to learn how to pronounce letters."

"I can read it just fine."

Abraham considered her for a moment. "Is that so?"

"Yes."

"And how did you learn?" He became increasingly curious at her demeanor. It wasn't like her to lie, but the fact was she had not yet been taught to read Latin. It was new to her studies this term. Though she was advanced in many of her classes, Abraham just started her in language.

"I don't know. I didn't learn. I just know."

The priest scooped the book up off his desk, walked to the window seat. Placing the book in his lap, he gestured for her to sit next to him.

When she sat, he placed the heavy book in her lap. "Here you are, child."

She looked at him, not understanding.

He smiled at her. "My eyes are tired from teaching." He rubbed them to convince her further. "You may read to me."

"*Me* read to *you?*" She sounded surprised; the uncertainty made him think he had caught her in a lie.

"Yes. If you wish to hear *me* read the rest of the story you can wait until next week with the rest of the children."

She shook her head. "No . . . I'll read it to you now." Her voice was cautious as she leaned over the pages.

"This is where we left off." Abraham pointed.

Elidad's little finger touched the word as her eyes took in the page. Abraham waited patiently. Without hesitation, the words rolled off her tongue, pronouncing each word as if she had spoken Latin her whole life.

"{11:9} *Et idcirco vocatum est nomen eius Babel, quia ibi confusum est labium universae terrae : et inde dispersit eos Dominus super faciem cunctarum regionum.*"

Hiding his surprise, Abraham smiled down at Elidad as she quickly looked up for approval after reading the first verse. He affectionately rubbed her back.

"Good, Elidad. Now, can you translate for me into English while you read?"

She pondered his question.

"If you can't, don't worry, it is very hard to do. Some grown men can't do this, even after studying for years."

"I can try, if you want me to."

"It would please me greatly."

Elidad looked down at the page, her words starting slowly. "*And . . . the . . . Lord came down to see the city and the tower, which the children built. And the Lord said, Behold, the people is one and they have all one language; and this they begin to do; and now nothing will be restrained for them, which they have imagined to do. Go to, let us go down, and there confound their language, that they may not understand one another's speech . . .*" Elidad stopped reading to look up at him. "Father, why didn't they do what God asked?"

Abraham stared down at her, momentarily speechless with her ability to read and translate the dead language so skillfully. With his mind spinning, he had difficulty processing her question. "What did God ask them to do, Elidad?"

"In the beginning of the story, God asked them to spread out over the earth, but instead they built a city and then they built the tower."

"Yes, Elidad, you are quite right. They were supposed to spread over the land and have children. That is what God asked of them." He patted her on the knee. "You have a terrific memory."

"But if that's what God asked them to do, then why did they stay to build a city?"

Abraham was amused at her young mind trying to understand.

"Why did you sneak into my office to read the rest of the story instead of staying out on the playground with the rest of the children?"

She shrugged, thinking of the voice, "I don't know. Something told me to."

"Yes, but you have been told that during recess, you are to stay in the yard with the rest of the children. So you have deliberately gone against what you have been told."

Elidad hung her head.

"Most of us try to do what is right and what God commands, but if we don't constantly read his word and ask for his guidance, the lines of what he asks and what we assume he wants often get crossed. Even though it appears you have broken a small rule by leaving the yard, you have not hurt anyone, or anything, what you haven't thought of is what would happen if you were hurt or lost. How would we find you? By breaking the rules, you have put yourself in danger. I think, Elidad, man most often makes the mistake of *thinking* he knows what is best and forgets to listen to what God commands." Abraham shook his head with regret. "And for this, man pays the price. Not just at the Tower of Babel, but time and time again throughout history. People's intentions, most of the time, are pure and true, but the seduction of sin over time can change our perspective. We reason in our minds that we have good intentions, and therefore cannot be doing harm. But going against God's wishes will lead to harm, even if we cannot see what our actions have put into motion. Always remember, the pathway to hell is lined with good intentions."

A look of worry came across her face. "It is?" she whispered.

He laughed again. "It's a figure of speech," he said, patting her knee, "but I do believe so, yes. They did disobey God's request. They did not spread over the earth. They built a city and a tower. Remember, Elidad, they said 'Come let us build ourselves a city, and a tower whose top is in the heavens; let us make a name for ourselves, lest we be scattered over the face of the whole earth.' They wanted to make a name for themselves. They wanted to be famous. Pride has always been a wedge between God and man. Modesty has never been our strong suit."

Elidad nodded, she remembered.

"Over the long process of building the tower, the architect became arrogant with the idea of his accomplishment."

"How long did it take?" Elidad said.

"No one knows, really, but experts believe it may have taken some forty years."

Her eyes widened. "Forty?"

"Building was a new idea at that time. Bricks did not exist before this. This is the first time they made bricks out of clay and baked them until they were hard enough to use in the construction. There were no tractors or machines to help them. Everything was done by hand. Nimrod was a pioneer."

Elidad giggled. "Nimrod? Doesn't that mean stupid?"

Abraham chuckled. "It does now, because of Nimrod's actions. Because he defied God, he is known throughout history as being stupid."

Abraham looked sternly at Elidad. "This is not a thing you want to be remembered for."

Elidad made a sour face, shaking her head.

"The persuasion of sin is so great, Elidad, over the time of the build, constructing the tower was not enough. He believed that its completion signified that he himself was godly."

"People build buildings all the time. Why did he think his was so special it made him like God?"

"This was before buildings existed. A building of this size had never been erected—maybe not even conceived. He thought he was equal to God for creating it. So rather than using the tower to praise God, he thought it would set him apart *from* God. God knew of the tower from the beginning and was concerned. The human race pulled together in a way they had never done before. They accomplished this task by working together. If they had accomplished this, what else might they be able to do? What destruction would they bring to the earth? What harm could they do? So he waited to see what the completion of the building would bring."

"What *did* happen?"

"When the tower was completed, Nimrod marched to the top and shot an arrow into the sky, *at* God."

Elidad gasped, "Why did he do that?" Her eyes were terrified.

"To defy God and attempt to challenge him."

Elidad's hand sprung to her mouth as though to silence a cry.

"As you can imagine, Elidad, God was furious. In response to his actions, a great wind came across the land and the earth shook. The tower crumbled, destroyed by God's command. As the bricks fell, the people of the earth parted in fear . . . fear for their lives. Confusion washed over the people as they scattered, their looks began to change, and they spoke differently. The people of earth were divided."

"What did God do to them?" Elidad said.

"This is when God created the races. He knew that if we were separated by something as simple as different skin color and speaking different languages, it would be enough to keep us from working together. It would cause us to fight amongst ourselves."

"He *wants* us to fight?"

He smiled at her. "No, Elidad, he doesn't want us to fight. He gave us the free will to be peaceful and love one another, although we do not. By giving us differences, he gave humans another target to fight, other than our own Creator. Fighting our Creator would be a war the human race would lose. God would be forced to end our existence."

"Would he do that?" Elidad said in a small voice.

"God has no wish to destroy the human race again; we do that just fine on our own."

"What do you mean again?"

"He has tried repeatedly to save us, Elidad. He has wiped mankind from this earth in an attempt to make us pure again, and in the end he has found that no matter what course of action He takes, humans will continue to be perverse by the temptation of sin. That is why He was forced to come up with another way for us to be saved."

The airplane's roar filled Elidad's ears while she studied a photo of her and Abraham. His arm was around her shoulders, they sat closely on the steps in front of their row house. Their smiles were as real as the happiness in the air that day. The day she left on her mission. Eight short years ago, she was fifteen, and Abraham's hair was darker, no sign of grey in his beard yet.

Aiden moved to a seat facing her, pulling her attention away from the photo.

"I'm sorry," he said.

"For what, being an asshole all the time?" She put the picture back in the open Bible resting in her lap.

"I'm sorry you have to look for him," he said, ignoring her comment.

"So am I."

CHAPTER THREE

The car that picked them up from the airport came to a stop in front of Abraham's townhouse. Old brick, wrought iron, and leaded glass stared back at them as they stepped out on the car-lined street. A horn screamed somewhere in the distance. Elidad glanced up and down the road. She noticed the night was darker than usual, most of the streetlights had burned out on the block. She took an extra moment to inspect their surroundings, and saw nothing unusual. Steam was rising from a grate in the gutter, its pungent smell wafting towards them on the breeze.

"Lord . . . what a hellhole," she said.

"This is a nice neighborhood," Aiden said.

"I meant New York as a whole. I hate it here. Abraham always tried to get me to come home. I just don't like the city anymore. Every time I left it just got harder to come back." She forced a laugh. "Stubborn old man. He got me here anyway, didn't he?"

After climbing the front steps to Abraham's door, Elidad set down her bag, fumbled around in the darkness, and ran her hand down the frame.

"What are you doing?" Aiden couldn't see in the dark.

"Looking for a key, unless you would like to sleep on the front step tonight." Her fingers continued blindly searching until she felt a slight crease in the wood.

Pulling a knife from her boot, the blade shimmering in the darkness, she used it as a wedge to pry the piece of wood trim away from the frame.

"I guess it's a good thing we took the Church's plane." Aiden observed.

"Why's that?"

"The TSA wouldn't let you on a regular plane with a knife."

"So you think." She smiled to herself as her fingers found the key in its hiding spot, quickly replaced the wood, and unlocked the door.

"Go ahead," she told Aiden, putting the knife away and turning to find her bag in the darkness. As she threw it over her shoulder, something on the other side of the street caught her eye. It was the outline of a person. Fearful he or she had seen the spare key's hiding place, Elidad strained her eyes to see who was there. The street was so dark she could only make out an outline, but she was unable to tell if the person was male or female. Whoever it was stood motionless, but appeared to be staring straight back at her. Elidad felt a chill run down her arms as she attempted to determine who was there.

Had the Church sent someone to keep an eye on her and Aiden? It wasn't impossible, but she deliberately didn't tell Aiden where they were going to avoid being followed. Requesting a jet from DC to New York might have been a giveaway. But they could have been watching the house since Abraham was missing, just in case he came home. Once she gave the cab driver directions it wouldn't be difficult for Aiden to sneak a text message. Either way, she wanted to know if they were being followed.

Elidad heard a car pulling down the street, it began to pick up speed in their direction. She didn't dare look away from whoever was standing across the street; she didn't want him or her to get away unnoticed. As the car came barreling down the street the headlights moved across the place where the figure was standing, but nothing was there. The car continued on its way and Elidad took a deep breath, shaking her head in bewilderment.

She bent down to grab her other bag, glancing one last time across the street, and paused. The landscape *had* changed. Where there had been a dark spot, the outline of a person, now there was nothing. She shifted nervously. Was it her imagination? Had her exhaustion finally gotten the best of her? If someone had been there he or she couldn't have moved before the headlights passed over.

"Do you need help, Elidad?" The sound of Aiden's voice behind her made her jump. She was glad he couldn't see her in the dark.

"No, I just thought I saw something," she replied as she turned to walk through the door. "It was nothing."

"Well, I need some help, I looked for a light switch, but I can't find one."

Elidad moved across the room and flicked the switch. In the light, she took a deep breath and exhaled a sigh of relief. Home at last.

"Now I know where you get it," Aiden said, looking around the room.

"Get what?"

"Your decorating skills." He smirked.

The living room had been turned into a study. Every wall was covered with bookshelves; books were scattered in every direction.

Elidad thought Abraham's study looked much different from her own. There were strange potions above pilot lights in glass vials waiting for Abraham to come home and light a flame to what experiment awaited him in their beakers. A metronome ticked like a clock next to a dozen flasks with varying colored liquids inside. There were open books scattered across all the tables. Composition notebooks were piled about the room, admittedly much like her own home, but she gave Aiden a dirty look for his comment anyway.

Elidad cautiously approached Abraham's desk, remembering how he used to look when he sat there. His readers on the edge of his nose, he would nod to himself possessing the information on each page, as if he were talking to an old friend. When she was young, she would crawl into his lap and he would read her whatever had captured his fascination for the month. New findings on the Dead Sea Scrolls, a new archeological dig in Israel.

She pulled the leather chair away from the desk and sat on the soft cushion. She touched the top of his desk as if to smooth the surface with her fingertips.

"We came here first to see if we could find out what Abraham's been working on," she said.

Aiden had been silently watching Elidad. "I was wondering why we didn't just go to Mexico."

"If the leaders in the Church won't tell you what he was working on, it must be important. And if it's important, it could be the reason he's missing. It doesn't make much sense to go to Mexico, not knowing what to look for. We could waste a lot of time there and find nothing. Its better if we have a starting point."

Elidad rummaged through the items on his cluttered desk, hoping to find some clue. One large book was lying purposefully on top of the other stacks of seemingly random mess. It was old and looked as if it might fall apart in a light breeze. The pages were frayed on the edges and black from years of people fingering through it. Elidad laid its spine on the desk while holding it upright. Letting the book fall open on the desk, she leaned over to see what page it opened to automatically. She read the top of the page aloud. "*In Heaven, his name was Morning Star (Lucifer), he was named this because he was God's most beautiful angel only the morning star could contend with his perfection. Even in a position of close fellowship to God, Lucifer could not be gratified. He was overly pleased with his supernatural gifts, his immortality, his closeness with God. And eventually, his pride became so great that he was angered at having a commander of any kind. He desired control of his own destiny and so he rebelled against God and all the Heavens. He recruited an army of equally discontented angels and waged war against God.*"

Elidad scanned the desk top again. Her eyes came upon an open Bible with highlighted passages, and she continued to read aloud.

"*And there was war in heaven: Michael and his angels fought against the dragon; and the dragon fought and his angels; and prevailed not; neither was their place found any more in heaven. And the green dragon was cast out, that old serpent, called the Devil, and Satan, which deceived the whole world; he was cast out into the earth, and his angels were cast out with him . . . Therefore rejoice, ye Heavens, and ye that dwell in them. Woe to the inhabiters of the earth and of the sea for the Devil is come down unto you, having great wrath (Revelation 12: 7-9, 12).*"

She looked up to meet Aiden's eyes. "I have no idea what he's working on," she admitted. "There has to be something in here somewhere, though. I thought maybe he'd been sent on an exorcism, and that's why they didn't tell you what he was doing. I thought maybe it had been difficult and that's why he hadn't been back. But this is not wording for an exorcism." She pointed to the highlighted page.

Aiden frowned. "Abraham is an exorcist?"

Elidad rolled her eyes. "Yes. He's been with the Church for the majority of his life. Of course he's an exorcist."

"How do you know that he wouldn't use those verses in an exorcism?"

"Because I know. The last part, 'Woe to the inhabiters of the earth and of the sea for the Devil is come down unto you, having great wrath . . .' that part would give a demon strength—empower it—and not weaken it."

"How do you know that?" Aiden asked again.

"You know why." She wasn't in the mood for games.

"I want to hear you say why or how you know. *I* didn't know that."

"Because, Aiden, *I* am an exorcist, *you're* not. Didn't you hear the rumors? Didn't your friends tell you? You've been with the Church long enough. I'm sure you heard."

He *had* heard the rumors, but he didn't believe them. Why would Abraham or anyone teach her how to be an exorcist? Why would they allow a female to do a priest's job? Is that why they decided to let her go? Had the line been crossed?

"We need to find something in here that will tell us where to start looking for Abraham," Elidad said firmly, cutting across his thoughts. She had no intention of discussing it further.

CHAPTER FOUR

For the next several hours Elidad and Aiden pored over books, searching for clues as to where Abraham might have gone. Looking up at the clock, Elidad realized it was almost midnight.

"There are a lot of rooms upstairs," she managed to say through a yawn. "If I were you, I would take the third door on your right. That bed is the most comfortable. I'll be in the room at the end of the hall, in case you get scared." She laughed, her voice trailing behind her as she exited the room.

She was now out of sight; Aiden could hear her making her way up the stairs. After he turned out all the lights and made sure the door was locked, Aiden turned toward the stairs. Standing at the bottom, he realized he had been in this house many times, but had never been upstairs. Standing there by himself, he let his thoughts take him back to the first time he'd been there.

"Aiden, I don't understand why you are so angry," Abraham told him.

"You don't understand, Abraham," Aiden blurted back.

Abraham smiled. "That is what I just told you, child. I *don't* understand."

The priest left him flustered. "Abraham, why does she have to be in our grade? She's little; she belongs with the other little kids."

"Aiden," Abraham said patiently, "we teach you to be accepting and understanding of others around you. I know this is a big change for your class, but you have to realize this is a big change for Elidad, as well. None of the kids in your class have been accepting of her move. Think about how stressful this is for her. She is three years younger than you."

Aiden tried to speak but Abraham held his hand up to stop him.

"It cannot be helped, Aiden. I know she is young, but she is smart, well beyond her years. She needs to be in a higher grade."

"Three years ahead?" Aiden couldn't see how she could be *that* smart. She barely talked, and none of the other children ever saw her study. How could *anybody* be that smart?

"Yes, three years, perhaps more in the future."

Aiden rolled his eyes at the thought.

"What I don't understand, Aiden, is why the students are so upset about her move. Why are they so troubled they thought it the right choice to send you to my home?"

"We don't want her around," Aiden said flatly.

"I am hearing that, Aiden, but what I am not hearing is *why*."

"The teachers make us include her in *everything*. She's annoying, and she's a tattletale. We can't do anything without getting in trouble. We can't have fun anymore."

Abraham nodded his head, smiling with acknowledgement. "So, Aiden, what I am hearing from you is that you all think Elidad should be refused the schooling she needs to challenge her mind. She should be refused the schooling that potentially will help her help other people and spread the word of God, and the reason she should be refused this is so that you will not have to be obligated to include her in what you do?"

Aiden opened his mouth to speak but Abraham cut him off.

"And she should be refused her education because you don't want her around so that you can go about your day breaking the rules and getting away with it? Is this what I am to understand?" His eyebrows rose, daringly.

Aiden hung his head. "Well . . . When you put it that way, I guess it doesn't sound so good."

Abraham rose from his chair and crossed the room, gesturing to Aiden that it was time to leave. "Aiden, it is a blessing that your peers look to you to be their speaker. It takes courage to be the voice for others. I know it took a great deal of courage for you to come here tonight." He placed his hand on Aiden's shoulder. "But in the future, perhaps you should fully analyze your purpose to make sure your argument is one of good cause."

"Yes, Father. I'm sorry," Aiden said quickly.

"Nonsense. I am glad you came here tonight."

"You are?" Aiden said, surprised.

"Yes, I am proud of your willingness to speak out for others, and I presume this will be a lesson you will not soon forget," Abraham said, opening the door.

Aiden stepped through the doorway and turned back to shake Abraham's hand. Glancing up to the top of the stairs, Aiden saw Elidad, tears streaming down her face, duck quickly around the corner. His stomach turned. Elidad heard everything. That night he was glad she heard what he said, and hoped his words would keep her away from the rest of the kids at school. He had actually bragged to the others about how he had made her cry. It only increased his popularity.

Aiden looked up at the top of the stairs, remembering the look on Elidad's face. He felt the sickness he had felt that night—regret. Aiden was ashamed now, and wished he could take it back. Since then, he'd asked God for forgiveness many times for his arrogance. Aiden was sure God could forgive the mistakes of a foolish boy, but he wasn't sure Elidad could.

Exhausted by the long day, a long flight, and hours of reading, Aiden quietly made his way up the stairs and down the long hall. Seeing a light shining from an open door, he paused, catching a glimpse of Elidad standing in a white towel in front of the mirror, her profiled silhouette giving away more than he intended seeing. Steam was drifting into the hall from the bathroom, bringing with it the light scent of jasmine. She was stunning, her figure perfect, water beading on her olive skin.

"Third door on your right, Priest," she said, not turning toward him.

Her voice snapped him out of his thoughts. "Right," he said quickly as he moved along, embarrassment motivating him to move faster.

Inside the room, Aiden dropped his bag and immediately crawled into bed. As he closed his eyes he could still see Elidad's figure etched in his mind. He shook his head and silently asked for forgiveness before drifting to sleep.

CHAPTER FIVE

Elidad was awakened by a sound in the middle of the night. She lay there, intently listening. She began to slow her breath to enable herself to hear well. *Did* she hear something? Or had she been dreaming? She sat up, straining her ears. Pushing the covers back, she gently glided across the floor toward her door she left slightly cracked. Hearing nothing, she decided to check down the hall. At Aiden's door, she pressed her ear against his sealed room, but all was silent inside. Convinced nothing was out of place, she retreated toward her bedroom, but paused. Turning back around, she noticed a dim light coming from downstairs. Earlier, she'd gone down after Aiden went to bed to make sure all the lights were off. Peeking around the corner at the top of the stairs, she could see a dim glow coming from the study. Perhaps Aiden couldn't sleep and decided to keep looking for clues. Elidad crept down the stairs, but she found the house quiet.

She moved cautiously around the corner, and found a fire burning in the fireplace, but the room was empty. Maybe Aiden had gotten up and started the fire, neglecting to turn off the light. It *was* a little cool on the second floor. She went to the hearth, drawn in by its inviting warmth. Holding her hands to the fire, she could feel the heat touching her fingertips and smiled as it crawled up her arms. She loved seeing the coals burn bright, gold and orange, crackling merrily.

A noise behind her jolted her out of the hypnotic stare, making her jump to her feet. Turning slowly, her intake of breath came fast across her lips. She stood as still as a statue, unable to move.

Staring at him a moment she finally was able to find her words. "Abraham, when did you . . . I mean . . . you can't be here."

He smiled back at her. "I assure you child, I am not."

"Where have you been?" she demanded, putting her hands on her hips. "The Church thinks you've been missing for months. I came all the way out here to find you." Suddenly angry with him, she waited anxiously for his explanation, but he didn't offer one. He just sat smiling at her.

"Abraham, this isn't funny. You can't just fake a disappearance to get me to come see you. What if the Church found out?" She felt silly chastising him. If she hadn't put off coming to see him, he might not have pretended to be missing.

"I am here with you now, Elidad. That's all that matters."

That's all he had to say for himself? He offered no explanation, and she was undeniably frustrated. How could he make her worry like this? Could he even understand what she'd been through the last couple days?

She wanted him to explain himself, but she could tell he had no intention of doing so.

"The Lord works in mysterious ways, Elidad," he said softly.

"And you try to follow His lead on that one?"

Abraham looked down at the open Bible lying on his desk and read it out loud. "Woe to the inhabiters of the earth and of the sea! For the Devil is come down unto you, having great wrath, because he knoweth that he hath but a short time." Abraham's gaze met hers as he finished the verse; his smile was gone.

"Abraham, why won't you talk to me?"

"Our visit will be short, child."

"Why? I just got here; I may as well stay now."

"I am proud of you, Elidad; you have done well with what you have learned."

His statement shocked her. She needed to hear him say that a year ago. Why was he telling her now? Was the last year of silence enough for him to realize how much he hurt her?

"Thank you," she answered, "but why aren't you answering me?"

"If you would listen, Elidad, I will answer your questions. But you continue to look for *your* answer, rather than listen to the ones I am giving you."

She looked at him dumbly, trying to decipher his words. She hated it when he talked in riddles.

"You are blessed, Elidad. Your mind has always been open. Don't let anything change that about you. You will need your faith to carry you through what is yet to come."

She was trying to absorb all he was saying, but her irritation was getting in the way. She wished he would just come out and say what he meant.

"What is to come?"

"I don't have much time. Elidad, I want you to remember, *the Lord thy God is one who goes with you to fight for you against your enemies to give you your victory.* Trust in Him, and you will find your strength."

"Why don't you have much time? Where are you going?" Before she knew it, she was shouting at him. She hoped the urgency in her voice would inspire him to answer.

Abraham pressed a single finger to his lips. "Shhhh . . . He is here, listening. He is always listening, Elidad. Remember, keep your faith."

He was talking like a mad man. Elidad was furious with him. She wanted to shake him. The room seemed to get hotter with her anger; the fire behind her was now searing her back. She took a step toward him, but stopped instantly. Abraham's eyes began to glow an eerie and unnatural green. The Bible on his desk burst into flames, and Abraham jolted to his feet, pushing his chair back. He opened his mouth to scream but all that came out was a bright green light. Horrified, Elidad stood still, not knowing what to do. The shock in her chest cemented her feet to the ground. She felt helpless. The room grew hotter and hotter until all the books on the desk began to burst into flames.

Abraham staggered backward, colliding with the wall, knocking a crucifix to the ground. When it smashed onto the floor, pieces of it shattered across the study. Finally regaining control of her senses, Elidad rushed toward Abraham to help, but was grabbed from behind. She turned to face whoever was holding her back.

A dark figure, like the unknown person who stood across the street, had her by the arms. She struggled to free herself, but his grip grew tighter. His face was so well-shielded beneath a dark hooded cloak, even though she was at arm's length, she wasn't able to see his face.

His hand was at her throat, and she began to kick and fight for her life. He was squeezing the breath from her. Her lungs hurt, desperately trying to move air past his constricting grip. Elidad tore at her assailant's flesh, attempting to inflict as much pain as possible. He didn't flinch, and his hold did not loosen. Elidad continued tearing at his skin, but as she did, her hands began to burn. She tried to claw at his face. When her fingers made contact with his skin, her hand caught fire. Every time she fought, the touch of his skin burned her as if she were reaching into molten lava. She could see the layers of skin on her hands bubble and peel back off the bone.

Elidad tried to scream in pain, but the only sound she could hear was the breath being choked from her. That and the searing of her own flesh was loud enough to muffle Aiden's voice.

"Elidad!" She heard Aiden calling for her. "Elidad!"

She continued swinging at the dark figure in front of her.

"Elidad, stop!" Aiden's voice was clear and angry. She opened her eyes and stopped swinging her arms, realizing she was still in bed, with Aiden trying to hold her arms down.

"You were dreaming," he panted. "I heard you screaming from down the hall. When I came in, you weren't breathing. When I tried to wake you, you attacked me."

Tears were streaming down her face. "It was Abraham; he came to warn me."

Aiden reached forward to touch her face, and drew her to him. "It was just a dream."

She shook her head. "No, it wasn't."

Aiden put his arms around her. As she allowed him to hold her, she held up one of her hands behind his back, turning it over and over. She studied it front to back, amazed it wasn't burned or covered in blisters. She had expected to see the flesh falling off, just as it was moments ago.

"It was so real," she whispered.

Aiden wasn't sure if she said it to him, or herself. It didn't matter; they sat in silence as he held her in the darkness of the room, her body trembling against his.

CHAPTER SIX

"I'm fine, Aiden, really." She was looking back at him, standing in the doorway as he closed his bag and zipped it shut.

"Do you always dream like that?"

"Yes."

He frowned. "You always stop breathing?"

"Well not like that, but nightmares, yes. No one has the job I have without . . ." She paused for the right words. ". . . Side effects."

"Maybe you should consider a new career."

"Funny, I was about to suggest the same thing to you."

"Why should I?"

"I think it scared you more," she said as she walked out of the room. He rolled his eyes when she was gone.

Aiden poked his head out of the room to see where she was going. She was standing in front of a door with her hand pressed against it.

"Are you sure you're okay?"

"Will you stop asking me that?" She was annoyed.

Turning the handle, she pushed the door forward and disappeared into the room. Curious, Aiden followed her. There was very little in the room. It looked like everything had been stolen out of it. There was a bedroll on the floor with a very small pillow leaning against it. Candles surrounded the mat: some stood on their own, while others were in tall holders. All of them showed how long they had been there, their wax dripping down onto the floor, pooling against their bases. Aiden thought it looked like a room from the middle ages.

There was only one table in the corner. Pictures of Jesus were the only decorations adorning the walls. Each picture was different, but all depicted his teaching and crucifixion.

The only personal item in the room was a Holy Bible, lying on the floor next to the bedroll.

"What does he use this room for?"

Elidad smiled. "This is Abraham's room."

Aiden looked at her in surprise, searching her face to determine if she was telling the truth.

"You of all people should appreciate it."

Confused, he didn't understand what he was supposed to appreciate.

"Isn't this what you preach? Being close to God has nothing to do with worldly possessions?"

"Yes, but I've never seen any other priests, or bishops, live like this," he said. Wide-eyed, he looked around the room again.

"And that's what sets him apart from all of them." She contemplated her statement. "One of the many things that sets him apart. He lives what he preaches. He believes that we all carry God within us. We just have to choose to be close to him. He would always tell me that God talks to all of us, we just have to listen . . . It's a choice." She stopped abruptly.

"What?" Aiden knew something had come to her.

Elidad dashed out of the room, and Aiden followed closely as she descended the stairs. She slowed as she came around the corner into the office, as if she expected to see the dark figure jump out of the shadows. She looked from corner to corner as she walked toward the fireplace where she sat in her dream.

She looked into the ash.

"What are we looking for?"

"I don't know. But he told me in my dream that if I listened, he was giving me the answer to my questions, just not the ones I was asking. I was so angry with him. I kept asking where he had been, but he kept talking about other things."

"Elidad, it was just a dream. I'm sure it felt real . . . Everyone has dreams like that."

She shook her head. "This was different, Aiden. This meant something."

He looked up to the sky for help; there was no talking her out of it.

"I know how it sounds. But it *is* different. I can't describe it." She sat at the hearth. "I was sitting here and he just appeared at his desk. He read me a passage from the Bible that was open on his desk. After he read it to me, his eyes began to glow, and the Bible caught on fire. He tried to get away from whatever it was inside him. I wanted to help him, but that's when the man grabbed me." Though she hadn't seen his face, she decided last night the mystery person was a man. His build and his energy were manly. "He grabbed my throat," she described as she stood, lightly touching her neck, remembering the burning in her hands. "I was on fire." Elidad crossed the room to where Abraham's Bible still lay. She picked it up by the binding and ash cascaded out of it, down to the desk and floor. Stunned, Elidad looked to Aiden to confirm he was seeing what she saw. They watched as the pages of the Bible fell like drifting gray snow. What was a Bible the night before, was now a pile of ash.

"How?" Aiden whispered.

"I don't know." She stared at the empty binding in her hand. The cover was untouched by whatever flame had burned the pages within.

"Elidad, you aren't doing this to be funny, are you?"

"This isn't funny, Aiden," she laid the Bible back on the desk as if it were a ticking bomb. She stepped back and looked at Aiden again, his eyes still on the Bible. Elidad glanced back at the fireplace, worried the shadow man might be there after all. She was terrified of him, but decided to keep that to herself. Instead, she moved around behind the desk to stand where Abraham stood in her dream.

"Abraham told me *he* was listening, that *he* always listens."

"Who?"

"I don't know. But when he told me, his eyes started to glow green and the Bible caught on fire. He stood up and stumbled backwards," she explained as she mimicked his actions. Her back hit the wall when she flailed her arms wildly, bumping the crucifix hanging behind her. She turned her head towards it as it swung on its nail. "When he fell back against the wall, he knocked the crucifix down, and it broke." Elidad pulled it off the wall. Turning it over in her hands she inspected the back. There was nothing. No distinguishing marks. "It doesn't look special."

"It was only a dream, Elidad." Aiden was trying to sound reassuring, even though he was beginning to doubt that was the truth.

She smiled, hearing the uncertainty in his voice. "I hope you're not scared, Priest. This is only the beginning."

Aiden fidgeted. "I'm not scared. It was only a dream."

"I told you, you aren't ready for this." She winked and simultaneously threw the crucifix to the floor.

She and Aiden both turned away from the fragments that flew in all directions. Even with their heads turned, the sound of something metal hitting the ground was unmistakable over the shards of pottery cascading to the floor. Turning back, Elidad crouched over the majority of pieces to carefully paw through them. Gently overturning the clay, she uncovered a large gold key. Its color was dull and scratched from what Elidad guessed to be decades of use. It was as long as her hand and had an intricate design cut into the shaft. Rare gems sparkled like fire and were pressed into the metal.

"I have seen this somewhere," Elidad said thoughtfully, as she held it up for Aiden to see. "Look familiar?" Aiden didn't answer. "Why was Abraham hiding it?"

"It's important," Aiden said quietly.

Elidad's eyes snapped from the key to him. "How do you know?"

"I don't think I am supposed to tell you."

"Aiden." The anger in Elidad's voice was apparent.

"I know . . . I know . . . I *will* tell you, but I am pretty sure I'm not supposed to, that's all." He took a deep breath. "When a new bishop of records is elected, there is a secret initiation for him. During that initiation, the old bishop passes a key to the new one. The key that is passed is very similar to this one. Almost identical."

"What do you mean almost? How do you know it's not the same key?" Elidad asked.

"Because, that key is silver and this one," he pointed to the key in her fingers, "is gold."

"How do you know they are identical? When did you see it?"

"I was allowed to be present at the last inception. I am the youngest priest to have ever attended the ceremony, and my presence was tolerated only with the recommendation of Abraham. Look at it. If you saw one just like it, you would know."

He was right. You wouldn't forget what it looked like, and she couldn't imagine another key resembling this one on accident. It was unique. She wasn't an antiquarian, but she was sure it was old, and the stones were real.

"Please tell me you know what this means," Aiden asked hopefully.

"I have no idea. What are the keys for?" She was equally hopeful he would have an answer.

"I don't know," Aiden admitted.

"You never asked?" Her eye twitched with annoyance.

"You don't ask questions like that, Elidad. It was an honor to be present. I just assumed it was an old ritual. I thought it represented something, but was simply decorative, like a nice necklace. I didn't know we would find another one just like it hidden in Abraham's office after he had gone missing. How was I supposed to know it was important?"

"It is important. Important enough Abraham wanted you to know about them. Why else would he have asked you to be present during the ceremony?"

"Maybe it's just a coincidence," Aiden offered.

Elidad shook her head. "You said yourself: you are the youngest priest to be present for the ritual. I don't think it's a coincidence. He wanted you to know about the key. Did he think somehow you would find *this* key? And if so, why would he enter *my* dream?" Her voice trailed as she turned the key over.

"Enter your dream?" Aiden echoed. "Now you're really sounding crazy."

She ignored him. "I might know someone who can help with this." Elidad turned her attention back to Aiden, looking him up and down. "Did you bring anything else to wear?"

"Like what?" He sounded insulted.

"You know . . . normal clothes."

"These *are* normal clothes," he said, looking down at his dark pants and clerical shirt.

"Yea, for a priest," she smirked. "It doesn't matter." She waved off his attempt to object. "I have a friend we need to go see. She might be able to tell us about the keys, but she won't be around till later. Meet me here at eleven. I'll be back then." Elidad turned, slipping the key into her pocket.

"Should I go with you?" Aiden called after her.

"No. Stay here."

"Where are you going?"

"Out." He barely heard her reply.

CHAPTER SEVEN

"You can let me out right here," Elidad instructed her cab driver. The sidewalk was full of pedestrians, like herded cattle pushing in different directions. Elidad sighed, wondering why God hadn't destroyed this city yet. Every street was lined with sin, breeding evil on every corner. A person could get mugged on the street and no one would notice. She was positive people would *see*, but no one would notice.

Elidad turned down a small alleyway where, nestled between large modern buildings, set back from all the commotion on the street, a single storefront was hiding. The door was encased in old sturdy stone. The stone was hard and unmoved by progress. The newer buildings surrounding it seemed frail against the hardened structure of this timeless architecture.

The wooden sign above the door was just as old. Weathered by years of punishment from the elements. The letters, flawlessly hand painted, looked as if they had been recently redone. Elidad tilted her head back to take in the full view: "Isaac's Import Books & Treasures." Smiling to herself, she pushed through the front door as a bell cheerfully chimed to announce her arrival.

Elidad loved the cluttered chaos that dominated every square inch of the store. It would take months to make an itemized list of everything. No place was left vacant. Piles of trinkets were stacked on top of piles of gadgets. Masks hung on the walls, accompanied by old paintings and wrought-iron art. Totem poles stood proudly on the far wall with dream catchers cluttering a corner, hanging like chandeliers from the ceiling. There were glass containers with potions and powders lining a wall behind a sturdy counter where an antique cash register showed its age. Elidad stood at the counter, expecting someone to greet her. At the end of the counter a stack of chests leaned precariously to one side, some with leather straps and metal clasps. She smiled to herself. Isaac had given her a trunk when she left home to further her studies as a missionary in Brazil. She ended up taking it with her around the world and every time she opened it she imagined herself standing here, in the shop.

Elidad ran her fingers down the smooth, polished counter. It was strange Isaac hadn't come out front to greet his customer. Perhaps he was out back receiving new items for the store, probably haggling over the price of an antique. At the end of the counter, Elidad pushed a curtain aside and slipped into a private room that was hidden behind it. It was a small library, cozy, with a large leather sofa along one wall. Elidad had fallen asleep there many times growing up. She and Abraham had spent many late nights here with Isaac, the two of them telling her stories of their travels. She loved every story and memorized every detail, often replaying them in her head, imagining herself in their place. Their stories left her dreaming of the day when she would see the world on her own.

Isaac was a good man, and a good friend to Abraham. He was intelligent, knowing the value of every antique that crossed his path. There were few things about which he lacked knowledge. Elidad hoped Abraham would have told Isaac where he was headed, and what he was working on. She placed her hand over the pocket where the key rested, wondering if Isaac would know about it. Would he know what it was for? She hoped Abraham would have told him, knowing this would be the first place she would come.

"I'm sorry, you can't be back here," a voice said softly behind her.

Elidad turned to face the man who spoke. She looked him up and down. "I'm sorry, who are you? And where is Isaac?"

The man smiled back despite her tone. "Forgive me. I thought you were someone who wandered in here off the street; you are not. You must be Elidad." He bowed formally.

She eyed him carefully. He spoke formally, not looking much

older than herself, maybe twenty-five.

"How do you know who I am?" She was sure they had never met.

"A picture Isaac keeps of you and Abraham behind the counter. I have heard many stories about you two." A smile came across his face. "I feel as though I know you already."

"But you don't."

It wasn't like Isaac to leave the store or have someone else run it. The store was his life; she had never seen him take days off other than holidays and Sundays—those days the shop was closed.

"So where is he, then? Isaac, I mean." Elidad hoped her demand came across as sharply as she meant it.

"On leave."

She frowned. "To where?"

"The Holy Land. He said he wanted to make the pilgrimage one last time. Life is too short. He said his life was getting shorter by the minute."

Elidad couldn't help but allow a wisp of a smile skim past her lips. "That sounds like something he would say."

She considered the man standing in front of her. *Would* Isaac have left the store to just anyone? Who was this man and where did he come from? Isaac didn't have any family left, the closest family he had were Elidad and Abraham, and with both of them absent, perhaps he felt forced to choose someone to run the store that he wouldn't have chosen under normal circumstances.

"Who are you?"

"How rude of me. Forgive me for not introducing myself." He appeared genuinely embarrassed for not offering an introduction earlier. Bowing to her again, he said, "My name is Lucian De'Lucius. I have known Isaac through the antique trade for many years, and I was given the opportunity, and *honor*, of keeping Isaac's shop while he is away." He stood straight again to meet her eyes. "He told me you may show up, and if you did, I was to give you anything you want."

"Isaac told you I might come?" Elidad was still skeptical of Lucian but if Isaac trusted him with the store, perhaps she could, too.

"Yes, months ago. He said that while he was away would be the time you would choose to visit."

Elidad smirked. "I wish he would have told me. I don't suppose he said anything about hearing from Abraham, did he?"

Lucian furrowed his brow as he thought on it. "No, I think Abraham went on a mission. Isaac had not heard from him in a couple of months, but he wasn't concerned. He said Abraham was in the middle of something important and had been gone longer than he originally anticipated. Abraham was supposed to come back to watch the store, but he sent word that his trip would take longer and he would be unable to fulfill his commitment. Isaac was in a difficult spot; he told me he didn't want to put his trip off any longer. His plans were made and tickets purchased, so I offered to run the store until Abraham came back. I had no idea I would be doing it for this long." He seemed amused. "I do enjoy it."

"Have you heard from Abraham at all, or did any letters come here for Isaac from out of the country?"

"No." Lucian shook his head. "Isaac was the last one to talk with him. I am still waiting for his return, or Isaac's."

"When is Isaac supposed to be back?"

"Another month, as long as nothing prolongs his stay."

"I would count on Isaac making it back first," Elidad told Lucian.

His eyebrows rose. "Did something happen to Abraham?"

"I don't know. But it's not like him to be gone this long and not tell anyone why."

"I don't mind staying as long as I'm needed. This really has been fascinating, and some days challenging."

Elidad searched his face, trying desperately to read him. Was he being sincere? What was so fascinating about antiques? His tone was even; she didn't feel like he was being sarcastic. How could he be serious?

"Fascinating?" Elidad repeated.

"Yes, quite."

He had a soft look about him, though he was a well-built man. She could see the form of his chest through his shirt, and his short sleeves revealed his sculpted arms. He didn't look the type to be hanging around antiques all day and being pleased about it.

"How did someone so young become so interested in antiques?" she asked, realizing her tone was patronizing.

He smirked. "How does someone so young become so interested in devoting her life to God?"

"Touché."

"After all, antiques are just artifacts of the past." He offered, "The Bible is another artifact that helps you understand the past, a past that you are dedicated to knowing and sharing with the world. Perhaps we are interested in history in very similar ways."

Elidad found his view interesting. Not many men in her life could pique her curiosity so quickly.

Lucian's hair was dark, slightly shaggy, with wispy curls on the ends. His eyes were friendly—an intriguing green against his dark skin. He was proper in his posture, like he had been educated and raised well, or more likely, well off. He was confident enough; he knew he was attractive, but seemingly modest about it. Elidad could feel her face begin to flush as the realization of *how* attractive he was began to sink in.

"I grew up spending most of my time in my uncle's antique store," Lucian said.

Elidad turned away, crossing the room in an effort to hide her embarrassment.

"It wasn't as large as this store, but it was a busy place in the town I grew up in."

"Where are you from?"

"Port Jervis."

"That's a small place; I can't imagine anything being busy there," Elidad said jokingly.

"My uncle utilized the internet. It was where we lived most of the time. Buying and selling antiques all over the world, I can't say we stayed in one place for long. We spent most of our time—and always felt most at home—in Port Jervis. I think my uncle liked to pretend we came from a small place."

Lucian's accent was noticeable, and until now she had not been able to pinpoint where he was from—now she knew why. He had grown up all over, picking up whatever accent he was around, trying to fit in as a kid. She knew how that felt.

"Is there anything I might be able to assist you with?" he asked politely.

The truth was, she *did* need help, but she wasn't sure she could trust him yet. Abraham had gone to great lengths to keep the key a secret, and it might be the reason he was missing. "I don't think so. I am not even sure what I'm looking for, really. I am hoping I will know it when I see it. I have a feeling I will find something in the shadow books."

His smile became twisted. "Into some light reading, are you? I hope you don't plan on sleeping tonight."

Turning to walk to the bookshelf behind her, she mumbled to herself, "Not if I dream like I did last night."

"Bad dreams?"

"You could say that." Elidad was surprised he heard what she said. Her fingers rifled down the books on the shelf until they came to a small black snakeskin cover with the words "Fallen Angels" embossed in a deep, gleaming red.

"Well, I shall leave you to it, then," Lucian said as she tilted the book off the shelf until they both heard a click. She replaced the book back in its place, turning immediately to the sound of a groan beside them. They stood in silence as the floor fell away to reveal a staircase beneath. "Let me know if I can assist you, Elidad," Lucian told her.

"Thanks," she said, smiling more comfortably at him. "I will."

He tipped his head toward her before turning to leave the room as she started down the stairs.

CHAPTER EIGHT

Below, Elidad could see what she knew to be a single torch burning in the darkness. The spiral stairs echoed every step she took toward the light. Above her, the hole in the floor began to close. Hearing the door lock into place above, she continued her descent. These stairs were one of the many wonders that Abraham showed her in her life. The stone walls surrounding them were thirty yards away in every direction, and encompassed them on all sides like a cylinder, but never touched. It was as if the stairs were hanging in midair by magic. There was no handrail on the staircase, just wide open sides making her feet naturally drawn to the middle of the steps. The edge gave her an insecure feeling, like standing cliffside.

When she finally came to the landing where the torch was burning, Elidad paused to look up at it. The stand was just as she remembered. Gold and gems crowned its resting place. Mirrored pieces were pressed into the gold to reflect the light around it. The torch was nothing less than beautiful. Pulling it down from its stand, she could feel the heat from the flame kissing the top of her hand. After walking to the edge of the landing, considering the darkness below, she tossed the torch over the edge. Elidad watched as it fell silently into an infinity of darkness. In an instant, the golden glow was only a speck in the dark. Soon its light was extinguished by the obsidian ocean beneath, but as usual, no sound came to signify the end of the fall. Waiting in silence, she remembered the first time Abraham brought her here. Back then she had been afraid of the dark, even with him by her side tightly holding her hand.

"Where do the stairs go, Father? How far down do they go?" she had asked, trying to break the silence of the deep blackness.

"I pray, child, that you will never have to know the answers to those questions." His voice echoed around them. Elidad could still hear it in her mind—the sound of warning heavy in his voice. Even as a child she knew not to keep asking. His words made her *more* afraid of the darkness and whatever was hiding beneath them.

A flame sparked up in the void behind Elidad. She turned to see the torch burning rightfully in its place on the pedestal. This time, in the flame's light she could see a passageway on the opposite side of the stand. Elidad passed the torch, entering the dark tunnel. As she continued into the darkness, torches began to light themselves along the way. It was as if they were alighted by her presence, ignited by the echo of her footsteps that followed her down the long corridor. The passage came to an end where a stone wall proudly displayed two torches, flickering in a light breeze that was pushing down the hall. She considered them for a moment as she removed her necklace. On the end of the heavy chain was a straight pendant in the shape of a rectangle. The metal was thin and had a design carved on the face of it. Elidad held it in her hand as she stared up at the burning torches.

The stone wall was oddly built. It looked like there had been an archway where a passage opening had been at one time, and was now closed off to trespassers. Elidad stepped forward and began to trace a grout line on the wall, starting at the floor. Tracing the line up over her head, she followed it back down to the floor again on the other side of the stone. Standing up, she knocked on the wall, her fist reverberated on the stone like a bell. As the wave of sound rolled through the wall, a keyhole appeared in the rock. Holding her pendant in her hand like a key, she inserted it into the glowing hole and turned it. The light that illuminated the keyhole began to move around the seam between the stones that she had traced. The ground began to quake as the arch before her became a door and groaned open. Elidad stepped over the threshold. The door moaned in protest, and slowly closed behind her.

Luxurious high-backed sofas were crowded in the center of the room, their claw feet perched neatly next to one another. Each high-back was home to multiple beautiful pillows, each more detailed than the previous, all outlined with gold cord. On the far wall a fire roared in a fireplace which ten men would have fit into easily. The mantle above held a massive clock showing the movements of planets, rather than the hours in a day. All of its hands glistened as they rotated, each signifying its own planet.

Elidad had always thought this room belonged in medieval times, like she had passed through a time portal to a king's private library. In the corner was a table fit for the Knights of the Round Table. Seven chairs padded with plush pillows were gathered around it. Each chair was carved by hand and signified a different bird of prey. The birds on the back of each chair looked alive. The reflection of firelight gleaming in their eyes. Their claws were inlaid with ebony and their feathers brushed with gold and silver. The fire touched everything in the room. Ten glass cases lined one wall, each containing a different book.

Elidad remembered when Isaac had installed the cases. He had bragged that they had some humidifying technology to keep the books safe. He had been so proud, only the largest museums in the world had the same technology. This library made the one upstairs seem like a small bookshelf. The shelves disappeared into the darkness above, giving the illusion that they never ended, going on forever into the sky, or rather, into the underground of the city. Elidad had often wondered how all these books came to be in this room. There were truckloads in here, all containing important information on innumerable topics.

Priests in the Church came here when they needed information on things that couldn't be found anywhere else. Elidad had come with Abraham, many times as a child, in the middle of the night to lead various people of various importance into the depths of the hidden library. At times, Isaac and Abraham would bring books up to people at the library upstairs, depending on the situation. The library downstairs was kept a secret from most.

"Why do you have to bring them books, Father? Why can't they go get them themselves?" Elidad asked, hating the climb back up the stairs.

Abraham looked at her in his understanding way. "Unfortunately, Elidad, not all men can be trusted."

"Then why do we bring them the books at all?"

"The people we bring books to have good reasons to look at them. They have good intentions for the information. So we allow them to see the books and learn from them and once their research is complete, we will return the book to its rightful place, all the while keeping the library's location a secret."

"What if they find out where the library is? What if they go when we aren't around?"

Abraham shook his head, "This is a concern, and we try to make sure this does not happen."

"How?"

"The store always has a storekeeper, but the passageway is protected."

"How is it protected?"

Abraham paused to consider her question. "The library has a spell on it."

"A spell? Like witchcraft?"

Knowing this would be a hard concept, he patted her arm as if to reassure her. "No, not like witchcraft. Just a good protective spell. Harmless."

"What does it do? How does it protect the library?" Her question came out as a whisper; she knew Abraham was entrusting her with a very important secret. The Catholic Church looked down on all magic, even the good kind. Elidad was amazed that Abraham would have anything to do with magic.

"The spell only allows a man with pure intentions to walk across the threshold," he answered.

"What will happen if they don't have good intentions?"

"They will find themselves in the alley out back."

"In the alley?" She giggled. "How do they get there?"

He shrugged, "The path they find on the landing leads them to the alley, rather than taking them to the library."

"You're teasing me," she laughed, accusingly.

"I'm not. I have seen it work with my own eyes, many times. I count on it to work when neither I nor Isaac are around to protect it."

Abraham's face became sincere. "You must not tell anyone what I have told you. No one in the Church needs to know. It's very important that you keep this a secret."

She shook her head in agreement. "I won't tell anyone."

"I don't want you talking about the library with anyone," Abraham asserted.

"I won't, I promise."

CHAPTER NINE

Standing in the middle of the library, looking up in awe of the bookshelves, she felt inconsequential. In a room of such grandeur, it was easy to imagine a spell looming within these walls. Large ladders were on every side of the room, stretching high into the darkness above. The ceiling that was unseen, and the stacks of books beneath it, appeared to go on infinitely. It was truly magical.

Elidad pushed the ladder nearest to her down its track. It hissed to the middle of the wall, where holding it in place she stepped on the bottom to engage the brake. Looking up, she climbed toward the darkness.

As she neared the top of the ladder it became difficult to distinguish titles on the book bindings from the lack of light. Looking down at the room, it appeared oddly far away. At this height, a fall from the ladder would be fatal.

Continuing to climb, the obscurity of her surroundings became more consuming with each push up. She knew her destination was close. Her hand reached forward to find where there should be an opening. Feeling into an open space, Elidad stepped off the ladder onto a ledge. The opening couldn't be seen from the ground. It had been hidden by darkness; only a select few knew of its existence.

Elidad ran her hand down the wall in the hidden space until she came to a tabletop where an igniter was resting. She picked it up and used it to light an oil lamp that was on the same table. The flame became intense in an instant lighting up the small area around her. There were mostly books in this hidden cove. Only a few relics were placed with the books and were just as dark and eerie as the books they accompanied. These items were hidden for a reason. She had no trouble imagining why they were referred to as the shadow books. Each containing a differing severity of evil.

Elidad walked directly to a large book resting on a pedestal standing in the center of the back wall. This book was oddly different, not only by looks, but by the energy it emanated. Elidad picked it up and quickly turned back to the ladder. She hated staying in this cove for too long; it made the hairs on the back of her neck stand up. Quickly, she placed the book in a basket and hung it on a hook on the backside of the ladder. Putting out the oil lamp, she expeditiously made her way to the room below.

Looking up where the basket was hanging, she was unable to see it. Reaching around the ladder, she flipped a switch. A string of hooks began cascading to the ground, the basket slowly coming into view.

Elidad was always amazed at how the fire kept itself alive over the hours she pored through books. She carefully turned the pages in the Black Book. Though the pages were heavy and thick, she always thought of them as being fragile. The Black Book, as she and Abraham had always called it, had no name, no author, and no stamp of a publisher. She was sure no publisher would put their name on it, or have any hand in creating it. It was a cryptic dictionary of legends, nightmares, and evil symbols and signs. It was extremely difficult to read, skipping over information, while referencing events and tragedies in the past. Turning to the book would lead Elidad to look in other books for pieces of information to put a story together. The crazy ramblings within the Black Book's cover were often incomplete, twisting truths to represent a skewed version of the past.

She had always wondered where the book came from, but never thought to ask. Elidad knew the book was important, or it would not have been hidden with the shadow books. All the shadow books had been confiscated by the Church and its crusaders. Elidad, herself, had recovered some of them.

The Church had approved many raids on satanic churches and various locations of cults. They had even secretly handled serial kill-ers and body possessions. Any information was logged and gathered and brought to Abraham and Isaac for safekeeping. Elidad knew there were other keepers, and more information. The Church was too smart to keep this kind of information under one roof. It was too dangerous. She wondered how much they actually controlled. Abraham told her of one other room like this. It was hidden under the Vatican. The Catholic Church had been crusading since the fall of Christ—acting as a medieval type of terrorist taskforce. She never had enough interest in that Records Room to ask about it. She knew they would never let her near it.

Looking at the book, she wished she'd asked Abraham about that. He would be able to tell her where it came from and who recovered it. She wished she'd taken the time to talk to him in the last year. How had so much time slipped away? She missed him now more than ever.

Sitting at the large table, Elidad continued to finger through the menagerie of printed pages, intertwined with feather-inked scribbles. She went through each page intently for hours, hoping to find something about the key. She thought maybe she had seen it in passing sometime in a book. She felt like she should know its purpose. Abraham should have told her what it was for. He meant for her to find it . . . he must have . . . he came to her in her dream, pointed her in the right direction, so why didn't he leave any other clues?

The hours of page turning revealed nothing. She was growing tired and began to feel overwhelmed when there was a faint knock, pulling her attention from her research. She looked up to see the door groan open. Lucian was standing in the doorway. In his arms was a tray displaying a dainty tea pot, two tea cups, and a sandwich on a plate. He walked to the table and placed the tray beside her.

"Forgive me, I did not mean to disturb you," he said, stepping back.

Elidad smiled up at him. Relieved at an excuse for a break, she pushed the book away to pour some tea.

"Please," he stepped forward quickly, "allow me." He reached for the pot before she could place her hand on it. Elidad pulled her hand back to allow him to serve her. She watched as the hot liquid cascaded into the cup below. Steam rose into the air bringing a fruity, flowery smell. She looked fondly at the china set. The dark pot was brushed with a shimmering gold dragon. Isaac had served her countless cups of tea with it. On the tray next to the tea set, the sandwich looked amazing. It was stacked tall and cut perfectly in squares like it had come from a restaurant.

"Is that for me?" she asked, as her stomach growled.

"If you would like it," he offered.

"I *would*," she smiled. "I was just thinking about how much I was missing Isaac's cooking. How long have I been down here? I am starving."

"About eight hours," he answered, pushing the sandwich toward her. "I thought you might be hungry. I have eaten twice since you have been down here."

Elidad took a bite. It was delicious. Way better than anything Isaac would have made.

"Thank you for bringing me this. It's really good."

He smiled. "It is my pleasure. It is nice to have company."

"Don't you get busy in the store? It used to be busy all the time."

"It still is. The customers are mostly older men and women, all of them having deep, interesting conversations . . . about antiques," he said with only a flicker in his eye to give away his sarcasm.

Elidad laughed at his candidness. He was quite charming.

"Did you find what you were looking for?" he asked, looking at the open pages of the Black Book.

"Well, the problem is, I still don't know what I'm looking for."

"Well, that could be a problem. No wonder you have been down here so long. And how long will you be looking for your mysterious answer?"

"Not much longer." She looked at her phone for the time. "I have some things to do. I'm meeting a friend later."

"Whatever you're looking for, it must be something dark." He gestured to the book lying open.

"Maybe," she shrugged. "I'm not sure."

"If you are looking for something good, I think you have the wrong book. I hate to be the one to tell you."

"I guess you better stick with antiques, then, because apparently your strong point isn't my kind of history." She assumed he must be some kind of crusader, like she was. That would be the only way Isaac would have trusted him to watch over the shop.

"You think so, do you?" He teased. "Then what is my lack of knowledge allowing me to miss? If you are looking for something good, why would you go to the shadow books to find information on it?"

She took a breath. "I have found that when looking at history, most of the time when something is important to the Church, whether a relic, an important piece of the past or future, it will be equally important to the opposing side."

"Opposing side?" His eyebrows rose. "What do you mean *the opposing side?*"

She shrugged, feeling silly. "Evil."

"So if you aren't with the Church, you are evil?"

She considered him. *Was* he a crusader? His words led her to believe that perhaps he was not.

"If you are not with God, your soul is susceptible to evil. Your soul is like a big open box, and you have to fill it up with things that are pure and good. Every day we submerge our souls in an ocean of evil, and if it isn't already full, you leave room for the darkness to seep in. So I guess the answer to your question is yes, you have to choose God or evil; there is no walking the line."

"I hope I didn't make you feel uncomfortable, asking. I like to try to understand you crusaders."

"We crusaders," Elidad repeated. "What does that make you?"

He smiled at her question. "A humanitarian, perhaps."

"A humanitarian? What makes you that?" Elidad wanted to know how Lucian fit in and how Isaac thought he would be the best keeper of the library while he was away.

"I have worked hard to fight for others. I have received my PhD in law and archaeology and a degree in Latin."

"And what do you do with all that education? Hang out in a busy antique store to bide the time?"

Lucian smiled at her. "That is a privilege of late. However, before Isaac asked me to assist him, I spent most of my time overseas on digs and fighting for lost artifacts."

"What kind of fighting?"

"The legal kind, of course. Most of the artifacts that we try to recover are not really lost, but stolen. Taken from digs and sold on the black market. We do our best to recover them."

Now it was easy to understand why Isaac trusted him. His life was dedicated to preserving artifacts and keeping them in their rightful place. She found herself intrigued by his work. He had to be very intelligent to complete the kind of schooling he had, as young as he was. He could only be a few years older than she, probably closer to Aiden's age.

"Be careful not to lose yourself down here, Elidad." He gestured to the book in front of her.

She could feel his words rise in her cheeks. "I'm not lost," she snapped. "I have a reason to be here." Her anger was driven by a previous conversation Abraham and she had had before she was cut from the Church. Abraham had questioned her use of the Black Book; he thought she was using it too much. She was hurt by his accusation, insulted that he would be concerned.

"My intentions were not to insult you, Elidad, though I have done that quite effortlessly." Lucian's tone turned apologetic. "I am sure you know what you are doing. Perhaps I sound a little like Isaac?"

"Maybe just a little," she replied dryly. Elidad stood and closed the book. "And a little like Abraham." She stood, to shake off the stiffness in her body, closing the book. "I have to get going. Thanks for the sandwich."

Lucian offered his hand as though to shake hers. Elidad reached forward, he embraced her hand in between his. "Again, Elidad, please accept my deepest apologies. I did not mean to insult you. It was my pleasure to have made your acquaintance, finally." He bowed forward and lightly kissed the top of her hand like a gentleman, the kind she only knew of through old black and white movies. His light touch to the crown of her knuckle sent shock waves up her arm, causing a slight—and hopefully unnoticeable—blush to rise in her cheeks.

She instantly forgave him.

CHAPTER TEN

When Elidad reentered Abraham's home she was greeted with silence, with the exception of the ticking clock in the entry. She found Aiden in the study, asleep in a chair with a book laid across his chest. She took a step forward to wake him, but paused. *Why had he really come to help her?* She wondered. She had always known him as the spoiled upperclassman who did everything in his power to contradict her opinions or her work. As she moved into—and beyond—his class his apparent devotion to making her life miserable grew steadily with her education. How could a teenager with so much jealousy and arrogance become this person before her . . . this kind, serene man? Was he genuine? His determination to help Abraham felt real.

Growing up, she found it difficult to look at Aiden for any length of time because he always upset her, but now, as his breath rhythmically drug across his lips in his sleep, she found it easy to take in his features. His blond hair was stylishly cut short on the sides and longer on top; he always kept it neat. The ends were slightly lighter, brightened by the sun. His brows were dark, making his blue eyes stand out when he was awake. He recently had begun letting his beard shadow his face; Elidad assumed it was to appear older than he was, but his features gave away his youth. He worked diligently to accomplish what he had in his young career, that maturity shone through his determined eyes. Elidad had seen fire in him many times while fighting for what he believed in—things he was passionate about—and she admired him for that. Throughout all their differences, Elidad could not deny that there was a certain allure about him. He had always been popular with the girls at school. Back then, she couldn't see the attraction, but now there was no denying it. She shook her head at herself. Just because she could acknowledge she found him attractive didn't mean she had to like him.

Perhaps she should let him sleep. He would be better off to stay here by himself than go with her tonight. Elidad turned to leave the room quietly, deciding it would be best for both of them.

"Elidad?" Aiden said with a groggy voice.

Her footsteps had awakened him. She pivoted in his direction.

"What time is it?" he asked, rubbing his face.

"Ten o'clock."

"Where are we going at eleven?"

"To meet a friend of mine. She might know something about this key, but I was thinking, maybe you should stay here and sleep. It'll be a quick trip."

"No, I'll go with you. I slept a little. I can go."

"You don't need to be with me everywhere I go, Aiden. You can stay and rest."

"Yes, I do need to go. The Bishop wants me to be with you. If he knew you were out all day, and that I had no idea where you were, I would be in a lot of trouble. They could call off the search." His voice was stressed. Elidad knew he was worried about Abraham, and probably worried about her. Maybe she should have called to let him know where she was, and that she was safe.

"I just don't think it's a good idea for you to go with me tonight, that's all." She held up her hand to stop his protest. "If you insist, I don't give a shit, you can go. But don't say I didn't warn you." She threw a bag at him; Aiden caught it in his lap.

"What's this?"

"Clothes."

"I have clothes."

She laughed. "The clothes in the bag are more suitable ones. Put them on."

"What's wrong with the ones I am wearing?"

"Nothing, if you want to get your ass kicked."

Aiden was standing in the entryway when the clock chimed the eleven o'clock hour. He looked at himself in the floor-length mirror. The clothes Elidad gave him were definitely different than his own. Being a priest, he was accustomed to seeing himself in black, but this was incomparable. He looked more like a person in a magazine than a servant of God. The outfit clung tightly to his build, drawing attention to his muscular physique. The jacket broadened his shoulders, making him look more masculine and less passive.

He heard Elidad as she started down the stairs. Looking up to express his disapproval of his new wardrobe, he lost his words when his eyes caught sight of her. Her hair was pulled to one side, with her long, dark locks cascading over one shoulder. Her eyes were smoky black and her lips bright red. He found himself wondering what they would feel like, soft and smooth.

Stiletto-heeled boots were zipped up past her knee, and the dress she was wearing, if you could call it that, stopped short at her thighs. The dress left little to the imagination. Aiden continued to watch as she descended the stairs.

"You know, Priest, it's not polite to stare." A tinge of mischief pulled at the corner of her lips as she picked up her coat. Aiden took the coat from her and held it up. She turned, allowing him to help her. Her dress was backless, dropping well below her waist. Aiden staggered for a moment when his eyes fell upon the tattoo on her back. It covered every exposed inch of skin. The detail was amazing. Studying the artwork closely, he quickly realized what he thought was a cross was actually a sword. The hilt was at the nape of her neck and the hand guard stretched across her shoulders, with the tip of the blade ending exactly between her hips. The blade was sunken into the chest of a demon; his lifeless body slumped below her waistline, his hands gripping the sword that was his demise.

Though it wasn't all visible, he assumed it was what Elidad saw as her life. The only thing captured in this piece—from his immediate interpretation, anyway—was sadness.

"See something you like?"

He looked up to meet her eyes in the mirror, realizing she'd been watching him. "I'm sorry. I didn't know. It just surprised me."

"It's okay."

"I've never seen a tattoo look so much like a painting before."

"Well, now that you have, can we go?"

CHAPTER ELEVEN

Their cab zipped down side streets leading to an industrial zone lined with old warehouses.

"Where are we going?" Aiden asked. Their clothing didn't seem to match the side of town they were in.

"You'll see, we're almost there."

The car turned once more before pulling into a street crowded with parked cars. Five valets stood out front of an old building as a stream of cars came flowing in.

Aiden tapped Elidad's arm. "That is an Aston Martin Vanquish." His astonished face was nearly pasted to the window. "That one . . . the car the valet is getting into."

Elidad frowned. "Is that a problem?"

"That car is worth over two hundred thousand dollars. Of course there's a problem. Who would valet park that?"

Elidad laughed. "Aiden, this may come as a surprise, but some people have a little more money than we lowly servants of God." She snapped her fingers to get his attention. "Will you please try to act normal?"

He nodded his head. "Okay."

"When we get out of the car, please keep your mouth shut. Just let me handle the people."

"All right."

The car stopped in front of the curb and a man opened the door for them.

There was a long line of people waiting to get in the door; it stretched the length of the immense building that took up an entire block.

"You can get back in the car and go back. Now's your last chance," Elidad quietly offered.

"No, I can do this," he told her as he stared at the line. Elidad knew he was calculating how long it would take them to get through the door. She walked straight for the front of the line where the large bouncer stood with his clipboard. He was separated from them by a fat red rope.

"Name." The bouncer's voice was as big and intimidating as the rest of him.

"Elidad."

He looked down at the clipboard. "Nope." He responded stone-faced, and turned back to the line of eagerly awaiting patrons that dominated the sidewalk.

"Check again," Elidad demanded.

"Get lost, bitch." The hulking man turned toward her and brought his clipboard up, pointing the way for her exit.

Before Aiden had a chance to see Elidad's reaction, the clipboard was snatched from the bouncer's hand, and the mammoth man was knocked to his knees. A woman in line cried out in fear. Everyone at the front of the line was now staring. A tall, thin, pale man who seemingly appeared from nowhere held the bouncer firmly by the back of the neck.

"Fool," the man spat. "Are you trying to get yourself killed?" The thin man was calm in his demeanor, yet he had an emanating intensity about him. Aiden was surprised at how effortlessly the bouncer had been subdued. The pale man looked up at Elidad. "My deepest apologies, my dear, a new man," he sneered, aiming his disgust toward the bouncer. "You know it is difficult to find good help these days. What is one to expect when you make yourself so scarce over the last couple of years?

"I assure you, he will not make this mistake again."

Elidad smiled back. "It was just a simple misunderstanding, Dedrick. All is forgiven. Besides, you know, I never would have done anything in front of all these witnesses."

"Of course not, dear," he agreed, letting go of the bouncer to extend his hand to her. "You would just plan something for later." His brow arched with a slight movement that spoke volumes.

Elidad took the arm that he offered.

"Come now, Elidad, I will escort you myself." Dedrick led them through the door. The three of them entered the building, leaving the bouncer to his shame, still kneeling on the sidewalk.

"It is so nice to see you, my dear. It really has been too long. I had wondered if we would have the pleasure of seeing you again. Leucosia assured me the time would come again soon." Dedrick looked over at Aiden. "And who is this striking young man you bring with you? I don't believe I have seen you in the company of another before tonight."

"Dedrick, you know I wouldn't stay away forever. I would have to come back to visit you once in a while." She winked, deliberately ignoring his questions about Aiden.

Aiden could see Dedrick distracted by her charm.

Dedrick escorted them to an elevator that stood open in the short entry. Elidad stepped inside and Aiden mimicked her action.

Dedrick bowed to kiss her hand, his silver hair catching the low light of the elevator. "Don't let it be so long next time, my dear." He stepped backward as the doors closed between them.

"Friend of yours?" Aiden asked.

Elidad pushed the button for the basement, and drew in a deep breath. "Remember, Aiden, when we get down there you need to stay close to me. Don't talk to anyone, just keep walking."

Aiden sighed. "I told you, I can handle this. I will be fine."

"We'll see." Her voice was doubtful.

The elevator groaned as it sank beneath the ground floor.

CHAPTER TWELVE

When the ping of the bell sounded the end of their descent, the doors drew open and the light of the elevator was consumed by the dark before them. Aiden found the throb of the music hypnotic as it raced across the floor to his feet and pulsed up his spine.

"Aiden, stay close. Don't lose me through the crowd." And before he could say anything, she stepped into the pulsing ocean of bodies.

As Aiden walked briskly after her, it was increasingly difficult to not be overwhelmed. Perhaps Elidad had been right. Maybe he should have stayed at Abraham's.

He had heard of high profile night clubs, but had never been in one. The sin oozed from every corner of the room. He would have to go to confession just for walking into this place. He tried to avert his eyes as his surroundings began to sink in, but everywhere he looked he found something new to make him feel uncomfortable and out of place. Just being a witness to this place made his soul heavy.

There were topless dancers gyrating on catwalks and swinging in iron cages, dancing above the crowd. Every woman in the place was scantily dressed, making Elidad's outfit appear conservative. What clothing they wore was held up by threads; other outfits appeared to be painted directly onto their bodies. If there was ever any question whether or not nuns' clothing made a difference, his belief that it did was now solidified. He struggled to keep up with Elidad as his eyes strayed from scene to scene.

Some of the dancers moved like spiders, floating effortlessly up and down large sweeping pieces of fabric that cascaded, mimicking waterfalls, to the ground. He had seen this type of acrobatics before in a Cirque Du Soleil performance but it was much different here.

These women were like black widows, descending upon the crowd to harvest their souls. They reminded him of dark angels, inspiring all that danced beneath them to commit what evil they could. He shuddered at their image.

Why were they here? What friend of Elidad's would be in a place like this? Surely not one that could be of any use. He wondered if she would bring him here solely for her amusement—as a cruel joke. As he continued pawing his way deeper through the crowd after Elidad, the faces around them changed, growing darker and more dangerous. What type of people frequented a place like this? Deeply disturbed ones. These people didn't come to confession . . . but they needed to. They looked at him as he pushed by, their eyes glowing with odd-ly-colored contacts under the black lights. He hoped he didn't look as out of place as he felt. Did they know he didn't belong? There was no telling what they might do to a man of God in this place. That's why Elidad had been so hard on his appearance, and offered so strongly for him to stay behind.

Someone grabbed him by the arm abruptly, breaking his train of thought, pulling him off course. He was shocked to see a beautiful woman standing beside him. She was almost as tall as he, six foot he guessed. Her skin, like a rose petal. Auburn hair framed her face, an ivory Cleopatra.

"Where are *you* going, love?" she asked, stepping closer to him, placing her hand on his chest. The warmth from her hand radiated through his clothing. Her touch consumed him. "Where are you going?" she asked a second time. Her words were heavy, blanketing him in a thick fog. The heat from her hand began to sear his skin, but it was impossible for him to pull away. His mind felt clouded at the enticing smell of flowers, so sweet he could taste it on his tongue. Hot, dry air sinking deep into his chest. Her smile was beautiful, even in the shadows of the dark club he could see how green her eyes were, deep like a tropical ocean. She was mesmerizing.

"Aren't you going to ask me to dance?" Her lips were pouty as she posed the question.

He could hardly hear the music anymore. It was just a faint, distant distraction in the back of his mind. She was so beautiful, the only sound he heard now came from his own heartbeat, a deafening pounding in his chest. He longed for her to speak again.

"No, he isn't." Elidad's voice was like a clanging gong in his mind. She gripped the woman's hand and ripped it from his chest. Aiden felt as though all the air in him went with it. He fell to his knees, gasping for air on the ground, bracing his chest. Looking up at the mysterious woman, he wished her hands were on him again.

Elidad was facing her, still holding her arm tightly. "Didn't anyone tell you, you should keep your hands to yourself, *Sophia*?"

"I didn't mean him any harm," she said as she struggled to free herself from Elidad's grip. No luck. Aiden wished he could come to her aid, but was still winded, and didn't possess the strength to bring himself to his feet.

"Honest," she continued, "I was only going to have a little fun. He was too sweet to pass up; I thought we might have a good time, that's all . . . If I would've known he was with *you*, I would've left him alone." Her words were apologetic but her eyes were not. "Besides, Elidad, he's too innocent for you." She looked over at Aiden, who could still feel her hand on his chest.

This is what the healing touch of Christ must feel like, Aiden thought.

"What are *you* going to do with him?" Sophia demanded.

"Just leave him alone," Elidad ordered as she stepped in their line of sight.

Aiden felt a loss inside at the disconnection from Sophia's view. He wished Elidad would move.

"Mother said you were coming." Aiden heard Sophia's perfect voice above the music from behind Elidad's shoulder.

"I guess there are no surprise visits for her," Elidad said.

Sophia laughed. "No. No surprising her, and no hiding anything from her." She sounded resentful of that fact.

Elidad released Sophia's arm and turned to retrieve Aiden. Sophia smiled at him before turning to walk away. He only caught a glimpse of her angel face before Elidad grabbed his shirt and pulled him to his feet. Spinning him around Elidad gave him a hard shove. She kept her hands on his back to push him in the direction they were walking before he was distracted. As they pushed their way through the crowd, Aiden could still feel the Sophia's hand on his chest. He could feel the warmth of her touch on his skin and taste her on his lips. He had never felt this way before. His mind was clouded and confused; he wasn't sure what just happened. The farther they walked, the clearer his mind became, the more he realized *something* just happened. But what that something was, remained a mystery.

Elidad grabbed Aiden by the arm and shoved him into a dark outlet that was unoccupied, along the outer edge of the club. His back was pushed against the wall, and Elidad's face was close to him so he could hear her talk.

"Shake it off, Priest," she told him.

"Elidad, I don't understand. What happened? Did she give me some kind of drug?" He was concerned.

The smile that came across Elidad's face felt condescending. He didn't want to look at her. He averted his eyes, over her shoulder, searching the crowd. In his mind, he knew he was looking for Sophia. He hoped, with all his soul, he would see her again.

Elidad snapped her fingers in his face to bring his focus back to herself. "Aiden. Pay attention."

"What?" he answered, looking at her again.

"She did not slip you a drug. She has that effect on men. She is a siren," she answered casually, as though this was a normal discussion.

Aiden looked her in the eyes, fighting the sudden urge to laugh. The look on her face told him she believed what she was saying.

"Like a mermaid?" His words were more condescending than her eyes were a moment ago.

"Sirens can be mermaids, but those sirens are rarely seen," she said.

Aiden stood silent, staring at Elidad with a blank look. "Why are you messing with me? This isn't funny." Maybe the woman *had* slipped him a drug and now Elidad was telling him some tale that would distract him from the panic that was sure to set in if he found out it were true. Or maybe Elidad was slipped a drug too . . . a drug that made her believe in sirens.

Elidad looked around before continuing. "I was hoping to have this conversation with you later. We don't have time for it now, so listen carefully, because I'm going to give you the fast version. The original sirens were cursed women, given wings and feet of birds, but their bodies and faces remained the same. Their voice and their song are poison to men's minds. Unfortunately, you just got a big dose from a very strong, very old siren." She looked down, adjusting her dress. "To be honest, this isn't quite the way I expected you to be introduced to all this. I thought I would ease you into it."

"You're not serious." He searched her face for any sign she wasn't.

"Aren't you a man of God?"

"Yes. So what? You're a woman of God," he responded, unsure of the point she was trying to make.

"Aiden," she said patiently, "how did you become a man who devoted his life to a higher power, a power that you cannot hear, or see, or touch? Don't you believe there are things in this world that you don't know about, but are very real?"

"We would know," he shook his head.

"Don't be as naive as the Vatican wants you to be." She was obviously annoyed. "Have you heard of sirens?"

"Yes."

"Then we do know about them, don't we? Their existence has been desensitized, over the years, just like the existence of God. Their story has been manipulated over time, but the basis is true."

"You were right: I shouldn't have come with you," he blurted out, before he could stop himself.

"If you are going to be with me on this trip, you need to know this, and accept it. We are going to stumble across things that you can't explain, but you are going to have to accept."

He was flustered. Elidad almost felt sorry for him, the ideas and emotions that were whirling around in his mind would be unbearable.

"There are varying degrees of temptation, Aiden, but have you ever wondered how a man that comes to confession every week can up and leave his wife and kids, and spend their life savings on a woman he just met? Or without warning just disappear one day leaving their family with no word as to why or where he has gone?" she asked.

He didn't understand what she was trying to tell him. "So sirens are evil?" He was becoming increasingly fearful. How many more of them were here?

"Sirens are like all the beings on this earth. They have a choice to be good or evil. Aiden, I know this is difficult for you, there is so much about this world that you don't know, but you will have to be a fast learner here. This is why I didn't want you to come with me. Your whole world is going to come crashing down around you. You are going to learn, some things you don't believe in really do exist. We don't have time for me to sit and explain everything to you, so you're going to have to keep an open mind and stay calm," she said, trying to be patient.

"I do have an open mind," he protested, "but sirens? Really?"

"I know, Aiden. I know how it sounds, and how it feels to say it out loud. But you need to pull it together because we have to go. We need to keep moving. We are here trying to get information that will help us find Abraham. That's all that should matter to you." She faked a reassuring smile.

"We're here so I could get my chest ripped out by a seductress," he said sarcastically. "Thanks for the warning. What's next? You going to tell me I should believe in Santa Claus?"

Elidad shrugged. "It's better than being afraid of getting your throat ripped out by a vampire."

"Oh, sure. Next you'll tell me they're real, too," he said, rolling his eyes.

"Keep an open mind, Aiden." Her smile was daring as she turned away.

"Well . . . They're *not,* are they?" His voice was weary. "*Are* they?" He trailed off after her, pushing through the crowd, trying harder this time to stay close.

Elidad pushed their way up to the bar at the back of the club. The bartender was pouring multiple drinks, many of which were brightly colored, producing an ethereal mist that danced eerily out of the glasses. Aiden wasn't familiar enough with a bar to know what the bartender was serving, but he had never seen anything like it.

The bartender himself was a thick man. He had tattoos that started on the back of his hands and crawled the length of his arms, up the side of his neck to the top of his clean-shaven scalp. His eyes were a deep blue and, like others in the club, were glowing in the dark. When his eyes reached Elidad thought, Aiden saw a glimmer of a smile in recognition, but as soon as he thought he saw it, it was gone. She must have been friends with him, if a man like that could be friendly to others. His nod towards Elidad was obvious. Elidad gestured to Aiden to come up to the bar as the bartender reached beneath the counter and pulled out two glasses. They were a unique shape, tall and slender.

The bartender reached underneath the counter again to produce an equally unique-shaped bottle containing a liquid looking similar to water. *Vodka*, Aiden thought. The large man held the bottle unusually high over the glass in which he intended to pour it. When the liquid hit the air, it shimmered out of the bottle like gold flecks. Once it hit the bottom of the glass, the drink turned a brilliant, glowing purple. Aiden watched as the substance started to churn inside the glass, producing a dark mushroom cloud that plumed from the bottom and swirled until the whole glass was filled a dark black. The top of the liquid sparked into flames. Elidad put her hand over the top.

Aiden could see the flames go out with the lack of air; its smoke filled the empty top of the tall glass. When Elidad turned to hand Aiden the glass, removing her hand from the top, the smoke, as black as the liquid inside, billowed out.

"No, thanks." Aiden held up his hand in refusal, and regretted that decision when he saw the bartender glaring at him, obviously disgusted that Aiden had turned down the drink he had just made.

"You don't say no to this drink, Aiden." Elidad shoved it into his chest. "And where you're going, you'll need it. Trust me."

Aiden took the glass from her hand. "Where am I going exactly?" He had to strain, listening for her response over the music that vibrated off every wall.

"With me, of course." She was smiling as she picked up her own glass and held it up to toast with him. "Here's to new understanding."

"Cheers," he reluctantly responded.

Aiden looked down at the dark liquid and decided it was better to not fight it and took a sip. His senses were instantly electrified when the smoke, though dark black, tantalized him with a beautiful candied smell, urging him to press his lips against the glass. The liquid burned down his throat—the sensation was like nothing he had ever felt before, nor could compare to any experience. The burn of the drink was addictive. Gradually, he could feel the liquid pulse through his veins. His toes and fingertips tingled with a warmth he could feel in his bones. He felt a comfort that was reassuring and invigorating. As he eagerly drank again, he swore the bartender winked at him.

CHAPTER THIRTEEN

Before he knew it, Aiden was pushing through the crowd again after Elidad. They were headed toward the back of the club where he could now see a long hall hidden in the shadows. The hall was narrow and darker than the club that continued to quake behind them.

"Here we go." Aiden could barely make out Elidad's words as she started down the hall.

They pushed past what appeared to be VIP rooms that were on both sides of the passage. Aiden's head was light; he could still feel the drink's warmth inside him, pleasantly dulling his mind. The hall was lined with people. Aiden tried to keep his eyes from making contact with any of them. He feared they could identify something in him that proved he was different, and would know he didn't belong. The drink was strong enough to numb his senses, but not his insecurities.

Each of the rooms they passed contained private dancers—girls in glass cages—like the ones hovering above the dance floor behind them, each with a different costume and glowing eyes. It seemed to be a common theme in this place, the glowing eyes. They must have some meaning of which he was not familiar.

Every room was different from the next, and the people within were different, as well. It was like this was the place where extras and movie stars came after work, dressed in their wardrobes. Their costumes were excellently detailed, their makeup flawless. Each room looked like it contained different species.

The next room they passed mocked a desert with a setting sun in the distance. The people who inhabited the room looked scaly, their eyes inhumanly narrow slants. Aiden wondered how they made their eyelids blink so convincingly. A clear membrane passed over their eyes, like a reptile's. The dancer in the middle of this particular room had a long amphibian tale that swayed to the music, wrapping around her body rhythmically.

Aiden shuddered. All the people here were trying to fill some void in their lives. These people needed God. As they pushed on, each room was more elaborate than the one before. The dancers inside mimicked the theme of the room. Whatever fantasy you wanted, you could find here.

A man in the next room caught Aiden's eye as they walked past. His smile glowed in the blue light of the room. Aiden shook his head trying to release the fog in his mind. It had to be the drink. Aiden swore the man smiling at him had fangs. He laughed at himself, thinking of their conversation earlier. He was letting Elidad mess with his mind. Vampires! How absurd.

Elidad paused in the hall outside a door. She grabbed Aiden and pushed him up against the wall and eased her body into him.

"What are you doing?" he whispered as people passed by in the hall, the hall that Aiden saw as a highway to every deadly sin.

Elidad smiled, reaching up to play with his hair as a couple passed them closely. She leaned into him more, her mouth pressed against his ear. He could feel her breath, warm and intimate. His heart began to race in response.

"Try to look like you're enjoying yourself. We don't want to attract too much attention," she whispered.

"You think this is inconspicuous?"

"Look around." Her breath on his neck sent chills down his back.

Obediently, he looked down the long hall. She was right, there were many couples just like them, some more intimately embraced than he was comfortable seeing. He put his face in her hair to hide from their graceless display. Her hair was soft, a light perfume lingered there that he had never noticed before.

"Loosen up, Aiden."

He put his arms around her to show that he was playing along. It felt awkward at first, but some instinct inside him enjoyed the twinge of indulgence. He ran his hands down her back, pulling her body closer to him. He could feel her breath rise and fall as he held her closely against his chest.

"Careful, Priest, I might think you *are* enjoying yourself." He could hear the smile on her lips. She continued, without pulling away. "We are going in this room, and you need to follow me closely. Don't stop moving. You are going to need to concentrate on me and where we are going. There will be a woman in the center of the room; she's a siren. The only reason she's in that room is to keep people from finding the passage we are going to walk through."

Aiden swallowed hard, realizing Elidad wouldn't have taken time to prep him if she didn't think this task would be difficult for him. The fear in him began to swell again. Elidad continued with his briefing. "She won't speak, or sing, so you will be fine if you are strong and keep moving. Keep your eyes on the floor and follow my feet. There are mirrors all over the room. Even if you make eye contact through the mirror, *you are done*."

"Right, eyes down. Follow you. Got it." He hoped he didn't sound as worrisome as he felt.

"The door we are going through isn't like any others you have seen. It'll be strange, so don't be afraid."

"Too late," he admitted sheepishly.

"It'll be fine, just keep your eyes on me. If you look at her, you'll stay in that room until you pass out from exhaustion or hunger, which could be days."

And there it was. The reason why she was taking the time to explain what they were doing. He could be stuck in there for days. They didn't have days to waste, he would be stuck in the room, and Elidad would be gone. Elidad stepped back from him and smiled, reassuringly. He faked a smile back as his stomach turned. Aiden watched as Elidad stepped into the room, her silhouette washed over with a blue light. He instantly focused on her feet, as the rush of fear completely engulfed him.

When he stepped into the room he couldn't help but look up a little, away from the center of the room where the dancer would be positioned. The outside of the room was lined with a dozen or so people, mostly men. They all were motionless, fixated on the forbidden dancer in the middle of the room. None of the people appeared to notice him or Elidad walking across the room. They remained in their zombie-like trances, brain-dead to anything else. Only their breath betrayed their motionless demeanors . . . even their eyes refused to blink.

Worried he might catch a glimpse of the mirrors that lined the walls, Aiden focused on Elidad again, her warning in his mind. *You could stay in that room until you pass out from hunger or exhaustion . . . it could be days.* Aiden believed her; the people who were here now looked haggard and worn.

When he and Elidad entered the room, he had the distinct feeling someone was watching him. He knew it was the siren, bearing down on him, in her attempt to keep him here. Aiden wanted to look up at her, but knew he couldn't. With every step, it became harder to focus on Elidad; it took everything inside his mind to keep from turning toward the dancer. His mind screamed with an urgency he had never felt before.

Perhaps he could sneak one quick look—it couldn't hurt. Elidad would never notice. Aiden's hand went to his chest, where he could feel the touch of the other siren on his skin. He could taste the sweetness on his tongue. He wished *she* was here, in this room, so he could see her again. His mind began to race. Perhaps this siren in the center of the room would look the same—maybe they were sisters. Maybe this woman would be *more* beautiful than Sophia, if he could just see her magnificent face. He knew she *wanted* him to look at her. She longed for him just as much as he longed for her. Without thinking he slowly raised his eyes. He would only glance at her quickly. Elidad wouldn't notice, and there couldn't be any harm in just a quick peek.

CHAPTER FOURTEEN

As he began to look up, rather than seeing the siren, he saw Elidad dissolving into a wall-sized mirror in front of them. The shock of seeing her melt away took his mind off the siren behind him. Elidad's skin turned liquid as it was absorbed by the mirror, his heart raced, and fear climbed up his throat. He was fearful of what he saw, and even more fearful of being in the room without Elidad. The shock of the moment gave him a second of much-needed clarity. He must not look at the siren, though he wanted to desperately. Before the siren had time to pressure him into looking at her, he reached his hand forward and felt the cool, unusual touch of the unknown. Reaching forward into the glass was like reaching into a pool of water, without being wet. He fought panic when something on the other side of the mirror grabbed his arm and tugged him through.

"Quit messing around. We have to get moving." Elidad's voice was sharp. Aiden couldn't see her in the darkness in which they were now standing, and was relieved she spoke, reassuring him of her presence.

"Elidad, what in God's name is going on? Where are we? I thought we were going to meet your friend." He panted with panic. "I feel like Alice, chasing a freakin' white rabbit here. I'm convinced that woman *did* slip me something out there. Over there . . . wherever the *hell* we came from."

"I have half a mind to slip you something myself." She punched him hard in the shoulder. Aiden winced at the pain. He clutched the sore spot with his opposite hand, hoping she wouldn't notice in the darkness.

"I warned you, Aiden. Remember? I told you not to come with me. I knew this was going to be too much for you, but you were convinced I was hiding something from you. You had to come, so here you are. Freaked out, and slowing me down."

"Slowing you down? You wouldn't be here if it weren't for me." His fear disguising itself as anger. He wanted to hit her back. Perhaps God wouldn't see if he hit her here in the dark in whatever hell she had brought him.

"I could have made it here by myself just fine," she argued.

"Oh, bullshit, Elidad. You would still be sulking in that shithole apartment you call home if I wouldn't have come to get you. You've been there for months, feeling sorry for yourself, wallowing in self-pity. You've ignored any cases that came your way. Maybe if you would've pulled your head out of your ass a long time ago you would have known Abraham was missing." He was sorry the instant he said it, but it was too late to take it back now.

He didn't see it coming. Aiden hit the ground as the full force of an angry punch caught him in the stomach. He hit the hard stone floor, wheezing, gasping for air. He felt like he was going to throw up. He had never had the wind knocked out of him, but he was sure this was what it felt like.

"We are here to see my friend, Leucosia." Elidad's voice was calm, like nothing had happened. Aiden was beginning to recognize that when her voice was calm, she was at her most dangerous.

"Leucosia is not an ordinary person. She is a siren, one of the three original sirens."

Aiden could hear Elidad's feet moving in the darkness, and hoped she hadn't planned on kicking him while he remained on the floor, as he still hadn't found the strength to push himself to his feet. "You see, Aiden, sirens are prophets; they know the future and the past. They can be a pain in the ass when it comes to getting a straight answer, but I thought Leucosia was the right one for us to see, considering our current state of confusion. With no real direction on where we need to go, since you and the Church leaders are so full of information, we need help. So here we are."

"You are taking me to see the queen of sirens?" Aiden panted as his feet found their rightful place beneath him. "The woman up there nearly ripped my chest apart." He wasn't trying to hide his worry anymore, and he felt like he was teetering on panicked insanity. "Are you crazy?"

"I told you, you weren't ready for this. I tried to get you to stay at the house . . . but *no*. This is what you wanted. So this is what you got, and now you're stuck. There's no going back now."

He could picture the angry look on Elidad's face as she spoke.

"Try to concentrate on what we are hoping to accomplish here, not how scared you are. Keep your mind focused," she told him.

Aiden saw the glow of a cell phone in Elidad's hand. He was surprised she had one. He recognized the whine of a flashlight app before it began to glow brighter. Elidad reached into her pocket and pulled out a single match stick and struck it against the rough wall. It instantly spat out a blue flame that gave off a smell of flowers, rather than sulfur. The longer the match burned, the more intense the light became.

Aiden watched as small embers fell from the match, fizzling out before they hit the ground, reminding him of the sparklers that children played with for the Fourth of July. He had to look away from her hand; the light grew so intense he could no longer see the shape of her fingers.

Elidad threw the match, now resembling a small flare, out in front of them. Neither of them spoke as it slowly drifted featherlike to the ground. When the match fell, it hit water instead of solid ground like he had expected. When it came in contact with the water's surface, it stayed alight and began to sink the same way it had drifted in the air. Aiden couldn't take his eyes off it. The process was amazing. Elidad watched it drift slowly to the bottom of the deep pool, he knew she was thinking the same thing.

Aiden began to realize they were surrounded by water, standing on a flat rock barely big enough for the two of them. The water reflected the blue flare's cooling color around the open space surrounding them. The surface of the water shimmered like diamonds; it was the most beautiful sight he had ever seen, since he laid eyes on Sophia. Witnessing this beauty was calming; he could feel the stress in his shoulders begin to lighten.

Finally, the match found the bottom of the lake, and the whole body of water became alight, displaying its vast, wide banks beaming from far and wide. It was so bright, they both squinted at its overwhelming luminescence.

The water before them began to churn and bubble. Fearful, Aiden took a step back from the edge. Dark figures under the surface began to rise out of the churning water. They were stepping stones forming a path outward across the near ocean-sized body of water in front of them.

Elidad turned to Aiden. "You can't stay here. You are going to have to come with me," she warned, turning and hopping out onto the first step. "I know this is hard for you, Aiden, but you wanted to come, so here you are. Now that you are here, you have to keep moving forward. If you stay here, the light will burn out, and if we don't get to where we are going before then, we will be in a lot of trouble." She hopped on the next rock with Aiden following her lead. "The sirens in the club will be the least of your worries." Her voice trailed off.

Aiden didn't bother to question her, and continued to make his way out across the stones after her.

"Sirens were the playmates of Persephone, the goddess of the underworld, you know." Elidad's voice rang out across the water and echoed off the rock walls of the seemingly underground cave.

"The goddess of the underworld? I thought you believe in God and the Devil, not theology."

"I do. But God, Jesus, and the Devil have followers: angels and demons. The ancient Greeks knew of them, and knew their names, but the evil angels convinced them that *they* were gods. Foolish humans, one of the many pet peeves God has, you know . . . 'thou shall not have any gods before me . . .' the first commandment." She added, "So you can bet that one bothers him the most. Anyway, they convinced the Greeks that they were gods and the Greeks began to worship them as God and that was the beginning of their downfall, but we don't have time for that history lesson, we'll have to save that for another day."

"So the short version is: you brought me here as a sacrifice to get the information you want?" Aiden asked sarcastically.

"Don't tempt me . . . Do you want to know or not, Aiden?"

"I apologize, please continue with your story of terror." He dramatically flailed his hands in the air.

Elidad knew he was being sarcastic to hide how afraid he was, but she laughed at him anyway, it was better than him being hysterical.

"The point I was trying to make here, Aiden, was that these 'gods,' as the Greeks called them, were supernatural beings and many of them still live. They aren't gods; they are angels, demons, or beings of some kind.

"So Persephone, the daughter of Zeus and Demeter—who was the goddess of the harvest—was so beautiful everyone loved her. Even Hades wanted to have her for his own. One day when she was collecting flowers on the plain of Enna, the earth suddenly opened and Hades rose up and abducted her. It is said that the sirens were present when she was taken, and chose not to interfere. Angered by this, Demeter changed them into birds, leaving their female faces. Demeter cursed the sirens so that they would be able to find their friend Persephone and when they did, their beauty would be enough to subdue Hades. This distraction would allow them to rescue Persephone and fly her back to the safety of her parents. Sirens are the daughters of the river, Achelous, and the muse of dancing, Terpsichore.

"Well, that would explain all the water, dancing, and mind control, I suppose." Aiden's sarcasm continued.

Elidad ignored his tone. "So, you have heard in some legends that the three siren sisters were mermaids. The confusion started a long time ago. The sisters lived on an island where they would sing on the shore. Unfortunately, they were unaware that sailors passing the island could hear their song, and were drawn to the island because of the power the girls' singing possessed. The men would navigate their ships to the island, and not seeing the rocks that lined the outside edge, many of them sank. It truly is sad that so many lost their lives." She shook her head regrettably.

"How many lost their lives?"

"Too many, but that isn't the point. One sister fell in love with a merman and they had children together, so, because of their union, there actually *are* siren mermaids."

"But you're talking about men *losing their lives* over these sirens . . . and you thought it'd be a great idea to bring me to meet one? Or three?"

"You wanted to come."

"You said we were going to meet your friend. Friend? Not a woman who is cursed, half bird, knows the future, and makes me feel like I have no control over myself? I might have made a different choice if you would've told me all that."

"Yeah, you'd have made a different choice, like to call someone to put me away in the loony bin. You had to see it for yourself, Aiden, or you would have just thought I was crazy. *Anyway*, Leucosia, who happens to be the middle sister, was tired of being partly responsible for the accidental deaths that had been occurring on the island. She and her sisters were having a hard time getting along; one of her sisters thought they should use their power over men to their advantage while Leucosia did not. Leucosia wanted to live alone, as far away from people as she could get, so she left her sisters to find her own way in the world. A few thousand years went by, add a dance club, and here we are."

"Well, I'm glad I'm caught up."

"Not even close." Elidad wasn't sure if he would ever be. "I'm just trying to fill you in quickly."

"Well, at least there's some good news." Aiden appeared mildly pleasant.

"And what's the good news?" Elidad asked.

"I don't see how things can get much crazier, at this point."

"Don't tempt fate, Priest. It wouldn't be good for either of us." Her voice was stern.

"I don't believe in fate, Elidad, I believe in God."

"And until an hour ago, you didn't believe in sirens, either." She was clearly agitated, adding, "You don't think God has something to do with fate? You don't think there are things that are prewritten? We impact fate with our choices, but most of the time, human kind is pretty predictable, Aiden. God can see ten moves ahead of us, like an expert chess player. God has control over the future. That, my dear, is fate, isn't it? Something other than ourselves having control of our future?"

He had never thought of it that way, so he opted not to say anything further on the matter.

Elidad stopped. "Seventy-seven," she said, as she turned to face Aiden.

"What does that mean? It won't kill me, will it?"

"No, seventy-seven won't, but the rest might." She was referring to the stones they had been following. "Aiden, you need to stand on this stone to follow me. You are going to have to follow me, just like through the looking glass." She needed him to know how important her instructions were. "You have to stand on *this* stone to get where I'm going."

"Okay, I get it. I might be a little freaked out, but I'm not stupid. I'll stand on that rock." He pointed to it.

"All right then, I'll see you on the other side, Alice." She winked at him as she stepped off the stone into the radiant blue pool, and slowly melted away, out of sight.

Aiden jumped onto the rock where she had been standing and looked up. "Lord, this woman may be the death of me. Please give me the strength to deal with her." He shook his head in disbelief and stepped off the rock.

CHAPTER FIFTEEN

This was a similar experience to the one before when he reached—
and was pulled through—the mirror. This time, the eerie feeling of
being suspended between two places was exceedingly longer than the
looking glass. He felt submerged and weightless in water, like time
was forcefully slowed as his body floated through this passage. Aiden
was *only* aware of the pressure from all sides of his body, and as he
sank further under the surface, the pressure intensified. He imagined
himself like the little blue match, floating slowly to the bottom.

Just as he felt his body melt into the pool, he now felt himself
melting out of it. His feet touched a hard surface. When he became
cognizant of his surroundings he realized he was standing face to face
with Elidad. As his mind became clear, his senses came alive, bringing
with them the familiar smell of flowers that he would now recognize
anywhere. It was that beautiful sweet smell dancing on his tongue
and burned through his brain.

Aiden looked around to determine where he and Elidad were
standing. They were in an enormous cave with the murmuring sound
of moving water surrounding them. Over Elidad's shoulder Aiden
could see a riverbank lining the shore on which they were standing.
It appeared they were on an island in the middle of a massive, rapid-
ly-flowing river. The island was brightly lit amidst the dark emptiness
of the cave.

"Someone new to my home?" The voice behind Aiden sent shock-
waves through his body.

Aiden could feel the heat and the pressure in his chest at the sound
of her voice. He wanted to hear her speak again. Was this the same
beauty he had seen before? The longing for her returned and pulsed

through his veins. He had to turn to face her; he felt like he would not survive another second if he was forced to face away from her any longer.

When Aiden turned, it was as he knew it would be. *She* was the most radiant beauty his eyes had ever known. Her skin glowed like the sun, so illuminating, it was difficult to look at her face for any extended amount of time, but he couldn't bear to look away from her deep blue eyes. Her eyes shone brighter than gems, burning through the depth of his soul. His breath quickened, and his body shook like a drug addict suffering from withdrawals. The garb she wore looked as if it had been spun from silk and woven with clouds, and floated about her perfect figure, long and slender. Wings broad and powerful, snow-white and enticingly soft, stretched out from her back. Her beauty was unimaginable . . . incomparable. She was what Aiden had pictured angels to look like.

"I'm not, you know." Her voice rang out in splendor across the cave.

"Not what?" His own voice was foreign to him. It took all the strength in him to speak in her presence. With every part of his body, he ached to be near her.

"I am not an angel. They don't have chicken feet." She moved one of her claws forward, the corner of her mouth slightly lifting.

Aiden's attention was drawn down. He hadn't noticed her feet until now: Rather than being seated in her position like he assumed, she was perched like a bird, resting on a large tree limb. Her feet were rough and leathery, her large talons clinging to her resting place.

He looked back at her face, at those stunning eyes. Her beauty tore at his soul.

She brought her hand to her lips in a sensual gesture, like blowing him a kiss, but instead blew a fine dust off her hand into the air around him. The dust sparkled about his face like snow falling in a full moon's light. It fell against his skin, with a cool heavy touch. It appeared beautiful, like frozen fog twinkling like diamonds in the air on a freezing, sunny morning, until it had a moment to rest on his skin. Aiden began to realize that the dust brought with it a darkening sadness. He shivered as he began to feel confused and betrayed. Why would she bring this curse upon him? How could she bring him this pain? The sensation he was feeling was emotionally draining, like he was losing something. Something was slowly slipping away from him. What was it? What was the void growing inside him and leaving in its place a churning black hole of sadness and despair?

He looked up to the face of his sweet angel. Her smile was still warm and inviting, but the brilliance of her skin began to dull. He no longer found it difficult to look at her. His depression was astounding; his whole being was encompassed in a cloud of dampening rain and misfortune.

With Aiden's attention no longer fixated on her beauty, slowly, their surroundings began to come into focus. He was beginning to feel like he had awakened from a beautiful dream, into a sad, dreary reality.

"Like all things, it will come to pass." Leucosia's voice warmed the chills on his skin.

She was responsible for the misery he was experiencing. She *meant* for him to feel this pain.

"Why?" he asked her, the hurt in his voice apparent.

"I know it is difficult now, but it will be easier as time passes. It will be the best for you where you are going."

"Where am I going?" Aiden frowned.

Her beautiful laughter echoed off the walls. "With Elidad, of course." She winked at him like she knew what Elidad told him earlier at the bar. Leucosia turned toward Elidad to acknowledge her presence for the first time. "It has been too long, my friend. I was pleased to see you were going to visit again."

"I know . . . It has been a long time. I have been . . . busy." Elidad was reluctant with her answer.

Leucosia's eyebrows rose. "Is *that* what you call it? Busy?"

Elidad sighed heavily. "I don't get out much anymore."

Aiden could see the remorse in Elidad's face.

"You will soon make up for that, my friend." Leucosia smiled down at her.

"Great," Elidad replied. "That doesn't sound promising."

Leucosia continued to smile. "We all have a path, Elidad. Yours has been a little overgrown lately. It will soon come clear to you."

"I see your daughter is well." Elidad made a lame attempt to change the subject.

Leucosia shook her head. "She is another that needs to find her path. I have told her I do not wish to see her in the club as much as I do. Lingering here too much leaves her in jeopardy of being led astray." She shrugged ever so slightly. "But like all children, she has a mind of her own and will need to find her own way, even if it is the more difficult one. But that's not why you came to me today, is it?"

Elidad looked down at her hands. "No, it isn't. You know that."

Aiden thought he heard a quiver in Elidad's voice when she spoke.

Leucosia smiled pleasantly at Elidad. "I *do* know. I also know you humans like to feel you have given information freely. You get uncomfortable when others know more than you."

"Leucosia, you have never had to worry about that with me." Elidad reminded her, frowning. "Since when have your gifts ever made me feel uncomfortable?"

"Never, but your friend is having a hard time with this experience. I thought I would attempt to make it a little more comfortable for him." Leucosia and Elidad looked over to Aiden as they spoke.

"That is very considerate of you, but you shouldn't worry too much about him; he'll get over it. We just need your help," Elidad said dryly.

Leucosia pondered her words. "Perhaps you should be more concerned with his welfare. It wouldn't hurt you to show more concern for your kind."

"I don't know if Elidad qualifies as one of *our* kind." Aiden interjected himself into the conversation.

Leucosia laughed out loud. "Funny *and* handsome, Elidad. I am glad you will be entertained throughout your travels."

Elidad crossed her arms. "Oh, yeah . . . me, too. *Ecstatic.*"

Leucosia spread her wings. The force of their extension whipped the air around them. She floated elegantly to the ground to stand face to face with Elidad. "Have you stopped to consider, Elidad, that perhaps you are not the right one for this quest?"

"Why wouldn't I be?"

Leucosia lightly placed her hand on Elidad's shoulder to quiet her impulse to argue. "For the reasons you already know, Elidad. Your soul is in a dark place, even you must realize this. You know this to be a problem, a very dangerous problem, for someone of your profession."

Elidad shifted uncomfortably, glancing at Aiden, wishing now more than ever she had left him behind and not brought him with her.

"Careful, my friend," Leucosia's voice a tone of warning, "susceptible is a troubled soul."

"I know," Elidad replied quickly.

"You do know . . . and yet you throw caution to the wind."

"It's Abraham, Leucosia. I have to look for him."

"I know you feel obligated, but have you looked for direction? Do you know that this is what you are *meant* to do?"

"This *is* what I am meant to do," Elidad replied definitively.

Aiden knew what Leucosia meant. *Had* Elidad asked for direction? Was she just taking off to find Abraham on her own, or did she look for guidance from her Creator? Leucosia's advice sounded like something a priest would say. Leucosia might have more insight than he thought. At Leucosia's words a thought began to occur to him: Elidad had been so depressed over what happened with the Church, had it caused her to lose faith? Was that the reason she hadn't been working? It wasn't like her to not help people in need, and yet she locked herself away in her flat, ignoring jobs that would have been easy for her to complete. Did she need to find faith before she could continue her work? Perhaps this assignment was going to be more complicated than he thought. Maybe he had been wrong to ask her for help.

Aiden's mind continued to become clearer with his concern for Elidad. The feeling of loss that had been overwhelming moments ago began to fade, and with the newfound clarity, their surroundings became more peculiar. The large tree that Leucosia had been perched on when they arrived was an unusual, creepy-looking tree. Standing over them, tall and intimidating. The bark, midnight black, was a perfect contrast to Leucosia's skin. Its gnarled limbs appeared to be carved of ebony. The tree looked like an art piece. There was not a single leaf on any of its branches to signify life—yet somehow he could *feel* it was alive. In the ground, where its roots dug deep to find their strength, flowers found a home growing wildly thick and full at the tree's base. These were the flowers producing the victimizing smell that once overwhelmed his senses. They were beautiful, different than any flower he had ever seen. They were similar to an Echinacea plant, in bright radiant colors, their foliage deep, dark green with blazes of lime green striping each leaf.

Aiden also noticed that under Leucosia's perch were strewn numerous statues of men. There was something strange about the statues, piled like mounds in an ancient battlefield, anguish and agony on their faces. The men's arms and legs contorted and twisted upon one another in a gruesome display.

"A reminder of the past, Aiden." Leucosia's voice snapped him out of his observation of her lair. She, too, was looking at the statues as she spoke.

"I suppose we all have our pleasantries." He was astounded at his ability to be snide with her despite how obsessed he had been a short time ago. It was amazing how drastically his emotions had changed. He started their meeting thinking she was the love of his life, and now only felt anger for her.

"Men in your world build memorials to ensure memories will not fade, because when memories fade, history repeats itself. Memorials are built not always to agree with the act, but to commemorate the loss so others will not turn a blind eye to the same actions in the future."

"We need your help, Leucosia." Elidad interjected herself between their intense stares.

Leucosia turned away from Aiden. "Yes, of course, the key."

Surprised, Aiden glanced at Elidad, searching for her reaction.

Elidad pulled the key from her pocket. "Yes, we are here because of the key."

Leucosia eyed the key closely. "It is missing its sisters."

"What do you mean, sisters?" Elidad said.

"I have never seen them all," Leucosia admitted, "but I have come across one, now two, in my time on this earth. However, I do know their story." Walking away from them, Leucosia beckoned for them to follow. Aiden and Elidad followed the short distance to a pedestal towering over the wildflowers encompassing it. Aiden thought it looked like a birdbath in a garden, but the only bird in this garden was Leucosia. She bowed over the pedestal after positioning herself on the opposing side. With a delicate finger, she gracefully touched the water, her finger sending out a perfect ripple across the surface.

"The key you hold has three other parts." Leucosia spoke without looking up from the water where a fine mist had begun to form in the air above. "Each of the keys is forged from a different metal of this earth," she said, waving her hands through the mist. The mist churned like a tormented wave before taking the shape of four identical keys, each its own distinct hue.

Aiden stepped back from the display. It was like they were looking into a hologram. He wasn't sure *what* he was seeing. How did the mist become a vivid picture before his eyes? What kind of witchcraft was this?

"When the keys are brought together," Leucosia continued, "they will meld to form a single united key." The mist twisted together and became one, as Leucosia described. "This single key will become a unique metal, one that is unknown to man. The strength from its united power is indestructible. The metal it becomes is the only material strong enough to turn the lock for which it was built."

"What is it meant to open?" Elidad asked.

Leucosia waved her hands once again over the water, the mist churning in response to her force. The new image it displayed was of a weathered, leather bound book. Metal bindings held its sides, braces from each corner met in the center where a heavy lock covered most of the cover.

"The book has been passed through the ages, from a time when man lived closer to the word of God. A time when man lived on this earth as one race and spoke one language. I trust you remember the story of the Tower, Elidad?"

Elidad nodded.

"What is she talking about?" Aiden asked out of the corner of his mouth.

"Babel," Elidad answered without taking her eyes off the book floating before them. Aiden would know the story from the Bible.

"The book was a gift," Leucosia continued. "Your kind was not able to manage this gift entrusted to you. Time after time, throughout history, man rebels and like so many times in the past, our Creator has to take your gifts away from you. They are taken away until you have suffered enough, and you may actually be able to appreciate them." Leucosia pointed at the mist. "The key opens this book. The key was divided when man was divided at the tower." Leucosia angrily slashed at the mist again, and it churned to show flashes of Nimrod shooting an arrow into the sky and the tower crumbling to the ground in response to his defiance.

"Unity was a blessing you were *given*, and over time you proved it was a blessing you were not worthy of receiving. You think you would have learned after severing the unity you had with your Creator." Leucosia touched the top of the water lightly again, putting a stop to the churning mist and its display. "By this age, there is no telling where the remaining keys are." She looked at Aiden. "Unfortunately, men's memories fade too easily."

"What is in the book?" Elidad asked. "What is so important that God wanted the key to be divided?"

Aiden's mind was churning like the mist. He was trying to keep up, but the insanity of it all was too much. How had Leucosia made those images appear? What dark dungeon had they come to with this bird woman?

Leucosia's smile was uneasy in response to Elidad's question. "Just as the keys unite themselves, the book will reunite the world."

"What do you mean, reunite the world?" Elidad glanced at Aiden. "You mean as one race again?"

Leucosia grimly nodded, "That is correct, Elidad."

"How is that possible?"

Leucosia smiled. "All things are possible. You know that."

"Yes, but God divided us for a reason, so how can there be a way to override that? It *can't* be possible. It's God's wish for us to be divided, for our own good."

"Elidad, the book was a gift from God, intended to be protected by people. He gave you this book so when your Savior came again, and you are ready to embrace divine love and forgiveness, the ones that earned it would receive the ultimate gift: the unity of your kind, and the unity of this world."

"The unity of the world?" Elidad looked back at Aiden, who shrugged, signifying he wasn't understanding any of it.

"After being divided, each of the keys was given to a strong leader of man. Four angels were chosen by God and given one key each. They were sent in human form to earth to protect the keys and ensure the keys were given to a man whose family line could be trusted to protect them."

Leucosia's finger touched the water's edge and a picture showed again. "Hezekiah, the first human chosen, was a leader of a people who fled to mountains when the world divided. Amin was a leader of people who skillfully mastered the fires of the earth. Shui, a strong man, led people to the waterside. Behitha, a man who was named after the eagle, led his people to their home in the windy cliffs of the high desert. These men were different, and were at far ends of the earth. The angels felt that the reuniting of the keys would be next to impossible."

"Why would he give us a way to be one race again?" Elidad said, frowning. "We already proved we couldn't handle it."

Leucosia laughed, her voice echoing off the cave walls like a song. "Elidad, you of all beings know our Creator makes choices we will never understand until the end of time. None of us can understand His movement or decisiveness. It is like a simpleminded person playing chess with a genius. He already knows how the game will end, before you have moved your first pawn." Leucosia sighed. "He created you and gave you free will, one of the few creations on this earth that has free will. The beasts of the air, earth, and water operate on instinct. *He* gave *you* a choice. It is very sad you often choose wrong, resulting in your own destruction." The sorrow was heavy on her breath. "Time and time again He only wishes for you to choose *Him*. I cannot help but think the book is much like the Tree of Knowledge."

"How do you mean?" Aiden said, failing to see the connection.

"Your race was given an option to be obedient and live a perfect life in the Garden with your Creator. All He asked of you in return was that you not eat the fruit of one tree. The tree was an option to live a different life than what He had given you: a way out." Leucosia's eyes became stern. "Don't you see? He has the power to *make* you love Him, but He wants you to *want* to love Him. He wants you to *want* to be with Him, to know Him. What is a love if it is forced? He always gives you choices to be obedient and walk with Him for eternity, or go on your own way and perish. He simply wanted the keys to be protected until your Savior came again, until a time when you all shall be ready to be one again." She forced a laugh. "I wonder myself if there will ever be a time when you are truly ready . . . But God is all-knowing, and if He says there will be a time, it will come."

"What happens if the book is opened before we are ready for it?" The concern in Aiden's voice was apparent.

Locking eyes with Aiden, Leucosia touched the surface of the water. The mist instantly swirled above the still surface. "The world will unite as one. The evils of the world will reign, and the people will blame God." She pushed her hand through the mist, which churned to display bloody battlefields, famine, and loss. "They will declare war on the Creator of all, and the world will lose."

"Where are they?" Elidad asked. "The keys, I mean."

Leucosia touched the water and the picture fell from view. "You know it's not that easy, Elidad."

Elidad sighed, "It is that easy. All you have to do is tell me."

"You know I can't. Even if I could, I am still not sure this is the right path for you. My views are hazy, and the future is uncertain. I am not comfortable pointing you in a direction with a limited view."

"Then where is Abraham?" Elidad asked forcefully.

Leucosia went to her side, placing her hand on her shoulder again. "He would not want me to tell you, Elidad. He of all people believes in finding your own way. You will have to find your path on this one."

Elidad brushed her hand aside, walking away. "Is he still alive? You can tell me that."

"Yes, I can. And yes, he is. He is waiting for you, Elidad. He knows you will come. I will also tell you that finding one key has set you on course to find the next, and in turn shall set you on a path for you to fulfill your destiny. Whether that be right . . . or wrong . . ." She turned toward the water before finishing her thought. "Finding the keys was Abraham's path. He truly believed that. There is sadness in his heart. He is overwhelmed with the fact that he has not completed his task. He knows you will feel obligated to complete it for him.

Keep the faith, Elidad, for you will need it where you are going."

"That's what Abraham told me in my dream."

Leucosia turned back to look deep into Elidad's eyes. "Was it a dream?" she asked, moving to touch the water in the birdbath and wave her hand through the mist once more. "Perhaps you should reconsider all the signs."

A silver canister appeared in the mist, displaying an intricate detail that was carved into the gleaming metal. Leucosia delicately placed her hands around the floating image and plucked it out of thin air. "Things are not always what they seem." Leucosia smiled pleasingly as she handed the canister to Elidad.

Elidad took it, wide-eyed. Aiden was sure Elidad had never seen Leucosia perform this trick before.

"It's beautiful," Elidad said, turning it over in her hands.

"Even more importantly, it contains a liquid with the power to heal. Only when you are in dire need will this be of use to you. Use it wisely and it will be a blessing."

"How will I know I am in dire need?"

"When the cells of ancestry gather at your feet with fleeting fear chased by cavernous thunder, this will be the time."

Elidad's mouth opened as if to ask for more information.

"That is all I have to say about it." Leucosia's voice was stern, and with her words the mist swirled again and a piece of metal appeared above the bird bath. It looked like the hilt of a sword, missing its blade. Again Leucosia pulled the item into reality with her beautiful, fragile hand. She handed it to Elidad. The metal, cool in her hand, was thick and heavy. The handle was ordained with orbs, inlayed in the hand guard and the base, where the blade should start. The handle was intricately designed, the detail was beautiful and would assist in the grip of the weapon, if it was complete.

"What is this?" Elidad asked her.

"An indestructible weapon. If you must use it, it will bring you victory over your enemies." Leucosia closed Elidad's hand around it.

"How?"

"Only with purity and justice in your heart will it come to you."

Bewilderment flashed over Elidad's face. "I will take care of it. Thank you."

Before Elidad could ask another question, Leucosia pointed behind them. Aiden and Elidad turned. A black box made of stone was resting on a pedestal. Aiden followed Elidad to where it was displayed. The box had a white design of birds and flowers cut into it. When Elidad lifted the lid there were two matches inside. They were just like the match Elidad had used to light their way after they left the club, revealing the stones in the water.

"Two?" Elidad asked without turning toward Leucosia.

"There are two of you," Leucosia observed.

Elidad put one into her pocket and handed the other to Aiden. He looked at her, puzzled. "Put it in your pocket," she directed. "So, Leucosia . . ." Elidad's voice was thoughtful. "If this book is so important, how many others will be looking for it and the keys?"

"Many are the numbers that wish to see God's word proven wrong . . . *legions* of them."

Aiden and Elidad glanced at one another again, neither of them successful at hiding their fear.

"Sounds like we have some challenges ahead of us," Elidad said. "I think we should get started."

Leucosia elegantly bowed to Elidad. "Until we meet again, my friend. I wish you well in your travels. I wish you would consider my concerns, though I know you will not." Leucosia walked to Aiden's side, placing her hand caressingly on his face. "And you, Charming. Our next meeting will not be so painful for you, so don't forget your way." A smile came pleasantly to her lips.

Aiden, still angry with her, looked in her eyes. A flash of gray washed over her blue eyes, as if the life had suddenly fled from her. Leucosia's body was still, statuesque. No breath passed her lips. Aiden glanced at Elidad, nervously.

"She's having a premonition," Elidad said.

When the gray left Leucosia's eyes, she was looking into Aiden's again. "Perhaps you shouldn't forget your coat. I hear Canada is cold this time of year."

Aiden frowned. "I'm not going to Canada."

"Thank you, Leucosia," Elidad said as she grabbed Aiden's arm and pulled him away, "he'll keep that in mind."

"Ready?" Elidad asked, dragging Aiden as they walked toward the water's edge.

"I guess." He looked back over his shoulder at Leucosia who lightly waved her fingers in the air to send them off.

At the water's edge the familiar stepping stones were waiting. Aiden followed Elidad across the stones. He couldn't decide how far under the earth they were. There was no telling how far they had fallen when they descended through the water. When he came through, he felt suspended for what seemed like an eternity.

The night left his head spinning as the island behind them became a faint glow of light, slowly being swallowed by the darkness that encompassed it. The lack of light was making it hard to see the stones in front of him.

"Is the match still in your pocket?" Elidad asked over her shoulder.

Aiden's hand went to inspect. It wasn't there. He just put it there a second ago . . .

"It shouldn't be. So if it isn't, don't worry," Elidad assured him.

"What do you mean it shouldn't be? Where *should* it be?"

"It's gone. You won't find it until you need it. Do you remember how I used it?"

"Yes, I think so. You just struck it on the wall, right?"

"Yes, but don't forget to go to the bar and get the drink first. It's important."

"Why do I need to remember, and why do I need a match when you have one? Why can't I just come back with you?"

"I don't know, Aiden. As you can see, Leucosia is not always overflowing with information. She just tells you what you need to know, and the rest is up to you. But you can assume you will be here without me."

"When?"

"Aiden, I don't know. You know as much as I do."

"Right." The thought made him uneasy. By himself? Why? Where would Elidad be? He wasn't sure he could handle being in the club without her. He *was* sure, however, he wouldn't make it past the woman with the burning touch.

Elidad stopped abruptly on a large rock. "Come on." She wanted him on the same stone with her. He could tell she was looking for something in the dark in front of them. Aiden couldn't see what she was looking for, but he heard a click and as she pushed it forward, a light shone in response around a door. She pushed hard against it and stepped into a bathroom stall. Elidad walked over the toilet and pressed her back up against the stall door. Aiden followed as the door closed behind them.

"When we leave here, try to look like you're enjoying yourself in a nightclub bathroom with a woman."

"What? Why?" He felt like he was trying to keep up all night.

"Try not to look like you just found out from someone of another species that the world might end soon . . . Okay?" She harshly tapped his cheek with her hand like it might snap him out of a dream. He couldn't wrap his mind around everything, but nodded in agreement anyway.

She grabbed him by the back of the neck and forcefully rubbed his shoulders. "Smiling couldn't hurt."

He forced a smile and Elida laughed at his lame attempt. Aiden couldn't help but laugh himself, imagining what he looked like.

"That's better. Are you ready?" He nodded again. Elidad took him by the hand and opened the stall door. The bathroom was full of women primping themselves in front of mirrors. Some were smoking, some doing their makeup, others passing pills around. One of the women didn't have a reflection. Aiden could hear the pulse of the music as all the women in the bathroom turned to look at them exit the stall together, Elidad leading the way. Aiden found himself being led back to the club of transgression.

CHAPTER SIXTEEN

Neither Elidad nor Aiden spoke a word as the car came around the front of Abraham's house. Aiden stared out the car window, the night's events racing through his mind. He wanted to believe the woman who stopped him in the club slipped him something, but how? Did she poke him with a needle? Did she have something on her hand and that's why her touch burned so badly? If so, how did it go through his clothing? Maybe it was a dream and he would awake to find himself in bed.

He was afraid to talk about it with Elidad, fearful she would have no recollection of the night's events. What would he do if the night *didn't* happen the way he remembered? Would he find himself in a padded room by daybreak? The further they pulled away from the club, the less real it all seemed. His reality began fading like memories do, distorted and odd in his own mind.

The brakes of the cab whined as they pulled to a stop. Elidad leaned forward to pay the cab driver. They walked up the front steps, just like they had the night before.

"How likely is it, all the street lights on one block burn out at the same time?" Elidad thought out loud.

"Maybe it's not the bulbs, maybe it's something electrical," he suggested. Aiden noticed Elidad looking from side to side like she expected someone to be waiting for them. "Who are you looking for?"

"No one," she replied.

He knew she was lying. Elidad swung the door open and allowed Aiden to walk in before her. She looked back over her shoulder one last time before entering the house.

She *was* lying. Over the day she found herself constantly looking for the person who'd been watching them last night. She *felt* like someone had been watching them since they came to New York. She usually was good at spotting a tail, but whoever this was, was better than average. Seeing nothing outside on the street, she closed the door and locked it behind them. Standing in the foyer she closed her eyes to inhale the familiar scent of leather and a wood-burning fire. It made her feel a little more at ease; the feeling of home was encouraging.

Though Abraham wasn't here she could imagine herself walking into the study to find him reading a book by the fire. She could picture him, the way happiness creased the edges of his eyes when he embraced her. Seeing him in her memory stirred something in her chest. Would he come to her in her dreams again, or would he let her sleep tonight?

Elidad went into the study and plopped down onto one of the large chairs facing Aiden. They sat in silence for a long time.

"I'm sorry you weren't prepared for that," Elidad admitted, truthfully.

Aiden snorted in response.

"If I would've told you, you would've thought I was crazy," she protested. "It was better for you to see for yourself. It was a good way to ease you into it."

Aiden stared at her in disbelief. "*Ease* me into it?" He took a breath. "Walking through walls to meet a cursed woman with wings is your idea of *easing* me into it?"

"Well, I certainly don't think taking you to an exorcism would be a great way to ease you into it." She was agitated with the fear that began to surface in him, again. "Imagine trying to wrap your mind around that for the first time, Aiden. Imagine if *that* was your first encounter with the supernatural world. Seeing demons inside people is not like what you see on TV. It's real. It's scary. You won't sleep for weeks. You would wish the worst thing you saw was a beautiful woman with chicken feet."

"The Church has done exorcisms since Christ. That's normal," he argued. "Sirens aren't normal. The only time I've heard of them was in folklore. I had no idea there was any truth to it. Some warning would be nice next time, that's all."

Elidad's eyes narrowed. "Just because you've heard of exorcisms doesn't mean they are normal. And don't kid yourself; attending an exorcism would not be less shocking than where I took you tonight. You might have preconceived notions on what an exorcism is, but you'll never be ready for it. If you attend an exorcism, and live through it, your life will never be the same. The demons exiled from the innocent will haunt your memories, your dreams. The experience will be burned into your heart and soul. Being present for an exorcism is to *know* and live pure evil. The only way you can try to describe it is to say seeing that kind of evil, that close up, is to have a true understanding of what hell is like. It will be the only time in your human life that you can even come close to understanding how evil, evil really is. Knowing evil like that changes you. It's not an idea; you know it, you smell it, it calls out to every strand of hatred in your body until you begin to question your own sanity. You start to question the purity of your faith. No one is ever ready for that, Aiden. In no way can you prepare someone for what that feels like, and there is no way to know if someone is ready to endure that kind of strain. Exorcists are not demonproof; they can be possessed just the same as anyone else. And given a choice, a demon will choose a priest over an innocent any day."

Aiden sat silently, taking in what she said before gathering a response. "I know I didn't attend an exorcism tonight, but I ensure you, my life will never be the same."

"It won't, I'm sure of that. But now you're not so blind to what's out there. This way, if something else comes along, hopefully you won't have a meltdown. Maybe you'll be able to handle things a little better moving forward. Because, Aiden, you need to be ready for more. As we look for Abraham it's very likely we'll come across some strange things. You need to be ready. I hope all the contact you have with this other world will continue to be with good creatures like Leucosia, but I'm afraid that's not the way it's going to be."

Aiden frowned. "How do you know she's good?"

Elidad was surprised at his question. "Leucosia? I just know."

"Did you see the statues she had around her?" His insides objected at the thought of the men's faces, the agony they portrayed.

"Yes, I did. She told you: they are a reminder to herself to ensure she won't allow history to repeat itself. That's why she lives down there, Aiden. She tries to keep herself away from men."

"She doesn't want history to repeat itself because she killed all those men," Aiden pointed out.

Elidad could see why Aiden thought Leucosia was bad. "She didn't kill all those men. Her sister did. She's vowed not to stand by when wrong is being done, ever again. She has vowed to intervene."

"You think she lives down there to stay away from men? She probably prays on them in dark alleys when you aren't around," Aiden argued spitefully.

Elidad shook her head. "I know it's hard for you to imagine what it's like for her to live with that curse."

"Curse?" Aiden laughed mockingly. "Could've fooled me."

"Yes, well, you are an idiot, and idiots are easily fooled." She glared.

"I just don't buy the curse thing. It looks to me like she enjoys resting on her evil throne, in her lair of darkness and despair. Look at that place." He waved his hand in the air. She assumed he was speaking of the night club. "It's evil. Nothing good can come from that place."

Elidad couldn't help but laugh at his childish outburst. "Aiden, I know how it looks when you walk in, but it's really not what you think."

"Really? Because I think it's an evil pit of lust and sin, and that's exactly what it is."

"To someone like you, it would appear that way, but there is much more to it than that. The club is the only place on this earth that good and evil exist under one roof and do not destroy each other. It's a safe haven for all species. A lot of good has come from that place."

"*Good*? Really?" Aiden's voice was doubtful.

"You don't have to believe me," she shrugged. "You can ask your boss. Almost all the funding for that place comes from the Catholic Church."

"Bullshit," he blurted.

"No. No bullshit. It's a frontline on their war on terror . . . not the domestic kind, the spiritual kind. They have helped a lot of damaged souls there. If you can believe it, one of the rooms we didn't pass is a place of worship; you can actually find people praying back there." Elidad smiled widely. "If you like, I can put you on a list; you can put in some mission time there."

He made a face at her.

"Honestly, there have been some real breakthroughs, peace treaties that kept wars from happening. The club is a good thing, and Leucosia is on our side. She didn't have a choice to be a siren, she was cursed. Being a siren is part of her DNA now; there is no reversing it."

"Where are her sisters?" he asked skeptically.

"One is missing, the other is dead." Elidad shrugged.

Aiden's dark eyebrows rose. "Dead, how? I thought they were immortal."

Elidad nodded in agreement. "Yes, but all immortals can be killed, Aiden. Even Dracula." A mischievous kind of smile came over her.

"So how did she die?" He ignored Elidad's taunting.

"I don't know."

"How do you know she's dead, then?"

"Aiden, I just do, okay?"

"How is her other sister missing? I thought Leucosia can see the past and future. Since she's an all-knowing seer, how can she not know where her sister is?"

"I'm sure she does know where she is; she just chooses not to share that information."

"Why?"

Elidad stood. "What is this, fifty questions?" She sat on the fireplace hearth and began to stack kindling. "She doesn't want to tell anyone where she is because the Church sentenced her to death."

"Since when does the Church condemn people to death?"

"Since the beginning of its existence. Where have you been? Crusades, witch hunts, they never stopped. Her sister isn't exactly a person, is she? It's much easier to sentence a siren to death. No one will notice her missing."

Aiden folded his arms. "Yes, but it's not like it's the eighteen hundreds, Elidad."

"You're right. It's not, they've gotten much better at assassinations since then. They know better than to do it out in the open. Riling up lynch mobs doesn't work anymore. Do you know how many unsolved murders there are in the U.S. every year?"

Elidad's mind raced considering how much more to tell him. How much would Aiden accept? She struck a match to light crumpled paper under the stack of wood. He'd have to know it all if he was going to help her find Abraham. Her dream, the club, Leucosia was only the beginning. He'd have to know more. Getting caught by Sophia in the club was easy, it was a safe place. There was no telling what they would run into on the road. He needed to be ready.

"They call us Crusaders." Elidad smiled at how it sounded out loud. "I'm not sure how many there are, exactly. I just know a handful that work out of the same area I did. I've seen a few others on jobs I was called to help on, out of the country. I'm sure there are a lot more. They consider us blood avengers."

"Like in the Old Testament?" Aiden's voice was cool. "You're an *executioner?*"

Aiden said the word cruelly. The hair on her arms sent a chill through her skin in response. "Kind of. More like, law enforcement."

"Who's law?" Aiden asked. "What happened to 'though shalt not kill'?"

"We mostly take care of demons, anymore. Demons aren't technically alive and they aren't technically dead. We just send them back to where they came from. I've heard of human assassinations, but that takes years to get a *yes* vote from the council."

"Why do they want Leucosia's sister dead then?"

"She is not so good," Elidad said, reluctantly.

"Evil, you mean."

"Not totally . . . she just plays both sides. She works for anyone who'll pay. She doesn't hold back information when she should like Leucosia. She'll tell all . . . if you have enough money, that is. But working both sides doesn't go over very well with the Church. It's hard to have any kind of advantage if you have a double agent in the mix. She really isn't all that bad; she just lost her way."

Aiden threw his hands up. "Are you listening to yourself? Good and bad, those are the only ways. You can't walk the line. She is bad, she is evil. And if their other sister went and got herself killed, I'm sure she was evil, too. Why else would anyone want her dead enough to go through the trouble of finding a way to make it happen? All you are telling me is more reason to believe that Leucosia is bad news. She comes from a whole family of bad news." He crossed his arms dramatically.

Elidad sighed. "So, are you telling me you wouldn't allow a child into your church because his father was a murderer?" She held up her hand to stop him from replying. "No. Because it's not the child's fault what path his father chose. You continue to help him; you teach him and believe with all your soul that he'll take the higher path. That's what we do every day: believe in people. Believe in good, and just because things appear to be complex or difficult doesn't mean we give up hope. History wasn't written by people who gave in at difficult times, Aiden."

"I'm not giving up. I'm just saying she might not be as good as you thought."

"You are judging her without knowing her. You gave up on her without giving her a chance. Her soul is good, and like the rest of us, she tries to do the right thing. That's why she has those statues. To remind herself every day of why she's there, why she does what she does, and a reminder to not become like her sisters."

"All right, Elidad, if you trust her, that's fine. I still don't know what to think. But this is your deal. You say you can find Abraham so we are doing this your way. That's all I am here for, to find Abraham."

Elidad sat back in her chair. The fire she started was crackling merrily, beginning to give off heat. Aiden watched the flames intently, despising their joyous flickers amidst his feeling of anger and loss.

Elidad sighed. "Leucosia and her sisters found an island that was free from the inhabitance of man. They tried for ages to live on the mainland, but as people began to cover the earth, it was difficult to keep themselves away from others. The girls loved the seclusion of the island. For once, they felt free from their curse. They could live their lives and sing without there being consequences. Unfortunately, times changed, man progressed, technology moved forward. Man began sailing the oceans, exploring.

"Leucosia and her sisters had no idea what was happening in the modern world. All they did was sit on the beaches of their island and sing together. They passed the years away in harmony. There was no warning that men were on the horizon, in ships, listening to their song. The water carried their voices across vast amounts of space. Unable to resist the call, sailors set course for the unknown island. They were so eager to reach the island, they didn't slow their ships, ramming into rocks, and sank. The majority of the men aboard died.

"Other ships were too large, and weren't able to get close enough to the island, so they jumped into the sea attempting to swim to the shore. Misguided by the sirens' song, they were swept out with the tide. Some made it to shore. The girls were happy to have company, but as time passed, things began to change. The men fought over who would spend more time with the girls. When the violence grew, the sirens decided to turn away the most vicious of them, before they began killing each other. The men who'd been turned away by the sisters eventually took their own lives.

"Leucosia told me the men would stay by their sides until they were too weak to move. They were unable to live normal lives. They were slowly wasting away, starving to death at her feet. Leucosia was sick with grief. She went to her sisters Calandra and Ignacia to ask her for help; they needed to do something with the men. The sisters decided to gather the men and fly them back to the mainland to heal. They would be free to live their lives without the weight of the siren spell.

"Months passed and the sisters again found peace on their island with their solitary lifestyle. One day, a ship arrived on the shore. The men they saved had returned, bringing others to be damned with them. Calandra was furious. She cursed them. She told them they deserved whatever fate they would suffer. Leucosia pleaded with Calandra, trying to remind her it wasn't their fault. The men lay victim to the curse. Calandra wouldn't listen.

"Leucosia and Ignacia shared her fear and frustration. They knew these men would perish, as so many had before. But Leucosia and Ignacia didn't blame the men. Calandra snapped. I think her heart was so heavy, she couldn't stand the pain. She needed to blame the men, rather than feel responsible herself. By blaming them she was able to desensitize herself. New men began arriving on the island mysteriously. Leucosia and Ignacia suspected Calandra was sneaking off in the night to sing on the shore. She intended to draw as many to their doom as she could.

"When they came ashore, she would allow the men to swoon over her, seducing and teasing them. Then she began commanding them. She demanded they build structures in her honor and expected great feasts. They did whatever she wished. When the men became too weak to function, she would end their lives." Elidad ignored the horrified look on Aiden's face. "She slit their throats. It was quick. She told her sisters she only killed them to put them out of their misery.

Though Leucosia and Ignacia didn't agree with it, they allowed it. Seeing the months of pain the men endured before starving to death, they felt it was merciful. When they began to discover men's bodies, mutilated, they became concerned. Leucosia and Ignacia confronted Calandra about the dead men. Calandra told her sisters one man, obsessed with her, began killing the others. She assured them she would handle the situation, and for a time, it did stop.

"Years passed, Leucosia and Ignacia stayed on their side of the island, neither caring for the jungle. Calandra loved the jungle and would disappear for days. Leading men over the dangerous terrain.

"Leucosia told me that she and Ignacia felt like their wings were a part of the siren curse so they tried to not use them. They would walk everywhere to be as human as possible.

"I'm not sure why, but Ignacia decided to fly to the far side of the island and explore. Walking under the dense canopy, she came across a structure. It was obvious men built it for her sister. A statue of Calandra stood out front. Ignacia, overtaken by the beauty of the architecture, couldn't help but investigate its detail. The building was immense, a wall protecting its outer edges.

"When she entered the grounds, she wandered through a short passage to the center of the building. The building was a crescent moon shape. Rows of seating lined its walls, facing a blood-soaked altar. Examining the alter Ignacia became fearful. What was it for? She had to find out. Eventually, she came across a door that led to a secluded side of the building.

"Silently slipping through a door, she found the first sign of life. Two men, working in the heat, didn't notice her. Ignacia watched in horror as the men picked up a mutilated body as if it were a bale of hay. They moved the body from a cart and flung it on top of a pile of rotting corpses, mounded in a ditch. From where she stood, Ignacia could see their hearts and tongues had been cut out.

"Ignacia flew to Leucosia to tell her what she found. They were heartbroken with the level of deception from their sister. She had a colony of men capable of incomprehensible things. And their sister . . . what part did she take in all of it?"

"She did it, didn't she?" Aiden asked. "She killed all the men?"

"Yes. She did. She was a mass murderer, before there were mass murderers. She slaughtered those men, torturing them, making her followers watch . . . they *wanted* to watch."

"So what happened?" Aiden asked. "How did they stop her?"

Elidad shrugged. "I'm not sure."

"You're not sure," Aiden repeated scornfully.

"Yeah, Aiden. I'm sure it's hard for you to imagine, but it's just not something that comes up in a conversation. *How did your sister finally come to her demise? Did you kill her by yourself or did you and your other sister decide to do it together?*"

"How do you know that's what really happened? What if her sister's not dead? What if you just think she is?"

"Look Aiden, if she was still alive, we would know. The world would know. She wouldn't hide in some cave like Leucosia, okay? She hid what she was doing from her sisters, but not from anyone else. She didn't care. She thought she should rule this world, and I think she was setting out to do just that. And the truth is, she did have a reason to hide it from her sisters because they are still alive, and she's not. Abraham believes her, why can't you?"

Aiden frowned. "Abraham knows her?"

"Of course he knows her. How do you think I met her?"

"I hadn't really thought about it. How did he meet her?"

Elidad smiled. "I don't know. I hadn't really thought about it."

Aiden wrinkled his nose at her tone.

"I would assume he was given the task of watching over the club from the Church. Maybe he volunteered. He was trusted with everything they had. He could've done hundreds of jobs anywhere in the world."

"I can't imagine him stepping foot in a place like that." Aiden shuddered at the images racing through his mind.

"Well, he was. More times than I can count. Probably more times than he can count." She smiled to herself.

"So, why did it change for me? What did she give me?" Aiden asked cautiously.

Elidad locked eyes with him. "You mean the antidote?"

"If that's what you call it."

"That's what she calls it: the antidote."

"If it's an antidote, why doesn't she give it to all men she comes in contact with?"

"Her curse is her only defense," Elidad answered, as if it should've been obvious.

"Defense from what?"

"People. Did you see her?" One of Elidad's eyebrows rose. "Can you imagine what would happen if she couldn't protect herself? She needs to have some upper hand on people if she is discovered. Otherwise, she'd end up in a zoo, or on some kind of display. How could she defend herself if she couldn't distract them with her beauty? Now, she can sing a song and people are so mesmerized she can slip away without them knowing what happened. Without that, she'd end up in an autopsy room in some government area."

Aiden frowned. "Her daughter walks around just fine. I didn't see any wings or talons on her. She looked normal."

Elidad crossed her arms. "She isn't cursed. Leucosia is."

"So, not all sirens are cursed . . . just the three sisters are?"

"And he gets it, folks," Elidad announced loudly to the room, throwing her arms up in victory. "But there are only two sisters, and their descendants have their bloodline, though they don't have the same curse. They are beautiful. The girls were beautiful before the curse. Their children will have some effect on people's minds, but not the same level. Sophia, the woman in the club, Leucosia's daughter, she had that effect on you because she was touching you. She is old, and she is very strong."

"Like how old are we talking?" Aiden inquired.

"Too old for you, Priest," Elidad smirked. "A hundred and forty-five."

"You're kidding."

"Nope. Sorry. That's the truth. And she isn't immortal either. Leucosia and her sisters found that out the hard way. That's the worst part of their affliction: they outlive everyone, even their children."

"That's terrible," Aiden admitted.

"Terrible. Also, another reason she doesn't give out the antidote, all the ingredients to make it aren't easy to find. That's probably the real reason she doesn't give it to just anyone."

"What are the ingredients?" Aiden's curiosity was selfish. He wanted to know what he'd been given.

"Just one ingredient is hard to get, actually."

"What's that? Napalm?"

"No. Angel's blood."

Aiden's jaw fell open.

"Don't look at me like that. It's not as bad as it sounds."

"Really?" Aiden's voice was a little higher pitched. "She is running around with the blood of an angel in a vile, and it's not as bad as it sounds? I don't care who you are, that sounds bad. How in God's name did she get angel's blood?"

"That's exactly how she got it. In God's name, with his permission. Angels don't do anything without God's blessing, Aiden. You know that. Leucosia had been trying for decades to find an antidote to the sirens' song, but was never successful. But then, one day, an angel came to her and told her God had a plan for her. He gave her a vile of angel's blood. They are one of the only beings on this earth immune to a siren. With the vile she was given instruction to make her dust."

Aiden closed his eyes and rubbed his face. "Maybe I *should* go home," he admitted.

Elidad smiled. "Don't get my hopes up. How are you feeling, by the way?" There was a slight note of concern in her voice.

"I'm fine, why?" He pulled his hands out of his way so he could look at her.

"Just making sure. The antidote is strong. Sometimes there can be . . ." She was looking for the right words. ". . . side effects."

"Side effects. Like what? A third leg?" The words hung in the back of his throat like a jagged pill.

"Calm down. If you were going to have any, you would be showing by now. And no, nothing is going to grow on you. It's more like depression. That's all."

He threw his hands up. "Oh, that's all. I'm glad I had a say in all this."

"You did, remember. I told you to stay here." Elidad pointed to the floor. "But you wanted to go. And if she would have asked you, you would have told her yes. You would have done anything she wanted. Have you forgotten that already? You do have some side effects going on. You are angry with her. You feel betrayed. Don't you?"

He was angry. She was right, he did feel betrayed, like finding out he'd been cheated on for years. He felt like Leucosia stomped on his heart and threw it away. That was the real reason he didn't like her.

"Maybe a little," he answered quietly.

"A little, huh?" Elidad said, doubt evident in her question. "It will pass, Aiden. It's just leveling itself out in your system. You'll be fine. Just don't try to kill yourself or anything."

He didn't answer. She suspected he wasn't really angry with her or Leucosia. Elidad understood how he felt. Learning the truth about the world was a hard lesson, and it would be especially hard for him. He had spent his life living by the rules. He did everything he was asked, and he did it blindly. Elidad knew the pain of finding out that in return for your devotion, the Church hid the truth from you.

"The things they keep from you . . . they think it is for your own good," she said, trying to make him feel better. "The dark ages were hard times. Too much evil was on the earth when magic roamed freely. After the Crusades the Church decided it would remove itself from any links to magic. They cursed it as devil's work and destroyed everything having to do with it."

"It *is* devil's work."

Elidad smiled. "Calling upon the Holy Spirit to help you remove demons is as close as you can get to magic. Jesus performed magic: he raised people from the dead, and turned water into wine. They weren't illusions, they were acts performed to show the world the Glory of God. Not the mythical kind, the Devine kind. Magic is the use of techniques to exert control over the supernatural. If we know him, we can call upon our God against our enemies to fight *His* battles, and win. That is magic. We just call them miracles."

"I've never heard anyone put it that way."

"Of course there are people who call on the Devil, and that is evil magic. *That* is who we fight. *That* is who we need to expel from the earth, but we can only do it armed." Elidad took a breath. "The evils of the world would rather operate out of sight, too. It's easier to attack the unsuspecting."

CHAPTER SEVENTEEN

Elidad and Aiden sat staring into the flames that began wrapping their hot grip around the larger piece of wood on the pile.

"How did you find out about all this?" Aiden finally broke the silence. Elidad looked at Aiden.

"It was nine years ago, when I was sent to a village in the Amazon." Her words were reluctant.

"It was my first missionary assignment out of the country. I was young . . . too young for the job. But the Church allowed me to be a protégé, with my record and personal references from high ranking priests."

"You were fifteen," Aiden said, not pulling his eyes away from the fire.

Elidad looked over at him. "Yes, I was." Her surprise was apparent.

"I was jealous," he admitted. "They wouldn't let me do anything like that until I was eighteen. I wanted to go when I was younger, too, but they denied my application. They wanted us to do other things like inner city programs, something in the states, Mexico, Canada, or Hawaii. Safer places. But *you*, being the next Mother Teresa . . . they let you do anything."

"They sent me to a small village in the jungle. There were little resources and we were a two-day hike from the closest village. Our only hospital consisted of a doctor that just graduated, a volunteer from the Peace Corps, and a medicine man. People often died from common diseases in the village due to a lack of vaccines and medicine.

"Missionaries had been coming to the village for years, and some of the villagers converted as a result. The Church wanted to keep a presence there, keep the word of God flowing. Our goal was to build a church, even if it was a grass hut with dirt floors. We made plans and gathered materials for months. Everything was done by hand—we worked hard for that church. When nearly all the materials were gathered and we had constructed frames for the walls, the chief's son, Samuel, got sick. At first it was a little cold. We kept him in the hut that was our makeshift hospital. His symptoms got worse. The chief was furious with us and was convinced it was our construction of the church and his tolerance of a 'new way' that brought the curse upon his family. He told us if we were not able to heal his son with our God, we would all be put to death.

"Naturally, we were afraid for our lives, and the boy's. What little medicine we had didn't touch his fever. He was getting worse, not better. We were out of options, so we prayed. We prayed over him, night and day. After a week, the priest I traveled with pulled me aside and told me he was certain the boy would die. He wanted me to be prepared for our fate. At that point, there was nothing we could do but wait."

"What happened? I had no idea you came so close to becoming a martyr."

"We were scared," she admitted. "I was more afraid for Samuel. I didn't want him to die. He was only seven years old, and he was in a lot of pain. He was a sweet boy. He loved helping us in the jungle and spent months following us around. I didn't know what else to do, so I got my Bible out and opened it to Psalm 103."

"*Bless the Lord, O my soul: and all that is within me, bless his holy name. Bless the Lord, O my soul, and forget not all his benefits: Who forgiveth all thine iniquities; who healeth all thy diseases; Who redeemed thy life from destruction; who crowneth thee with loving kindness and tender mercies; Who satisfieth thy mouth with good things; so that thy youth is renewed like the eagle's.*" Aiden recited the passage perfectly.

Elidad smiled. "It was the only thing I could think of. I was pleading with God to help all of us."

"And it must have worked."

"Not quite. Not like you think."

"What do you mean? You're here now."

"True. But it wasn't a miracle cure. At the conclusion of me reading the passage, Samuel began to seize. His body shook violently, foam came out of his mouth, and his body flailed on his cot. I was terrified. I thought that my actions caused him to seize. Maybe the chief was right. Maybe it was our intrusion on their village that brought this curse to them. I had to fight off thoughts that made my faith waver.

"To keep him from hurting himself, I put my Bible down to hold Samuel's head against the bed while another person held his arms. When I put the Bible next to him, he began screaming. His cry was bloodcurdling. Other villagers came rushing in, fearful we were hurting him. All we could do was hold him down until the episode passed. But instead of it passing, it grew more intense. His eyes rolled back in his head and voices came out of him that were not his own. I know now, he was speaking in tongues, but back then it was the scariest thing I'd ever seen.

"We were forced to tie him down. His strength intensified and we were barely able to keep him on the cot. The priest I served with grabbed me by the arm and dragged me into a corner of the room. He told me that we would be held accountable for the boy's condition. He was scared. He insisted we needed to leave . . . sneak away in the middle of the night before we could be killed. I pulled away from him. How could we just leave Samuel to die? I felt responsible. How could the priest just want to sneak away?

"I remember him telling me: 'Forget him. He is nothing. He is damned to hell. You can stay here and go with him, or leave with me.'

"I was floored. I couldn't believe what he was telling me. I was fearful, too, but I didn't want to leave Samuel. I looked over at Samuel, his body bruised and beaten. His arms and legs now bleeding, cut from the restraints. I looked back at the priest, and he was gone. He left me there, alone. At fifteen, I never felt more alone. I stood in the corner of the room, dazed. What would I do?"

"What *did* you do?" Aiden was hanging on her every word.

"Just then, one of the villagers burst through the door with their medicine man. He'd been at a nearby village. It took a week for the messenger to bring him back.

"The medicine man was intimidating. He towered over everyone in the room. Piercings glinted against his charcoal skin in his nose. Bone stuck through his neck and ears. He looked like a walking voodoo doll. He took one look at me and pushed past to Samuel. He picked up my Bible off the bed and threw it at me. The boy's screaming instantly subsided. 'Yours?' he demanded.

"I was afraid to answer, but I said *yes*.

"'Not time for that yet,' he told me.

"I didn't understand, but I was too afraid to ask what he meant. He softly pushed his hand against the boy's forehead, pulling his eyelids back. The medicine man looked at one of the women and barked orders. He waived his hands as he spoke, women scattered like mice in response, as Samuel wriggling under his touch.

"I was surprised he spoke English so well, we hadn't heard him speak in anything but his native tongue. I couldn't take my eyes off Samuel. His body was warm from the constant struggling with the restraints. His breath was labored; his chest slowly rose and fell with a raspy sound.

"'Your priest left you', the medicine man stated as I looked down at the Bible, shaking violently in my hands.

"'I won't go', I told him. I looked back at the helpless boy. 'I won't leave him.' It took all my strength to lock eyes with the medicine man. 'Do you know what he has? Do you know what's wrong with him?'

"'I do.'

"'Can you make him well?' I was afraid of the answer, but I had to know.

"'I can. It will not be easy. But he will be well again.' He looked me up and down. 'You will stay, and help me make him well.'

"That's all I wanted.

"The first woman he sent running with the wave of his hand burst through the door, her arms full of various items. She knelt to place them in the center of the room at our feet. The medicine man knelt to inspect what she brought. When he did, I noticed a crucifix dangled from his neck, and a cross tattooed on his arm. He handed a bowl to the woman, and she rushed to a corner of the room and frantically started a fire, placing the bowl on the flames, water full to the brim.

"'What is wrong with him?' I asked.

"'He is possessed. I am surprised your priest did not know,' he answered.

"'How do you know?'

"He held out his hand. 'Give me your Bible.'

"I obeyed without question. He took the book and placed it on the boy's chest. His violent reaction was instantaneous. His grueling screams filled the room. Skin crawled over his bones in an unnatural way, as he pulled against the restraints. His head lifted as he swung it from side to side, clearly trying to remove the Bible. The medicine man picked it back up and handed it to me.

"'How could your priest not know?'

"I shook my head. 'I don't know. He didn't. I didn't.'

"'I wouldn't expect you to. You are young,' he observed.

"'My name is Christian.'

"'Christian?' I repeated.

"He smiled. 'Yes. My given name you would have a hard time saying, but I decided to take on the name of the beliefs that have changed my life. From now until I die, I will be Christian.'

"'How long have you been saved?' I couldn't think of anything else to ask.

"'Five years. I was a little boy when your people came here. They brought magic that saved my father's life. The magic of the syringe. The medicine they injected him with was something we had never seen. The priests prayed over him, and in a few days, he was well. My father sent me to help the missionary, the man who cured the medicine man. They taught me how to use their medicine and I learned of their God.' He smiled. 'My God.'

"I was astounded at his story. How unique for a medicine man to be converted to a Christian. Here in this place, he knew how to save this boy, and in turn, save me."

Elidad took a breath. "At that moment in my life, I knew, God intended for me to live. It was a miracle.

"As I stood in the middle of the room, Christian and the woman worked circles around me, preparing for the ceremony. When the time came, he began chanting, his arms reaching up to the sky; the boy beneath him began shaking. The woman helped light incense, waving it over both the cot and Christian. Samuel's body surged like electricity was being pumped through him. He opened his eyes and again only the whites were showing. The boy leaned forward, trying to bite Christian with sharp, jagged teeth.

"I, too, thought I knew what an exorcism was, Aiden. I read about them in books and had many conversations with Abraham about what he'd seen. I knew the process: identify the demon, get the demon to tell you its name, and finally command the demon to leave the victim's body. But until I was present for one, I could never understand.

"As the demon began to surface in the boy, his skin began to change. His body appeared to take a different shape. His voice wasn't his own. As his appearance changed, the room around us felt like it was changing, as well. Every evil element around us felt like it was closing in, tightening its grip. Fear and hatred in my own soul rose in my chest. I found my thoughts drifting to the priest that left me there by myself. I wished bad things would come to him for what he did.

"I couldn't believe I was thinking like that at such a crucial time. My thoughts should have been about Samuel, not revenge, not hatred. So I began praying . . . praying for the boy, and praying that God would keep me from evil thoughts.

"When my eyes were closed tightly, the room filled with a rancid smell. It was repulsive, like rotting flesh. When I opened my eyes again, the innocent boy was gone, and an evil demon lay strapped to the bed. Christian waived his hands over the demon, producing out of nowhere a small, brightly colored bird. Christian held it firmly in his hands as it pecked and struggled to free itself as though it knew its fate. Christian produced a knife, slit the bird's throat, and let its blood drip down onto the body below.

"The demon shook and laughed, the blood absorbing into its skin. 'Yes,' it hissed. 'Give me sacrifices of blood, and I shall spare this child.'

"'Tell me your name, demon,' Christian demanded.

"The demon screeched, 'I am Vamdemon! I demand you give me your sacrifice, or bear my wrath!'

"'The only sacrifice I give is my own body. Therefore, I urge you, brothers and sisters, in view of God's mercy, to offer your bodies as a living sacrifice, holy and pleasing to God.'

"The demon screamed at his answer of scripture. Christian looked over his shoulder at me, like he expected me to know what I was supposed to do. I opened my Bible to Psalm 61: 1-4. *Hear my cry, O God; listen to my prayer. From the ends of the earth I call to you, I call as my heart grows faint; lead me to the rock that is higher than I. For you have been my refuge, a strong tower against the foe. I long to dwell in your tent forever and take refuge in the shelter of your wings.*

"At the sound of my voice the demon screamed, but under his cries, I swore I heard Samuel's voice.

"My heart leapt as tears streamed down my face. To hear Samuel's voice gave me hope. I wanted to go to him and hold his hand, but I knew the demon still had control of him.

"Aiden, that exorcism still bothers me. When I'm alone at night, I still remember how I felt, what I smelled in that room, the sound of Samuel's screams. I have nightmares about all the exorcisms I've attended."

"Did the boy survive?" Aiden asked.

"Yes, he did. And he gave up his inherited right to be the chief of his tribe to be a priest in his village. He built his church, and he teaches Christianity to hundreds that would not have heard the word otherwise."

"That's amazing." Aiden's mind was buzzing.

"It *is* amazing. Just remember, through the toils and troubles of our life, we are only serving one God. Religion is perfect, the Bible is perfect. Man is not. Unfortunately, man does what he thinks is best, and most of the time, he makes mistakes trying.

"Don't lose faith because man's actions have tainted a pure thing. God is always the same, no matter how dirty the glass is you're looking through. Sometimes we just have to open the window to get a better look."

Aiden leaned forward rubbing the back of his neck. "Wow. You can give good advice." He looked up to meet her eyes. "Maybe you should listen to yourself sometime."

She stared at him. He was right. She smirked. "God *does* work in mysterious ways, doesn't he?"

"So that's when you went missing?"

"I wasn't missing. I was right where they left me . . . kinda. I stayed in the village, but began studying with Christian from that time forward. He accepted Christ, but he also had a vast knowledge of demonic possession through his tribe. They were keener on diagnosing possession than we are. With less distractions from the modern world they are more in tune to issues of the soul when they arise."

"They let you stay there after the boy survived his possession?" Aiden was surprised.

"The chief was happy that his son lived and Samuel was adamant that we stay to tutor him. We spent the rest of our time building the church. When it was built, we went to the surrounding villages to let them know there was a house of God for them to visit. Christian had been telling people about Christ for years; there were many people excited about a place where they could go to learn more. We touched so many lives, Aiden. It truly was amazing."

There was a long pause, filled with the ticking of Abraham's metronome and the crackling fire. The day wearing hard on Aiden's dark brows. Elidad wanted to give him time to absorb everything. She watched him as he stared into the dancing flames.

"So, now what?" Aiden asked finally.

"I don't know," Elidad told him truthfully. "Leucosia told us that I needed to reconsider all the signs, that I only understood part of Abraham's message."

"You found the key . . . what more can there be?"

"I don't know, but you can be sure if Leucosia says there is more to it, there is. I keep playing the dream through my head and I can't figure out what else I missed."

"I'm sure it was hard for you to concentrate on everything while you were being choked to death and all," Aiden said lightly.

"You're right."

"I know. You're lucky to be alive, let alone remember anything," he said, honestly. "Why didn't Leucosia just tell us what he was trying to say?"

Elidad smiled. "Welcome to the life of a seer. I told you they can be a pain in the ass. They can't interfere too much, or it can alter the future. A good seer will give you guidance so you can find your own way, without outright telling you what's going on.

"That's why the Church doesn't like her sister—she will tell anyone everything they want to know, if they have money. That's not good for anyone."

"So, what am I right about, then?" Aiden asked.

"It was hard to concentrate on anything other than being choked, so maybe Abraham already told me what he needed to." Elidad got out of her chair and moved across the room to the large desk where the burned Bible still lay.

She opened the cover, revealing a small amount of ashes still inside the binding. "When Abraham read from the Bible it burst into flames, and that's when the dark figure started choking me. Maybe he attacked me to keep me from understanding what Abraham was saying." Elidad flicked at the ash, attempting to brush it away. Some of it smeared on the inside cover.

Something about the cover caught her attention, a line that didn't belong. She leaned in to get a closer look. Realizing what was there, she scooped up some of the ash from Abraham's desk and smeared her hand from side to side on the inside of the cover. As her hand brushed across the surface, a symbol began to appear where it had been hidden before.

Watching Elidad inspect the book Aiden crossed the room to stand by her.

"What is it?" he asked.

"It's a symbol."

"I see that. But of what?"

"It's a symbol on an old tombstone."

Aiden looked at her. "How do you know that?"

"Abraham took me to see it when I was young. We went in the summer, a family vacation. The tombstone's in a graveyard of a church. The church overlooks a bay in a tiny town. Abraham always talked about that trip, how he wanted to go back.

"He liked to take rubbings—it was kind of a hobby. I took the rubbing of this tombstone, because of the pretty symbol." She shrugged. "I was young. I liked pretty things."

"Okay," Aiden said thoughtfully. "Then what is that tombstone doing imprinted on the inside cover of his Bible?"

She shook her head. "I have no idea, but we are going to find out."

"How are we going to find out?"

"We are going to the church," she answered, as if he should have known.

He stared at her. "Without knowing why, we are going to go to this church, and hope there's some answer, or direction, for us?"

"Yep. That's the plan." She smiled broadly.

"How far away is it?"

"Maybe a four-hour flight."

He shook his head in disagreement. "Why on earth would we fly four hours away not knowing if we are going to the right place?"

"Oh, Aiden. Don't get all huffy. The Church will be paying for it. We'll take their jet. Besides, you can feel good about going there, the church is in Trinity."

"So. What does that matter? And you know, this is exactly why they sent me to go with you. To keep you from doing pointless things on the Church's dime."

"Trinity is in Newfoundland." Her tone was condescending.

"I have never been there. I have no idea what I'm missing." He was too tired for her guessing game.

She faked an irritated sigh. "Newfoundland is a province of Canada."

Aiden rolled his eyes. "Right. I should have guessed. Canada."

Shortly after the plane lifted off the ground Elidad looked out the side window at the twinkling lights of the city below.

How peaceful it all looks from up here, she thought.

She wondered what they might find in Canada. Would the little church give them some hope of finding Abraham? Would he have left something there for her? She wished he left a clue, something more than a dream and a shadow of an image inside a book.

She knew their path was leading them to the church, but Aiden's doubt made her second guess herself.

"Dang it." Aiden was annoyed, rummaging through his luggage.

Elidad turned to see what he was doing. "What's your problem?"

He frowned at her, aggressively closing his suitcase. "I forgot my coat."

CHAPTER EIGHTEEN

"I don't want to go to Canada," Elidad shouted.

Abraham smiled back at her. "I understand why you are upset, Elidad, but it can't be helped. No one knew the school was going to receive this gift. I planned this vacation a long time ago. You know that."

Elidad felt terrible inside. She knew what he was saying was true. He *had* been planning this trip for a long time. Their tickets were purchased nine months ago. He'd been talking about going to Trinity for years, ever since he found an article on the town in a travel magazine. He kept the magazine on one of his many bookshelves, a blue tab stuck out of the pages with his hand-written note: "Trinity." Every time he talked about it, he would pull the magazine off the shelf and open it for her to see. She knew he wanted to go on this trip more than anything. And now she didn't want to go.

Recently, a wealthy alumni of the school passed away leaving a large donation to the school. The donor left instructions for the school describing how she wanted her money spent. She wished for the entire sixth, seventh, and eighth grades to go to Disney World.

"We can go to Disney World another time, Elidad. Our trip will be wonderful; I know you will enjoy it."

The tears streamed down her face. When she really considered it, she wasn't sure why she was so upset about it, anyway. It's not like she would have fun with the other kids. Even there, she would be an outcast, but somewhere inside she hoped that in a land of make-believe the other children would see past her differences and accept her for who she was. She knew that was hoping for too much, but over the last few days, it was all she fantasized about.

Abraham put his hand on her shoulder. "This trip is very important. If it wasn't, we would go to Disney World."

Elidad remembered looking up into his face, so sincere, and so full of regret. She knew he didn't mean for her to feel any pain.

"Why is it important?" she asked.

Brushing away her tears, he said, "Just wait until you see the bay. It is just beautiful. The town's population is just three hundred people, but there are fifty architecturally significant buildings." She knew he was trying to appeal to her historical interests. Throughout her middle-school years she'd grown fond of history. He knew pressing the historical background would make it easier to win her over.

She sighed. She *had* wanted to go to Trinity, and the more she thought it over the more she knew she would enjoy her time with Abraham more than she would enjoy the trip with her classmates.

The people in Trinity took pride in their town and preserved it as though it were a museum. The structures were perfect. The grownups in the town loved that Elidad was so interested in the buildings and history, despite her age. They all treated her like a princess, making her feel accepted and important.

When they finally made it home, she knew her trip was more fun than Disney World. She was glad Abraham had remained so adamant about going.

"Where to now?" Aiden's voice snapped her out of her reverie. He'd just finished piling their luggage in the trunk of the car they rented.

"The Grover House. That's where we are staying until we can figure out why we're here. It'll take us a while to get there."

"The Grover House," Aiden repeated. "Sounds fancy."

"It's nice. Nineteenth century." She shrugged. "Why stay in a hotel when the Church is footing the bill?"

She snickered under her breath at his glare of disapproval.

CHAPTER NINETEEN

The town was small and picturesque. Everywhere you turned, a new scene masqueraded as postcards images. Beautiful landscapes you would find covering a wall in a tourist trinket store.

Just as she remembered, the town held true to its heritage. Many of the buildings looked the same as when they'd been built, nineteenth century.

When they pulled up to the Grover House, the bay lay behind it, a few boats bobbing in the backdrop. Aiden and Elidad both hesitated, taking in the serenity before exiting the vehicle.

Elidad smiled to herself, remembering back to when she and Abraham had been here before. It was summer then, and the sun managed to peek through the clouds. She spent hours playing on the bayshore, building sandcastles and digging for shells.

"You have been here before?" Aiden asked, still looking across the water.

"This is where Abraham and I stayed for a vacation, one summer."

As they unpacked their belongings from the car a dog came bounding out of the house to greet them. Elidad smiled, "Hello, Max." She knelt on one knee to greet him.

"You two have met before?" a woman's voice asked from the porch.

Elidad and Aiden walked toward her, their arms full with luggage. The woman smiled at Elidad, apparently recognizing her face.

"Well I'll be, I *do* remember you. Course you're all grown up now, and such a beautiful young lady you've become.

"It's funny . . . I told Bill your name sounded familiar on the reservation. He told me we've had over three hundred people board here since we bought the place; every name sounds familiar to me.

But I told him your name was different. Yours is unique. I might go a hundred years and not meet another Elidad." She smiled confidently, pleased she'd been right.

"Yes, and you are Betty, right?" Elidad asked.

"Oh, yes, dear. I'm sorry. She offered her hand to help Elidad with her luggage. "You have such a good memory."

Elidad shrugged. "You and your husband were so nice to us when we visited before. We had a wonderful time. I wouldn't forget that."

"You are too sweet. How is your father?" she asked.

Aiden tensed at the thought of Abraham.

"He's well, thank you. He says to say hello." Elidad smiled, not skipping a beat.

"So nice to hear, dear," Betty said as she held open the door. "We're glad you came back." She eyed Aiden. "I'm assuming you two aren't on your honeymoon, seeing as you've booked two rooms."

"Right," Elidad answered. "This is Aiden. We're here on business, unfortunately, not pleasure."

Betty frowned. "Not too much business 'round these parts."

"No," Elidad admitted. "Research mostly, for a book."

Betty smiled. "Well, how lovely. I'll show you to your rooms then. Come along, Max," she hollered back over her shoulder.

Elidad unpacked a few things from her suitcase and hung them in the closet, wondering how long they'd be staying. Not knowing exactly what they were looking for was a little disheartening, but she knew without a doubt they were meant to come to Trinity. Abraham tried hard to point her in this direction, and the dark figure did what he could to keep her from finding her way.

She hoped what they came for was Abraham. She smiled, thinking about how much he loved it in Trinity. It wouldn't be difficult to convince him to stay as a substitute priest in one of their churches.

He always wanted to come back. He spoke of it many times. Maybe he'd grown tired of waiting on her, and decided to come alone. Could he lose six months assisting one of the priests in town? Would he stay to fill in for another priest without notifying his superiors?

Elidad pictured her and Aiden stumbling on Abraham at a local church, taking care of daily tasks. In her heart she knew it wouldn't be that easy, but it was a good dream.

Leucosia's warning rang through her mind. *Finding one key will lead you to the other, and in turn that will set you on your true path . . . to your destiny.*

A chill came over her. Her true destiny. Leucosia's words sounded infinite. It didn't sound like this was going to be a short trip with all the answers at their first stop.

That night, under the brink of pure exhaustion, Elidad didn't remember falling asleep, and was only aware that she had when she awoke in the darkness.

Hearing footsteps in the hall, she lay still, wondering where Aiden was going. His room was the only other on the floor. Maybe he was checking on her. Her previous nightmare scared him more than it scared her. He told her many times, if he hadn't woken her, she would have been strangled to death. He was exaggerating. How could anyone suffocate in their sleep? People can't hold their breath until they die. It's physically impossible. Maybe he was coming to make sure she was still breathing.

Elidad's eyes caught a slight movement as the door handle slowly turned. She wasn't sure why, but she held in her breath as it clicked open. The door slowly pushed forward. Elidad exhaled with surprise to see Lucian standing in the doorway. She propped herself up on her pillows to consider what she was seeing. Was he really standing in her room?

She wasn't awake enough to ask him what he was doing here. Her surprise kept her from speaking at all. He quickly made his way to the side of her bed and sat beside her.

He was without words, engulfed in moonlight. Elidad could feel her heart race as he moved closer.

In this opaque light, his form was flawless. His masculinity invoked a weakness inside herself. A place she could usually keep hidden from others; a place delicately vulnerable. The sound of his breath was steady. Through the darkness, Elidad could feel the tension between them. She sensed he wanted to reach out to her, and she wanted him to, but was frozen by her own wavering sensibility.

Lucian's lips quivered a tentative, insecure smile. It appeared he was looking for some indication his intrusion was welcome. Her stomach felt heavy at the thought of Aiden. How would it look if he came to her door? What would he think if he found the two of them together in her room? Her head was spinning. She didn't want to think about it. Thinking complicated things too much. Aiden complicated it.

Lucian reached forward and softly caressed her face, lightly pressing his index finger over her lips to silence her doubt before she had a chance to voice it. His skin was warm but his touch sent chills, like a shock wave, through her body. His hand moved away from her mouth, traced her jawline with a stroke of his finger, gently caressing the nape of her neck to her shoulder. She closed her eyes, not wanting the moment to end, allowing herself to linger in the mix of sensations. An advantage she never permitted herself to take.

In response to his touch, she pressed her hand on his chest. She could feel the pulse of his heart. It was so strong under her hand it almost muffled the sound of the footsteps coming down the hall. Elidad's own heart skipped a beat, knowing this time it had to be Aiden coming to her room. He would find them together, in the dark. What would his reaction be? Would he be angry?

She became overwhelmed with worry as his footsteps grew nearer.

Elidad opened her eyes to the bright morning light, her own hand pressed against her face. Relief came over her as she looked around and found herself alone—the pace of her heart identical to that of her dream. A light tap on her door startled her.

"Yes?" she answered, trying unsuccessfully to sound calm.

The door opened slightly. She was glad to see Aiden standing in the opening, albeit with a slight twinge of regret when she realized it wasn't Lucian that came to wake her.

"What's wrong with you?" Aiden asked.

"Nothing. I just had a strange dream."

"Oh, Lord. I hope it wasn't like the last one?" He was concerned.

Elidad lay back on her soft pillows to stare up at the ceiling. "Don't worry. It was nothing like the last one."

CHAPTER TWENTY

Elidad decided it would be best to make their way to the nearby inn for breakfast. She thought it would be the perfect place for them to catch up on the local gossip. Maybe they would get lucky and over-hear conversations of strange happenings in the area.

Like the rest of the town, the inn was picturesque. Their table looked out over the bay. A thick coat of heavy fog dulled the sun's morning rays.

Eavesdropping on people made it easy for Elidad to avoid conversation with Aiden. After her dream she felt uncomfortable making eye contact with him. She wasn't sure why, but she felt like she had betrayed him in some way. Just because he had taken an oath of celibacy didn't mean she had to. She felt silly for feeling guilty about being attracted to Lucian.

As she listened to the chitchat, Elidad began to realize how much she liked simple talk about ordinary lives. Ordinary was a luxury she would never have. She envied them—careless in a way, naive to what the world was really like.

What would she give to be blind to everything? What would she give to unknow what she knew?

"Envy." She let the word slip out of her mouth.

"What?" Aiden looked at her confused.

She was embarrassed he heard her. "It's a deadly sin, that's all."

He frowned. "I know that."

"Well, dears, how ya doin' over here?" The waitress saved Elidad from having to explain her outburst.

"Very well, ma'am." Aiden smiled.

The waitress put her hand on her hip. "Are you two here for your honeymoon?"

"Who, us? Nooo . . ." The word hung on his lips as he shot an uncomfortable glace at Elidad.

"Oh dear, I didn't mean to put you on the spot." The waitress laughed as she patted his shoulder. "We just get a lot of honeymooners here, that's all."

"We are here for work," Elidad informed her, in an attempt to save Aiden.

The waitress sighed. "Work is not the best reason to come here, but at least it's a beautiful place to work. What do ya'll do?"

Aiden was glad she hadn't directed her question at him; he wasn't sure he could come up with anything on the spot.

Elidad smiled at her politely. "We are here to study early habits of the Christian settlers here. We are writing an article on the old churches in the area and the ideal state of many of the historical buildings."

Aiden gaped at Elidad. He was floored at how effortlessly she rattled off her lie. This was the second time she astounded him with her ability to deceive. He wouldn't be capable of possessing that skill.

"Your community has taken such great care of your buildings. We think other towns should follow your example on the care and preservation of historical landmarks." Elidad sold a convincing story.

Turning his attention to the waitress, Aiden could see the pride well up inside her.

Aiden smiled, seeing Elidad work like this. She always had a hard exterior, but was smart enough to turn on the charm when it was convenient. Aiden was also beginning to realize she was nice to most people, just not him.

"Well, dear, I am sure glad someone is smart enough to take note on the subject," the waitress said, still beaming. "Have you been to any of the churches yet?"

"No," Elidad told her. "We just got in last night. We'll spend most of the day looking for the oldest, best preserved buildings. Do you have any ideas on where to start?"

The waitress thought hard. "I would go to St. Paul church. It's beautiful."

"Oh, yes," Elidad agreed. "That church was built in 1892, right?"

"You've done your homework. You know a lot for being so young. How old are you, darling?"

Elidad felt blood rush to her cheeks, but she kept her smile. "I'm twenty-three." Age had always been an obstacle in her life.

"I didn't mean to embarrass you, dear, you are just a smart girl, and good for you. That's nothing to be ashamed of." She patted Elidad on the back.

Elidad ignored her attempt to smooth things over. "Has there been anyone else new in town? We are supposed to meet some colleagues."

Aiden frowned, not understanding why she was making up fictional traveling companions.

Making quick eye contact with Aiden, Elidad ever-so-slightly shook her head, not wanting him to give them away.

The waitress's pen went to her chin in thought. "Not lately. A few weeks ago there was a man. But no one since."

"Maybe they came early?" Elidad pressed.

"I doubt it." The waitress frowned.

"Why's that? Sometimes our colleagues like to get a jump on things."

The waitress looked over her shoulders to make sure no one was listening before sliding into the booth next to Elidad.

Leaning into the table to speak with a soft voice, she said, "I don't think he was your colleague because he left. Maxine from the inn told me he was gone before his week was up . . . he didn't bother to check out."

"Really?" Elidad's eyes widened with pretend shock. "Who would do that?"

"I know," the waitress agreed. "He just left. Left some of his belongings in his room and didn't even bother to turn his key back in. I suppose Trinity wasn't what he had in mind for a vacation."

Elidad shook her head. "Some people."

"Right? So that's why I don't think he was your friend. If he was, he'd still be waiting for you. He wouldn't just leave."

Elidad nodded in agreement. "You're right. Our colleagues wouldn't just disappear. I guess they haven't shown up yet. Thank you so much for sharing. We appreciate it."

Someone from another table waved the waitress down. "Let me know if you need anything else, dears." And with that she was off again to attend to her daily duties.

Aiden leaned across the table. "Do you think it was Abraham that was here before us?"

Elidad shrugged. "I don't know."

Aiden sighed. "I still don't know why we are here. I doubt this mysterious man was Abraham."

"I doubt it, too," Elidad agreed.

"Then why are we here, Elidad?"

She sighed. "We came here because Leucosia told us we would be going to Canada."

"No, she didn't. She told me not to forget my coat because it is cold in Canada. That's all. We could be wasting time here, Elidad. Abraham could be in trouble and we are on a wild goose chase." He flailed his hands in the air. "Are we even looking for him? Or are we looking for these keys?"

Elidad rubbed her forehead. "I know it's a lot to wrap your mind around, Aiden. We came here because I had a dream that led me to a key that led me to a book with a hidden symbol on the inside of the cover. We came here because I know where that symbol is, on a tombstone, in Canada, in the yard of a church, only five minutes away from here. We are here because someone I trust who can see the future told us, in a roundabout way, that we would end up in Canada, you without a coat. Which really was the case, wasn't it?" She was trying hard not to be annoyed with him, but wasn't accustomed to explaining herself.

"If that church is only five minutes away, then why are we here?" Aiden looked like a scolded child.

She smiled back at him. "Because we've got to eat, don't we?"

Aiden rolled his eyes.

"Besides, we need to wait until we're sure there will be someone at the church working."

"Why do we want someone to be there?"

"Because, we might need to get into the church."

Aiden's eyes widened. "Why do we need to get into the church?"

Elidad shrugged. "I don't know, but we are going to look there first, before we dig into the grave."

Aiden scowled. "We wouldn't."

A crooked smile pierced her lips. "You wouldn't, but *I* would." She was amused at the fear in his eyes. "You are a man of God, aren't you?"

He gave her another dirty look. "I hate it when you ask me that. Why?"

"Because, for a man of faith, you sure don't have a lot." She chuckled. "And you sure suck at following signs. You need to learn how to follow with your heart, Aiden, not your mind. Your mind will deceive you."

"We only came here for one reason: to find Abraham. That's it. You are deluding yourself with these dreams, thinking you are on some holy quest or something." He sneered back.

Elidad's eyes sharpened. "Get one thing straight, Priest: I came here for more than one reason. *You* came here for only one: to tag along with me as I go about my business. I am going to work this the way I think it should be worked, and if you have a problem with that, then maybe you need to rethink your choices. If Leucosia tells me we need to look for the keys, I will. I don't work for the Church anymore, Aiden. You do. You need to tag along with me, not the other way around. That means we do this my way." Elidad leaned back against the booth. "If you think finding these keys sounds like a holy quest to you, then by all means, get your damn sword and banner ready," she said, holding up her fork like a flag, "because we are marching into battle."

"But that's not all she said, was it?" Aiden asked her.

Elidad placed her fork back on the table. "What do you mean?"

"She told you this quest might not be for you. She said you needed to ask your Creator for guidance, remember?" He took a cautious breath. "She said your soul was susceptible to evil."

Elidad smiled. "All of our souls are, Aiden. Even yours. That's kinda the whole challenge of life, don't you think?

"She said she can't see the outcome of this whole thing and that's why she is hesitant. That means this will be difficult for me, and probably you. That's when seers have a hard time telling the future, when the lines of good and evil no longer have a clear boundary. We'll be at a crossroads, and every decision will affect the future."

Aiden sighed. "Well, that's encouraging."

Elidad laughed as she held up her coffee cup in a salute. "Just another day on the job."

CHAPTER TWENTY-ONE

When they pulled up to the front of the old building, it was easy to fall in love with the quaint little church. The gothic architecture was simple but elegant against such a beautiful backdrop. The small church had been in operation since the mid-nineteenth century, and sat proudly beside the bay. The red and blue accents around the windows were appealing and the steeple stood tall above the water, towering like a lighthouse.

Aiden and Elidad walked toward the cemetery hugged against one side of the church, outlined with a small white picket fence. The headstones that the fence corralled were weathered and worn from years of coastal climate abuse, making it difficult to read some of the writing etched on them.

Aiden was surprised to see dates from the early eighteen hundreds. As his eyes scanned the dates, he realized how tragic and hard life had been. Their lifespans were short, and no doubt difficult. Many of them only lived to be thirty years old; others a mere twenty.

Aiden felt like he was being watched. Looking up, he caught Elidad staring at him. He insecurely shifted his body weight. He realized she had been watching him carefully as he surveyed the graveyard.

"Amazing, isn't it?" she asked.

"Actually, yes."

"It makes you appreciate the life you have. To realize how hard their lives were, and the difficulties that made their lives short." Elidad made her way through the graves to stand by Aiden. "Did you see it?"

"See what?" But before she answered, his eyes came across the next headstone in the row in which they were standing. The emblem was precisely the same as the one embossed on the front cover of Abraham's Bible.

The rest of the tombstone was illegible. The face worn and eroded, washed completely away.

Elidad was not mistaken. It was the same marking, without a doubt.

Recognizing the look in Aiden's eyes Elidad stepped closer, putting her hand on his arm. "I know this is hard for you, Aiden, and it *is* crazy. But it will only get crazier. I don't know what else we will find, or what will happen. You need to be ready for anything."

Aiden continued to stare at the blank tombstone.

"Aiden, you could go back home. Tell them this assignment was too much for you . . . maybe they'll still help me."

He shook his head. "No. They won't." He turned his face to her. "There are rumors of Abraham using magic, so they won't allow him to come back easily. That's why they were hesitant to come to you in the first place. Since you left, they think you and he have been meddling in the dark arts, together. In the beginning, the fear was that he came missing on his own accord—that maybe he switched allegiances."

Elidad began to pull her hand away from Aiden's arm and he put his hand over hers to hold it in place. He looked deep into her eyes. "I came because I don't believe the rumors. I came so when we find him he can clear his name, and yours."

Elidad forcefully withdrew her hand from his grip. "Why didn't you tell me earlier?"

"Because it wasn't important then. I'd only make you angry, like it is. You being angry doesn't help your situation, or Abraham's. Elidad, it doesn't matter why they sent me. I only came for one reason: to help you and Abraham. I told you, I love him, too. He is the reason I am the person I am today. He would never do anything that would put a wedge between him and God.

"I will stay with you until we find him. You might think I am slowing you down; I am trying hard not to. I am trying to be as helpful as possible." He took a deep breath. "Elidad, I will follow you anywhere."

She was overrun by emotion, his sincerity dissolving her anger. She knew how hard it was for him to admit he was at her whim. He'd always been a leader and conceding would be difficult for him.

Though it was demeaning, feeling like she was given a babysitter, her views on his presence began to change. It began to feel like he *was* there to help her and Abraham.

She had to admit, it was nice to have someone to travel with. It was nice to be able to talk things out with another person, instead of having a hidden life. He was right: telling her wouldn't have helped the situation. She would've started this journey angrier at the Church than she was already. Refusing their help from the beginning, they wouldn't have made it this far. She might still be in her apartment, trying to figure out the meaning of life.

"I hope you're not hiding anything else from me, Aiden."

"I'm not," he assured. "That's everything."

Elidad walked to the tombstone and kneeled over it. She needed to stay focused. They needed to find out why the tombstone was important. She reached forward and touched the stone with her bare hands. It was cool and dusty under her fingertips.

Elidad closed her eyes and bowed her head and quietly whispered words aloud. "Dear Heavenly Father, I pray you will hear my words. I need you now, dear Lord. I need you to guide me on the path to righteousness. *If* this is where you intend to lead me, Lord, please give me some guidance. May we find our way, doing your work, in your glory. In Jesus' name, I pray. Amen."

"Amen," Aiden whispered behind her.

As she opened her eyes, head still bowed, something in the grass reflected the daylight. Elidad bowed a little closer to the ground, reaching out to touch whatever it was.

It was a chain, hidden in the dirt. She pulled at it, but the grass was reluctant to give up whatever it was. Elidad grabbed handfuls of grass, she could smell the greens as she threw them away. A big tug on a large handful began to unearth it more.

"What is it?" Aiden asked.

"I can't tell." Elidad pulled a little harder and it came loose in her hand. When she held it up, even being caked with dirt and grass, she knew what it was. It was a necklace, almost identical to the one she wore around her neck. The necklace, given to her by her father.

"What is it?" Aiden repeated.

"It's a key," she told him.

Aiden frowned. "Not the keys we are looking for?"

"No, not the keys we are looking for. But indeed a key."

With her words, the front door of the church swung open and a large, booming man stepped out to greet them.

"Hello friends," he said merrily. The way he held up his hands, Elidad knew instantly he was the leader of the church.

He was an older man, not as old as Abraham, perhaps in his late fifties. His demeanor emanating happiness and love.

"Hello." Elidad was smiling her pleasant smile, tucking the necklace into her pocket. "Good day to you."

Aiden again was mesmerized by her ability to turn on the charm. Her ability to act was award winning.

"Good day, indeed," the man beamed back.

Aiden and Elidad made their way through the headstones to meet him. The man extended his hand. Elidad reached forward, allowing their hands to embrace. She was pleased with his firm, honest handshake.

"My name is John Michel Stevens, the rector of the cathedral," he brightly introduced himself.

"I am Elidad, and this is Aiden, my collogue." The two men shook hands.

"Ellie at the cafe gave me a call, said you might be heading this way," John informed them.

Elidad glanced at Aiden with a smile. "She did, did she?" Her voice sounded surprised, but Aiden knew it was part of the act. He wondered how she knew the waitress would call ahead to make their presence welcome.

"We are so happy to have you here. How can we be of any assistance in your quest?"

Elidad and Aiden looked dumbly at one another.

"Our quest?" Aiden asked.

"You are here seeking the truth. You are interested in how we take care of this magnificent structure. You are going to share it with others, aren't you? In a magazine of some sort?"

Elidad laughed. "Yes. We are."

John smiled broadly. "A true quest. If it results in others preserving their churches, then surely it's a quest ordained by God."

Riddled with guilt, Aiden sighed. "I hope so."

"I'm sure of it," John told Aiden as he briskly hit Aiden's shoulder, a gesture of reassurance.

"Oh, John, you are too sweet. We hope we are not a bother, showing up on your doorstep like this. I feel terrible we were unable to contact you in advance. We would love to spend some time with you and your church. Unfortunately, our colleague hasn't made it to town yet. He was supposed to set up appointments for us. We just found out he didn't make it. You'll have to forgive us. If this isn't a good time, we can always come back."

"Nonsense, my dear. You are not a bother. None of us should be bothered with the works of the Lord." He smiled. "We would love to share with others the history of this church. Its story needs to be shared. Did you know, people have been worshiping God in this house for over a hundred years?"

Elidad's eyes grew with excitement. "I did know, but just to hear you say it gives me goosebumps."

John was ecstatic to see her interest. "It is a wonderful thing; a true blessing."

"John, if it isn't too much to ask, we would love to have a tour of your church, whenever it's convenient for you, of course."

"Of course," John said enthusiastically. "You didn't come all this way to stand on our threshold." He smiled, turning to open the door and waved them in.

The pit in Aiden's stomach began to churn with their deceit. John seemed an honest man of God; a genuinely good person. Aiden didn't join the Church to deceive people, especially people like John. He wondered if this was how Adam felt when Eve led him astray.

Aiden's eyes met Elidad's for a second before stepping into the church. He meant what he told her. He *would* follow her anywhere.

Inside, the church was in pristine condition. The pews smelled like rich polish and gleamed like crystal. Anyone who entered the structure could tell there were many invested hours of polishing to achieve this level of care. The boards beneath their feet creaked softly like tall trees in a gentle gust of wind. It was warm inside with the sun shining through the stained-glass windows, despite the foggy haze that'd been looming all day.

"Magnificent." Elidad's hushed voice fit the moment.

Many years of worship these walls housed. The prayers heard, the love that was vowed, and all the sorrow that was comforted. John was right: It truly was a blessing.

"You said your friend was supposed to come and set up meetings for you?" John inquired.

"Yes, that's right," Elidad confirmed. "Unfortunately, we haven't been able to get in contact with him. He didn't set up a single appointment for us. So, here we are, and no one is expecting us. We'll waste a lot of time trying to meet with people. That's why we sent him ahead, so that part of the work would be done."

John shook his head. "That is a shame. I hope your friend is well."

"Oh, I wouldn't worry about that, John. He's a busy man; he always has a million things going. He just fired his assistant so he's been a little flaky. I'm sure he'll show up soon."

"There was a man staying at the inn, maybe a month ago, that came to look at the church," John offered.

"Really?" Elidad looked at Aiden. "What did he look like?"

"About the same age as me, a little nervous, but a very nice man. He dressed a little like this guy," he said, pointing to Aiden, "but not as quiet."

"Did he say why he was here?" Elidad asked.

John frowned. "Just to pray." He shrugged. "I went back to the office to do some work, and when I came back he'd quietly slipped out."

"Well, then I suppose he wasn't our man." Elidad smiled. "Our colleague would have hounded you for hours. But I'm sure you get people in to see your church all the time. Look at how beautiful it is." Elidad waved her hand over the wood. "You and your congregation must work so hard to keep it in this condition."

The rector smiled widely. "We do work hard," he agreed. "I'm so glad you can see that. It's nice to see young people like you so passionate about history." John looked down at his watch. "I'm sorry to say, I have to cut our visit short. I have an appointment with one of my parishioners at her home. She gets a little feisty if I'm late." He winked at Elidad.

"You make house calls?" Aiden asked.

"One of the benefits of being in a small town. We can spend most of our time with our flock, connect with them on a personal level. There are quite a few members of the church that have a hard time getting out every Sunday. I make it a priority to go and visit them when I can. You two are more than welcome to stay and look around the church while I'm gone."

"That is so nice of you, John. We would love to spend a little more time here, if it's not too much trouble," Elidad said.

"Not any trouble at all," John assured. "Just leave the door unlocked when you leave. It's that way most days anyway."

Listening to John's car drive away, Elidad promptly began walking up and down the church floor, investigating the walls and pausing at cracks in the floor. Aiden thought she looked like a birddog pacing frantically through tall grass to pick up a bird scent.

Elidad was so intent on what she was doing she hadn't noticed Aiden watching her. He waited intently, hanging on her every move. He felt slightly helpless, not knowing what she was looking for. He was forced to stand quietly and wait. He was afraid to distract her from what she was doing. Whatever it was looked important. He knew she'd be angry with him for breaking her concentration.

Aiden nervously glanced at the door, straining to listen for any car that might pull up to the church. His palms hadn't quit perspiring since they walked through the door. He wasn't used to lying. Even having permission to be in the church, his heart reminded him, they were doing something wrong. They might get caught.

Running her fingers down the wall, Elidad stopped abruptly.

"What?" Aiden was afraid to ask.

"Look." Elidad pointed to the wall beside her.

There, next to her on the wall, was a crucifix. It was an exact replica to the one that hung on Abraham's wall. The same crucifix Elidad shattered to find the key that sent them here.

Aiden looked at the door again, and back to Elidad. "Elidad, you can't just break it."

"Relax, I'm not going to . . . yet." She pulled it off the wall.

"Elidad, I'm serious. He'll be back, and we don't know when. It will look bad if we're here cleaning up your mess."

Ignoring him, she turned the crucifix in her hands. She gave it a good shake like she expected there to be another key inside, but there was no noise. On the back, stamped in gold, were Latin words pressed into the clay.

"In the name of God, I command you to open?" Aiden read over Elidad's shoulder.

Elidad looked at him. "Wow, *your* Latin has gotten better."

He made a face. "The last time we had Latin together was five years ago. I *hope* it's gotten better since then."

She laughed. "It's been a little longer than I thought."

"What do you think it means?"

"I think they want it to open something."

His brows pressed together. "Really? And what was your first clue?"

She hung the crucifix back on the hook and repeated Aiden's words in Latin. "*In nomen od Deus, imperium istud istud ad aperta-um.*" The words rolled off her tongue in a commanding voice. She pulled down on the crucifix until they heard a click.

A groan came from the floorboards. Aiden jumped to the side as the floor began to slowly fall away.

When the floor was done shifting, the scene felt all too familiar to Elidad. As she stood on the edge of the opening, a faint glow came from the darkness beneath. Elidad knew there would be a torch burning on a landing below the winding staircase they were looking down on.

"Ready, Aiden?"

"For what?" He looked over at her wide-eyed, failing to hide his panic-stricken voice. "We don't know what's down there."

Smacking him on the shoulder, she started down the familiar spiral toward the light below. "And there's only one way to find out."

His hesitation was brief. Elidad heard his footsteps behind her. Suppressing a laugh, she wished she could see the look on his face.

CHAPTER TWENTY-TWO

When Elidad and Aiden reached the landing, they found a single torch burning on a pedestal, just as Elidad anticipated. The handle was gold with mirrored pieces inlaid around all sides of it. It was just as beautiful as its twin on the landing under Isaac's shop.

How many rooms were there like the one beneath Isaac's shop? She never considered there could be others.

As Elidad looked up at the torch burning brightly, Aiden circled around the landing to inspect the torch and its pedestal.

"It's beautiful," he said, not taking his eyes off the stunning artifact.

"Yes, it is." Elidad always thought so.

Aiden turned to look over the edge of the landing. "It keeps going, doesn't it? Where do you think it ends?"

"I'm not sure," Elidad answered truthfully.

"The problem is, Elidad, once we go down, we're going to have to walk back up."

Elidad smiled. She'd never thought of the severity of that before. Once Abraham warned her not to follow the stairs down, she never considered it again. But Aiden was right: it would be a treacherous climb back up.

The stairs appeared to go on into oblivion. If someone chose to take that walk, perhaps the most severe punishment would be to have to walk back up, but she doubted it. She remembered the tone of Abraham's voice when he told her, "I pray, child, you will never have to know." Elidad shuddered at the memory.

"I don't think we have to worry about what's down there just yet," she told Aiden as she took the torch from its stand.

"Change your mind, then?" he asked, making his way to the stairs to go back up to the church.

"Nope," she answered, holding the torch over the edge of the landing.

"What are you doing?"

"Nothing," she answered as she released the torch over the ledge. In the last second of light, when the torch fell away to be devoured by darkness, she could see Aiden's face. She had to cover her mouth to suppress a giggle.

"What do you think you're doing?" Aiden asked frantically.

"What did it look like? I threw the torch over the edge," she answered matter-of-factly.

"Well, *that* was obvious. What isn't obvious is why. How in God's name will we find our way out of here now?"

"Be patient, Priest. Take a breath." Elidad was enjoying herself at his expense.

She was confident things would work the same way they worked under Isaac's shop. She knew it was cruel not to inform him, but it was good for Aiden. He needed to harden up.

The torch caught fire in its stand just as she knew it would. Her mischievous smile flickered at Aiden in the dancing light.

He stared at her in disbelief. "How did you know?"

She shrugged. "I just did." Elidad walked past him to enter the long hall that materialized in the absence of light. Elidad didn't need to turn to face Aiden to know the look of surprise on his face when he realized the hall appeared in the new torch light.

"Does anything normal happen when you are around?" Elidad heard Aiden's voice trail after her as the torches on the wall began to mysteriously light their way.

Elidad laughed. "And what would be the fun in that?"

"Normal is fun," Aiden said flatly. "Maybe you should try it some-time."

"Believe me, Aiden, if I could, I would." Elidad stopped to face him, the end of the passage at her back. "Maybe *you* should get out more, because I really don't think there is any such thing as normal."

"There are many things *close* to normal, Elidad. But your life, chasing tombstones for hundreds of miles, dreams that almost kill you, and creepy hidden passageways under hundred-year-old churches is most definitely not my definition of normal. It's not my definition of fun, either."

Aiden looked around them realizing they reached a stopping point. "It's nice we came all this way to find a dead end."

"Maybe." Elidad took the necklace she found in the grass out of her pocket. This was the first time she had a chance to inspect it. The markings on this piece of metal were slightly different from the one hanging on her neck.

"What do you think that's for?" Aiden asked.

"I told you, it's a key." Elidad knelt down and began tracing the grout lines in the wall.

"What are you going to do . . . dig your way through?"

Elidad ignored his snide comment and stood up, taking a step back as the grout lines began to glow. She looked at Aiden as he took a step back. Elidad moved forward as the keyhole began to glow. She inserted the pendant into the opening in the stone, turned it, and knocked three times.

When the door creaked open, Elidad was just as surprised as Aiden to see what lay on the inside of the stone door.

"*What is this place?*" Aiden whispered. He moved forward, only brave enough to peek his head through the opening, careful to now step over the threshold.

"I don't know, but there is only one way to find out." Elidad gave him a hard shove forward.

CHAPTER TWENTY-THREE

"For not knowing anything you sure got us here like you knew right where to go." His accusation was clear. "I think you know a little more than you're letting on. You've been here before, haven't you?"

Elidad looked around the room. "No, I haven't. I swear. You might be right though; I do know a little more than I told you. But I haven't ever been in this room." Elidad took her own pendant out from under her shirt so Aiden could see it.

"Look familiar?" She held open her hand with the pendant she found in the graveyard.

Aiden looked from one pendant to the other. "You already have one?"

"Abraham brought me here, to Trinity, when I was a little girl, but he never brought me *down* here. I'm not sure if he knew it was here, but it couldn't be a coincidence.

"The pendant I have opens a room, a library, under Isaac's shop in New York. That's where I went when you waited for me at Abraham's house. I had no idea there was another room. When I found the necklace in the graveyard, I thought there might be a possibility, but I still didn't know for sure." Elidad looked around, adding, "But this room is totally different. It's nothing like the place I know."

They both fell silent, taking in what encompassed them. The room was spectacular. The Trinity church had been built close to the bayfront and this room, directly under it, was on the bay, as well. Like the library under Isaac's shop the ceilings were high, but unlike that room, one wall was made of glass. It was like an underground aquarium with the bay floor stretched out before them.

Elidad couldn't help but walk towards the glass wall. It was so beautiful, so alluring, with multi-colored sea anemone pulsing with the ebb and flow of the tide. Schools of tiny fish swam by, showing off glistening scales with glittering reflections.

Close to the glass wall a table had been placed in the center, making a perfect viewing spot. The table appeared to be hand-carved, the detail intricate and attentive. Each chair at this table represented a different fish from the sea. It looked like a sister to the set Elidad adored in Isaac's library, the likeness of which was eerie. Had the same person carved them? They were so alike, they had to have been. And what about the rooms? Were there others? When and how were they built?

Aiden walked to the table and took a seat. "I need to sit down for a moment." He was exhausted with the shock of the week weighing heavily on him.

Elidad handed him the pendant she found in the graveyard. "I think you should keep this."

"Why?" He was surprised.

"I already have one." Her hand went to where it rested on her chest. "Just don't lose it."

Aiden took it from her and placed it around his neck.

Elidad inspected the tabletop. There was a large stack of books in the center, some left open, others leaning against each other.

"Anything interesting?" Aiden asked as he pulled a small stack towards himself.

Elidad pushed another pile around. "Not really." She shrugged. "Informative books, kind of like encyclopedias."

"On animals?" Aiden opened the book on the top of the stack.

Her eyes rose in interest. "Books on yeti."

He frowned. "What's that?"

"You don't know?" She grinned.

"I know, surprising. You know something I don't. Will you just tell me what a yeti is?"

"The Abominable Snowman, ring a bell?"

Aiden's mouth fell open. "You're kidding?"

"Nope." She smiled back, then turned to inspect the room.

"Yeti." Aiden repeated the name as he looked over the book in front of him. "You are talking about snow monsters. Like *real* snow monsters."

Elidad turned back to face him. "You are the one that a siren put a spell on . . . then fixed it, with her magic dust . . . and you *still* have to ask."

Elidad walked over to the fireplace where a flame was brightly burning.

"Someone must have been here recently," Aiden said.

"What makes you say that?"

"The fire's still burning."

"The fire always burns . . . it never goes out," Elidad told him.

The fire under Isaac's shop would burn for hours. Elidad never saw anyone start it or touch it in any way to make it burn. It just continued, without end. "But I think you're right. I think someone was here before us, recently, anyway."

"Can you repeat that, please?"

"I do think someone was here before us." Elidad said again.

"No, no . . . not that part. The part where you *actually* think I'm right."

Elidad grabbed a pillow off the closest sofa and threw it at him. Aiden laughed as he knocked it down, just before it touched his face.

Elidad stood over the coffee table, eyeing the items lying on top of it. There was a half-drunk bottle of water, the cap beside it. Next to the bottle, a book lay open. She picked it up.

All the pictures in the book were similar. The pictures began in the front as paintings and moved on to black and white, changing to more modern photos. There were some captions, notes taken on the animals in the pictures. A bear and wolf were shown over and over again, the same animals, page after page. Each of the animals was white, deceptively whiter than the snow beneath them. In the colored pictures they had flaming blue eyes—a blue that would shame a perfectly cut sapphire stone.

Elidad sank slowly to the sofa as she began to realize the animals in the pictures didn't have shadows behind them, and were eerily flawless.

Thoughtful, she took in a breath and laid her head back on the sofa. When she did, her eyes were drawn to a spot above the fireplace. She hadn't noticed when they came into the room but the clock above the fireplace wasn't a clock. It was similar to the one she knew in the room under Isaac's shop, but this one didn't keep track of the time. It looked like it was built to keep track of the tide and the moon phase that controlled it. She would love to stay in this room and inspect it, attempt to find its secrets, but they wouldn't have time for that.

Who was the keeper of this place? She wondered. Was it the rector? How would he have lost possession of his key? Maybe he had his key and the one they found was an additional one. Isaac, Abraham, and Elidad all had keys to the library. Maybe this key belonged to Abraham. Did he leave it for her, hoping she wouldn't need to find it?

Leucosia said his heart was heavy that he was unable to complete his task, and he knew she would feel obligated to finish it for him.

"Here's something." Aiden's voice pulled her out of her thoughts. He was pointing to the page in a book lying open on the table. "It says here that this guy," he held up a picture of a mean looking yeti for her to see, "is Ardemis. He's the leader of the yeti, and he is not a nice one. He runs a tight rule: anyone who questions his tactics is considered a traitor and executed. And he does the executions, himself. That keeps the troops afraid of him. Sounds like the yeti are a cuddly bunch." Aiden placed the book back on the table. "It's dated ten years ago. I wonder how long they stay the leader."

"I don't think it's a democracy, Aiden. They probably rule until they can't rule anymore."

Aiden raised an eyebrow. "Yes, until the next charming leader comes along, I suppose."

Elidad noticed a jacket beside her on the sofa. It was a nice coat, expensive, and looked freshly pressed. She picked it up to rummage through the pockets. Something in the right pocket rattled. She withdrew a room key for the local inn. It was the missing key the waitress told them about earlier. The key that was never returned. Elidad held it up for Aiden to see.

"The man who went missing a few weeks ago?" Aiden got up from the table and crossed the room to inspect it for himself.

Elidad nodded. "It has to be." She handed the key over to him, and continued going through the pockets. Aiden watched to see what else she would find. She pulled a crumpled piece of paper and a pen out of the inside jacket pocket. Elidad handed the pen to Aiden and straightened the paper.

"It's the address to this church," she told him as he inspected the pen. "Somehow he knew the room was under the church, but hadn't been here before. Otherwise, he wouldn't have to write down the address."

"This is a nice pen," Aiden told her. "Expensive." He turned it in his fingertips, and paused. Swallowing hard, the color in his face melted away.

"What?" Elidad asked, afraid he was going to be sick.

"There's an engraving on it."

"I didn't notice," Elidad admitted. "What does it say?" She reached out for it.

"Bishop Blankenship," Aiden said, barely audible.

Elidad looked at the pen, and indeed it was carved clearly on its clip. She looked back at Aiden, his worry still apparent. "What?" she asked him. "What am I missing?"

"Blankenship is the bishop that was given the other key, the key that I recognized. It was *his* anointing that I attended with Abraham."

Elidad looked down at the pen in her hands.

"What would he be doing here?" Aiden asked.

"Researching, I guess," Elidad shrugged. "That book was open to yeti?" She looked over at the table where Aiden had been sitting.

"Maybe he is just interested in animals that live in snowy areas." Aiden glanced down at the open book in Elidad's lap.

Her fingers turned the pages as her mind was racing. Why would he be here? Was he trying to find Abraham, she wondered? Elidad stopped turning the pages and bent her head to look closely at the book, pulling her finger down the page where it was inserted in the binding.

"I'm afraid to ask," Aiden said, watching her. "It's not going to burst into flames, is it?"

Elidad tipped the book in her lap forward and pointed to the pictures of the two animals. "I know what this is." Elidad's stomach felt hollow. "I can't believe I didn't remember. His name is Ghelgath," she said, pointing at the photos in her lap. "This is what he looks like in two of his favorite forms."

"His favorite forms? He can choose what he looks like?" Aiden's tone was reluctant.

"He is an ice demon, a high demon. I think he would make the yeti you found in that book look nice and cuddly. Ghelgath can change from a wolf to a bear, a dragon, or a man. I'm sure there are others, but those are the ones that have been documented."

"Why would the bishop have come here to do research on him?" Aiden asked.

"I can't imagine." Elidad looked down at the book, her finger still touching where the pages came together. "There's a page missing."

"What do you think is missing from it?" Aiden asked.

"A page that has a map, showing where Ghelgath lives, I would imagine. Look." Her finger pointed to a fragment of the page left in the binding. "What does that look like?"

Aiden leaned down to look closely. It did look like a piece of a map. "Why would he need that?"

"Remember what Leucosia told us? She said others would be looking for the keys. Not just people with good intentions."

Aiden shook his head. "No, not the bishop, he's a good man. He wouldn't. Not how you're thinking."

"You never know, Aiden. We are all capable of evil. He came here looking for something, found it, and left. He took a page with a map out of this book, left his belongings behind and didn't bother to go back to his room to check out. He had to have gone straight to the airport and gotten on the first plane out of here. He was in an awfully big hurry."

"So you think he went looking for Ghelgath, for what?" Aiden continued to shake his head like it would make the riddle come together.

"I'm not sure. Maybe he thinks he can talk Ghelgath into giving him something for the key. It would be a stupid idea, but he might try."

"You're trying to make the bishop look like a bad guy. What could Ghelgath give him? It's impossible. He's a good man. There has to be another explanation. What would he hope to get from a demon that would be worth his soul?"

"Envisioning money and power is enough to persuade most people." Elidad, like Aiden, couldn't understand what would drive a man to meet a demon. "He will just end up dead, and Ghelgath will end up with the key. And once he has it, I don't think we will be able to take it from him. Ghelgath is as ruthless as they come. He is known for destroying his enemies and keeping them frozen like statues— prizes from his victories."

"Lovely," Aiden replied.

"He destroys anything and anyone that's in his way. He doesn't care who they are. He's never shown loyalty to anyone, other than himself. Other demons won't go near him for fear they'll be devoured. We are going to have to try to find the bishop before he gets to Ghelgath."

"He is two weeks ahead of us. How are we going to stop him?"

Elidad shrugged. "We'll just have to pray the weather has kept him at the bottom of Mt. Denali, until we get there."

"How do you know all this about Ghelgath?" Aiden asked. "How could the weather keep the bishop from finding him, and where's Mt. Denali?"

Elidad smiled. "I know the yeti are on Denali because that's what it said in the book you had on the table over there. I know where Ghelgath is, and about him, because just like with all high-ranking demons, we had to memorize details about them in demon studies. So that's the only place Blankenship could be headed. He came here to find a map to Ghelgath and see what else was on the mountain with him."

"Demon studies? Where did you take that class?"

"Our school," she answered.

"Funny . . . I don't remember that being an elective."

Elidad smiled. "I don't think they offered it to just anyone."

"Of course not. Just the specially gifted." He bowed his head dramatically.

"Mt. Denali is in Alaska," Elidad told him. "You might know it as Mt. McKinley. The government changed the name, years ago. Most people in that area still call it Denali."

"Alaska?" Aiden shook his head. "How can we possibly stop him?"

"I know it seems like we'll never catch up but Mt. Denali is one of the most turbulent mountains in the world. Its weather is unpredictable. It could take weeks to put together a group to climb, and he can't do it alone. If the weather is bad and he has a hard time finding people for the excursion, we might catch him before he leaves base camp."

Aiden took a breath. "And if we don't find him there, then we leave and go look for Abraham? Because, Elidad, that's what we're supposed to be doing. Looking for Abraham, remember?"

"We need that key, Aiden," she said forcefully. "Remember what Leucosia said? Finding one key will take me to another, and in turn lead me on a path to fulfill my destiny . . . whatever that means."

He sighed. "She did say that, but she also said she wasn't sure if this was the right path for you."

Aiden could see the contempt rising in her face.

"Elidad, what are we going to do if he started to climb? Climb a mountain, confront your *high-level demon*, and steel his key from him? You said yourself you don't think we can get it from him once he has it." His mouth grew dry at the sound of her wild plan. "Do you even know *how* to climb?"

Elidad crossed her arms, stubbornly. "I climbed Everest."

He forcefully closed the book and tossed it onto the coffee table. "Of course you did."

"And let me guess, you've never climbed?" She knew the answer by the look on his face.

"Does the rock wall in my gym count?" His sarcastic banter was easier to deal with than his usual panic.

"Not really, but all we can do is go there and try, Aiden. That's all I'm asking you to do. We probably won't have to hike. The bishop might know where Abraham is, or he might have something to do with Abraham missing. We won't know till we find him. But what we do know, is the world will be in a bad way if Ghelgath gets that key."

Aiden shook his head. "Abraham probably went missing in Mexico, which is a long way from Alaska." He watched Elidad closely. "At least we are heading west, I guess."

"Have you ever been to the west coast?" Elidad asked, trying to distract him from arguing.

"I went to Disney World when I was in eighth grade. Didn't you go on that trip with us?"

Elidad smiled. "No, Abraham brought me here, to Trinity. He told me it would be a much more memorable trip. He thought this trip would have more meaning in my life than Disney World."

Aiden snorted. "As usual, Abraham was right."

"Yep, he's good at that, isn't he?"

"You ever feel like his tendency to be right might not just be a coincidence?" Aiden asked.

Elidad laughed. "All my life."

CHAPTER TWENTY-FOUR

The flight to the world's most dangerous mountain was a long one. The little plane, provided by the Church, fluttered in the turbulence of the high altitude. Elidad looked over at Aiden, who seemed more than a little uneasy as the plane continued to shudder.

They changed planes in Anchorage, going from a jet to a little four-seater, and since then, Aiden had been a man of little words. She was sure it was because he spent most of the flight praying for their safety. The plane seemed more like a child's toy compared to the lush jet they flew across the country in.

She fought back the urge to give Aiden a hard time about his unease, thinking it better to let this one slide. He was already terrified they might have to climb a mountain when they landed, she didn't need to stress him further.

"We'll be landing on a little air strip owned by a tour company in the area," Elidad shouted to Aiden above the roar of the engines. "It's the closest we can get to the mountain. After we land we're looking for a man named Jedidiah. I was told he's the best one to get us up and down quickly and safely. He usually lives at base camp during the hiking season."

"I thought we weren't sure we were going to have to climb, and we were going to try not to," Aiden reminded her.

"Just in case," she replied.

"How did you get this guy's name?" Aiden asked, thankful for the distraction from the shuddering aircraft.

"A friend of mine has climbed with this guy before. He told me Jedidiah has climbed Denali a few dozen times. He knows the area and will know how to get to where we want to go."

"And where exactly do we want to go?" Aiden asked.

"The back side of the mountain—the side no one is allowed to climb." Elidad could see Aiden's face change. "We probably won't have to go up there, Aiden. I'm sure the bishop hasn't left yet. But if we do, at least we have a map." Elidad smiled.

"What map do you have? I thought he took it with him. The page was ripped out."

"It was a large book," Elidad answered, "and all those pictures were from years and years of different people watching Ghelgath. All the book's writers mapped where he lives in detail. There were four maps in the book, and they were all of the same place. I just took a picture of the maps with my phone."

"What are we going to do if the bishop is still at the base camp? Ask him nicely for the key?" Aiden was trying to imagine how that conversation would go.

"We'll just steal it from him."

Aiden frowned. "And what will we tell him if he asks us why we are there? Won't he be a little suspicious?"

"He'll have a guilty conscience. We'll tell him the Church told us to follow him. He will know why we're there; he won't bother to ask. Did you have a chance to call anyone at the Vatican before we boarded?" Elidad wondered if Aiden would tell her the truth.

"No," he said, shaking his head, "not enough time. I'll have to call when we land."

"You won't have to. I already did. The bishop took leave for six months. He told the Church his mother was dying of cancer and he was going home to care for her."

"Maybe his mom *is* sick. Maybe he *is* taking leave to go take care of her. Maybe we're going to Denali for nothing," Aiden sheepishly protested, feeling compelled to stand up for the bishop.

Elidad pulled a file out of her bag and sat closer to Aiden. Opening the file, she removed a photocopy of a newspaper clipping, handing the page to him. "His mom died in a car crash fifteen years ago."

Aiden looked down at the page and back up at Elidad. "How did you get this? Where did you find a copy of an old newspaper clipping of his mother's death?"

"I got it from the Vatican," Elidad responded, with a mischievous smile.

"Who at the Vatican talked to you, or sent you information? No one is supposed to be in contact with you."

"People like me." She raised an eyebrow. "I'm sure that's hard for you to understand, but people do like me. I happen to know a lot of people who work for the Church that can get me the information I need. The Church keeps files on all the people that work for them, or anyone it has direct contact with. They have files on demons, angels, sirens, even me and you. Can you imagine my file?" She laughed, holding her hands up a foot apart. "Huge, I'm sure, more like a book."

"I'm glad you can find humor in all this, Elidad." Aiden shook his head. "Why would the bishop lie? What does that mean?"

Elidad's smile fell. "It means he wants to be gone for a long time before anyone wonders where he is, or before they wonder what he's doing. He doesn't want anyone looking for him anytime soon. Also, this newspaper clipping was in his file, so who else knew his reason for leaving was a lie? These personnel files are locked and only a few have access, but someone has to know his mother was already dead. It's not a good sign. I just hope we can get to him before he can get to Ghelgath."

"What if the clipping isn't real? Maybe his mom is still alive?" Aiden suggested.

"I thought you might say that." Elidad turned her phone around for him to look at. "I Googled it."

Aiden looked at the image of the same newspaper clipping, its replica in the small town newspaper archive database. There was no denying, the Bishop's mother had been killed.

Before Aiden could ask another question, the pilot yelled over his shoulder they would be beginning their descent.

Elidad quickly moved back to her seat and fastened her seatbelt.

CHAPTER TWENTY-FIVE

Looking out over the white surroundings, Elidad felt the cold deep in her lungs with every breath. She loved that feeling and smiled. Aiden, standing on her right, seemed miserable as he looked over the mountain of white.

"You going to be okay?" she asked.

"I doubt it," he sneered. "Are you sure the bishop isn't here?"

She laughed. "You were with me. There are only forty people in base camp and the ones that have been on this hill for two weeks told us he went up eight days ago, remember?"

"Are you sure he's not just hiding in one of the tents?" Aiden flailed his hand in the direction of the small tents clustered together.

"I'm sure, Aiden," she answered, knowing he was worried about the climb.

"Who, in God's name, would be up here if they didn't have to be?" Aiden threw his hands up in the air with his question.

"That would be me." A gruff voice answered behind them.

Aiden and Elidad turned to face the man who spoke.

His voice fit his appearance, representing a stereotypical mountain man. His eyes were dark, his hair was greasy, and his smile, a sneer through his shaggy goatee.

The man wore new gear that looked heavily used. His hat must have been a lucky one, Elidad thought; it looked like he hadn't taken it off for ten years.

"My name is Jed," he said as he offered his hand.

Elidad reached out to shake it. His rough fingers encompassed her small hand in a firm embrace. His skin felt chapped and scaly from the unforgiving Alaskan weather.

Jed's eyes locked with hers in an intimate moment of interrogation.

"Jed, as in Jedidiah?" Elidad asked.

His look never changed, but his eyes shifted to suspicion. "That's my given name. No one calls me that 'cept my momma and the Law."

Elidad smiled at him. "That's a shame, it's a good name. I assure you, we are not the Law. I hope you aren't insulted if I call you by your given name."

Jed's face broke into a rickety grin. "Hell lady, you can call me whatever you want if the price it right."

Elidad smiled back. "I'm sure we can come up with some kind of compromise. I hear you are expensive, but good."

"I'm not expensive if you live through your climb," Jed offered.

"True." Aiden nodded in agreement.

"Who has been spreading those nasty rumors about me?" Jed asked, pretending to care.

"Daniel Song told me you were the man I needed to talk to, said you could take us to where we needed to be."

Jedidiah's face changed back into a suspicious glare. "And how do you know Daniel?"

Aiden looked from Elidad to Jed. Aiden knew who Daniel Song was. Aiden spoke with him on a few occasions when he traveled to the Vatican. The man they were talking about had the figure of a boy—a petite man who was strangely quiet. Aiden always thought it was fitting for him to work in records, working endless hours in an empty room surrounded by files; he didn't seem the people type.

By the look on Elidad's face, Aiden knew she was pleased to have Jed's undivided attention.

"I work with Daniel," she responded, "just like you do. We help him keep his files up-to-date." Elidad locked eyes with Jed. "He pays gatherers like you and me to collect information."

Jed shifted, looking from side to side. "Maybe we ought to go inside," he said as the wind began to push hard past them.

Aiden was glad someone else wanted to get out of the weather. The temperature began to drop as the wind moved faster across the mountain. Jed led them to a large wall tent. It was pleasantly warm with a wood stove blasting heat, desperately fighting the cold.

Jed threw his gloves on a table and sat in a chair covered in animal pelts. He pointed at two chairs, and Elidad and Aiden sat.

"We're looking for a man," Elidad started. "He would've been eager to get up the mountain. He may have told you he was a priest, but possibly not. He might've been here a couple of weeks ago. Word around camp is, he started his hike eight days ago."

Jedidiah shook his head. "Yes, a week and a half ago. There was a man wanted to get up the mountain. Desperate, I would say. Said he was dying, wanted to make it to the top before he was so sick he couldn't. Said he thought it would bring him closer to God."

"Who took him up?" Elidad asked.

"Mike. He's the only one crazy enough," Jed told them. "I didn't want no part of it. Desperation like that makes a man do stupid things on a mountain. Stupid enough to get himself—and whoever he's with—killed. He couldn't pay me enough."

"We think he means to meet Ghelgath," Elidad said bluntly.

Aiden stared at Jed for his response.

Jed opened a box, carefully withdrawing a pack of cigarettes. Leaning back in his chair he popped one in his mouth and lit it. "Man was dumber than I thought." He took the first drag. "And had a bigger death wish than I thought."

Aiden stared at him. How could this man, in the middle of nowhere, know more about demons than he knew himself? People from his own Church, that he devoted his life to, trusted this man more than they trusted him.

Jed didn't seem the type of man to be afraid of anything, but Elidad, speaking Ghelgath's name, made him noticeably uneasy.

"We came here to stop him before he was able to make it up the mountain. Unfortunately, we missed him so we will have to climb after him. Before we came here we found some of his research," Elidad said. "What do you know about the yeti?"

Jed's eyes shifted from Elidad to Aiden. "Not much." He shrugged. "They've been laying low, staying quiet over the last nine years; it seems there might've been a shift in leadership. They don't bother humans anymore; they are almost nonexistent, no sightings."

"What do you know about Ghelgath?" Elidad asked. "I know who you are but I don't know your story, or how you came to *watch* him."

"I know a hell of a lot about him," Jed admitted. "He's the reason I'm a gatherer. Most people don't start with one as bad as him, but he seems to have *chosen* me. He's the reason half those idiots out there think I'm crazy." Elidad knew he was referring to the other climbers on the mountain.

"How did he choose you? I can't say I've heard of a specimen choosing its gatherer." Elidad urged him to tell his story.

Jed exhaled smoke out of his nose. "Ghelgath isn't what you would call a common specimen. He's different from the others."

"I can imagine," Elidad admitted. "I heard he killed his last gatherer."

Jed nodded in confirmation. "Kills almost everyone and everything." He inhaled his next drag and before blowing it out, added, "Except for me."

Elidad and Aiden waited patiently as Jed pulled another cigarette out of his box and used the one he was smoking to light it, taking a labored drag.

"I had come to live on the mountain for the hiking year, like I always do. It was my third season as a guide, and I climbed the mountain four times already . . . this was seven years ago." Jed took another heavy drag of his cigarette. "A group of six men came to camp, wanting to climb the mountain. It was going to be an easy job. The man in charge had a lot of money; he'd been climbing for some time, knew what he was doing.

"I wouldn't have to worry about his entourage; they were all tough and done climbs with him in the past. They looked to be ex-military to me, most of them, anyway. I got the feeling they were his bodyguards—more than friends—but I was paid to take them up the mountain, not to ask questions. Either way, it didn't matter to me. They paid in advance, and I didn't expect them to reach the summit. I figured we would hit fourteen hundred mark, as long as the weather stayed in our favor.

"The climb was slower than I thought it would be. For all the experience they had, they sure took their time. The man in charge stopped at every fork in the trail for a damn photo op. It was frustrating, to say the least. I just wanted to get the job over with. These guys weren't the kind of people you look forward to spending quality time with, but they weren't the kind of people you hurried along, either. To tell you the truth, I didn't say much about our pace for fear I would get a heavy shove down the mountain. That bastard was confident enough in himself, I'm sure he would've tried to make it down the mountain without a guide if I pissed him off enough." Jed's cigarette went to his lips again. "Most people climb because they love the mountain, and the challenge, but this man just wanted to show off to his friends how great and powerful he was.

"Early on in the climb one of his men came back from taking a piss, and he was a little shook up, telling us he'd seen a wolf not too far from camp. He carried on all afternoon about the wolf, and how big it was. Said it was the biggest wolf he'd ever seen." Jed smiled. "He didn't take too kindly to me pointing out that he lived in the city. I didn't reckon he'd seen too many wolves in his life.

"It didn't shut him up, though. He went on and on about how this wolf was *big*, and just by looking at him he could tell he was smart. He went on and on about how abnormally white he was and talked about his crystal-blue eyes that looked right through you.

"I went and looked around the camp. There were no tracks, and the wolves up here are gray, so I thought the guy was half cracked, or the elevation was getting to him."

"Ghelgath?" Elidad asked.

Jedidiah exhaled a big puff of smoke. "Oh, yeah, but I had no idea then." He took another drag. "The man pissed me off, scaring everyone. I couldn't get him to shut his mouth. All the climbers were scared and spent more time looking to the horizon for the damn wolf than on where their feet were going. I wasn't about to let him get me killed.

"So on the way back up to fourteen camp, I pulled him aside and warned him to keep his mouth shut; he was distracting the other climbers. I told him I didn't believe he saw any wolf, and if he had, it wouldn't matter. We were approaching the fourteen thousand post, and there would be no animals past that point. Even if the wolf was starving, he wouldn't push up that far."

"You were headed *back* up the mountain?" Aiden asked. "Why did you come down?"

Jed looked at him with a blank stare, and turned to Elidad. "He doesn't know what the hell he's doing, does he?"

"No," she answered honestly.

Looking back at Aiden, he answered, "When you climb a mountain like this you can't just do it in one shot. You have to go a little at a time. When you reach higher altitudes you can stay the night, then you turn back around and go to the camp you were at before. You climb up and down, up and down, it's more like climbing the mountain three times."

"Really?" Aiden shot a scowl at Elidad.

"If you don't do it that way you get elevation sickness, and you're as good as dead," Jedidiah said. "They will retrieve your body in the spring, if you're lucky.

"On our climb, the weather had been perfect," Jed continued. "Before we reached the fourteen we could see a system moving in. There was no way we would make it to the seventeen camp before it hit us, so we set camp where we were. We spent hours digging our tents into the snow, so by nightfall we were exhausted." Jed looked at

Aiden. "The wind up there at minus forty degrees and sixty miles an hour will rip through your tent and tear it to shreds. You have to dig down into the snow as much as you can in hopes that the storm will blow over you."

Aiden stared at him. "Wow, this is sounding like more and more fun all the time."

Jed's lips parted to allow smoke to pass through a crooked smile. "By the time the storm hit we were all in our tents, thank goodness. It was a bad one. It continued on through the night and into the next morning. I told everyone to stay in their tents until I came to get them. I didn't want them getting lost; it was total whiteout conditions. The second morning, the storm lifted and the winds died down, so I decided it was time to regroup and head to the next camp.

"When I came around the front side of their tent to tell them it was time to get ready, I stopped dead in my tracks. My feet felt like lead. The white wolf was standing outside the two tents. Blood was smeared across the snow and his white coat. It was like a horror film with body parts scattered everywhere . . . there were so many pieces . . . I couldn't tell who—or how many—had been killed. I stood as still as I could," Jed told Elidad and Aiden. "The rangers say the worst thing you can do is run, because wolves like the chase. I tried to lighten my breath," Jed snorted at his memory, taking another drag, "as if it would keep him from seeing me."

Jed shook his head, the color draining from his face with the memory. "That bastard had a human arm in his mouth, blood pouring from his lips, and all I saw were those damn blue eyes. Just like that man gone on and on about, and I didn't believe him. He was right, you could feel them, deep inside you, like he was looking into your soul. I thought he was an idiot when he told me the wolf was smart, but I'll be damned if I don't tell you, you *can* feel him thinking. You could see his mind working when you looked in those eyes."

"How did you get out of there alive?" Elidad asked.

Jed shrugged his shoulders. "I have no idea. If he wanted me dead,

I wouldn't be here right now, I'll tell you that. He crouched down, I thought for sure he was going to pounce on me, but instead he bounded off. Left me there, in the middle of a murder scene. No one else survived. The only thing left was scattered pieces of flesh."

"What did you do then?" Elidad's heart raced with the thought of being that close to Ghelgath.

Jed took another desperate drag of his cigarette as if it contained the antidote for his memories. "The only thing I *could* do. I got the hell out of there before he came back."

Elidad shook her head. "What did you tell everyone when you came back without your party? Did you talk to the police?"

Jed blew smoke out his nose like a dragon with a snort of disgust. "Those assholes? I told them the truth: we were attacked by a wolf. They sent a party to our location. They didn't find anything. No blood, no body parts. They think my party fell, and I had a hard time with the shock of the accident. They think I created some ulterior reality to deal with the tragedy. Idiots. I was hellbent on saving other hikers so I talked to the press and they ran my story about a white killer wolf. That's when Daniel Song showed up. He told me about Ghelgath, and what he was. *I* thought *he* was the crazy one. But the money he was offering was real. He gave me a high-powered camera and a journal, and all I had to do to earn the money was keep a log book and take pictures. Told me that he needed people like me to gather information. He told me there were people like me keeping tabs on creatures like Ghelgath all over the world.

"He told me it was divine intervention that kept me alive on that mountain that day and I was meant to help the Catholic Church. He swore God has a plan for me." Jed smiled, adding, "I don't know about all that. I'm sure God has a plan for all of us. Since that day I have been a little more of a believer than before, but I just can't help but think, after dining on six grown men, maybe Ghelgath had his fill. Maybe I just didn't look as tasty as the others when he was hungry. Can't say that bastard didn't have it coming though," Jed added.

"Who?" Elidad asked.

"That cocky bastard and his entourage. All of them had it coming." Jed leaned forward to put his cigarette out in a beer bottle full of butts. "After they went missing the press had a field day over the story. He was some high-profile businessman. They think he faked his disappearance so he could flee the country."

"Why would they think that? I thought you said the police believed you lost them all in a fall?" Elidad asked.

"They did, at first. After the press got ahold of his story and more came out about him, they weren't so sure. A pretty girlfriend of his had been missing for a few weeks before our climb. Apparently, he was so concerned with her welfare, he left town to climb Denali. While we were on the mountain, her body surfaced. She was found in a river, close to an apartment he leased for her, unbeknownst to his wife." Jed struck the flint on his lighter, staring into the flame. "That girl's body was half digested by fish. They hadn't gathered enough evidence to press charges for murder, and weren't sure if they ever would. They assumed he killed her because she was pregnant with his child." Jed looked through the flame into Elidad's eyes. "If he had the balls to do it himself. Which I doubt. No matter, the water destroyed any evidence and I'm sure his bodyguards would have lied for him, giving him an alibi. The feds managed to drive up some racketeering charges, and a little tax evasion. Either way, he was looking at prison time. Someone must've had a hard on for him."

Jed leaned across the table toward Elidad and Aiden. "I know they *all* had something to do with that girl's death. She'd been beaten to death and tossed in the river tied to a rock with a climber's rope. Somehow, her body came loose and surfaced. It was a miracle they found her at all."

Elidad shifted in her chair, digesting everything Jed told them. "How many times have you seen Ghelgath since?"

"Maybe twenty or so times, mostly from a mile away. Only close up two or three times. But he knows, every time. No matter how far away I am, he looks right at me and sometimes I swear he winks, just to let me know he's looking back."

"Maybe Daniel was right," Elidad suggested.

"About what?" Jed asked.

"Divine intervention."

"I doubt that. If I come across him again, he won't hesitate to kill me, or anyone else for that matter." He glanced at Aiden. "If the mountain doesn't kill us first," he added with a wink in Elidad's direction.

Jed appeared to pinpoint Aiden's fear. He knew Aiden didn't want to make the climb. At his remark, Elidad decided she liked Jed, and he would make a good companion up the hill.

"He'll be fine; he's strong enough." Elidad was trying to convince herself just as much as Jed.

"And if he's not?" Jed looked doubtful at Aiden.

"I'll carry his body down the mountain myself," Elidad said flatly.

"Better you than me." Jed flashed Aiden a wicked smile.

Aiden frowned. "I'm sitting right here," he said, pointing to himself, "I can hear what you're saying."

CHAPTER TWENTY-SIX

It seemed like an eternity since their first encounter with Jed till now. In fact, it'd only been twenty-four hours.

Aiden and Elidad were standing shoulder to shoulder, looking at their nemesis, Mt. Denali, the drifting snow tainted with calamity. The mountain was beautiful, though saturated with dangerous obstacles that would threaten their lives, leaving their fates untold.

Aiden sighed. "Elidad, I think you should go without me."

"You'll be fine." She sounded sure enough for both of them.

"I've never climbed before, Elidad, and experienced climbers die on this mountain every year." He was surprised he had to argue his point. He thought she would be happy to let him stay behind.

"Yes, they do," she agreed, "but the good news is, we aren't going up to the summit." Elidad sighed. "As much as I would love to . . . we aren't . . ." Her voice trailed off as she continued to dreamily gaze upon the mountain.

"You would love to?" Aiden was dumbfounded. "Why on earth would you *want* to climb a mountain like this . . . pure insanity?"

"Just wait a few days . . . you'll see," she answered as if she had some secret he was not privy to.

"I will wait. But I'm sure I still won't understand. Unless I get elevation sickness and I'm totally out of my mind."

"What we are looking for isn't at the top of the mountain, and we are going where not a lot of hikers go. If we're lucky, we'll find the bishop low. There have been some heavy storms so maybe we'll catch up to him quickly," Elidad said.

"How much lower down?" Aiden asked seriously, looking around. "Like here, in base camp?"

Elidad shoved him playfully. "You wish, smart ass."

"I do wish. And if I was smart, I wouldn't follow you up there." He pointed to the mountain.

She shrugged. "You don't have to go if you don't want to."

Aiden sighed, defeated. "I told you, I will follow you anywhere." His eyes were fixated again on the mountain; this time she knew it was to avoid her eyes.

The shock of his statement distracted her from teasing him further. This had become a repeated statement for him lately. Was he making it clear his orders were to go where she went? Or had he finally accepted the fact that she was right and the best way to find Abraham was to follow the path of the keys, which is what he was most likely doing when he went missing? When Aiden said it this time, it *felt* different.

Elidad cleared her throat. "Jedidiah said we need to be ready at six a.m., packed and ready to hike. Get as much rest as you can. We are going to be pushing our bodies pretty hard over the next week or two."

"Two weeks?" Aiden's voice was overwhelmed.

She smiled reassuringly. "We don't know how long we'll be up there, for sure, we can only take one day at a time, Aiden. It's not as bad as it sounds. One day at a time, one step at a time."

"Right," he answered, "one step at a time. I'll try to remember that."

That night, lying in her sleeping bag, Elidad prayed that God would give them the guidance to carry them to their destination, safely. Through the howl of the wind, Elidad could hear Aiden's breathing, and knew he wasn't asleep. She was sure he was doing the same thing.

Elidad loved sleeping on a mountain. Something about the crisp cold air and the hush of the wind was comforting. With all their work and jetlag, Elidad fell into a deep sleep without trying.

When the alarm went off in the morning, she stirred only to snooze it. She lay there for a moment, thinking to herself, this was the hardest part of climbing—getting out of a warm sleeping bag.

"Aiden," she called out in the dark, her voice carried by the wind pressing through the side of their tent.

"I heard it," he answered.

"Just making sure."

"Why am I here again?" Aiden asked himself out loud.

"Follow me anywhere, right?"

"I'm officially retracting my statement."

"Once we start moving you won't notice the cold."

"Will that be because I'll be so frostbitten I won't notice how cold my extremities are?"

Elidad laughed. "I thought you said you hadn't climbed before."

When the three of them were packed and began to move up the side of the mountain, Aiden started to realize why people chose to do this for fun.

Climbing made you appreciate the small things: one foot in front of the other, team work, and stability. Every step was demanding, and every step after that was gratifying. The landscape was serene and everything within sight was breathtaking. Aiden felt like they were discovering a whole new world. A world that was peaceful and pure, a world untouched by man. With all the overwhelming beauty, it felt like he was crawling his way up the mountainside to discover what his Creator *wanted* him to see. He had no idea, until he saw it with his own eyes, that such purity lived on the earth.

On the fifth night, the three of them huddled in one tent as a storm ruthlessly rushed down the mountain.

They were exhausted from frantically digging into the snow. They worked for hours trying to allow enough room for the tent to be hidden from the wind. The storm had blown in so fast, and their fatigue grown so severe, they decided it would be better to squeeze into one tent to save time, and consolidate body heat.

"How long will this last?" Aiden asked, climbing into his sleeping bag, his body shaking from the cold.

"No telling," Jedidiah answered. "Could be overnight, could be a few days. It'd be best to try to sleep through it. It's better to lay low in a storm, gain energy by sleeping and stay warm. That way when it ends, you're ready to go again."

"Sleep?" Aiden asked. "How do you sleep through all this noise?"

The storm sounded like a freight train passing by; they had to shout above the wind to talk to one another.

"Better take advantage of the rest now, while you can," Jed told him. "You'll be surprised at how easy it is to sleep. You're more exhausted than you think. Sleep will come easy."

Jed was right. It was easy to fall asleep. Aiden hadn't even noticed that he had until Elidad's voice woke him.

"You've got to be kidding me," he heard her shout above the wind.

"We have to get out," Jed answered.

Aiden stuck his head out over his sleeping bag and knew instantly what they were talking about. The tent imploded under the pressure of the wind, and was now frantically whipping around them.

Aiden groaned, "Could it get any worse?"

"Come on, Aiden," Elidad commanded. "We have to reset the stakes."

Reluctantly, Aiden got out of his sleeping bag and pulled his heavy coat out of the bag with him. Over the last few days he learned that leaving his coat in his bag ensured it would be warm in the morning. Now it proved even more useful since he didn't have to rummage through the collapsed tent to find it.

When Aiden finally found his way out of the tent, Elidad hung a light around his neck. Even with each of them having individual lights it was difficult to see as the ruthless fall of snowflakes stung their faces.

Elidad was standing on a corner of the tent frantically looking for the stake that was buried in the snow. "We have to get the tent back up. If it flops around in the wind it can rip, or hurt someone," she shouted to Aiden.

Before Aiden could get the tent in his grip to help her hold it down, the corner she was holding whipped out from under her. Jed clung to the tent as it flipped like a kite in a wind tunnel. A gust of wind dropped down quickly while Elidad and Aiden tried to take hold of the fabric. Jed's feet began to slide. He was being drug downhill while another gust of wind whirled around them, ripping the tent away. They watched in horror as the tent sailed away into the darkness.

Elidad sprinted after it, lunging and diving, but it eluded her every attempt. Aiden started after her, but Jed caught his arm. "Grab this bag," Jed commanded.

A couple of their packs were thrown from the tent as it whipped in the wind. Aiden looked in the direction Elidad had gone.

"Grab it," Jed told him. "It's our gear. We can survive without a tent, but without gear, we're all dead."

Aiden obeyed and put the pack on his shoulders. Jed hoisted his pack on his own shoulders before beginning their search for Elidad.

The cold air burned in Aiden's lungs as he began to realize the severity of the situation. Elidad ran off so quickly. The clothes she had on weren't nearly warm enough, and he was afraid her heavier coat was in the tent. What if she only had her under layers and her light jacket? Even with her outer layers the threat of frostbite and hypothermia were very real.

Aiden and Jed pressed into the mountain, now calling out her name. Their voices were carried away on the angry wind. Aiden felt hopeless. She could be standing five yards upwind and would never hear them calling out for her. Continuing toward the mountain, a rock wall shot straight out of the ground and towered over them.

Aiden looked back at Jed. "We can only go up or down," he shouted over his shoulder.

Jed answered, "The wind goes down, it would have taken the tent down, that's my best guess."

A guess. Elidad's life rested on a guess. With every step forward

Aiden pleaded with God to give them direction, to take them to the place where she was. He prayed for God to give them the strength to continue until they found her.

It became apparent why more climbers were killed going down the mountain than up. The wind pushed them from behind, making it more difficult to find solid footing. Aiden clung to the wall face for stability, pausing to catch his breath.

Turning to Jed, Aiden couldn't resist the impulse to ask, "Will we find her?"

Jed's face was without expression. "In this storm, it's not likely."

Aiden knew the answer, but it was more difficult to hear Jed say the words.

"We have to try," Aiden told him.

Jed agreed.

CHAPTER TWENTY-SEVEN

Aiden turned down the mountain, carefully choosing his footing. He stayed close to the rock face where the wind wasn't as violent.

How could Elidad be so stupid? Running off into the dark after the tent? She was supposed to be experienced; she should've known better than to be split up from the group.

As the two men came around a bend in the rock, Aiden noticed an oddity in the rock face, a dim light glowing from behind it.

Aiden turned to Jed. "What's that?"

"I have no idea," Jed yelled back. "Looks like a light. I think we better go have a look."

When they came closer they could see the light moving up and down as if to signal them. They could see an arm holding it.

Elidad was pressed into a nook of the rock where the wind would blow around her. She was waving her light up and down. She stayed close to the opening to flash her light so she could be found, and used the rock for cover from the storm. She was trembling violently in the cold.

"In here," she said through chattering teeth before slipping back into the crevice when they were near enough to hear her.

Aiden looked over his shoulder to make sure Jed was still behind him before stepping into the dark. The opening in the rock was larger than it appeared. Aiden expected it to be a tight fit with the backpack he had on, but there was plenty of room. Jed broke a glow stick behind them, and the light began to glow more intensely until they could see the form of the large cave surrounding them. He threw his bag down to dig in it, pulled out a sleeping bag, and threw it around Elidad's convulsing figure.

"Did you find that tent?" Jed asked her.

She only shook her head in response as Jed flashed a light in her eyes and inspected her ungloved hands.

"Your big coat is in the tent?" he asked.

Elidad nodded her head yes, adding, "But I did get the small bag of food that was on my pack."

Jed took the backpack from Aiden and produced another sleeping bag from it. He laid it down on the ground. "You did good," Jed told her, adding, "even though you almost got yourself killed. This cave will save us. It's probably twenty degrees warmer in here with the wind off of us. We can ride out the storm in here."

Elidad climbed into the sleeping bag on the ground in an attempt to get some of her body heat back.

Jed looked over at Aiden. "You two will have to share a bag."

"Excuse me, what?" Aiden asked even though he knew what Jed was saying.

"You heard me. We lost our bags, and we only have two extras." He shook his head. "I can't say I've heard of people losing their sleeping bags *and* a tent in one night. Look at her. Hypothermia's already started to shut her down, she's probably feeling a little drunk, her mind moving slowly. She needs all the warmth she can get right now before she starts losing fingers and toes."

Aiden was afraid for her. He'd never seen anyone's body shudder so hard in protest to the cold. With no other options, and too exhausted to argue, Aiden climbed into the sleeping bag with Elidad.

Aiden's body heat was like a life preserver in the churning storm, every sense in Elidad's body embraced him as if he were just that. They lay there for some time before her body began to quiet into a light shiver. Her exhaustion washed over her mind and pulled her down into a deep sleep.

Elidad's mind swam with bad dreams. The sound of shattered glass, and the key falling to the floor, was an eerie sound. Abraham overtaken by a green light, reaching out to her, but she was unable to help him. The shadow man standing on the street following her; the surroundings changed. They were now in the cave, and he was here, in the shadows of the cave, watching her and Aiden.

When the morning broke, Elidad found herself still clinging to Aiden, his arms wrapped securely around her. The previous evening felt like a bad dream, distant and withdrawn. The hypothermia, still weighing on her thoughts, an uncomfortable stiffness settled deep in her joints sometime during the night.

As her thoughts became clearer, she was relieved Jed hadn't offered to share his bag with her. Unable to protest, she couldn't imagine waking up in a sleeping bag with him.

Elidad realized Aiden was also awake.

"I'm sorry you had to share the sleeping bag with me," she told him, breaking the silence.

"All that matters is that you're okay. I thought for a little while we weren't going to find you last night."

"So did I," she admitted as she unzipped their bag and sat up. In the sleeping bag they hadn't noticed the light in the cave.

Jed was sitting up eating his breakfast. "Must be a beautiful day out there," he said, pointing to the light above.

"Where are we? How's it so bright in here?" Aiden asked, in awe of their surroundings.

"Ice cave," Jed told him. "The light goes through the ice."

"It's beautiful," Aiden answered.

Layers of ice were compressed together reflecting different shades of blue and green. The sun sparkled on stalagmite forms that reached upward from the ground. Beautiful was not a word that captured its true glory.

"You don't find too many of these caves," Jed told them, "but when you do, they never cease to amaze."

Jed threw them each a silver pack of food. After Aiden and Elidad finished eating they began to pack the sleeping bags and flashlights.

"So what's our best plan of action?" Elidad asked.

"We try to make it back down the hill without getting ourselves killed," Jed answered.

"Down the hill?" Elidad didn't understand.

Jed looked at her with a scowl. "You don't have all of your gear. We are not continuing up the mountain."

"Why not?" she demanded.

"Because, that's the way it works. If you aren't prepared to hike, you don't," he answered.

"We have to keep going, Jed. I know it's dangerous, but we have to find the bishop, and Ghelgath. This is more important than me not having a coat. We don't have a choice."

"No," he said defiantly. "I *do* have a choice. I am going back down, today. You can get yourself killed without me. I won't take no part in it." He pointed at Aiden. "You better come with me, boy. She'll get you in trouble. There'll be nothing you can do on your own up here."

Aiden looked helplessly from Jed to Elidad.

Furious, Elidad stood up to emphasize how important this was, shouting, "We have to keep going. We are *all* going!" Her voice reverberated through the cave.

Jed and Aiden stared at her. She recognized the fear that washed across their faces. She hadn't thought she yelled that loud, or convincingly, but it appeared both men were terrified by her actions. She paused, waiting for them to argue, but they held very still like they were afraid to move. Realizing they were not really looking at her, she slowly turned to see what had them so mesmerized.

In the opening of the cave, a wolf was crouched, his beauty indescribable. Ears pinned back, his lips were pulled up displaying a terrifying snarl. Every inch of him was white: his nose, his eyelashes, his gums from where his razor-sharp teeth protruded, even his heavy breath in the cool air. His definition only came from darker shades of white.

Elidad thought, if this was her last second on earth, she would die with the knowledge of perfection. How could something so beautiful be so evil?

As the wolf took a step toward them, all three stepped back.

CHAPTER TWENTY-EIGHT

Elidad stepped backward, bumping into ice. The walls that gave them shelter and saved their lives the night before, now encompassed their doom. The only way out was directly behind the wolf.

A deep growl rumbled through his body, pulsing across the ice, making the hair on Elidad's arms stand on end. The way Ghelgath was crouched, it was clear there would be no compromising with him. His aggressive stance showed he was ready to kill. He was larger than a natural wolf, and noticeably different from a typical animal.

Though terror was beginning to take over Elidad's mindset, she couldn't help but be enchanted by his beauty. The photographs they found in Trinity were unable to capture the magic of his existence. Elidad felt like this was the first time she witnessed a true absence of color, a crystal-clear white. His eyes were the same striking blue as they were in the photos, but in person the blue moved and swirled like churning water; they were eerie and hypnotic.

Ghelgath had them cornered. Elidad glanced to the small pack she was able to retrieve the night before. She hadn't told Aiden, but it was the pack where she hid the weapon that Leucosia had given her. Leucosia told her it would be a weapon in her time of need, and she needed it now. But she would be dead before she could close half the distance to it.

Sadness began to fill her chest. She failed. Abraham was on his own. She began to pray he was okay and didn't need her help, wherever he was. Thinking of Abraham made her stomach hurt. He *did* need her help. Her path couldn't end here.

Defiantly, she walked toward the wolf. His lips quivered in a bloodcurdling snarl, his gums fully exposed, making his teeth look longer. Ghelgath held his ground, waiting for what came next.

Kneeling to the ground, Elidad looked up to the heavens. "In you, O Lord, I put my trust." Behind her, she could hear Aiden begin to recite the words with her. "Let me never be ashamed; Deliver me in Your righteousness. Bow down Your ear to me, Deliver me speedily; Be my rock of refuge, a fortress of defense to save me. For you are my rock and my fortress."

As Elidad finished the words, looking to the sky, she heard Aiden's quick intake of breath hiss across his lips. Knowing the beast had lunged forward to make its kill, she accepted her fate and closed her eyes.

She felt nothing . . . no pain came. Surprised in the delayed attack and hearing a commotion, she opened her eyes as the wolf flew across the cave, whimpering. Ghelgath crumpled against the far wall. Picking himself up, he shook off the pain, growling with rage. The hair on his back stood on end, his face a portrait of evil continuing to display his razor-sharp teeth.

Elidad, confused to find herself alive, not understanding what was happening, turned to Aiden and Jed for an answer.

She froze, standing face to face with another white beast. Directly behind her a yeti stood, towering over her. His face was dark black and leathery, similar to an ape's. His chest, fingers, and toes were the same dark skin; everywhere else on his body was covered in a long, white, wispy hair. He pulled Elidad behind him before screaming an intimidating roar at Ghelgath, exposing his fangs and pounding his chest. Ghelgath lunged forward, snapping his jaws at the yeti in response.

Elidad was surprised. The yeti was much larger than Ghelgath, and yet the wolf didn't look like he intended to back down. Ghelgath paced back and forth, snarling at the yeti, the large snowman grunted and pounded his chest. With no indication he was prepared to attack, Ghelgath sprang toward Elidad. The yeti extended his arm in time for Ghelgath's iron jaws to lock around it and save Elidad.

The yeti howled in outraged pain. He shook his arm until the wolf released him. Blood stained the yeti's white fur, a crimson trail running down his arm. His roar intensified as it echoed off the ice walls in the cave. As his roar became louder, the wolf hunkered back, defeated.

Ghelgath's actions were odd. A second ago he appeared determined, convinced he would be victorious, yet so quickly he changed his attack. He slowly backed his way out of the cave opening as the yeti's roars encompassed the small space. And just like he appeared, he was gone again.

Elidad's mind was spinning with the events that unfolded around them. When she looked over her shoulder to see where Aiden and Jed were, her eyes caught sight of a ledge high above their heads on the inside of the cave. None of them noticed the ledge this morning, it was so high up. But now, with a line of seven yeti standing on the ledge, there was no mistaking it was there.

All the yeti above were roaring, pounding their chests just like the one next to her. *They* were the reason the single yeti's roar was loud, and the real reason Ghelgath's advances turned to a retreat. They were the reason the wolf was gone.

Aiden rushed to Elidad's side, his abrupt movement catching the yeti off guard. He turned growling, bearing his teeth, ready to ward off an attack. Then, understanding Aiden was a friend, the yeti allowed him to go to Elidad.

"Are you okay?" Aiden asked, looking her over.

"I'm fine," she assured him. "He's the one who took the brunt of it all." She looked over Aiden's shoulder at the wounded beast. She was sad for him as she watched his blood pooling on the ground.

"I wouldn't feel too sorry for him," Aiden whispered. "I'm sure they were just fighting over who gets to eat us," he said, skeptically.

"I don't think so," Elidad disagreed.

The injured yeti was holding his arm quietly.

As Elidad watched the blood continue to trickle down his white fur and gather in a puddle at his feet her mind began to swirl. She looked over to Jed and the packs that remained. "Jed, where's the pack with the food in it?" The tone of her voice was noticeably elevated.

"What is it?" Aiden asked as Jed slowly brought the pack to her.

She knelt to rifle through it. "Do you remember the riddle Leucosia told us when she gave me this?" Finding what she was looking for, she pulled the metal canister into the light. "When cells of ancestry gather at your feet with fleeting fear chased by cavernous thunder, this will be the time." Elidad smiled triumphantly. "Cells of ancestry is blood, fleeting fear is the wolf, and cavernous thunder . . ." She looked up to the ledge of yeti whose voices scared away the wolf. Elidad's eyes locked with Aiden's. "Now is the time." Turning toward the cowering giant, Aiden stopped her. "Elidad, are you sure you want to go over there?"

"If I wasn't sure, I wouldn't go, Aiden," she answered calmly.

"Somehow I doubt that," he told her.

She smiled as she pulled away from his grip. The yeti's eyes were suspicious as she approached him. Elidad held up the canister for him to see. She unscrewed the top, and his large nostrils flared in an attempt to capture any scent that drifted from it.

"It's medicine," she assured.

He drew his arm into his body as if the vile were poison, displaying his fangs as a warning.

"Oh, come now. It won't hurt you, honest." She tried to be convincing.

He continued his defiant look and held a position of defense against the small human.

"Why are you even trying, Elidad?" Aiden asked. "He doesn't understand you."

The yeti glared at Aiden and hissed at his comment.

Elidad laughed. "Are you sure about that?" She didn't wait for his answer. She shook the canister in front of the yeti and took a sip and swallowed. "You see," she told him, "it is just fine." Her voice was soothing. "You saved my life. Please, let me help you."

The beast looked up to the other yeti on the ledge. The yeti in the center of the seven was larger than the others. His face was hard. The entire group looked to him for his decision. He considered for a moment, sighing a heavy breath in thought before nodding his head in acceptance.

Elidad looked back at the yeti beside her. He sniffed the air again as she held up the canister.

"Give me your arm," she commanded.

He sheepishly held his arm forward, watching her intently.

Elidad's hand disappeared into his wispy white fur as she grabbed his arm. She expected his hair to be wiry, but it was soft like goose down. The wound was deep, and lay gaping enough to see bone exposed under the torn flesh.

Elidad poured the liquid into his wound. It was thick, dropping like mercury out of the canister. The yeti whimpered in protest, pulling away.

Elidad held fast to his muscular arm. "Don't even think about it," she warned. His brows creased together as he grunted in response. He could've pulled completely free if he wanted to, but allowed her to hold him in place.

"How's it going to work if you fidget?" she asked, as if he were a child. "Stay still."

He watched as she poured another drop into the wound. The silver liquid moved in the void of flesh connecting with the other drops. Elidad leaned in and lightly blew on the liquid moving it over the surface of exposed bone. His flesh began to glow. The warm color intensified and the silver moved vigorously. Tentacles with jagged barbs grew out of the silver blob and attached themselves to the yeti's open skin, drawing it back together. The more air that passed over the torn flesh the quicker it began to heal and gradually began to close. Every creature in the cave watched in amazement.

Elidad held up the canister, ordering, "Now drink."

With his good arm he took the metal vessel from her hand, which was minute compared to the size of his paw.

"Don't drink all of it," she warned.

He paused to listen for her direction.

"Just a drop is enough. Don't use it up," she instructed.

His eyes flashed upward to the large yeti on the ledge again. When there was no protest to her request he did as he was told and handed it back to her.

Elidad walked slowly back to her pack to put the metal container inside.

"Well, now what?" she asked, looking up at Aiden and Jed. "Even if they do let us go, we probably won't last more than a mile."

"You think?" Jed asked. "A half hour ago you were ready to hike without a coat."

"Ghelgath is not going to let us march down this mountain. He came in here after us. I think he might know why we're here, and he didn't look like he came to talk," she pointed out. "As soon as our protectors are gone, I think he won't be too far away."

The yeti that saved Elidad approached their small human huddle. The humans stopped talking, wondering what he would do next. He leaned forward to grab Elidad firmly by the arm. Aiden stepped between them and the yeti roared, determined not to be swayed by Aiden.

Aiden stumbled backward as the yeti scooped Elidad up in one arm with a sweeping motion. In two leaping bounds they ascended the ice wall to join the other yeti high on the ledge above the two men, left standing in the ice cave.

Before she realized what happened, Elidad found herself looking down on her friends. She frowned at the beast who was holding her. "We can't just leave them here. They'll die."

The yeti stared back at her. She could sense him considering her demand before making a grunt to the other animals on the ledge. Before Elidad had a chance to catch her breath, two of the massive animals descended upon the men below, collecting them and their belongings, and brought them up the wall. With the others right behind them, the beast carrying Elidad turned to an opening at the end of the ledge. The mouth of a long tunnel was cut into the ice, appearing to lead further into the mountain.

The yeti clung to each of its travelers like they held parcels stamped with fragile. Elidad was amazed at how effortlessly they traveled over the rough terrain, moving faster and faster, they pushed deeper into the ice.

CHAPTER TWENTY-NINE

In the distance, Elidad could see large doors sculpted from ice and guarded by two yeti. Each of the animals was wearing an iron helmet and holding axes that were large enough to cut a car in half. The group moved toward the doors at a quick pace. The yeti carrying Elidad cried out to the two guarding the doors. The animals moved quickly to drag the doors open for the herd of yeti, allowing them to pass without pausing. The colossal-sized doors screeched in protest at being moved.

Elidad felt her breath sharpen at the sight of the cave. The open space around them was a few hundred feet tall and the doors before them came to half the height of the cave. The entourage of yeti paraded by the guardians of the doors. Their shinning helmets nodded recognition to the yeti as they passed.

On the other side of the doors, the group slowed to a casual pace. On this side of the guarded entry, the ice fell away to a monumental opening. Below them, carved as far as the eye could see, was a crystal city. It glowed like a diamond under a showroom light.

The yeti descended a large sweeping hill on a path leading straight for the city center. Elidad looked over her shoulder to exchange glances with her human companions.

Enormous pillars of ice jetted up from the floor to support the ceiling that enclosed the city in ice. As they followed the path lower into the city the pillars rose taller over their heads. Elidad noticed that each one was carved with exquisite detail.

The path turned to a street. The streets of the city were packed with yeti, mimicking the hum of a human town. Down the main street, ice buildings lined either side of the main flow of traffic where many yeti were hard at work. Some were busy skinning animal pelts, others stood over slabs of fish and meat displayed on ice counters. One building housed a metal works where tough-looking yeti sharpened axes and swords, others labored over mending armor. Elidad was so captivated by the city she wished the one carrying her would slow his pace so she could see inside each building. On a corner there was a structure partially made of stone. The building stood out on the street amongst all the buildings of ice. Inside, Elidad could see stones stacked like brickwork around a small flame. A yeti sat close to the fire, his hair shorter than the other yeti's, his black skin showing through. Above the flame, a bowl made of copper sat on top of the hearth. A large block of ice sat in the copper bowl. On one side, a luge exited the bowl. Ice water ran down into pitchers that the thin-haired yeti handed to others to take out of the building to be distributed to yeti waiting in a line.

None of the buildings had doors or windows, just openings. Deep in the city the temperature was consistent. Elidad guessed it was just below freezing. Being protected from wind, it was the warmest temperature they'd felt in six days.

In the center of the city was a large dome-shaped structure. It reminded Elidad of an igloo. The doors that appeared to lead into the building were just as large as the ones they passed through to enter the city, and guarded more heavily. They were headed straight for those doors. Yeti on the streets turned their heads to watch as the humans passed, while some followed the group, to see where they were going.

The two guards in the center of the doors crossed their axes to keep them from entering. They stood before the eight yeti guarding the doors, who looked dressed for battle. The one who carried Elidad made a sound to the others.

The guards exchanged looks. One of them sounded back, pointing to the humans. In response, the yeti held his wounded arm out for them to see and then offered Elidad forward in his other hand. One of the guards sniffed the air, his nostrils pulsing in and out before he finally conceded to open the doors.

It took two yeti to open this door. Elidad wondered what waited for them inside. She knew this building was special. It was so deep in the heart of their city, significantly larger and much more detailed than the other buildings.

As they were taken deeper into the building, Elidad was fascinated by how the ice walls were cut intricately with amazing detail. Beautiful designs covered every area, depicting the crowning of kings, and battles displaying the yeti fighting creatures she had never seen before. The carvings reminded her of paintings lining the walls of ancient pyramids.

The ceiling was translucent, allowing the outside light to enter the building without being filtered or dimmed.

The hall they were in opened to a massive space and another set of doors guarded once again by yeti wielding axes. These yeti did not bother to question the group holding the humans; rather, they only moved to open the doors for them to pass.

In this room, there was no mistaking where they were. Elevated on the top of an expansive set of stairs an elaborate chair made of ice, inlaid with gold and gems, sat proudly before them. In the throne sat the largest yeti they had seen yet, his body strong and wide. On his head was a heavy crown pounded from steel and decorated with perfectly cut jewels. Across his lap his hand rested on the hilt of a mighty sword.

This was their throne room, and before them, the king sat awaiting their entry. His eyes fixed on the humans as they were brought before him. Elidad cringed, remembering what Aiden read about the ruthless leader, Ardemis, in the books beneath Trinity.

All three of them were placed at the king's feet. Elidad was glad they were together; she felt stronger with Jed and Aiden at her side.

The two beasts grunted and growled between each other, and the other yeti behind them chimed in occasionally. They were like animals, but it was apparent they were having a conversation. Their city was more advanced than animals living in the wild. Elidad wondered why they were brought before the king.

In a low voice, Aiden asked, "Now what?"

"I don't know," Elidad admitted.

Jed snorted, without any concern of being heard by the yeti, "We'll be lucky to not end up as lunch."

"Our kind has never been fond of human meat," the king said, shaking with amusement. His voice was deep and distinguished.

The humans were awestruck, their mouths gaping to the king's sudden outburst of English.

"Forgive our rudeness," Elidad quickly interjected for fear of insulting him. "We had no idea. The others didn't speak to us. We didn't know you could speak our language. We weren't sure what to expect. We were brought here without explanation."

The king nodded his head. "And for that, I must offer my own apologies. It is forbidden for yeti to speak to humans without my blessing." He looked to the others with approval. "These warriors are dedicated and do me a great honor. Of course, yeti are forbidden to come in contact with humans at all, but if it cannot be avoided, they are to stay mute, or only speak yeti in their presence." A smirk came to his lips. "Humans are a lot more manageable if they believe they are the intellectually superior beings on this planet. Our life remains much simpler if we allow them to go through life not knowing any different."

Elidad glanced at her companions before taking a small step forward. "My name is Elidad," she introduced herself.

"And I am King Hiri." He moved his sword off his lap, leaning it against his throne.

"We are thankful to you and your warriors for saving us from the wolf," Elidad started. "We would not be alive if not for their bravery. We don't want to seem ungrateful to you, but we are not sure *why* we were brought here."

The yeti that carried Elidad moved forward with a grunt, holding his arm forward for the king to inspect. The king touched the spot on his arm that had gruesomely lay open an hour before. Now, the skin was merely a hint of a scar, only visible because his fur hadn't grown back.

Hiri looked again to Elidad. "Perhaps it should be our kind that is thankful to you."

"It was only a flesh wound. I was lucky enough to have something to help it heal quickly."

Hiri leaned forward. "No yeti has survived the bite of Ghelgath," he answered softly. "Indeed, it is Kade who is indebted to you."

Elidad shook her head. "Sounds to me like we are even. He saved my life first."

Hiri looked proudly at Kade before turning back to Elidad. "You were brought here, Elidad, because the yeti have been waiting for you."

Elidad shifted uneasily. She wanted to look to Aiden and Jedidiah for reassurance, but was afraid to appear weak.

"What do you mean, you've been waiting for me?"

The king stood before his throne and shrugged off a large cloak from his shoulders. He descended the immense steps to stand with the group of humans.

"Will you walk with me?" His invitation was pleasant as he extended a hand in the direction of the far wall.

Elidad didn't want to, but she didn't care to offend their hosts, either. All the information in the book Aiden found described the yeti as ruthless and mean. A race that should be feared, but these creatures were civilized and polite. Had the gatherers been wrong? What did the yeti want with her? How could they have been *waiting* for her? How would they even know about her? Elidad was sure they made a mistake.

"Our kind lives by the heavens," Hiri told them as they walked. Kade was the only yeti following behind, the rest fell away. "Since the beginning of our creation we have lived by the stars. Sadly, that is something man has forgotten how to do. Years ago, before your lifetime, a prophecy written about a woman was revealed to our ancestors. In the stars, they found a dark time for yeti. It told of a ruler, ruthless and evil, that would come to rule the yeti for twelve turns of the earth. And without reason, the ruler would disappear. All trace of him would vanish and the yeti would be free of his reign."

Elidad and Aiden glanced at one another. Elidad realized that's what happened to the yeti leader Ardemis, who they read about.

Hiri and the group stopped walking when they came to an enormous book resting on a pedestal chiseled from ice. "The yeti would rise up again, a righteous clan once more, and live peacefully in the safety of the mountain. The book," he gestured in front of them, "foretells a time when a human—a female who is beloved by God—will come to us." He turned to lock eyes with Elidad. "That *is* what your given name means, does it not?" Hiri's words, more a statement than a question. "Beloved by God?"

Elidad's eyes shifted from the book back to Hiri. She could feel Aiden's and Jed's eyes on her. "Yes," She whispered, reluctantly.

Aiden's heart pounded. He never realized, but he should have. After all, Abraham was the one who named her. *Beloved by God*, and wasn't she especially.

"There are hundreds of women who climb this mountain every year," Elidad frantically tried to rationalize. "I don't know how you could think it was me your ancestors predicted would come. Just because my name is close to what they predicted, doesn't mean it is me. It's a coincidence; we're all beloved by God, are we not?"

Hiri smiled pleasantly, turning to the book. He opened the cover, riffling through the pages. The pages were heavy canvas. Detailed pictures were painted on every page. The book looked to contain years of yeti history, like the building walls they walked past on the way to the throne room.

Hiri laid the book open almost directly in the center of the binding. The open page depicted a human woman with a sliver canister pouring liquid onto an injured arm of a yeti, a puddle of blood at their feet. In the picture, a white wolf running away in the background.

Elidad's heart sank. This time she couldn't help but look back at Aiden, he and Jed exchanging glances. There would be no convincing them they had the wrong human now.

Hiri turned the page, interpreting, "When the earth begins to warm for a period of a thousand years, a human will come to the yeti. The cells of ancestry shall gather at her feet with fleeting fear chased by cavernous thunder from her path. The human, with the power to heal the bite of the Great Wolf will be sent by God. The army of the yeti shall be led by the healer, and her sword. And with her sword, the healer shall slay the evil that lay within the Dragon Heart."

Elidad took a deep breath. "I'm not a healer." She stared at the page. "I just had something that helped, that's all, it was lucky . . . a coincidence . . . I'm not the one to lead you into battle."

Hiri gently placed his paw on the pages of the book. "There is no word in Yeti for coincidence. We don't believe in it. We know that everything happens for a reason, Elidad. It is true we are not perfect. Sometimes our translations of the stars are correct, other times we are close, but very few times we are wrong. Only God himself can decipher his own language; we merely try to translate what we can." Hiri pulled his hand away from the pages. "You may not be a healer, but you did heal my son. He would be dead without you." The king looked back at Kade as he spoke. Elidad recognized the look. He was proud of Kade; he loved him. It was his son. *She had saved the king's son.* A prince. A prince that undoubtedly grew up listening to his father's stories of the woman healer.

"Is this what you had that helped you heal him?" Hiri pointed at the metal canister in the woman's hand, the detail of which was similar to her own canister. Elidad continued to stare at it without answering. Hiri looked at Kade. Kade nodded his head yes.

"Do you have the sword?" Hiri asked Elidad.

Elidad stood still. She knew Aiden and Jed were waiting for her answer, too. She tried to avoid their eyes. She took a deep breath. She wasn't sure how she had gotten here. How did he know? Leucosia handed Elidad a piece of metal, telling Elidad it would be a weapon in her time of need. Though she'd never seen it, she knew it was a sword. "Yes. I do."

"Why did you come to this mountain, Elidad?" Hiri asked.

"Ghelgath has something we want," she told him. "Something we need."

"Something that will invoke the wrath of God? Something to bring forth the destruction of the earth before its time?"

Elidad looked up at his face, her eyes wide. Hiri gestured to the book on the ice pedestal. "I told you, it's all in there." He closed the book carefully. "And might I ask how you and your friends intend on retrieving this item from Ghelgath? You almost perished in the cave, overwhelmed by his power."

Elidad frowned. "He caught us off guard, that's all. Next time I'll be ready for him."

"That may be, Elidad, but perhaps we are in need of each other's help. The yeti live in fear of Ghelgath; he has terrorized this mountain as long as any of us can remember. You intend to find the place where he dwells. This will be an impossible task for you, as the path is difficult and long. Your bodies are too weak to make the journey. And even if you were able to make it, Ghelgath will attack you with his army, there are only three of you. You are bound to meet your demise before you are able to complete your task."

"His army? What army?" Aiden asked.

Hiri turned to him. "An army of frozen warriors. He commands the dead, so long as they are taken by the mountain. That is why I suggest you allow us to take you to his cave. Our army is ready and willing to fight this fight. It has been a battle long anticipated by the yeti. In showing a unity with us, the yeti army will be stronger." He turned to Elidad. "Your presence will give us the confidence we need to defeat his army. I only suggest that you allow my son to take you the distance you need to go. We will ensure that you make it to your destination. Then perhaps you will find what you came for."

Elidad glanced at Aiden and Jed. Looking back at Hiri, she sighed. "You make a good argument. Apparently we do need your help. There are things we didn't know about Ghelgath, like where to find him, and the fact that he has an army . . . we totally missed that. We would be honored to fight with the yeti," Elidad said honestly.

Hiri roared. "It is done, then." He turned and pointed to guards in the corner of the room, barking orders in Yeti. In an instant they were gone.

"Father." Kade spoke English for the first time. "Shall I take the humans to the baths to rest?"

Hiri looked at his son with soft eyes again. "Yes, they will need it. See that they are well kept. They will need food and furs."

Hiri looked back to the humans. "Rest as much as you need. We will begin our journey when you are ready."

CHAPTER THIRTY

Elidad was relieved to be back in Kade's arms. With everything that happened in the throne room she hadn't noticed how cold she was. His body heat kept her warm, like riding a horse on a snowy day.

This new tunnel they were following lead away from the throne room and grew darker as they sank deeper into the mountain's core. The tunnel grew smaller, only large enough for a yeti to get through.

"The baths are where our sick come," Kade said. "When yeti become sick our body temperature gets cold. If we become too cold inside, we are like humans, we will die. The water has healing powers. It will help you feel better and rest well."

"They sound wonderful," Elidad told him, hoping the water was as warm as she was imagining, and not mountain ice water.

They came to a stop in front of two large wooden doors at the end of the tunnel. Kade put Elidad down, and the other yeti following them deposited Jed and Aiden next to her.

"Wood doors?" Elidad asked Kade. "I didn't see anything else made out of wood in your city."

Kade smiled at her observation. "We have nothing else made of wood. Only ice, stone, bone, and leather." He reached forward to touch the door's smooth surface. "Stone was too heavy and the ice melts with the heat of the water behind them, so we could only use wood. Ages ago, a hunt party was sent to find wood strong enough to guard the baths. The hunters went past the foot of the mountain, before they were able to find a forest with large enough trees. On their way back they were hunted by the humans. Only a few of them returned completing their task." Elidad could tell this was an important story that was passed down through the generations.

Kade pushed the doors forward, and was greeted with a heavy, warm fog that lay on the other side. Drawn by the heat, the humans quickly walked forward, close behind Kade.

As they moved toward the rushing sound of water, the heavy fog bringing them warmth began to lift with every step. It rose high with the ceiling as the ceilings grew higher. The fog clung to the outer rim of the wall, allowing them to see their surroundings. Water cascaded from the ceiling, showering down to the rock beneath, where the stone was smooth, shaped from ages of water passing over its surface. The thin waterfall fell fifty feet from the elevated cave. The rock was as dark as coal, and the ceiling resembled a night's sky above. Elidad stopped to look at the twinkling.

"Diamonds," Kade told her softly.

"I've never seen a diamond sparkle like these, not even cut ones," she told him.

"Why would anyone cut them?" he asked.

"It makes them sparkle, I guess."

"That is sad. If you let them grow, they will mature into what they were meant to become." He pointed up. "Gifts from God. Light giving." Kade pushed forward to lead the way to the baths as the three of them lingered a moment, looking up.

Aiden nudged Elidad's arm. "Are you sure we are doing the right thing here, Elidad?"

"What other choice do we have? We need to find the bishop, we need the key, and they can take us to Ghelgath."

"Ghelgath almost killed you," Aiden pointed out.

"I wasn't ready for him. None of us were. I wasn't expecting him to come looking for us. I was too far away from my pack; I couldn't reach the sword in time."

"Maybe if we knew you had a sword that could be used against him, we would've been better prepared; we could have helped you," Aiden retorted.

Elidad made a face at him. "You were there when Leucosia gave it to me."

"She gave you that silver canister and a metal thing. I thought she was being funny when she told you it was a weapon."

"And I will have you both know," Jed interjected, "I was paid to take you up the mountain, not go into a warzone. I'm not the fighting type. I think I'll wait it out here for you two."

Elidad stared at him in disbelief. "You're kidding."

"Does it look like I'm kidding?" Jed asked. "That's the second time I've seen Ghelgath that closely, and was lucky enough to get out of it alive. Have you heard of three strikes and you're out? I'm just not going up to bat."

"Whatever." Elidad waived her hand in the air at him, turning to catch up with Kade.

Elidad took in a deep breath, acknowledging her solitude. Could she really relax? She wanted to. Looking around she was completely alone beside the water.

Kade brought them to an area where the cascading hot spring turned into slow moving water dipping in and out of rocks. Over decades, the water carved pools in the rock, staggered randomly under the diamond-filled cave. The pool in which Elidad was left to soak had a high rock surrounding it like a privacy screen. Many of the pools were separated by these walls, giving them a feeling of private rooms.

Kade led the two men away to soak in other places. It was nice to be alone with her thoughts, but in the silence she began to realized she'd become accustomed to company over the past few weeks.

Looking at the swirling water she remembered Leucosia's warning: *Finding one key will lead to the other, in turn leading you to your destiny.* Was her destiny to find Abraham? At this point she felt they would be lucky to get off the mountain alive, let alone continue to follow what little trail Abraham left. She hated feeling like everyone knew what she was supposed to do with her life—everyone but herself.

"*The healer and her sword of justice shall slay the evil that lay within the Dragon Heart.*" Elidad shook her head reciting Hiri's words out loud.

"Get into the water, Elidad." Aiden's voice startled her.

Elidad looked around, but didn't see him. "Where are you?" she asked, her voice echoing off the stone.

"On the other side of the rock. Get into the water," he demanded. "You'll feel better."

It did sound good. She dipped her hand beneath the water's surface. The warmth sent electricity up her fingers, causing her body to convulse in a shiver. Suddenly, she couldn't wait to get in. Shrugging off her clothes only took moments, but slowly lowering her cold body into the hot water took much longer. The water seared every cold nerve in her body making its warmth almost unbearable. As she submerged herself lower into the water she became aware of all the cuts and bruises on her body.

Her mind relived the past weeks since Aiden came to her door. It seemed ages ago since that moment. She was still far from knowing where Abraham was. Sadness began to fill her mind. Would she be able to complete this task? So many times her life was close to ending, from dreams to extreme weather, to mythical creatures wanting her dead, and tomorrow they would be marching into battle. How could she expect to make it through alive? The impossibility of her goal darkened her hope, formed into the shape of a tear, and ran down her cheek.

How could the yeti expect her to defeat Ghelgath? She was unable to stand her ground with the wolf. What would be her fate if she found herself face to face with the dragon? That was the prophecy after all: *The healer and her sword of justice shall slay the evil that lay within the Dragon Heart.* How could it be done? How could she slay one of the most powerful demons on earth in his most powerful form? She closed her eyes and splashed the warm water on her face, laughing at herself.

"Forgive me, Father, for doubting you and your wisdom," Elidad told the emptiness above. "Please forgive my fear. I put my faith in you, Lord, and I pray that you will carry me through this difficult time. I know you will not lead me to any battle, in your name, that I cannot conquer. I am your servant, and I pray you will guide us to do your bidding, in Jesus' name, Amen."

"Amen." Aiden's voice came from over the wall.

Elidad smiled at the twinkling lights and wished Aiden was a little nearer. She'd gotten used to his presence, and now, with the approaching battle, she didn't want to be alone.

When they finished their baths Kade appeared, leading them to an area where they could still feel the warmth from the hot water. The rock here was carved to form little caves all the way down the wall, three caves high. Each cave was large enough for a single yeti to lie in. It looked like a line of bunks, each cave lined with animal pelts.

"Do the yeti get sick often?" Elidad asked Kade.

"No."

"Then why are there so many beds?"

"For times of battle, the ones who can make it will come here. The water has healing power."

Elidad didn't doubt it. All the soreness in her muscles had gone, as were most of the scratches and bruises she acquired over the last week.

"Do the yeti stay here any other time?"

"No. If a yeti stays in a warm climate when their body is warm, they will lose their hair. Their body changes and they are unable to maintain the correct body heat to survive the cold."

"Like the yeti in the brick building, in your city?" Elidad remembered aloud.

"The water maker? Yes." Kade appeared surprised at Elidad's memory of the short-haired yeti. "Only one water maker is selected, for that reason. The water maker will never leave the city, but it is a great honor.

"You'll need your rest," Kade said. "There will be a guard outside your door. If you need anything, just ask." He pointed to the beds on the wall. "You will sleep here."

"I'll head downstream a little," Jed said, following the wall. "Not so loud down here, away from the waterfall."

Elidad, still angry with him, watched him walk away. She wondered if he was putting distance between them so he didn't have to feel guilty when they left for battle. He climbed into a cave and disappeared from sight. She and Aiden climbed into their caves. The beds were deeper and softer than they appeared in the light. Each bed was lined with a pillow cut into the rock. The smell of lavender, lemon grass, and thyme wafted through the fur. The mixture was light and perfectly soothing. After Kade left them, sleep wasn't difficult to achieve.

CHAPTER THIRTY-ONE

Elidad found herself in the middle of a battlefield, tears streaming down her face, a sword in her hands. She swung the sword with all her might. She swung it for what she believed in, she swung it for her life.

Frantically, she looked around, needing to find something. How could she find anything amongst all the chaos? People scattered, fighting, screaming, dying. Then, in the distance, her eyes rested on Abraham, his face filled with fear. She rushed to get to him, but the battle raged on, blocking her path. She fought furiously, trying to get closer to him. Every step she took forward felt like it drew her further away. Tears clouded her sight, but she couldn't wipe them away for fear the distraction would make her vulnerable to her opponents. Bodies fell before her as she sliced through the battlefield, and yet she was just as far from Abraham as before.

"Elidad." She heard her name above the screams of war and the clanging of weapons. She turned to see Aiden, collapsed on the ground, holding his chest where an arrow protruded.

"Aiden," she screamed.

Turning back to Abraham, she stood, torn. In opposite directions, who would she help first?

In the distance the wind began to blow, kicking a dust storm toward them. Elidad watched as it churned dirt and debris like an angry cloud of chaos. The cloud encompassed the battle field. When it fell around them, a deafening silence came over the quarrelers and their clanging weapons. The warriors continued to fight, their movement eerie, as all sound fell away. Blood pounding in Elidad's ears was the only noise not dampened by the storm.

The ocean of fighting bodies parted for the Shadow Man, leaving him an open path to Aiden. The dark figure that haunted Elidad, stalking her on the street, stood over Aiden. Reaching down, his fingers wrapped around the arrow in Aiden's chest, twisting it. Aiden's cries of anguish were stark against the numb hush. Elidad looked back over her shoulder at Abraham. He pointed to Aiden. "Go to him," he said.

Elidad raised her sword and sprinted to help Aiden as warriors began attacking her on all sides. The Shadow Man ripped the arrow from Aiden's chest and blood sprayed from his wound.

Aiden held his hands over his gaping flesh. "Elidad," he said softly, his voice hushed by pain. "Elidad . . . Elidad, are you okay?"

Aiden's voice was still hushed as she opened her eyes to see him in the faint light of the cave. Elidad touched his face. "I'm fine," she whispered, relieved he was okay. "It's you I'm worried about," she confessed.

"I'm fine," he told her. "I'm not the one having bad dreams again." He smiled, placing his hand lightly over hers. "Can I assume my fate is disastrous?"

"What?" She pretended to not know what he was asking. She didn't want to tell him about her dream.

"You were crying, in your dream." He reached forward to brush away a tear. "You were calling my name, and now you're happy to see me." A quiet laugh escaped him. "I don't think you've ever been happy to see me. I'm guessing whatever was happening in your dream, wasn't in my favor."

"It was just a dream," she said, pulling her hand away from his face to wipe her remaining tears.

"I hope it isn't a foretelling of my destiny tomorrow."

The thought sent chills through Elidad. She hoped it wasn't, either. What if it was? Would Abraham be there? Was Ghelgath the Shadow Man, and holding Abraham prisoner? If they found him, would the battle play out the same way it did in her dream? Would Aiden die?

Aiden affectionately squeezed her arm. "Get some rest. You need your sleep." He began to move away, but Elidad caught his hand.

"Stay with me." Her words were startling in her own ears. She could tell Aiden was surprised, also. "Just for a little while." She tried to make her invitation sound less needy. "I just don't want to be alone." But every time she spoke she felt like her words sounded more desperate. She was too tired to care. She really didn't want to be alone with the Shadow Man haunting her dreams, and if Aiden was close, she could make sure he was safe.

"Okay," he whispered.

Elidad rested her head back on the furs, her movement sending the aroma of the herb collection through the air. She was surprised at herself and her fear at the thought of Aiden hurt. A month ago, she couldn't stand to look in his eyes, and now she didn't want to be twenty yards from him.

Aiden lay down beside her. She was relieved to feel the security his presence brought. Hearing the rhythm of his breath was a constant reassurance of his safety. With all this, and the rushing sound of water in the background, she found herself slowly slipping back into sleep.

Groggy with exhaustion, before completely succumbing to her dulling energy, she slipped her hand inside Aiden's shirt, moving her arm across his waist. She could feel his stomach quiver as her hand brushed across his skin. Tucking her hand under his side, she pulled herself into him. She knew her action was subtle enough he would think she was asleep. She smiled, pressing her head into his chest. His arms wrapped around her, comfortably tightening, emulating strength.

This is what it must feel like to find solace in an impenetrable shelter.

CHAPTER THIRTY-TWO

When Aiden woke the next morning, or what he believed to be morning, he found himself alone. Sitting up in the twinkling light he looked around. "Elidad? Jed?" No answer. The sound of water rushing between its banks was the only thing he could hear. Lying back down, he stared at the mock stars above.

The night before had been a restless one for him, thinking only of their battle, foretold by the yeti. How could his task have been set so off course? His purpose was to help Elidad find Abraham. Now, here he was, striving to stay on top of the task at hand. The changes in their path from Abraham, to keys, to the bishop, left him in a whirlwind of confusion. How much further off course would Elidad take them? Would finding these keys really lead them to Abraham? Elidad was certain that following the path of the keys is what Abraham was doing when he went missing.

Aiden was sent to follow Elidad. She was the best at her job; she had a way of finding things others couldn't. She had a way of saving the unsaveable. But at this pace, he felt like they were on a psychotic downward spiral rather than a byway to an acceptable ending. Aiden sighed. He only wished she could save herself. Seeing Elidad afraid shook him. She'd always been calm and collected. He didn't know how to handle her any other way. Who was this fearful person? Not the girl he grew up knowing.

He wondered what she'd dreamt. The fear in her eyes when she woke still unnerved him. It might've been the first time she'd looked at him without a hint of resentment. Was it terrible to feel some pleasure, seeing the tears escape her guarded eyes? It was relieving to see she had some feeling for him. He never thought there would be a time he would catch her vulnerable, openly insecure. It made him feel connected to her, closer in some way. He felt a tug of guilt for feeling empowered by her insecurity. Seeing her vulnerable and asking him to stay, made him feel needed. It gave him purpose.

His hand rested on his stomach. He remembered the feeling that stirred when she pulled closer to him. He could feel his breath rise and fall under his palm with the memory of her hand on his skin.

A noise down the corridor shook Aiden from his thought. He sat up. Kade was rapidly approaching. When he came near he held out a stack of white furs.

"These are for you," he told Aiden. "They should fit you well."

Aiden separated the stack of heavy furs; pants, a shirt with a vest, and a coat. The leather's thickness would offer protection against the cold and padding against attacks on the battle field.

"Where's Elidad?" Aiden asked.

"With the king. They are discussing a battle plan."

"Why didn't anyone wake me?"

"Elidad thought it would be best if you slept. She said you did not sleep well," Kade answered. "Dress, and we will meet them."

Aiden changed. The leather was cool. Tailored in the ice city, the cold remained deep in the folds. He knew it was a small foreshadowing of the cold that awaited them outside the wooden doors.

Aiden wasn't excited by the thought of leaving the baths. It was comforting here. He would've liked to have been able to stay longer in the serenity of the cascading water and its foggy banks. He wasn't sure this war was meant for them, no matter what the yeti read in the stars. What if the bishop hadn't gone to Ghelgath? As far as Aiden was concerned, they hadn't found any concrete evidence that the bishop was actually looking for him. Aiden refused to accept that the man he knew and respected would give up his relationship with God for wealth and power. A man of his position would know how short lived that would be. He would know it wouldn't be worth it. Aiden couldn't pretend to understand anyone's motivation to gain wealth and power. But not everyone had firsthand experience seeing how those things destroyed lives.

Kade closed the doors soundly behind them and held out his hand to Aiden.

Aiden paused.

"It will be much faster," Kade explained.

Realizing what was being offered, Aiden stepped forward into Kade's hand. With a rush of wind biting at his face, they were bounding down the hall, the ice growing lighter as they moved along. Aiden was glad he wasn't walking, as the passage appeared much longer today. He wasn't sure his legs would've made the distance.

Entering the throne room, they discovered a small group of yeti, and Elidad, looking down at a map etched into the ice floor. Jed lingered on the edge of the room as if to disengage himself from the conversation. The rest were so enthralled in their planning, they were barely interrupted by Kade and Aiden's entrance.

"I think we are going to need to hit the gates hard and fast," Elidad was saying. "He won't be surprised we're coming. Are you sure no one knows what's on the other side of those gates?"

Hiri shook his head. "No yeti has ever returned from the other side of those gates. And all yeti are forbidden from that side of the mountain."

Frustration escaped Elidad in the sound of a sigh. "I suppose all we can do is guess that whatever is inside will be big and bad, and waiting for us. How much do you know about his army?"

"We have never seen his army, in this century, but there are inscriptions," Hiri said, walking to the walls of the throne room. Elidad followed him.

The inscriptions here were cut into a darker, duller ice. It lacked the gleam that the rest of the room had. The wall that Hiri touched showed a dragon standing over piles of yeti, a few fleeing for their lives. "It is not told why the battle began," Hiri said. "It only tells of days when the dragon's wrath destroyed the yeti.

"Ghelgath's army swept the land, destroying all that stood in its way. With his ability to command the dead he was able to fight the yeti with devastating force." Hiri turned to his new friends as if to ensure they would understand. "He has the ability to command the dead. All that are within reach of the high demon can be called to his aid. No matter who they were in life—good or evil—he is able to use them at his will."

"How's that?" Jed asked. "How can he have power over anyone that isn't living?"

"Dead bodies are just useless shells that carry nothing: no good, no evil. If the body is empty, it is susceptible to being used," Hiri answered. "All that fall during war are used against the offense. In the past, our warriors found themselves having to dismember their own allies to defend their lives." Hiri looked back to Elidad. "Once our warriors fall in battle, they must be considered the enemy. It is the only way to ensure our safety. There may be humans or yeti that we know and love, set against us to slow our attack."

Elidad remembered her dream. Would Aiden become a part of his army? "Maybe it would be beneficial for you to remind your troops."

Hiri turned to one of the guards by the door, grunted an order to him in Yeti, and in a flash he was gone. Hiri looked back to Elidad. "My son Kade will carry you through this battle. He is one of our finest warriors," he announced proudly, "and he does owe you his life."

Elidad shook her head. "He doesn't owe me anything."

Hiri held up his hand. "He will be the one to take you into the cave of the White Dragon."

Elidad knew it would be an honor for Kade to carry the Healer into battle. She imagined the inscriptions that would be chiseled into the wall when their fight with Ghelgath was over. Elidad turned to Jedidiah. "Can you tell us anything about Ghelgath's habits?"

"Not too much," Jed answered. "He keeps mostly to himself, sticking to his side of the mountain. If you want to see him, you have to go looking. He's been leaving humans alone for years. There haven't been any attacks, other than on my climbing party, even if he was tempted. I know he sees me when I photograph him. I'm not sure why he lets me. He left me alone on the mountain, too. Mostly he avoids contact with everyone."

Hiri grunted, "Not from our experience."

Jedidiah nodded, "I'm just telling you what I know. I know he is a mean bastard, but for some reason he's left me alone, let me live."

"He wasn't going to let us live in that cave," Elidad reminded him. "At least, he wasn't going to let *me* live."

While Elidad's statement rang through the throne room, the large doors on the far wall pushed open violently. A yeti decorated in shining armor holding an impressive helmet tucked firmly under his arm stormed across the room. A red cape, fastened around his neck with a bronze pin, flapped vigorously behind him. His face was fierce as he walked with purpose. This yeti did not appear to have a soft side. His attitude was as hard as the armor that shielded his warrior body. Ignoring the humans around him he conversed with Hiri in their native language. Hiri answered calmly and the warrior seemed agitated, never once glancing at the humans. Elidad guessed that by refusing to acknowledge their existence he was directly insulting them.

"In English," Hiri answered the warrior. "Our guests may know of the battle plan; after all, they will be fighting with us." Turning to the humans, Hiri introduced the disgruntled yeti. "This is Leonidas, our general. He fears that we have been mistaken, and suggests, perhaps you are not the chosen one."

For the first time Leonidas looked at Elidad, showing the offside of his broad face where a massive scar across his eye disfigured the right half. The scar started at the top of his forehead and trailed through his eye where it split his pupil in half, giving it an obscure shape. His lips were split and indented, the scar tracing to his chin. Elidad wondered how he survived such an injury without the miracles of modern medicine. Leonidas, nostrils still flaring with his objection, came closer to Elidad, sniffing the air around her.

"This human is small. How can *she* be the one to lead us to victory against the beast? She will only lead us to our demise," he said loudly glaring in Elidad's eyes, not hiding his disdain.

"She healed the bite of the wolf," Kade protested, holding his arm up for Leonidas to see.

"Does she have the sword?" Leonidas asked pointedly, not taking his eyes off Elidad, and yet not asking her directly.

"I do," Elidad answered, holding her ground. "Perhaps you would like to put the steel to the test?"

Aiden shifted his weight as he watched the tension grow in the general. He could crush Elidad with one hand, and she just challenged him, in his own city.

Leonidas turned to the king. "She has a brave heart," he snorted, "and a fast tongue. We will see if she can keep herself alive." He glanced at her doubtfully and bowed before the king. "As always, I am a servant. I will honor your command. I pray that we are not leading our army to a tragic ending, my Lord." Without another word, he turned and stormed out of the throne room, his cape whipping behind him in the same manner of his arrival.

Aiden whistled through his teeth, slapping Elidad on the shoulder when the door slammed behind Leonidas. "And just when I thought it couldn't get any tenser, you go ahead and pull it off."

Elidad glared back in response.

"He is an excellent warrior; he will be ready to fight," Hiri assured. "His army will know no hesitation in him."

"Maybe he's right," Elidad offered. "Maybe I'm not the one that your people have been waiting for."

Hiri smiled. "What do you know to be true?"

She could feel the eyes of the others on her. She wished the color that rose in her cheeks would fall away. "I'm supposed to be here."

Hiri nodded his head in agreement. "We have faith in the Lord. Faith that He, and you, will lead us to victory."

"God willing," she said, hopefully.

CHAPTER THIRTY-THREE

The sound of a thousand yeti was slightly muffled by the snow, like a distant drum beating a countdown of doom. Their war march was perfectly in time. Kade was carrying Elidad in one arm, a shield strapped to the other, and a sword in his belt. The sword swayed with each step. Looking down at it, Elidad was sure that if it were lying on the ground next to her, she wouldn't be able to pick it up.

The wind screamed down the mountain, covering the earth in a white blanket—perfect weather for their advance. Elidad wondered how they were going to hide a yeti army in daylight. God was truly watching over them. The whiteout was what they needed to ensure a hidden advance. The march slowly came to a halt where the ice began to form a steep canyon before them.

Aiden, who was being carried by another yeti, was brought to Elidad's side.

"Now what?" Aiden wondered aloud.

"We wait for our scouts," Kade answered. "This is a dangerous passage. If we were attacked from above, few would live."

Kade was right. Elidad was impressed at the yeti's intelligence on warfare. If they blindly passed through the canyon, they would be sitting ducks.

A yeti scout came barreling toward Leonidas. They conversed, then the scout took his place in line with the other warriors. Leonidas pulled a large stone from a pack fastened to his belt. It was clear like crystal and it shimmered like the sun. A diamond. One that grew mature enough to emanate its own light, not just twinkle. The canyon walls were so large, daylight was blocked from its depths.

Holding the stone above his head, they watched as it threw prismatic light down the canyon. Elidad squinted at the brightness of the diamond, it reminded her of the match lighting her way to Leucosia's lair. The last time they saw her, did Leucosia know Aiden and Elidad would come this far? Would she know Elidad would have to battle a dragon? Did she know then, the outcome of this day? Elidad wished she knew as she glanced over at Aiden.

Leonidas made a faint but distinctive roar that signified the beginning of their march down the dangerous passage.

Elidad felt a slight relief as the army came to the end of the canyon—the dangerous walk behind them. The terrain before them turned treacherous. Rocks and boulders cascading down, as if a landslide had left the rubble, some larger than buses, strewn about. The ground was riddled with bones of animals and humans alike. Ice hung from the ceiling like deathly chandeliers, threatening to impale all who walked below. Her momentary relief was quickly replaced with unease.

The passage floor was rough and uneven, and Elidad knew that she, Aiden, and Jed never would have been able to walk here on their own. The ice alone would've made it impossible. The yeti moved across the ground with ease, their claws digging into the ice.

At the end of the long, obstacle-laden corridor loomed an intimidating wall of ice. The advancing army came to a stop once more.

"Ghelgath's gate is at the top of this wall," Leonidas said, looking up, speaking in English for the first time since the throne room.

"Hiri said no one returned from the other side of the doors," Elidad said.

Leonidas turned his disfigured face toward her. "He was right, no one has."

"Then how do you know what's up there?" Elidad asked.

Leonidas's face stayed motionless. "Because some of us made it back from the front gate."

Leonidas waived one of his massive paws toward the wall, and the front line began to advance up the ice. The few hundred yeti moved cautiously over the wall's edge. The rest of the army watched intently . . . all were silent . . . hoping for their safety.

"You will have to hold on to me," Kade told Elidad, holding up the shield on his arm.

Elidad wrapped her arms around his neck as he pushed her toward his back. She held tightly with her legs, forcing them to support her weight so Kade wouldn't have to. Aiden and his yeti followed suit as Elidad and Kade began to climb the wall. Higher and higher they rose. With them, a wave of yeti crawled over the ledge together. Kade and Elidad's line pushed to the front, closest to the dreaded doors.

Kade stood in line with the other troops while Leonidas pushed past, turning his back to the ice doors. He was the only thing between the doors and the front line. The ground they stood on was flat and level, free of the rubble they'd encountered earlier.

Leonidas began pacing back and forth in front of his army, his cape vigorously trailing him. Ghelgath's ice doors stood a hundred yards tall, dwarfing Leonidas, the largest yeti Elidad had seen. Turning over her shoulder, she saw the yeti army, like an ocean of white dissolving into the snow-covered mountain.

Elidad hadn't noticed the shutter of nerves through her hands until Kade set her on the ground. The overwhelming task before her and her companions began to resonate through her body. She thought of those people she envied, the *normal* people who would never understand, or believe what was happening, or about to happen. She was glad she wasn't them. She was glad she had a choice and was able to fight for the people she loved. She hoped Abraham was here. She hoped Ghelgath had him and the key. She felt empowered by the yeti's prophecy. She, the Healer, would slay the evil that lay in the Dragon Heart. She would be victorious.

Elidad was grateful they were more than just two humans on this part of the quest. She felt a stir of anger, thinking about Jed refusing to fight with them.

The yeti army began to pulse with a war chant. Kade picked Elidad up with his shielded arm, drawing his sword.

Leonidas stopped pacing, his body moving to the yeti's chant. He roared, pounding his chest. Before his voice could echo through the cave, the front line cascaded forward, parting around him. The battle had begun.

Elidad's mind was numb as the cold wind rushing past her face caused tears to stream from her eyes. The weight of their advancing army hit the doors with force. Elidad and Kade were only fifteen yeti behind the fist to shoulder the weight of the doors. Even from Elidad's view she could tell they pushed open with little effort.

Shocked at the lack of resistance, the line of warriors lost its pace, slowing to a walk, and began moving cautiously. Elidad didn't think it possible, but her heart began to race faster in anticipation of an attack. She found herself continually glancing in Aiden's direction to check on him, the horrifying images of her dreams distracting her. She should have made him stay back at the Crystal City with Jed. Her concern for his safety was affecting her ability to stay focused.

What did her dream mean? Would they find Abraham here, in this ice hell? Would he be hurt? Would he be dead or given over to Ghelgath with the key by the bishop? Did the bishop sell his soul to Ghelgath? What would he get in exchange? What could be worth bringing an end to the world?

Elidad forced herself to look forward, and not check on Aiden again.

Behind the doors of Ghelgath's cave was a long hall. The ice was dark and uninviting. The cave was clear and open, but the ice here was discolored, dark in some places and light in others. As the troops pushed forward, nothing came to stop them. No defense was executed.

"This is too easy," Elidad said uneasily to Kade.

The hall was so long they would see and hear an approaching attack long before it reached them. As they continued forward, the passage became darker, light no longer filtering through the ice. Perhaps the attacking army was waiting in the darkness ahead.

"I agree," Leonidas said. He had caught up to Kade and Elidad. She wondered if he was going to stay by her side, to see her fail.

"I don't suspect it will continue to be easy for much longer," Kade said, producing his own light-giving diamond from his pack.

A shimmer at Kade's feet caught Elidad's eye. Looking down, her breath got caught at the back of her throat. "Tell them to stop," she forced herself to shout. "Tell them to fall back now!"

Below the surface of the ice, bodies were littered under their feet. Looking at the walls of the cave she realized the dark spots in the ice were bodies. In the dark they were hard to make out, but if you took the time to stare into the walls with a light, the figures were gruesomely unmistakable.

Leonidas immediately sounded a roar, echoing down the hall. Hiri was correct. Leonidas's army would know no hesitation in him. Though he protested Elidad's presence, he followed her lead without pause.

Before his roar of retreat had a chance to reach all the warriors behind them, the ground began to shake. Ice flew through the air like shrapnel, loud crashes and rumbling filling their ears as the walls and floors exploded around them. *The dead army had begun to attack.* Metal clashing and ice crumbling came at them from everywhere, bringing chaos to their line of defense. It felt like they were in an avalanche.

Elidad ducked as a sword came crashing down on Kade's shield. The hit surged through her body.

"Put me down, Kade," Elidad demanded. She could sense his hesitation. "Put me down!"

Sweeping his shield through a patch of frozen humans to clear a spot, he did as he was told.

Elidad threw open the thick, ankle-length coat protecting her from the cold. On her belt was a sheath made for her by a yeti blacksmith. In the sheath was the piece of metal Leucosia gave her. The yeti made the sheath fit the hilt perfectly so the hilt locked into place.

If you saw the hilt in the sheath, you wouldn't think the blade was missing. Many times, while she was alone, Elidad tried to wield the sword, but it never materialized. The only time before now that she needed it, she was unable to reach it. Elidad remembered Leucosia saying, "If you must use it, it will bring you victory over your enemies. Only with purity and justice in your heart will it come to you."

Elidad's heart raced as a yeti, his eyes frozen over, raced toward her. She closed her hand around the cold steal.

Kade, who was standing by her side a second ago, was too far away to help her now. She caught a glimpse of Leonidas as the undead yeti rushed her. Elidad slowly withdrew the hilt, hoping the sword would reveal itself.

The blade hummed as she pulled it free from its sheath. Hearing the drag of metal against metal, she knew the blade was there, with an aggressive thrust she released the end of the sword.

She ran to the top of a mound of ice to gain an advantage over the yeti that was advancing. With both arms she slash the metal through the air at her attacker, cleanly severing his head from his body. She stood in awe as the corpse crashed to the ground. Elidad waved the sword through the air again. The weapon was surprisingly light and easy to handle. She had trained with many weapons, but this one felt like it was *made* for her.

Ghelgath's dead army was made of various creatures: yeti, humans, wolves, dwarves, and some Elidad had never seen before. Hiri had been right about Ghelgath raising a dead army, but their faces were frozen and cold. Ice replaced their eyes as they fought. It was easy to tell the difference between the bad guys and her allies.

Elidad jumped off the ice, back to the ground. A man dressed like a climber, his face lifeless and blue, came storming toward Elidad. He swung an ax used for climbing at her head. Elidad whipped her sword, slicing through the metal ax head like it was a blade of grass. Another swing and the climber's arm was gone.

Another climber came at Elidad in a dead run. Seeing him out of the corner of her eye, she had no time to wield the sword. She dropped to the floor, rolling onto her back and kicking her feet into his stomach as he bent to attack her on the ground. Kicking as hard as she could, Elidad launched him over her body. He flew to the floor behind her.

Snapping to her feet, she held her sword ready. He advanced again for a second attack. Elidad swung the sword into his body, dislodging his torso from the remaining part of him. When she pulled the sword away, the corpse slumped to the ground, severed.

Across the battle-filled hall, though he was fighting off many attackers, she could tell Leonidas had been watching her fight. She sensed a glint of approval in his eyes.

Kade finally made his way back to Elidad's side. His presence gave her a second to observe their surroundings. Elidad noticed that when the yeti were overpowered by the dead army, the frozen ones would wrap their bodies around the warriors and sink into the ice below, taking their captives with them. Out of the thousands of yeti, only a mere few hundred were left in the passage with them.

Distracted in her observation, a man came up behind Elidad and wrapped his arms around her. She could feel her feet begin to freeze as her body began to lower into the ice. She desperately struggled, the ice moving up her ankles. Elidad could feel a tug pulling from behind. She leaned forward and was released by the frozen man. Looking over her shoulder, she saw someone other than Kade had come to her aid. Though her captor released her from his deathly grip, her feet were still stuck in the ice. She quickly stabbed the ice with the sword to free herself, and turned just in time to see Jed finishing off the man who attacked her.

"Nice of you to join us," Elidad said with a slight smile.

"Well, I thought you could handle it on your own. Apparently not." Jed gestured to the man at his feet. "It's a good thing I came to check up on you."

Jed pointed behind Elidad and she turned to see Kade wrestling with a dead yeti who was pushing him backward. Kade's body pressed against the wall and ice particles protruded from the hard surface absorbing him in.

Elidad and Jed sprinted to his aid. Kade pushed hard against the yeti making him stumble backward. Diving at the frozen yeti, Elidad drove her sword through his foot, pinning it to the ground. He was unable to move forward, giving Kade an opportunity to pull free of the ice that had not yet encompassed him. Kade knelt to scoop up his sword from the ground. Swinging it hard, he dislodged the yeti's head from the rest of his body. Elidad pulled her sword from his foot as his body fell back, shaking the ground.

Their numbers were falling quickly. Yeti on all sided of them were being pushed into the ice wall. Elidad watched another under attack stumble, causing him to fall on the floor. A dead creature pounced on him and they were both absorbed into the floor.

"We have to get to the other side of the passage," Elidad told Kade frantically.

He swept Elidad into his arm and sprinted toward the darkness, his roar echoing behind him. Any yeti that remained in battle were now on his heels. At the end of the passage, the vast open space grew more confined and the ice became hard dark stone. Kade withdrew his diamond, its light bouncing down the passage to light their way.

"Put me down." Elidad wasn't sure why she whispered.

She was surprised he heard her. He set her on the stone while the others came up behind them. Elidad was relieved to see Aiden set down beside her, Leonidas carrying him. Jed was deposited with them by another yeti she didn't know. Elidad saw the look of surprise on Aiden's face.

"Look who decided to show," Elidad said to Aiden.

"He probably shouldn't have . . . he didn't sign up for this," Aiden scowled at Jed, apparently not ready to forgive him yet. "We got slaughtered out there; there's hardly any of us left." Aiden was much calmer than she anticipated. She found his demeanor a little unsettling. She was used to him in a panic, not calm.

"We just have to keep moving," Elidad said. "His army shouldn't be able to function if he's dead."

"Elidad." Aiden grabbed her arm as she put the sword back in its sheath. "How are you going to kill Ghelgath when we can't even get through his army?"

The panic she knew so well was beginning to show on his face.

"I don't know, Aiden." She pulled her arm away from his grip. "But if we don't keep going we'll all be dead anyway. We have to try. We just can't stay and fight a battle we are clearly losing." Turning from Aiden, she took the diamond from Kade. The passage turned a sharp corner. *All we can do is push forward and try*, she thought. She had to face Ghelgath.

The darkness that greeted them as they made the corner was strangely different. The absence of light dimmed the brightness of the diamond. It was only able to illuminate a small space around Elidad. Everything beyond that was too dark to see. By the expression on Kade's face, Elidad knew he didn't understand it either.

A burst of flame came scorching toward them like a flame thrower, large enough to engulf a bus. The group went jumping and diving in all directions. Kade grabbed Elidad in his dive and she hoped someone grabbed Aiden and Jed. The fire was so hot, the stone on the wall behind where they'd been standing caught fire.

Learning from her mistake, Elidad hid the diamond in her pocket to extinguish its light and conceal their location, but it was too late. Another burst of flame bolted their way and she felt her body being hurled in the air as Kade jumped with her again. Kade pulled the large diamond from his pouch. The light, so bright, Elidad was unable to look directly at the stone.

What was he doing? Trying to get them killed? Before she could ask, Kade hurled the diamond in the direction from where the flames originated. Hitting the ground with a heavy thud it began to roll along the floor like a bowling ball, its luminescence growing in intensity as it moved. Brighter and brighter it burned as its momentum slowed.

A white reptile hand, jagged with talons, rose above it. Elidad's heart was in her throat, choking away her breath. The talons were long enough to pierce through her body and Kade's at the same time. The reptile claw came crashing hard on top of the light, the diamond disintegrating with little effort from the beast. Fragments were discharged in every direction like fireworks across the black space. As the small pieces came to rest across the floor, and the dust of the diamond settled on the walls, every remnant began to glow with its light.

As the light grew, the foot that stomped the diamond appeared to grow out of nowhere into a leg. Poised with tense muscle tissue, attached to a body the size of a football field, displaying outstretched wings twice as large as its body. Its neck nearly reached the top of the monumental cave in which they now found themselves standing. He turned his head dangerously to inspect the intruders standing before him. His crystal-blue eyes swirling in anger, as he released a shrill cry of rage.

Sharp horns spiked off the top of his head. He was just as white as Elidad remembered him. Every crevice of his body was flawless. His claws, his tail, with spikes on the end, hammered the ground every time he whipped it . . . every part of his figure was made to kill. Smoke flared from his angry nostrils. He opened his mouth, eliciting a terrifying scream more intense than his last, sending chills down Elidad's spine.

Kade put Elidad down. Finding her feet beneath her, she once again drew the sword. Advancing on the dragon, leaving the others behind.

She moved forward to fulfill her destiny.

CHAPTER THIRTY-FOUR

The sound of Elidad's heartbeat consumed her ears as her hands held fast to the steel, now shaking with the surge of adrenaline. Ghelgath reared back on his hind legs, beating his wings, stirring a violent wind around her as he screeched another bloodcurdling cry. His front legs crashed to the ground. It took all her willpower to not cover her ears with her hands as the gut-wrenching sound radiated through the cave like a nuclear blast.

His neck arched back, as he once again stomped his feet, attempting to squash Elidad where she stood. She dove through the air, rolling on her shoulder into a somersault. As she came around she swung the sword hard, cutting across the underside of his foot, barely escaping his attempt to mutilate her body.

Ghelgath screamed with pain, his head flailing with rage. Stomping his feet against the ground, blue blood as bright as his eyes smudged across the rock, spattering treasures and bones that were scattered around his feet. As he broadened his chest and flapped his wings, Elidad looked up at him in wonderment. She didn't know anything about dragons, and this one was the size of a building. She could spend days stabbing his body blindly and never once pierce his "heart of evil" as the prophecy had foreseen.

Angry he'd been injured, Ghelgath's head came wielding back toward Elidad. Before she could brace herself, he opened his mouth and discharged an ocean of flames meant to engulf her.

In that brief moment, all she could picture was the wall of rock that had been set ablaze by the scorching inferno when they entered the cave. She knew there was no hope. She brought the sword down in front of her face, as if to hide behind it, and closed her eyes in what she assumed would be her final prayer.

She could feel the heat wash over her: her nostrils burned, the white heat seared her lungs, and her breath became labored with the intensity of her looming death. It wasn't as painful as she'd anticipated . . . perhaps it already ended. Was she dead already? Was she paralyzed with the severity of her injuries? Whatever the reason, she was relieved to not feel her flesh melting away by the blast of flames.

Opening her eyes, she became aware that the dragon's flames hadn't stopped. She stood in the middle of the flames, sliced in half by the sword. Ghelgath's flames parted like the ocean parted for Moses, and held away from her body, leaving her untouched. She pushed hard against the pressure. It slowly, eventually, fell away. Elidad stood, stunned, waiting for Ghelgath's next move.

His ears folded back and his head cocked to the side, smoke drifting from his nostrils. Ghelgath's eyes whirled and Elidad could feel him pondering what just happened. His head came low to the ground, hovering just above, slithering like a serpent in the air. He remained outside of her striking distance, but lingered with intense curiosity.

The tension was agonizing. What was he thinking? Elidad wondered if he was contemplating just eating her. His blue eyes swirled like multifaceted sapphires under showroom lights. He held perfectly still, staring *into* her. The swirl of his eyes was mesmerizing, and she wondered if he was trying to hypnotize her. As she watched him carefully, the dragon began to fade away and in its place a fog slowly drifted to the ground. Elidad's heart pounded harder. Where did he go? How could she pierce the dragon heart if there was no dragon? Could this fog attack her, or enter her body? She wanted to look back at her friends, but didn't dare take her eyes from where Ghelgath had been.

Out of the fog came the figure of a man. Her grip around the sword's handle tightened. Ghelgath was stunning. His eyes were brilliant, just as they were in all his other forms, but less threatening as a man. He looked like an ice sculpture, a flawless model of man. Every muscle on his body looked like iron threads, woven together to form perfection. His body glowed white, brighter than the diamond hidden away in Elidad's pocket. His hands resembled the talons of the dragon that nearly ended her moments ago, long and lean, crested with dangerous white claws.

As Ghelgath neared her, he fell to his knees. To Elidad's amazement, he outstretched his arms from either side of his body as if relinquishing all control.

"Did she send you?" he demanded.

His question was confusing. Elidad didn't want to answer him for fear the wrong one would anger him. Who was he talking about? Was this a trick? She wasn't sure. His question was odd, his tone a strange desperate petition.

"Did she send you to finish it?" His eyes were pleading.

Again, Elidad wanted to look to the others for help. Was he just toying with her to get close before he closed in for the kill?

"Who?" Elidad asked, just above a whisper.

His brow creased in the center with his own confusion. "Leucosia. Was she the one who gave you the Sword of Justice?"

Stunned, Elidad stared into his eyes.

"Did she give you the sword? Did she send you to kill me?"

"She gave it to me, but she didn't send me here," Elidad told him, thinking back.

"It doesn't matter. She would know your path would lead you here. She would have known you would come to kill me. Let it be done." He looked up at Elidad. "Do what you came here to do, human. Let my suffering end." His words had an air of sadness that disenchanted Elidad's fear. She lowered the sword.

"What are you doing?" She could hear Aiden's voice behind her. "Don't trust him. He's going to kill us."

"How do you know Leucosia?" she asked, ignoring Aiden.

He looked at the ground beneath him. "I know her . . . with all of my soul." His face turned up to meet hers again. "That is how. With everything I am, I know her."

Elidad stared. "That's not what I meant."

"I know her from another life," he answered, "when evil was all I knew, and love was an unknown enemy." He continued to hold Elidad's eyes with an honesty she could feel in her bones. "I gave her that sword, many lifetimes ago," he said dreamily, staring at it.

Elidad looked down at the steel in her hands. "Where did you get it? Being a demon, I mean. How did *you* come to own the Sword of Justice?"

"I fought an angel for it and nearly killed him." Ghelgath took a breath. "He nearly killed *me*. Though I was the victor, I decided to spare his life. I am not sure why I allowed him to live. One thing is certain, that choice changed my life," he admitted. "My mind became clouded; I thought differently. I began to make *different* choices."

"What kinds of choices?" Elidad asked.

He smiled up at her. "Good ones. But that is of no consequence." His eyes went back to the sword. "That blade is the only one on this earth that can kill me." He held out his palm for Elidad to see blood still pouring from his wound where she cut the dragon. "It will kill an immortal . . . It will kill me as easily as it has made me bleed.

"It has great power. I doubt any on this earth know its true capabilities. You should know, when the sword is won through a duel, it has a link to the victor. It will eventually come back to the victor over time. I thought it was a myth, but over the centuries it has *always* found its way back to me, one way or another. I gifted it to Leucosia. If she is not the one to bring it to me, I do not want it, nor my mortality."

"I don't understand," Elidad heard herself say. She understood he wanted to die, and was throwing himself at her, but why? What part did Leucosia play in all this? Why didn't Leucosia warn her about Ghelgath and the sword?

Ghelgath studied Elidad's face as his eyes swam in circles. "I can show you, if you'd like."

Elidad felt comfortable enough to look over her shoulder to her allies, still cornered in the cave a safe distance away. They all shook their heads in disagreement.

She looked back into Ghelgath's blue eyes. The pain she saw tempted her curiosity. "Okay."

He slowly came to stand before her, his chiseled figure towering over her as he reached out his hand to grab her arm. His touch was like ice, sending goose flesh racing up her arms. Still guarded against an attack, Elidad braced the sword in her hand. Ghelgath's eyes began to move more vigorously, swirling like ocean waves, pulsing and churning. As Elidad stared into them, they moved more intently. His grip on her arm became colder until her skin burned and began to freeze with his frigid touch. She could feel the ice pulsing through her veins, moving across her body, settling deep in her lungs. The heavy distant hum of her thoughts began to slow, like the night hypothermia took over her body. She looked into his eyes, her fear fading while Ghelgath's touch consumed her.

Opening her eyes, she found herself in a field of fragrant flowers, the same flowers that surrounded Leucosia in her home. Only here, the sun was high overhead, with its warm rays falling upon her shoulders. This was not Leucosia's lair; Elidad was outside, in the open air, on a warm sunny day. An ocean breeze danced around her bringing the smell of the salty sea.

Elidad looked down at her hands, then to her surroundings. A moment ago she'd been in an ice cave with Ghelgath, and now she was here, in this flowery field. Did she die? Did he deceive her? Did he send her to another place, or another time? Was she transported away? She didn't think it was possible, but assumed anything *could* be possible.

Hearing voices in the distance brought Elidad back to her current surroundings. Not knowing who was talking, or why she was there, she ducked down into some nearby bushes. Hoping to stay concealed, she made her way carefully and quietly to where the voices were coming.

"This is enough, Calandra." Elidad paused. Without seeing her, she knew it was Leucosia's voice. Elidad pushed through the bushes until she could see Leucosia standing amidst the flowers, tears streaking her face. She was just as beautiful as she always was, even in her agony.

"You must stop this," Leucosia told the woman in front of her, the one she called Calandra, while pointing at the ground where blood-stained white and yellow flowers stood silent. The flowers dripped with scarlet as though a morbid rain had washed them all in the sin of a murderous death. Lying still, below the flowers, bodies of men covered the ground around the two sirens. Their bodies were mutilated, contorted in a grim scene. It was eerily similar to the statues that inhabited Leucosia's home.

Calandra's beauty was just as staggering as Leucosia's: her glowing skin, flawless, her robes, floating weightless around her perfect body. She had glowing locks of curls that draped sensually over her shoulders—different than Leucosia's straight hair. Their brow line was identical. There was no mistaking their bloodline was the same.

Reality came crashing down on Elidad: This was a memory of when Leucosia confronted her sister about the killing of men on their island. This was the incident that divided the remaining sisters and changed the fate of the world.

Calandra's voice rang with the hum of amused laughter. "Oh, little sister, don't you see? This is our destiny." She waved her hands over the dead. "Our gift is a blessing. We hold power over them . . . *all* of them. They gratefully give their lives to us. Think of the army we could command. No one would stand in our way. We are goddesses of this earth, and they should kneel at our feet. We shouldn't have to live out our lives in hiding; we should *own* them." The way she spat the words at Leucosia, Elidad could feel her hatred as she pointed her wicked finger at the bodies.

"This power is not a blessing. It is a curse," Leucosia yelled. "They have a God. *We* have a God. And *you* will have to answer to him."

Calandra's face contorted into a pleased smile. "And yet *your* God does nothing to help these fiends as I bring them to the end they deserve. He did nothing to help *us*. He keeps this curse upon us, though we have prayed for his help. He stands and does nothing!" Calandra's voice became a rabid screech.

Leucosia hung her head. "That's not the way it works, Calandra. You know that. This world is unkind and unfair because the Devil walks upon it. God is good and true to His word. One day, we shall be saved. Until that day, we must do our best to walk with Him. But make no mistake, sister: you are not God, nor are you godlike."

Calandra's face grew darker with hatred. "If you cannot see that this is a gift, sister," she said, her voice wavering in anger, "there will be no hope to save you."

"If you cannot see there is no future without God, there is nothing left for *you*. If death and despair are what bring you happiness, the Devil has already won you over. You are damned," Leucosia spat.

"I make my own fate!" Calandra screamed.

Leucosia shook her head. "You are wrong, and you know that. You have a choice—good or evil. There is no in between, no neutral, no going your own way. Try to walk that line and you will fall to the dark lord, every time." Leucosia's face turned hard and emotionless. "*You* are no sister of *mine*."

Screaming an eerie wail of anger and disgust, Calandra advanced on Leucosia, swinging a sword that moments ago had not existed. It was seemingly plucked from the air. Calandra swung it so violently the blade hummed as it cut through the air, coming to a dead stop at the nape of Leucosia's neck.

"You are weak, little sister," Calandra sneered. "Do not turn your back on your destiny . . . on *our* destiny. I give you one last chance to see the error of your ways. Come with me, and let us do what we were born to do."

"I do what I was born to do every day. I give thanks to the Lord. That is what *we* were born to do." As Leucosia finished her words, her eyes hazed over with a glow of premonition.

Leucosia's body was still; there was no movement or breath in her until the premonition ended. As the haze fell away from her eyes, the life returned.

"Do you see your own death, sister?" Calandra hissed like a snake.

Hearing a whimper from amongst the flowers, Elidad tore her eyes away from the scene to find Ignacia, Leucosia's other sister, pinned to the ground seemingly by her own fear. Only a hushed sob came from her as she watched her sisters intently.

Leucosia's eyebrow rose. "What do *you* see, Calandra?" Leucosia asked.

"Shut up," Calandra yelled. "I see plenty. I see me ruling this world, with or without you."

"How long has it been since your last vision?" Leucosia asked. "I hadn't realized they were gone. You are so clouded with evil, your soul is no longer your own. That is why you have lost your premonition. Do you hear that, Ignacia? Her premonitions are gone."

"Traitor," Calandra screamed. "You are a traitor!" She leaned across the blade, still at Leucosia's throat. "You try to turn my sister against me. The decree for traitors shall be death." Calandra swung the sword back as she spoke, preparing to strike. Leucosia held statue still, making no attempt to save herself.

No longer able to keep quiet, Elidad cried out for Leucosia to move, but none of the sirens noticed her. This was a memory—there was no changing the past.

Tears rolled silently down Leucosia's face as she awaited her fate. Calandra swished the sword through the air, meant for Leucosia's throat. Leucosia made no movement in her own defense. The sword collided with a crash. Elidad could see the shock reverberate up Calandra's arm.

The blade found a harder surface than its own . . . Ghelgath's hand. Appearing out of nowhere, his hand held the end of the steel at the base of Leucosia's neck. Ghelgath tossed the end of the sword away from Leucosia, sending Calandra a few steps back, stumbling over her victims lying hidden amongst the flowers. A stunning bright blue liquid trailed down Ghelgath's arm. He looked at it with fascination, as if he'd never seen his own blood before.

"You fool," Calandra laughed. "This is the Sword of Justice. Your immortality means nothing to it. It will kill you, just as easily as it has made you bleed." Calandra began to hum a sweet, lulling tune. Ghelgath's demeanor began to change as she sang.

"You insignificant beast, you think you love my sister? It is only a spell. Something like *you* could never love. And now, you will pay for your intrusion," Calandra threatened as she continued to sing.

Elidad knew no man could resist the song of the siren. And now, she knew it affected Ghelgath the same way. His face began to soften, his body swaying, powerless against her. Could Ghelgath love Leucosia? Why did he keep Calandra from killing her?

"Lie down among the flowers," Calandra commanded.

Elidad looked to Leucosia, hoping she would do something to help Ghelgath, and herself. Standing in quaking silence, she did nothing. Listening to her sister's words about Ghelgath unable to love appeared to hurt Leucosia. Was that the reason she refused to help him? Was she going to watch her sister kill him?

"Lie down," Calandra told Ghelgath. Ghelgath fell to his knees.

Calandra smiled a self-righteous smile, like a predator content its pray was ignorant to an impending strike. She moved to Ghelgath's side and ran her fingers through his hair, locking eyes with Leucosia. "No wonder you favor him so much, sister. He is quite beautiful, and how well he obeys." She smirked. "Perhaps he loves me, too." Calandra pulled Ghelgath's head back by his hair to expose his throat. "Do you think he would kill himself for me if I asked?"

Calandra laughed as the tears began to fall from Leucosia's eyes again. In a furious rage, Calandra stormed toward her sister. "He doesn't love you. He is a beast. And you are a god. He worships you. Stay with me and you can keep him as your pet."

Ghelgath brought his hand to his face as if to blow Calandra a kiss. Calandra's smile was wicked at his gesture. She continued to sing. The kiss he blew swished and swirled in the warm breeze forming snowflakes that rushed to her face. The icy wind that hit Calandra caught her off guard, freezing her song in silence. Elidad watched as the ice raced through her body, freezing her feet to the ground. An ice sculpture, surrounded by blood-soaked flowers on a warm breezy day.

Without the weight of her song holding him captive, Ghelgath was able to get his feet under him and close the small distance between him and Calandra.

Though the rest of her body was as rigid as a statue, Calandra's eyes were able to move. She was alive, frozen in place and aware of her surroundings, but unable to do anything else.

Ghelgath reached forward and wrapped his fingers around the sword in her hand. Calandra's eyes widened with worry. Ghelgath ripped the sword from her. She watched wordlessly as her hand shattered with the force of his strength. Elidad could see the pain in Calandra's eyes.

"You are right, Calandra, immortality means nothing to the Sword of Justice." With the words crossing his lips, Ghelgath drove the sword through her chest. Holding the end of the sword, he looked into her eyes. "I want you to remember the beast that killed you." Ghelgath blew, once more, into her face. The ice that consumed her disappeared. Blood began to pour from her wounds as she grasped the sword with one hand, the other mimicking the movements, her body not aware she was missing a hand.

Ghelgath lowered Calandra's body to the ground to lie with her victims. Standing over her, he ripped the sword from her chest. Calandra's hand found her wound as her breath began to wheeze past her lips. Coughing and spitting, she held up her blood-soaked hand in a final, fruitless gesture.

"I will see you in hell," Ghelgath said.

"She will die, I saw it," Leucosia said, looking to her sister as her life faded before them. Calandra's head turned at Leucosia's words. "I let you die to save my own life," Leucosia said. "That was the premonition. It was to be my death, or yours."

Ghelgath stepped toward Leucosia's side, kneeling before her. Holding up the sword for her to take, he lowered his head.

"I beg your forgiveness," Ghelgath pleaded. "I had no other choice. She would have killed you."

"I am not the one to look to for the forgiveness of sins," Leucosia said. "That is the burden of only one."

"Please, Leucosia, take the sword, as a token of my sorrow. Perhaps, one day you will find it in your heart to forgive my actions."

Leucosia took the sword from him. Her hand went to his chin to lift his face to hers. No words.

"I give you my life," he pleaded. "Just tell me one day you will forgive me, and my life shall not have been in vain."

Elidad was torn with the sadness in Ghelgath. She found herself hoping Leucosia would tell him she forgave him. How could it be difficult for her to forgive him for killing Calandra? She was evil, and needed to die.

Resting the sword across her hand, Leucosia eyed the steel, considering its every detail. Turning away from where Ghelgath knelt at her feet, she closed the distance to where her sister lay dying. Leucosia knelt at her side, placing her hand across Calandra's forehead as her breath became more labored.

"I tried to save you," Leucosia told her. "All you had to do was stop. All you had to do was listen, and you would have seen your fate the way I did. You stop listening to God, sister, and everything else becomes silent." Leucosia grabbed Calandra's hand as her body began to quake.

"I forgive you," Leucosia whispered as her sister took her last breath.

Moving her hand down her sister's face, Leucosia closed Calandra's eyes. Using the sword to push herself up, Leucosia stood over her body. She raised the sword high above her head, and came down hard to sever Calandra's head. Leucosia dropped to her knees and wept over her sister. Holding her hand out, Ignacia moved forward to take it. Ignacia seamed petrified with what she witnessed. Leucosia dropped the sword to touch her sister's lifeless body. Ignacia, weeping uncontrollably, did the same.

When all three sisters touched, a light came from the midst of them. Leucosia's and Ignacia's eyes froze in their familiar way, a premonition bringing them a glimpse of the future. Their bodies began to glow with an intense light as the living sisters turned their faces toward the sky. The light grew between them, becoming a beacon shooting to the heavens.

Ghelgath appeared nervous, rising from his position. He walked around the sisters, taking care not to touch them. He appeared concerned, not sure what to do.

The premonition lasted longer than any other Elidad had seen. She knew that time in a premonition moved faster. Sirens were able to see a lot without losing much time in their trance. When the gray finally fell away from the sisters, they released each other's hands.

"Did you see it?" Leucosia asked Ignacia.

Ignacia nodded her head.

"It can be changed. It can always be changed," Leucosia assured her.

"I know," Ignacia agreed.

Leucosia stood, and with the sword in her hand, she walked away from all of them—the sad group huddled amidst the wreckage of lost life. Ignacia stood, wiping away tears, spread her wings, and disappeared into the sky.

Ghelgath looked around helpless as Leucosia walked further away. "Leucosia," he yelled after her.

She paused mid-step, but didn't turn to face him.

"I did this for you, for your love. I saved you. Do you feel nothing?" he pleaded. "She would have killed you."

Leucosia's face rose upward, refusing to turn toward him. From where Elidad stood, she could see the tears begin to roll down Leucosia's face and knew she *did* feel something.

"I am a siren, Ghelgath. It is a spell. Calandra was right. You know nothing of love."

Elidad knew she was lying.

His face contorted in an array of emotions—anger, pain, confusion. "I know enough. I know there is no life without you. If you must leave me here, then leave me to my death. Do not torture me with an eternity without you."

"Though shalt not kill . . ." she whispered. "My death would have been her sin, and now it is yours. I have seen the future, Ghelgath. The punishment for the death of my sister will be paid. When I wish for the payment of your penitence for today, I will send someone to do my bidding. Until then, you can live with the death of my sister and the loss of my friendship as your punishment."

"How will I know who they are, and if they are sent by you?"

"She will be human, and she will wield the sword. I will send her to take away your pain." She looked up, her wings spread, and just like that she was gone.

Ghelgath crumpled to his knees in her absence.

CHAPTER THIRTY-FIVE

When Elidad became aware of the burning cold in her arm again, she found herself still face to face with Ghelgath.

This time, being in his presence was much different. The fear she felt before was gone, replaced by pity and sorrow. She didn't know a demon was capable of such love. She wasn't even sure a human was capable of such love. He truly preferred death over living without Leucosia. Standing here with him, reliving his memory, Elidad knew the pain was as real today as it was then. Elidad took in her breath quickly, realizing Aiden was standing right next to her, his face nearly as white as Ghelgath's.

"Are you okay?" He raised his hand to her face like he needed to touch her to reassure himself.

"I'm fine." She wondered how long it took for her to relive his memory. By the look on Aiden's face, she assumed it'd been a while.

"She didn't send me here to kill you." Elidad directed her statement to Ghelgath.

"That is of no consequence. She would have known your destination. She gave you the sword . . . that's all she needed to do. You heard her, she would send a human."

Elidad shook her head, placing the sword back in its sheath.

Aiden grabbed her arm. "Are you sure you want to put that away?"

She smiled at him. One minute she was in a battle till the death and now she was sheathing her sword. To the others, not seeing what she saw, it would be difficult to understand.

Elidad looked into his eyes. "I know this is hard to understand, Aiden, but we will be fine. He won't hurt us. I know he won't. You have to trust me."

Aiden glanced at Ghelgath, as if doubting her words.

Elidad looked back to Ghelgath. "I understand how you could see it that way, but maybe you're wrong. It's true—she'd know that I'd end up here. But maybe she gave me the sword so you wouldn't kill *me*."

Ghelgath's eyes whirled. "Perhaps you are right. Perhaps she only wishes to prolong my torture. Perhaps she never meant for it to end."

Elidad's heart sank. "Maybe she thought the siren spell would've broken by now, and you wouldn't be in pain."

Ghelgath grabbed Elidad's arm. Aiden stepped forward to come to her aid. Ignoring him, Ghelgath placed Elidad's hand on his chest. "The spell was gone after a month had passed, and still I ache for her." His blue eyes radiated the sadness in his soul. They stood tightly connected, Ghelgath holding Elidad's hand against him, Aiden right at her side, his hand on the sword.

"Who are we talking about?" Aiden broke the awkward silence. Ghelgath released Elidad's hand and they stepped apart.

"Leucosia," Elidad answered.

Surprise crossed Aiden's brow. "He knows Leucosia?"

"It's a long story. I'll tell you later."

"If you did not come to kill me than what did you come for?" Ghelgath asked.

"A man. We've been looking for him . . ." Elidad said. "We followed him here from the east coast. We think he has something . . . something that's important to us."

"A key, perhaps?" Ghelgath suggested.

Elidad and Aiden looked at each other. "Yes, a key."

"The key is in my possession, and it will remain here."

Elidad felt affronted. "But we need to—"

Ghelgath interrupted, "Keep the key away from all its other parts and anyone that wants to use them for evil. That is what I intend to do. I will keep it here. I will keep it safe."

That part hadn't crossed Elidad's mind. What were they going to do with the keys when the found them? They couldn't keep them all together. He was right. They needed to be separate, and safe.

"What about the bishop?" she asked.

"He will stay here, as well, as per his request."

Elidad and Aiden looked at one another. "He asked you to keep him here?"

"Yes, he wanted to remain with the key. I can show you, if you would like." He extended his hand.

"Okay," Aiden said, as he stepped forward offering his arm.

Ghelgath reached forward to grab Aiden's arm. Though chiseled, Ghelgath's face gave Elidad the feeling he was amused. "He wishes to protect you," Ghelgath said, his eyes locking with Aiden's as he spoke.

Before Elidad could say anything, she saw why Aiden had been so worried when she came out of her visionary state.

The ice began to pulse through Aiden. She remembered the burning in her veins as his skin turned a dull blue. When the ice got to his chest and climbed up his throat, his breathing stopped. He was frozen like the zombies that attacked them during the battle. Ghelgath's eyes were the same, lifeless stones on the bottom of a frozen lake. His hand and Aiden's arm, frozen together where they were joined.

The moments dragged on as Aiden and Ghelgath were frozen in time. Elidad felt much better as she watched the blue in Aiden's face begin to recede, and the life start to move through him once more. Ghelgath let go of Aiden's arm, and walked away, allowing Aiden to tell his story.

"The bishop asked him to keep him and the key here, just like he said. He didn't want to leave, for fear whoever was looking for it would find him and torture him until he told them where it could be found. He said he didn't trust his own human weakness. He said he'd rather sacrifice himself, to fall under the grace of God, than to be free at the potential cost of his soul."

Elidad looked to Ghelgath. "Why did you help him? What was in it for you?"

"He was absolved," Aiden answered for him.

Elidad looked from Aiden to Ghelgath.

"He baptized me," Ghelgath said, quietly. He took a breath and turned away, as if embarrassed to face them at his most vulnerable state. "Perhaps there is a place, even for demons, where forgiveness may ring through." His voice carried softly through the cave.

Elidad understood. The bishop found Ghelgath's one weakness: love. He was smart enough to use it to his advantage to help all involved. She felt a surge of respect for the bishop, who risked his life, protected the key, and saved a damned soul. Aiden was right, he was a true warrior of Christ. Perhaps there was hope for the Church after all.

"Why did you attack us?" Aiden asked, not so quick to be won over by Ghelgath.

Ghelgath turned to address them. "For that I am truly sorry. The bishop told me evil forces would not stop in their attempts to acquire the key. For so many years, the yeti have kept to their side of the mountain, and when you formed the war party, I assumed it was to get the key." He looked to Leonidas. "Please, accept my apologies. I did not know."

"An apology doesn't bring them back. How many did we lose today?" Leonidas was not going to forgive and forget, thinking of his fallen comrades."

"They were never gone," Ghelgath answered.

Leonidas frowned.

"None of them were killed. They were only captured. I will release them to you."

The small group of yeti murmured amongst themselves, relieved their friends and family were okay.

"What about in the cave? Why did you attack us there?" Aiden's persistence was intrusive.

"Aiden," Elidad turned to him, "calm down."

"Elidad, he tried to kill you. You wouldn't be alive if it weren't for

Kade, and he wants us to believe it's all a mistake? You're being very trusting."

"He is right," Ghelgath spoke, "I should have known. I am usually able to distinguish good and evil in humans. For some reason, in the cave, I thought you came for the key and intended to do evil. That is why I attacked. I have never been wrong before. I sensed evil in the cave with you." Ghelgath was stoic, sincere. "I cannot offer you any explanation other than my sole purpose was to protect the key. And if this is what you have set out to do, as you have said, then you will understand."

"Can we see him?" Elidad interjected. "The bishop, I mean."

Ghelgath's eyes churned the way they did when his mind was working. "You may see him, but only you three." He pointed to Kade and Aiden. "The others should go back to the gates. They will find their fallen warriors waiting there."

Kade gave the group of yeti direction. One of the yeti scooped up Jed, and obediently trailed back the way they came. Leonidas stayed behind, not so easily convinced to trust Ghelgath. "I will not leave the prince. Nor the woman. I was commanded to keep them safe."

"Very well." Ghelgath turned toward the dark void that his dragon body had filled, without another thought to Leonidas's presence.

Ghelgath held up his hands clasped together, and pulled them apart. The wall at the back of the cave separated the same way. When the wall pulled apart it revealed a pathway, into which Ghelgath beckoned for them to follow.

"This is the way," Ghelgath said.

The two humans and two yeti followed him down the newly conjured passage. After a short distance they found themselves in a space that felt like a large room, with lower ceiling, and walls carved perfectly flush.

Elidad suspected this was where Ghelgath spent most of his time. Ice statues filled the room, standing shoulder to shoulder with narrow walkways between the rows. If the beings had been carved of wood, or made of iron, she would think this was a collection of art, but she knew they all were once living creatures. Aiden tugged at Elidad's furs, probably astounded at the number of statues. He didn't need to bring it to her attention. The room was overwhelming without him having to point it out.

Leonidas split from the group to walk down one of the rows, coming to a stop directly before a frozen yeti that towered over him. Ghelgath watched carefully, following him.

"This is Ardemis," Leonidas stated.

"It is," Ghelgath said, searched Leonidas's face.

Elidad recognized the name, and by the look on Aiden's face, he did too.

"He has been here this whole time?" Leonidas asked.

"He has been," Ghelgath confirmed.

"Why?" Kade asked.

Ghelgath looked up at Ardems. "He was a persuasive leader, a *great* leader. He came to the yeti when they were most in need. Their army had been crushed by humankind, and their numbers were dwindling. He gave them hope, and leadership. He was a magnificent warrior. He led the yeti for decades, but unfortunately, in his time of power the perversion of greed and vanity began to darken his soul." Still looking at the frozen form that dwarfed him, Ghelgath asked, "Do you know the meaning of his name?"

"Butcher," Leonidas answered flatly.

"And that he was," Ghelgath agreed. "He persuaded himself to believe he was untouchable, and he was. No yeti was strong enough to defeat him, though they tried. He became so ruthless, in one year, he personally killed fifty of his best warriors. He taunted the yeti, daring them to overthrow his power. It became a game of intimidation. He would urge any of his warriors to take his throne and challenged them to fight him. When they did, he would beat them to death in front of the yeti so the others would be too afraid to stand against him.

"He became mad. Obsessed. He believed he needed an army just as powerful as he was. Slowly things in the Crystal City began to change. The strong would prevail, and the weak would be beaten and killed. He only kept the females for breeding and the small ones did hard labor. Happiness left the city. His only goal was to create the perfect army. An army that would not be defeated by mankind again."

"It was a dark time for the tribe." Kade confirmed. "None could fight against him. Many tried." He shook his head, it looked as if sadness were heavy on him.

"Why?" Leonidas asked.

Ghelgath continued to stare up at the yeti. "Your kind has always been a peaceful one. I keep to myself mostly, but the stench of evil sometimes is too much for me to bear. I wanted this mountain to be peaceful, one again. He thought his reign was eternal . . . until the day he met me."

That look again. Elidad swore she saw a glimmer of a smile pass over Ghelgath's lips. It was odd how someone so statuesque could show so much emotion with no quiver of a muscle in his face.

"So, is it a bad time to point out that all of these statues were actually living beings?" Aiden's question crashed through the silence.

"Some of them were not." Ghelgath pointed to the man standing behind Aiden.

Looking at him closely, Aiden saw the man's mouth open, like a cat hissing. Two sharp fangs, dangerously long, protruded from the top of his mouth.

"A vampire?" Aiden stepped backward into Elidad.

Ghelgath started back toward his original destination. "They are all varying degrees of the world's darkest figures. I assure you, none were missed."

In the center of the round room, there was an open space with a single pedestal. On the pedestal, the perfectly preserved bishop stood, his hands clasped tightly shut, as if interlocked for prayer. Looking around, all the other statues were facing the bishop who was directly in the center.

Elidad paused. "He's frozen? When you said he stayed here, you didn't say he agreed to be frozen." She looked at Aiden.

"I thought you would assume, I'm sorry," Aiden said. "Why do you keep them like this?" Aiden directed his question at Ghelgath.

Ghelgath affectionately gazed at the bishop. "To remind myself, in a world with so much evil and hatred, there are still those who sacrifice their lives for the sake of others. The bishop holds the key," Ghelgath told them, "the others guard him. If anyone enters the room without me, they will be attacked," he explained.

"So what's that, then?" Aiden asked pointing to a miniature dragon-like lizard scurrying up the wall. "Your pet?"

Ghelgath pushed Aiden aside, advancing toward the lizard, wide-eyed. They all stood in shock as he began shooting streams of ice at it, the lizard jumping and diving to avoiding being hit. All the statues in the room turned towards the lizard as the reptile scurried up the wall to a tiny hole in the ice. The little creature hissed a declaration of triumph, tossing what looked like a key into its mouth and swallowing it. The creature dodged swords and arrows that were being thrown at it from every angle of the room just before disappearing into the ice.

Ghelgath yelled as loud and unbearable as the screech that came from his dragon form. The shock of the sound caused the ice to crumble away in an avalanche, but no creature was found amongst the rubble.

"What happened?" Aiden asked, still not understanding.

"I think that little thing just stole the key," Elidad said.

Ghelgath pointed to the bishop still frozen in the center of the room, his hands opened. He held nothing.

Ghelgath looked back at Elidad, fire in his eyes. "You did come here to take the key." His face was dangerous as he stormed to her side. His rage was threatening, but Elidad didn't have time to defend herself as Ghelgath swooped her up with a choking embrace. The burning cold she felt at Ghelgath's touch, before, was now at her throat, and instantly the present was gone.

A flash of black came. Her mind was spinning, bringing back memories of her past. Flashes of a woman and a man standing over her, smiling down on her, peacefulness in her heart . . . then sadness and darkness, the woman's face again, pain stricken and sad.

She remembered being a baby in Abraham's arms, crying. She remembered being an outcast in her childhood, and feared in her adulthood. She remembered feeling loved by Abraham, and cherished by Isaac. In her unconsciousness, she became aware she was reliving parts of her life. Her life was flashing before her eyes. This had to be her end. But she knew she wasn't alone, someone else was here with her, watching *with* her, reliving real emotions.

Leucosia's words rang in Elidad's ears as she handed her the sword, plucked from the mist "only with purity and justice in your heart," and at the sound of Leucosia's voice Elidad's heart became heavy. She started to realize, not all the feelings were hers. Ghelgath and she were sharing the experience; she felt him as much as he felt her.

With the next flash, Elidad began to relive the fear from the dark figure that lingered in the street and tried to kill her in her dreams. She saw him, again, his fingers wrapped around her throat, his dark face inches from her own, empty from detail. She felt the pain of her flesh burning off her hands when she tried to free herself from his grasp.

The feeling she buried earlier, when Ghelgath told them there was something *evil* in the cave with them, began to surface. She wondered if the Shadow Man was somehow there, with them, following them. The uncertainty of not being able to find Abraham, and the weight of obligation grew heavy in her heart. Anxiety grew like a bulge in the back of her throat. Worry she wouldn't be able to find the keys and complete Abraham's journey made her physically ill.

When her breath came back, Ghelgath's hand was still at her throat. Aiden was being held back by Ghelgath's other hand and the two yeti were held in place by ice jetting out from beneath them, freezing their feet into place.

"I had to know." Ghelgath defended his actions as he released her. "I had to know you were not here to help that demon get the key."

Elidad, knowing for sure it was Ghelgath through her memories, tried to shrug off the violation out of necessity. "I thought no one could get in here, and if they did, they'd be attacked?"

"That is true. None should be able to enter without me knowing. The only way another could make it past my magic is with amazing power. There are very few powerful enough to deceive me."

"*You* are a high demon," Elidad said accusingly. "There should be almost no one as strong as you."

"Indeed."

"Who *is* more powerful than you?" Elidad asked.

"In this age of man?" Ghelgath thought. "It is hard to say. The influences of evil are strong; there can be more than I know."

"What about when you *did* know? How many high demons do you know, and how many of them know where to find you?"

"I cannot say," Ghelgath admitted. He walked away from Elidad to looked into the bishop's eyes. "I have been too far removed from the evil ways of this world. It is easy to get left behind when you spend decades hidden in a mountain." Ghelgath's hands closed the bishop's hands, like they'd been before. "How long has your dark figure haunted you?" He turned to Elidad.

Aiden shot a look at her. "The one from your dream?" Aiden demanded. "Is that who he's talking about?"

Elidad held Ghelgath's eyes, not wanting to answer, and not wanting to look at Aiden. She knew what Ghelgath saw in her memory. He felt what she did in the street out front of Abraham's and knew how she felt since they went to New York. Someone had been following her. Elidad knew. She'd allowed herself to live in denial, until this moment. Ghelgath made him real. The Shadow Man walked out of her dreams and into reality with Ghalgath's words.

"How do you know about the dark figure from her dream?" Aiden wanted to know, this time aiming his question to Ghelgath.

"It would appear, she has not only seen him in her dreams," Ghelgath informed Aiden.

Aiden's eyes widened. "What?" He looked at Elidad. "Is that true?"

Elidad shrugged. "I can't say for sure. I didn't want to worry you."

"*I* can say for sure." Ghelgath's voice was calm.

Elidad hated that he spoke with such certainty. He wasn't helping her smooth things over with Aiden.

"He has a desire for you," Ghelgath said. "Can't you feel it?" Ghelgath looked deep into Elidad's eyes. "Of course you can. You may have ignored it, but it is unmistakable. He is certain you possess what he needs. What I would assume can only be the keys."

"When did you see him?" Aiden demanded.

Elidad was at a loss. "Um . . . outside Abraham's house."

Aiden scowled at her. "You didn't feel like it was important to warn me? You almost died in your dream. Imagine what he would do to us in person." Aiden was furious.

"He is a high demon," Ghelgath interjected before Aiden's tirade could take off. "Not just anyone has the ability to inflict pain into dreams. That is a skill that must be achieved over time."

"Do you think he has Abraham?" Elidad asked Ghelgath, hoping she was wrong.

"I think it is likely, Elidad. As I said before, he is certain you have what he wants. Why wouldn't he take Abraham? It is a way to ensure you will come to him. I have seen you, Elidad. Only death will keep you from Abraham, and *he* will surely know this."

Elidad ran her hands over her face. Ghelgath *had* seen her. He knew more about her than she would admit to herself, let alone show to anyone else. He raided her space. Perhaps he felt the same. She knew more about him than anyone else. His emotion and passion were why she chose so quickly to trust him. Feeling how someone else felt and sharing his thoughts was a connection that could not be explained.

"Why is this happening?" Elidad asked desperately. "I don't know what to do next," she blurted out. "The best man for this job is missing." She made an exasperated sound. "We came here to find the key and Abraham, and now neither one is here. How in the hell am I going to find three keys?"

"There may be a way," Ghelgath said cautiously.

Elidad looked up to search his face. "How?"

"Ignacia."

Elidad's face dropped. "We can't possibly."

Ghelgath answered, "It may be the only way, or wait for *him* to find you. I am sure if you wait, it will be inevitable."

"Who's Ignacia?" Aiden asked.

"Leucosia's sister," Elidad answered.

"The crazy one, selling her soul to the dark side?" Aiden asked.

"Yes."

"Great." He threw his hands up. "That's a great idea."

Elidad scowled at him, and looked back at Ghelgath. "Will she tell us where to find the keys?"

"Perhaps, for the right price." Ghelgath smiled, adding, "She was always the reasonable one."

"No," Aiden shouted. "No, we are looking for Abraham, remember?"

"Aiden, we don't even know where to look."

"Yes, we do. Mexico. We haven't even tried there yet. Instead of going on this insane quest, we could be there, looking."

Elidad knew he was desperate and she felt his pain. All this work, all this way, almost losing their lives, and they would leave the mountain empty-handed.

Ghelgath made his way across the room and opened a chest. It was filled with treasures. Ghelgath plucked an item from the chest and handed it to Elidad.

"Give her this," he offered, placing an emerald necklace dripping with diamonds into her hand. "She may be willing to help."

Ancient and handcrafted, the jewels alone must have been worth half a million dollars.

"Thank you, Ghelgath," Elidad told him earnestly.

Ghelgath held her hands tightly. "Give me your word, when you find the key, you will bring it back here, to rest in its rightful place." He pointed at the bishop. "He gave his life. It can't end like this." His eyes were both sad and stern.

Elidad felt sorrowful for Ghelgath. The bishop knew nothing of the recent changes. Ghelgath knew what it felt like to have the meaning of his life ripped from his hands. She knew, Ghelgath imagined what pain the recent events would cause the bishop. Ghelgath was driven to make things right. The bishop chose the right creature to protect the key. Ghelgath would be passionate to see this to the end.

"I give you my word." Elidad pulled her hands from his icy grip. "It will come back to him."

CHAPTER THIRTY-SIX

"Now what?" Aiden asked. "I feel like we're wasting time here."

They were back at the warm baths in the Crystal City, desperately in need of rest.

"We can't make it down the mountain tonight, Aiden. Ghelgath told us he would create a storm to cover the yeti tomorrow so they can take us down the hill. But for now, we need to sleep. We are no good exhausted, and it's unlikely we would be able to fly out right away. Nothing is going to happen overnight, so lie down and get some rest."

Aiden was pacing back and forth in front of her. "Rest? I couldn't sleep if I wanted to. I'm still mad at you for not telling me about the Shadow Man."

"I told you a hundred times, I thought I was imagining it, and probably still would if Ghelgath wouldn't have said anything. Now, lie down. You're driving me crazy. I need to sleep."

Obediently, he plopped down on the soft bed next to her.

They did have a lot to do; who knew when this would all end? Would it end with her finding Abraham? She feared finding him meant finding the Shadow Man. There were few things in this world she feared. He terrified her.

Ghelgath thought it best to find Ignacia. Elidad knew she was in the Los Angeles area. Many dark demons lived in the depths of larger cities. They blended in better. With time clicking away, LA was a lot closer than Leucosia in New York. They did need direction, and Ignacia was a lot more likely to tell them where to go than Leucosia was. Ignacia liked to break the rules. Selling information about the future was the reason the Church had a bounty on her. Elidad hated breaking the rules in this way, but they needed some sort of help. Abraham had been missing for over seven months. Tomorrow would be another day, and another dead end. She prayed they were headed in the right direction.

Aiden's change in breathing pulled her from her thoughts. He'd fallen asleep.

Smiling at the fact that he "wasn't tired," she lay back on the pillow, and closed her own eyes.

CHAPTER THIRTY-SEVEN

The street was quiet when Aiden and Elidad pulled around the corner. Most of the streetlights were out on their stretch of road.

"We're going to get killed," Aiden said nervously as he looked up and down the street.

"Probably, if we are seen," Elidad agreed when she put the car in park. "Try not to look so white when we get out of the car," she told him with a smirk on her face. This was not the place for them to be at two in the morning, or any time of day. Elidad thought it best to go early, hoping they wouldn't be seen or bothered.

They sat in the car, Elidad taking in everything. In the early hours, this back road was like a ghost town, the hum of the city sinking in around them. Every window on the block had bars over them. Gang signs were spray painted on the buildings, garbage cluttered the gutters, and beat up old cars were left abandoned or neglected.

Across the street, one open sign hung crooked in the window, the glass blacked out around it. Elidad had a friend in LA who worked with the Church over the years as a gatherer. His job was to spot possible problem areas in and around the city. He worked like an undercover detective for the Church. He had ties with some upper demons and heard rumors of Ignacia hopping from place to place throughout the city. She never stayed in one place long enough to be found.

"Why are we here again?" Aiden asked.

"We have to see Ignacia. We need her help. We need to know how to find Abraham, and if we are lucky, the keys." Elidad was annoyed.

"I know that. But why here? Why not the night club a week from now?"

She smiled. The informant told them of the places where they could find her. The night club where she would make appearances was a high end club for the wealthy in Hollywood. A certain step up from where they were now.

"Because, this is much safer." Elidad slapped Aiden on the shoulder.

"Sure it is . . . as long as we don't die first."

"Precisely," Elidad smiled. "Honestly, Abraham doesn't have an extra week for us to hang out so we can go somewhere nice."

Aiden sighed. "Let's get this over with."

When Elidad exited the car she was cautious not to slam her door; they didn't need to draw attention to themselves. They could hear cars passing in close proximity, base thumping hard as they moved along. Without a word between them they hurried across the street.

The storefront was indistinguishable from every other on the street. Elidad's informant told her this place was a Santeria shop. It'd been raided many times for animal cruelty and sacrifice. The locals feared it. Even the gangs stayed away. It was the only store on the block that hadn't been robbed.

Elidad grabbed the handle on the door, glancing at Aiden for a second before pushing it open. Just inside, a wind chime made of bone hung from the ceiling. The door brushed it as it passed, announcing their entry.

Every place on the shelves was covered in candles, incense, and various trinkets. There were shrunken heads and voodoo dolls. On the far wall, glass jars with chicken heads and feet floated in a mysterious solution.

"Lock de door be'ind you." A woman's voice came from a corner of the room, startling Elidad and Aiden. They hadn't noticed her there, watching them enter. "You 'eard me." She pointed to the door.

Aiden did what he was asked.

"We are here—" Elidad started.

"I know who ya are, Elidad." The woman stepped out from behind the counter. She was a big black woman, her hair wrapped in a brightly colored turban, its knots exquisitely detailed. From her neck hung an array of jewelry displaying teeth, large beads, and bird talons. "I am Adisa," she said, pulling a bunch of incense off the shelf. It was a large bundle of herbs tied together with twine. She retrieved a silver lighter from her pocket and lit the herbs. As it began to smolder she put the lighter back in her pocket and grabbed Elidad's hand, inspecting it. Sternly, she nodded her head before turning toward the back of the store.

"You traveled a great distance to see us," Adisa said, blowing on the end of the herbs causing the smoke to billow from the end.

"You know why I'm here?"

"I know many t'ings, child," she answered as her eyebrows rose, "but most important, you came to get your cards read."

Elidad felt Aiden looking at her.

"No, I didn't come here to get my cards read. I came . . ."

"You *will* have yo' cards read," Adisa said forcefully.

Elidad sighed. "You know who I am. You must know why I'm here. I really don't think . . ."

Adisa made an agitated hiss at Elidad, waving the incense in a scolding manner. "You didn't come to t'ink, girl. You came to listen. You'll have your cards read. And any dat wish to see 'er will have to reveal d'eir wishes. It be no different for anyone. I'm de gatekeeper, and if you wish to see Ignacia, dat is de only way."

Aiden couldn't figure out what they were talking about. Reading what cards? And why was Elidad so set against it? He wished she would quit being stubborn and just let Adisa read her cards so they could get on with their meeting.

"Aha. You see," Adisa said loudly, pointing at Aiden.

Aiden looked from woman to woman. "What?"

"He t'inks you should quit being so stubborn," Adisa told Elidad.

Elidad scowled at him. Aiden shrugged in response.

Elidad looked disgusted. "Really? You're taking her side?"

"I didn't say anything." He wasn't sure how he'd gotten in trouble without saying a word.

"Apparently you thought it," Elidad told him.

"No, I . . . well . . . How would she know?" he asked defensively.

"Because she's obviously a seer." Elidad made a face. She turned her attention back to Adisa. "Fine, but make it quick. We need to see Ignacia. We don't have time for games."

Adisa held back a curtain made of shells and beads, leading them to a back room. As Elidad passed Adisa, the woman grabbed her arm. "De cards are no game, child. You'll see."

Elidad pulled away from her grasp and entered the room to find a small table in the center, covered in brightly colored tablecloths and scarves. The walls were draped from top to bottom in luscious materials, rich and deep with color. Incense was already burning in the room giving it a hazy, dull feeling. On a table in the corner lay the wings of an eagle, stones white and black polished smooth, the skull of a large animal, and other assorted trinkets.

Elidad plopped down at the table in the center of the room where three chairs were placed. She knew Adisa had been waiting for them.

When Adisa picked up a stack of cards Aiden realized she was going to read Elidad's tarot card. That's why Elidad was so against it. Aiden had never seen tarot cards being read. He watched silently as Adisa shuffled.

"What 'ur question, my dear?" the old woman asked through a shady smile, at Elidad's unwillingness to participate.

"I told you, I didn't come here to get my cards read," Elidad answered stubbornly.

The woman leaned in across the table squinting at them so as not to be mistaken in her intent. "An' I tol' you, no one passes wid'out 'um bein' read. So give me 'ur question or you can be on 'ur way, now."

Elidad sighed heavily, looking at the stack of cards in the middle of the table. "Where will this journey end?" Without being asked, Elidad reached her hand out and cut the cards.

Muttering under her breath about Elidad's stubbornness, the old woman began to lay the cards across the table. By the look on Elidad's face, Aiden suspected Elidad knew something about the meaning of the cards. She looked like she was trying to act like they didn't matter, but he could sense her unease.

The first card she turned over was the fool. "Ye began a journey," the old woman said aloud, "mostly physical, but it will become a spiritual journey fo' ya. You'll find 'appiness, but it will force ya to make decisions, later on. You must be careful you are not pushing forward too fast, too rash. Rash decisions will lead ya nowhere but trouble. You to be makin' decisions, an' you should do it wid a clear mind."

Her hand moved to turn over the second card. The woman's eyebrows rose. "You been 'avin' dreams, girl." Her tone was accusing. "Ooh, dem terrible dreams." Her finger touched the card displaying the Nine of Swords. "Dis card 'tis not a friendly one, it carries wid' it a weight o' despair and disappointment."

Aiden's eyes flashed to Elidad for her response. She didn't move.

"Dreams where de darkness chokes de life from ya."

Aiden shifted at the woman's words.

Adisa touched the card. "'E keeps comin' back? Dis darkness, 'e follows you, not only in your dreams. Your worry is just, girl. 'Tis de darkness dat will keep you from your path and may keep you from your destination."

This time, Elidad moved under the weight of Aiden's stare. She could feel his anger, being reminded that she hid the truth from him. Not telling him about seeing the dark figure across the street from Abraham's home, or suspecting he's been following them all along.

This seer was not as powerful as Ignacia, but she had the gift.

Paying no attention to either of them Adisa flipped the next card. "De Three of Swords, reversed." The woman shook her head. "You are lost; your confusion blinds you. The confusion in your soul parts you from your Maker." She touched Elidad's hand, adding, "Vulnerable is a heart wid'out spiritual connection."

Elidad pulled her hand away. "There are many things in this life that I may be separated from, but my Maker is not one of them."

Adisa cackled, "We all are separated, child. Dat is de curse of dis world, 'tis not? We were cast out from his side. 'Tis a sad existence, and a lonely one at dat."

"Elidad turned the next card. That card," Elidad pointed, "represents loss and treachery in my distant past, which I have. Hasn't anyone, for that matter? Any person off the street can relate to any of these cards." Elidad was snide.

"Hmm . . ." Adisa nodded her head in agreement. "A believer who does not believe."

Elidad hit the table with both hands, making the table jump. "I believe. But not in these cards that can be manipulated. Not your words that can be twisted."

Adisa laughed. "Everyt'ing in dis world can be manipulated, child."

Elidad snorted, muttering under her breath, "Some things more than others."

Adisa flipped over the fourth card. "Queen of Swords. An' you t'ought de cards were wrong. Dis is you, 'tis not? Inner wisdom and a sense of truth. You have suffered a great loss. Your soul weeps wit' de sadness of de unjust, but you will overcome adversity, overcome de discrimination of dese men." Her hand waived toward Aiden.

Aiden immediately held up his hands. "Wait, I had nothing to do with any sadness or unjust. I didn't do anything."

Adisa stopped to look into his eyes. "You were der' when de decision came and ya did nothin'."

Aiden was affronted by her statement. The words he was about to speak fell away, leaving him speechless.

"Enough," Elidad shouted. "Enough of this game. I want to speak to Ignacia."

"No child, da door will not open till de last card is turned." She pointed down at the table. "Your cards are left . . . we will know what is to come," she said softly in a powerful way, making it clear they would remain until the end. I have to know dat you did not come to cause harm. Wid'out de right cards, ya shall not pass."

Elidad sat back into her chair that was ordained with scarves and folded her arms.

"'Tis up to da fates wedder or not you'll move forward 'ere." Adisa pointed to the Queen of Swords. "She can skillfully balance opposing factions to meet 'er own needs."

"Turn the damn card," Elidad commanded.

With a smirk, Adisa turned the fifth card. "Lovers," she said quietly. "Dis is de best dat will come o' your quest. De lovers represent a struggle between two paths, difficult decisions to be made. Not necessarily about love." She smiled her sly smile. Looking at Aiden, she said, "But in dis case, perhaps." She turned back to Elidad. "Your commitments will be tested; your decision is best made wit' intuition, not intellect."

Adisa flipped the next card, displaying the Seven of Wands.

"Very soon you shall find strength o' nerve, great fortitude and courage in de face of de 'ardships dat are yet to come. Der' is an indication 'ere," she said tapping the cards, "dat t'rough sustained effort your success may be achieved. I see your time laid out before you as a test of your courage and determination, requiring much skill from you to ensure victory over ot'ers."

Adisa flipped over the next card as though she were eager to see what it was herself.

"Ten of Wands," she said, not looking surprised. "Your conduct *is* honorable. 'Ur good fortune 'ave become a curse for ya. A burden demanding your time, taking away what little life ya 'ad for yourself."

Elidad stared blankly back, without a word. Aiden could tell she wanted the reading to be over.

Five of Cups was the next card. "Ot'ers around you will influence your journey, as dey always do. Unfortunately, deir impact on your path will not be positive. Dese outsiders will only lead you to emotional letdowns as a result of broken engagements because of worry and regret. De dishonor cannot be overcome, resulting in loss and defeat."

Elidad glanced at Aiden, almost accusingly.

Adisa flipped the next card to display the Ace of Swords. The card was reversed.

"I see the misuse of power 'ere in your journey, but the misuse is not your own," Adisa told Elidad. "None de less, der' will be confusion and violence, as I am sure ya know, Elidad. You are not a stranger to violence."

Elidad smiled. "Is that why we have to play out this whole charade?"

"I told ya, everyone dat wishes to pass must have deir cards read. 'Tis not somet'ing made up just for you. But I will know more with what de next one tells me."

She flipped over the next card displaying the Devil.

Adisa took in a swift gulp of air, sitting back from the card as if it were a cobra ready to strike.

Aiden noticed this card also was reversed.

"If I were you," Adisa whispered, "I would choose another path."

"Why?" Aiden asked, not knowing what the card meant.

Adisa stared at the card.

"Because," Elidad answered, looking at Aiden, "as you can imagine, the Devil stands for pure, true evil. The last card of her spread is the final outcome for the answer to my question. It seems that all we will find on our quest is true evil. The prior card, not being a good one, indicates death."

"Whose death?" Aiden asked.

"It's my reading, so mine."

Before Aiden could say anything, Elidad leaned across the cards. "So if it is *my* life in danger, then you know Ignacia is safe. I want to see her now."

Adisa took her eyes off the cards to look at Elidad. "She is right. It is 'er own fate dat is discolored. She may pass." The woman's voice was loud, like her words were meant to pierce through the wall.

The incense began to whirl around the room at an alarming rate making it difficult to see. The smoke filled in from their feet and became thicker and thicker as it moved around them. Elidad could feel the weight of the smoke on all sides of her, the pressure growing in her lungs. The smoke encompassed everything, making it difficult to determine which way was what.

CHAPTER THIRTY-EIGHT

The smoke began to fall away, and their surroundings became clear. Adisa was gone as were the fabric-covered walls. This room was dark and hard like a dungeon. Small fires in sconces on the wall provided the only surrounding light. Elidad could smell the lamp oil that wafted off the flame in a black smoke, replacing Adisa's incense. Aiden and Elidad remained in their seats, everything else transforming around them. In the center of the room was a birdbath, reminding Elidad of a fountain in a park. Alight from the inside, the water twisted and turned as it cascaded off the center bath into the larger pool below.

"Elidad." A woman's smoky voice came from a corner of the room. Ignacia stepped out from the shadows. Her skin was light and radiant like her sister's flawless perfection, but there was a different aura about her. Her clothing floated about her, similar to Leucosia's, but hers were dark, like rainclouds being blown in as a storm formed. Her wings were similarly radiant, yet darkly shadowed as they settled around her body. Ignacia's hair hung straight and black, long past her shoulders. As she moved across the shadows of the room, it floated lightly behind her.

Until now, Aiden had been concerned that he might be mesmerized by Ignacia, the same way he had been with Leucosia. Her beauty was staggering, but he was not affected the same way.

Ignacia made her way to Aiden and lightly touched his face. "Such a handsome one. I see you've been to see my dear sister," she said, looking into Aiden's eyes. "Such a shame."

"You had a premonition?" Aiden assumed.

Ignacia laughed. "No, she is the only one with the antidote. Without her, this conversation would be going much differently for you."

The antidote. He worried it wouldn't last and her spell would work on him. He was thankful it still worked. Leucosia told him he would need it where he was going. Did she know they would be standing before her sister, looking for help?

Ignacia rounded the room, away from Elidad, in a seemingly deliberate attempt to keep her distance. Her wings followed her like a cape as she moved about.

"You have the sword?" Ignacia asked Elidad.

Since Leucosia gave it to her, she hadn't let it leave her side. "I do."

"Is that why she sent you?" Ignacia asked. "To *give* it to me? In the way she gave it to my *other* sister?"

"If that was her purpose, I assume she could wield the sword herself," Elidad answered.

Ignacia's smile twisted. "Yes, you could assume that, couldn't you?" Her voice was eerily cool. "You have been to see Ghelgath. He gave you his memory." She smirked. "Pathetic."

"Almost as pathetic as you, choosing to do nothing when Calandra tried to kill Leucosia," Elidad said.

"*We* don't share memories with mortals," Ignacia sneered. "Of course, *you* are not a mere mortal . . . are you?" She sat on the edge of the birdbath and stroked the water, her finger barely rippling the surface. "Oh, that's right," she said, locking eyes with Aiden. "She doesn't know." Ignacia giggled mischievously.

Elidad stared at her. "What don't I know?" Elidad was annoyed. Ignacia seemed to be toying with them. Elidad hoped playing along might help get them answers.

Ignacia touched the water and mist began to rise above its surface. "You are *not* a mere mortal. You have a purpose in this world. Your fate has been decided."

"You are starting to sound like your tarot card reader." Elidad was growing weary of the mystic talk. "Did you pull that shit out of a fortune cookie? Tarot Card Reading for Dummies?"

"You are scared." Ignacia smiled across the water. "And you should be. Everyone you have known, your whole life, has kept it from you . . . and yet you knew, didn't you? You felt it in your soul. You knew you were meant for more."

"We're all meant for more," Elidad said.

Aiden could tell she was trying to belittle what Ignacia was saying, but somewhere inside, Ignacia was hitting her at the core.

"Elidad . . ." Ignacia's voice was smooth. "The one who is beloved by God . . . Such a tragedy, your story. Destined to save humanity, cursed by God's grace." Ignacia laughed. "Some say it's a blessing, but look at you. God has set you on your path, and you've lost everything. Everyone in your life feared or despised you . . . your parents killed, taken from you."

"My parents' death was an accident," Elidad said. "Accidents happen."

Ignacia laughed again. "*Was* it an accident?" Her finger brushed the water again, and the mist lingering in the air just above the surface took shape to form images. A woman screamed, her voice emanating through the air as if she were standing before them. It was the same scream she heard in her memory with Ghelgath. In the mist, her body lay on the ground. A baby's cry rang out through the hardness of the room. A man, a dark figure, walked around the woman's lifeless body, to pick up the child. As the baby was raised, her face was turned. Elidad recognized herself in the man's arms. His face was never seen—a dark figure, his hood hiding his face, like the Shadow Man—as he disappeared into the night.

Elidad gripped her chair. Ignacia waved her hand through the mist, and the scene changed. There were sounds of a struggle, fighting and items being knocked down in the dark. Again, a baby cried. Her screams were agonizing, continuing on without relief. Once again, a body fell in the dark and a silhouette of a man stood over the body. Elidad watched intently as the silhouette moved across the room to a crib and picked up the crying child she knew to be herself.

"It's okay, Elidad. Shh . . . you are well, child." Before he turned, Elidad knew who it was. Slowly, as he pivoted to leave the room, Abraham's face came clear.

Elidad stood and waved her hands through the mist. "No, you're lying."

Ignacia smiled. "It doesn't work that way, Elidad. You must know."

And she did. The images couldn't be manipulated; they reflected a true incident. The memory couldn't be changed. Ignacia's words had to ring true about her vision. She was bound by magic.

"Abraham killed my parents?" Elidad said, furiously.

"You saw with your own eyes. The memory cannot be changed. Only humans can alter their memories."

"Why?" Elidad demanded.

Ignacia shrugged. "I suppose you will have to ask him yourself. *I* can only speculate."

"Where is he?" Elidad's face was fierce.

Aiden refused to believe. How could Abraham have done this? What would Elidad do to him when she found Abraham? He was her father, but only because he took her from her parents. He couldn't imagine the deceit she was feeling. The hurt had to be overwhelming.

"That's what you came to ask. You want me to tell you where he is." Ignacia's eyebrow arched. "This was free. A gift . . . for a friend to my sister. I pity you. My sister, such a good friend . . . She never told you, herself. Someone had to tell you, you poor girl. But if you wish for the waters to turn again, I don't take credit cards." She eyed Elidad. "But I *will* take the sword." Her hand reached elegantly forward, palm open.

"Not on your life." Elidad's face was daring.

Ignacia shrugged. "Suit yourself . . . you have so little time left, you will never find him without help. My sister will not help you, as you know. You have no other choice."

Elidad took a silk pouch from her pocket and threw it at Ignacia. Ignacia caught it and opened it.

Ignacia smiled. "You drive a hard bargain," she said, eyeing the jewels. "I suppose I can find it in my heart to get over the sword."

She reached forward and touched the water. Mist shot up from the water's surface, once again.

"Abraham's father, Josiah, was an archeologist. Hearing of the Dead Sea Scrolls, he felt drawn to the project. The air of mystery surrounding the scrolls enticed him so much, he packed up his family and moved them to the West Bank.

"One evening, while alone, Josiah found a cave with a single scroll." The mist showed a man entering a cave, opening a clay pot and removing a scroll from the inside. "Before calling the others to share in his findings, he relished his time, alone. He thanked God for his findings, and the blessing of being a part of history. During his prayer, Josiah was filled with the Holy Spirit. He was able to read the scroll, and understood its importance.

"The scroll advised of a child that would come to this earth. A girl who, as a woman, would shoulder the weight of the world. Throughout her life she would find the power to save the world from itself." Ignacia paused, changing the image of the water. "Or the power to destroy it." The water portrayed a scorched earth.

"Fearing another would abuse this knowledge; Josiah stole the scroll, wishing solely to protect the information and the child.

"As the years went on, he raised his son as a holy man. Abraham's life was devoted to God from birth. His total existence was devoted to protecting the scroll and the child about which the prophecy was written."

"That's impossible," Elidad argued. "Abraham would've told me."

"It would have been your own end," Ignacia told her. "It was safer for you not to know. The weight of knowing would have given you away to those who wished to destroy you." She again touched the surface of the water. "Not long after Josiah found the scroll and translated the true meaning of it, his life became a mountain of hardships. Tragedy began to find him wherever he went. The few men that were aware of his mission soon began advising him to quit. His friends suggested perhaps he was not on the right path, and was being punished. He would only respond affectionately. Many that have been touched by God have been forced to live through hardships, but solely at the hands of the Devil." Ignacia's pictures twisted and turned showing

Abraham's father working away in a study and teaching Abraham the importance of their mission.

"He taught his son everything he knew: what was to come, what the prophecy foretold, and how he would prepare himself and the child." Ignacia's description was unsettling.

"Unfortunately for Josiah he came to an untimely death when Abraham was only twenty-four years old." Flames blazed in the mist as the silhouette of a house stood engulfed in the carnage. "His home caught fire while he was asleep. They found his remains curled in the corner of his room. Unable to escape, he was trapped there." Ignacia's image was gruesome. "That is the reason you did not know him," she informed Elidad.

Elidad shook her head. "I didn't know any of this." She looked to Aiden. "Did you?" Her eyes narrowed, fearful this conspiracy had taken over her life.

"No." Aiden could feel the anger radiate off her. "I had no idea, I swear."

"Why me?" Elidad directed her question to Ignacia. "What makes me different? What would make Abraham kill my parents?"

Ignacia smiled. "Your bloodline. That is what makes you different. Your family line is one of the oldest and purest on this earth."

"What does that matter? Are we not all sons of Adam and daughters of Eve?"

Ignacia nodded. "True, but you remain different still. Your blood is purer than most, the descendant of kings, specifically the king of Israel. In turn, that bloodline became the King of Kings." Ignacia sat motionless in the light of the pool, waiting for their response.

Aiden leaned forward to rest his elbows on his knees, rubbing his eyes with his palms. He tried to speak with his face buried in his hands. "So what you are saying is that Elidad is actually a descendant of David?"

"That is exactly what I am saying. She is the descendant of Jesus Christ."

"How is that possible?" Aiden asked.

Ignacia smiled again. "Though many of your religion have fought the idea, many have thought Jesus had siblings, half brothers and sisters. Some are named in history, two sisters remained nameless." Ignacia touched the water to stir another picture. "Her name was Elidad. The closest sibling to Jesus, she adored him, and wanted to be like her big brother, walk in the light of the Lord. Her closeness to Christ was beautiful, and when he began to make enemies of the Romans, his sisters were taken away so as not to be used against him, or wrongly convicted."

Elidad stood back up out of her chair and walked away from Ignacia. "You lie. You're a liar."

"Now, Elidad . . . we have been through this. You know I cannot. If you keep calling me names, I will assume you don't wish to be my friend anymore."

Elidad shook her head pacing the room. "There's no way."

"There is always a way." She smiled broadly, apparently amused at turning Elidad's life upside down. "Much of the information about the children were hidden and erased from history; this was not a mistake, Elidad. It was made this way to protect *you*, the child about which the prophecy was written. It is fitting that you were named after your ancestor, for she too was a strong woman. The descendant of the King of Kings.

"The scroll was the only documentation reflecting the truth. Every ancestor of yours has had the opportunity to be the chosen child, but only you were born on a day when the moon eclipsed the sun." She paused, waiting for Elidad's mind to catch up.

"What was I chosen for?" Elidad wanted to know.

Ignacia touched the water, changing the images again. "To save the world from itself, but you already knew that. My sister has sent you on this course. Abraham, that fool, tried to save you from this task, and that is the reason he is missing now."

"Why would he kill my parents? How could that save me from

having to complete . . . whatever I'm supposed to do?"

"Maybe he wanted to ensure you would fail. Perhaps he thought he could save you from it. Who can say? Only Abraham, I suspect."

"You're a seer." Elidad crossed her arms, digging her fingernails into her flesh. "You can say."

"The lines are as foggy as your fate. No matter how badly you would like to hurt me, nothing will change that. Something dark clouds your future, I can't see what lies ahead for you. You turned the card of the Devil. Death and destruction are in your path. Perhaps that's why my sister didn't warn you. She left it to the fates to decide."

"You mean God?" Elidad asserted.

Ignacia held up her hand to inspect the jewels Elidad gave her. "He is not the only influence in this world, silly girl. And many times he allows the dust to settle as it may."

"He doesn't just let the dust settle. If that's what you think, you're in a lot more trouble than I am. You didn't answer my question: where is he?"

Ignacia made a face. "I thought you would be happy. I gave you so much *free* information. It's no wonder why my sister likes you so much. You're just like her: pushy." She touched the water and revealed a large chapel. "You know this place?"

Elidad did. "Metropolitan Cathedral."

"Right." Ignacia looked at Aiden. "Someone paid attention in world studies. This is the last place Abraham went. In the library he found a map in a book." Ignacia waived her hand. The book appeared in the mist and opened to a map. Ignacia leaned forward and removed the map from the image. She tossed it at Elidad. "The map will give you directions to the desert. Abraham thought it would lead him to the location of one of the keys, but he was wrong. Evil was the only thing he found. Much stronger than any you have seen before." Ignacia's mist flashed signs and roads that led to a desolate space. "There," Ignacia pointed, "you will find the barn."

"That's it?" Elidad asked. "He's in a barn, in the desert?"

Ignacia looked Aiden over. His face was no longer in his hands, but was chalk white. "I wouldn't advise anyone to enter the barn with you, Elidad. Abraham's soul will not be saved." Ignacia touched the water, the image of the barn fell like rain drops on the surface below. "And perhaps yours won't be, either."

"We will see about that," Elidad said.

"You may want to talk her out of it." Ignacia was talking to Aiden. "It is unlikely she will return. She may not have the opportunity to save the world from its demise if she doesn't live through this. It would be a sad thing, really."

"Like you care," Elidad roughly countered.

"Even *you* have never fought a demon this strong. He cannot be saved," Ignacia said, laying the jewels over her wrist, moving them back and forth, allowing them to sparkle in the low light.

"Is that it?" Elidad's tone was sharp.

"Do you have more jewels?" Ignacia asked, smirking.

"Come on, Aiden." Elidad stormed out the same way they came in, though there was no doorway.

Aiden sprang from his chair to follow. In a few steps, they were back in the storefront.

Ignacia watched them leave. Her eyes hazed over with a premonition.

"What do you see?" A masculine voice came from the shadowy corner, his green eyes eerily gazing at the seer as her premonition fell away.

"You were right. Telling her he can't be saved will ensure she makes it there. She will go to his aid, even though she's angry. She refuses to ask God for direction."

The little creature that scurried out of the ice cave in possession of the key emerged from the shadows. He climbed up Ignacia's wing and perched on her shoulder.

"You didn't get the sword," the voice said, remaining shapeless.

"What was I supposed to do?" Ignacia turned to face the Shadow

Man. "Take it from her? She would've killed me." Her left brow arched, accusingly. "Why didn't *you* take it from her?"

"Now wasn't the time for us to meet. I'm still trying to understand her, and the prophecy. Telling her that Abraham killed her parents will help. The angrier she is, the further from her Creator she will become, and the more vulnerable she will be."

"What will come of her?" Ignacia asked as her pet nestled against her hand. She adoringly stroked his scaly flesh.

"She will face her mortal father, and be forced to exorcise his demons. With her heart in such a dark place, she won't live through the exorcism."

CHAPTER THIRTY-NINE

"Elidad, he can't be saved," Aiden said solemnly, lightly touching her shoulder.

"You don't know that," she shouted, shoving his hand away. "Not everything the seer says is true. She's influenced by humans and her surroundings. Only God knows for sure what the end is like. Human minds change so rapidly with evil influences, the future's ever-changing. We can change our future. That's one of the things that makes us human. God granted us the gift of choice, the ability to decide. And I am *choosing* to save him."

She could feel Aiden's eyes in the rearview mirror before he leaned forward to say, softly, "You could lose your life."

"It doesn't matter, Aiden. Why can't you understand that? If it's the time God has set for me, then so be it. I'll give Abraham peace, no matter what."

She pounded the steering wheel as if it would make the car go faster.

Aiden was fortunate to be here. They had stopped to take a break from driving. Aiden lay in the back seat to take a nap, and when he woke up she was driving through the desert. He hadn't decided if she knew he was back there or if she'd intended to leave him and go the last leg of their journey alone.

Aiden smiled to himself. "I suppose that's why you're the best at these things." He shook his head, as if understanding for the first time. "No matter what you're facing, you always keep the faith. Some people preach this kind of devotion, but in the end, you live it, with all of your soul. I can only hope that in my lifetime I can embrace even a small portion of your kind of faith."

He looked up to meet Elidad's eyes in the mirror.

"What?" he asked, puzzled by her look.

"Don't think I'm going to make it out alive, huh?"

Before he could answer, Elidad slammed on the breaks, locking all four wheels, skidding to a stop before a decrepit building.

She clicked off the engine. Silence.

Aiden looked out the window. There was nothing on the horizon. No sign of life, other than fragments of debris, scattered by the wind. Plastic hung in the sage brush, waving like a flag. Aiden was surprised by the garbage dumped on every roadside.

No wonder why Abraham didn't like Mexico. Perhaps somehow he knew he would be held prisoner here. Maybe his body felt it, years before.

Aiden's eyes came back to Elidad as she picked up her Bible resting in the seat next to her. She held it in both hands and gently closed her eyes.

Aiden tried again, reaching forward for her arm. "Really, Elidad, you don't have to do this. Everyone that came before you failed and they may never be seen again."

To Aiden's surprise she didn't brush his hand away. She opened the Bible and removed a picture of Abraham and herself sitting on the front steps of their home.

"You let Ignacia rattle your faith. You can't trust everything she said."

"You told me she can't lie."

"True, but she can skew the truth, or misread signs. Just because she sees death in my future, doesn't mean it's mine. I could walk into that barn and find a dead cat. She said herself, the future was hazy. That's why you just have to make a choice and go with God." Elidad sighed. "Besides, Abraham would have done the same for me," she added, running her fingers over the picture affectionately. "I was only a baby when I came to him. He taught me everything I know. I need to help him."

"Even if he was the one who killed your family?" Aiden was hesitant to ask, but felt it was a necessity.

Elidad sighed heavily. "I wasn't put on this earth to judge. I was put here to do God's work. Abraham's fate is between him and God. We can all be forgiven."

She put the Bible in her pocket, left the picture resting on the front seat and got out of the car.

Opening the trunk, Elidad looked at the arsenal lying before her. Before they arrived in Mexico City, she placed a call to a friend, a gatherer, who ensured the car would be waiting for them. It was a local car, inconspicuous.

The trunk reminded her of Isaac's shop, filled with vials and potions, books, bones, canisters of mysterious contents, and bundles of incense. Among the packages there were various weapons, including guns, crossbows, and knives. If they'd been stopped and searched, they would undoubtedly spend the rest of their lives in a Mexican jail. Aiden stood silently by her side. She assumed he was thinking the same thing.

She reached forward, picking up the Sword of Justice. The hilt of a sword. She put the sheath on her belt and pulled the hilt from it. The sword hummed as she withdrew it, revealing the blade. Before this, it hadn't appeared without an impending attack.

"This is the first time I've been able to look at it," Aiden said.

"Me too," she agreed. "There's an inscription on it, and I don't know what it says," Elidad said, looking at the steel to read the words. "Destruction cometh; and they shall seek peace, and there shall be none."

They were both silent.

"It doesn't sound like a sword of justice." Aiden broke their silent thoughts. "It seems more like a sword of eradication."

"Sometimes justice needs to be firm. You'll notice the sword only appears when it's needed." She placed it back in its sheath. "After Ghelgath showed me his memory, I couldn't figure out why the blade didn't slash through his hand and Leucosia's throat at the same time. It didn't have any issues dismembering body parts during our battle against Ghelgath's army. It slashed through an ax like it was nothing . . . It's almost like the sword has a mind of its *own*. Like it can decide what's just and what's not."

"I don't know," Aiden said. "I suppose I can believe just about anything these days."

Elidad slapped him on the shoulder. "Well, there might be hope for you, after all."

"Elidad, did you notice how similar the Sword of Justice looks to the sword in your tattoo?"

Elidad's brows creased together. She hadn't.

"Oh, blessed be. I knew you would come."

The man who spoke seemed to materialize out of nowhere. Elidad and Aiden both jumped at his appearance, simultaneously taking a cautious step away.

"No one else could free him. I knew you would come." His voice wavered with emotion, wild hair blowing in the wind. His eyes shifted from Elidad to Aiden, then checked their surroundings.

Cuts and bruises covered his face and arms, his robes encrusted with dried blood and dirt. The pores on his nose were enlarged, caked with dirt. Elidad wondered if he'd been sleeping on the ground. When he moved, flies would buzz around, landing back on his soiled clothing when his movement slowed. Though torn, she could tell the robe he wore was a cassock. He was the priest that went missing with Abraham: Remiel. The same priest that sent the letter to the Church.

"Remiel?" Aiden's voice was accusatory. "What are you doing here?"

"I couldn't leave them," Remiel wailed. "Not while they're here, I couldn't leave them."

"Remiel." Aiden grabbed him forcefully, as if to stabilize the emotional man. "*Who* couldn't you leave?"

Remiel blinked. "The other priests, of course." Remiel directed his attention to Elidad. "They all fell . . . They tried to uphold the word of God." Tears were now cutting through the dirt on his face. "You're the only one that can save them . . . He told me *you* would be the only one."

"Who told you?" Elidad kept her distance from Remiel.

"Abraham. Abraham said you were the only one who could save him. He said you were the only one that could expel the demon inside him."

"Where is he?" Elidad shifted her weight, adjusting the positon of the sword.

Remiel pointed to the building, sobbing. "There . . . he's there, in that . . . that gateway to hell," he whispered, as if afraid someone would hear.

Elidad turned, picking a few vials out of the trunk and closing it. Turning toward the barn, she swiftly walked toward it.

"Elidad, you don't have to do this. No one will think any less of you." Aiden rushed to her, pulling her arm back, forcing her to stop. "You can't do this. Three other priests have tried, and only God knows what's become of them."

"Aiden." Elidad's voice was calm as she defiantly swallowed her fear. "I do have to do this. If I don't, their souls will be lost. Abraham will be tormented until Christ comes again. Their bodies are like prisons, and not like a prison where you get three meals a day and cable. A real prison of torment and torture. Their pain will be unimaginable. None of these men deserves this."

Aiden's eyes pleading, he held her arm as if letting go would seal her fate.

"You have to promise me, Aiden, if you don't see smoke by night-fall, you'll burn the barn to the ground."

"But . . ." Aiden's voice was weak.

"You have to do it, Aiden." She looked from the barn back to him. "There will be no saving us if I'm not out by then. You *can't* go in there. Don't come in after me—just burn it."

Aiden nodded in agreement, but wasn't sure he would be able to follow her orders if it came down to it.

Remiel rushed to their side, his hands on Elidad's feet, his face close to the ground. "Be strong and of good courage, fear not, nor be afraid. For the Lord thy God, he is that doth go with thee; he will not fail thee, nor forsake thee." Remiel rocked back and forth and began to recite the passage again. "Be strong and of good courage, fear not, nor be afraid . . ."

His prayer was consistent as Elidad pulled her arm from Aiden's grip and walked away from the two men. She could still feel the pressure of his fingers around her arm as she headed for the building.

Aiden caught up to her, again. "Elidad, you really don't have to . . ." His words fell away, like he knew how useless they were.

She turned to look in his eyes, amusement pulling at the corner of her mouth. "Careful Aiden, someone might think you were worried about me."

"I am."

A tightening in her chest slowed her breath, in response to his sincerity. "Promise you won't try to come after me. Just burn the building down."

"I don't know if I can." desperation danced in his eyes. His hand clasped around the back of her neck. "You'll just have to make it back, so I don't have to."

She smiled up at him. "I wish it were that simple."

"Me, too," he said softly.

"Just don't go in there, Aiden, I mean it. Your fear will kill you in there."

"What about you?"

"If it's my time, then it's my time. I'm not afraid of what's in there," she responded.

"I know, that's what scares me."

"God will deliver me from evil, in life or death, whatever may come to pass. In His plan, everything has a purpose."

Aiden looked in her eyes, touching her face. She placed her hand over his. He pulled her to him, pressing his forehead against hers.

Fighting the sting, threatening to develop into tears, Elidad closed her eyes. She could feel his breath against her lips. His aroma had become familiar in the past few weeks.

Breathing him in, she remembered how the heat of his body saved her life in the ice cave. She remembered how her fingertips felt their way across his skin in the Crystal City. Sleeping in his arms, he made her feel safe. In the cave, it was easy to forget he was a priest who'd devoted his life to God. She wished they were back there now.

CHAPTER FORTY

Only silence surrounded her when she crossed the threshold and paused to look about the vast space. It was an ordinary barn. Though there weren't any animals, she could smell horses and leather as she walked. Dry hay crunched under her feet as she made her way toward the back where the light grew faint.

A pungent smell carried on a small gust of wind sweeping across the barn. Elidad winced as the fragrance came to her. Instinct forced her hand to her face to cover her mouth and nose. She was familiar with the smell of rotting flesh, but this made her stomach churn. She pushed forward over the tufts of hay. With each step, the smell became more formidable, with the sound of hundreds of flies growing louder as she walked.

On the back wall of the barn a single door creaked back and forth in a draft that pushed redolent air toward her. Her heart throbbed in her ears as she attempted to peer through the slight opening. Her eyes couldn't focus through the shadows on the other side.

When she pushed the small door forward, the rotting smell came rushing to her with the full force of a geyser. Elidad gave herself a moment for her eyes to adjust before continuing.

No windows were in this room. Light found its way through the wallboards, not perfectly placed against each other, the outside light giving the walls an eerie glow. She could see hay particles dancing through spotlights, beams of sun, coming through the walls.

"Please Lord, be with me. Give me strength in my time of need," she whispered as she pushed past the door.

Perhaps Remiel was right, she thought. *Maybe this is the gateway to hell.*

The three priests that'd been missing were now found. All three were hanging from the rafters, a large noose around each of their necks. Elidad followed the ropes with her eyes from each body all the way up to the rafters. They hung in a triangle, precisely spaced from one another. One to the north, the others east and west.

Flies swarmed around them, gathering about their eyes, flying in and out of their noses and mouths. Maggots crawled over their bodies, occasionally falling to the floor below. They fell on a triangle drawn in the dirt, under the priests. Each priest hung directly over a tip of the triangle. She knelt to inspect the drawing. Its linear perfection was astounding. The lines appeared to have been stamped rather than drawn. The edges were sharp and straight; no human would've been able to draw it.

It was so perfect, and the design so detailed, it had to mean something. Her mind spun with all the images she'd seen over the years in the shadow books, and in the Church. She couldn't place it. Elidad tried to trace each line with her mind. She pulled her phone out of her pocket and took pictures of it. She sent the image to Aiden with the words "we need to find the meaning of this." She watched the icon spin, trying to send her text. She wasn't sure it would go through.

A movement in the center of the triangle caught her attention. Elidad got to her feet, readying herself. There was something lying on the floor under the three priests. From where she stood, it looked like a pile of linens. Her eyes couldn't find a shape within the pile. Elidad cautiously made her way around the room to get a better look. When she came around the pile, she could see a single hand outstretched from under a blanket. It was frail and malnourished, like a skeleton with skin stretched over the bone.

The only priest still missing was Abraham. All the others were hanging above her. Her breath began hammering in and out of her lungs as hope leapt from her chest. Without thinking, she stepped forward to see if it was him. As her feet crossed the line pressed into the earth, the room came alive. She had stirred the evil that'd been lying dormant. The wind screamed, blaring through every crack in the barn walls, seeking retribution for her intrusion. Dust clouded Elidad's vision, her heart became a lump in the back of her throat.

It had begun.

CHAPTER FORTY-ONE

The corpses at the east and west were closest to her. Their heads spun to face her, their mouths agape. Their faces contorted, changing from bodies resembling the men she'd once known to gruesome beings producing sounds that made her body shudder. Their high-pitched screams moved her skin. The hairs on her body stood, driven by their screeching. The sound hurting down, deep, in her bones. Elidad covered her ears, the howls bringing her to her knees. If she had something long and sharp, she would have dug out her eardrums to make it stop.

"He *only* is my rock and my salvation: He is my defense; I shall not be moved," she shouted. The screams were so consuming; she was uncertain if she had spoken at all.

The eyes of the priests opened; death had taken the life out of them. She watched as black veins began to move across their dull blue lenses, developing into black pupils. When they fully developed, awareness came to them. They began to flail and grab in her direction as Elidad pressed her fingers hard against her ears.

Something across the room caught the wind and flew towards her. Elidad held out her hand just in time to shield her head. She winced as metal sliced the palm of her hand, blood rushing from the wound. When she quickly replaced her finger over her ear, she could feel the blood dripping down her face.

"He only is my rock and my salvation: He is my defense; I shall not be moved!" She reached into her coat and pulled out her Bible, throwing it on the ground. Blood from her hand splashed down onto the open pages. She reached to the sky for strength.

"And now shall mine head be lifted up above mine enemies round about me: therefore I offer in his tabernacle the sacrifices of joy; I will sing, yea, I will sing praises unto the Lord!" The howling screams that filled Elidad's ears softened enough for her to hear her voice. "He is my loving God and my fortress, my stronghold and my deliverer, my shield, in whom I take refuge, who subdues peoples under me."

The screams of the two corpses changed to cries of agony; she knew the passages were taking a toll on them.

Elidad reached into a pocket and removed one of the vials she took from the car. Uncapping the vial, she threw holy water onto the screaming corpses. Smoke lifted from the skin where the water had landed. Their eyes rolled back into their heads. The corpse closest to her hissed with anger. Elidad threw the remaining holy water on his face. The demon inside howled with laughter. Flesh melted off the skeleton as if it were acid she'd thrown on it.

"In the name of the Father, Lord thy God, I command you demons to reveal yourselves to me!"

She felt his growling throughout her body. The atrocious sound resonating inside her. She wished she could turn and run, but knew she must stay.

"You came to save their souls, Elidad, but you cannot even save your own," he spat, the flesh falling in clumps to the floor. When his skin hit the ground, it melted into the crevices of the image on the ground, absorbed by the dirt.

"I command you: In the name of God, reveal yourself to me," Elidad shouted.

He screamed. His hand reached out for her and she jumped to the side.

"Tell me your name!" Elidad screamed her question to the other demon. He wasn't as strong as the second.

"We are banshee," he screeched.

The other corpse made a horrifying noise, his voice stirring the wind in the barn.

"In the name of the Lord thy God, I cast thee out, devil, demon of

Satan." Elidad's thighs tensed to stand strong against the wind. "And now shall mine head be lifted up above mine enemies!"

The banshee shrilled in unison. She could see the demons clawing at the bodies, desperately trying to hold on. Something from inside pushed them out. The broken-down bodies began to radiate a blue light. The demons' wails weren't aggressive anymore, they were fearful. Elidad watched the blue glowing light, trapped souls inside, trying to escape.

The weaker demon shot from the first body, flew around the room, a blue light chasing him. She yelled as they passed, "To hell with you, demon!" The demon flew straight into the center of the triangle. His impact shook the ground, but left the dirt unmoved. The blue light only followed him to the ground then cut back to the other body. The second demon screeched as he released the priest, both blue lights now chasing him. He flew into the ground the same way the first had. The ground shook forcefully enough to make Elidad stumble.

The blue lights lifted into the sky, disappearing through the cracks in the ceiling. Elidad had seen the souls of people she'd saved escape many times before, but this was a true triumph. She prayed she would be able to save the others.

Strangely, the wind didn't let up. The boards of the barn were moaning under the strain of the wind. Random pieces torn off the walls, flying past her, hitting her unexpectedly.

The last demon of the triangle opened his eyes and hissed as she came close. This body had been here longer. It was decayed more than the others. A body of a small man, it must have been DelFlur. She didn't care for him much, but it was sad to see him this way. An exorcist, whether she liked him or not, didn't deserve to be trapped by the things he spent his life fighting.

Elidad pulled another vial out of her pocket, throwing holy water on him. His arms shot out from his sides. She jumped back but the demon managed to catch a lock of her hair. Elidad threw herself away from his grip. She could feel the sting on her scalp as she fell against the ground, her hair still in the demon's hand. Her head throbbed with pain.

"Reveal yourself to me," Elidad shouted.

"No," the demon hissed through the priest's mouth, his face now a twisted smile. "You come with a heavy heart, Elidad. Your own mind will destroy you here." The voice was enchanting. "Did you come to find the missing? Or did you come to know what Leucosia refuses tell you?"

Elidad watched him carefully as she pushed herself off the ground.

"The future is yours, and all you wish to know, Elidad" he continued. "If you only ask, you shall be told."

To what was he referring? What could she know? Her mind began to spin. Did he know the answer to what really happened to her parents? Was Abraham the one that brought an early end to their lives, and if so, why? She *did* want to know.

"Yes, Elidad," he purred, "ask a question, and I will give you the answers you seek." His voice was strong and reassuring. "Give up this fight and the power of knowing shall be yours. He who has the power of knowing is greater than God, himself."

His words echoed in Elidad's mind, the longing for answers swimming in her head. She wanted to know. She longed to know. Why had Abraham hidden it all from her? As she held the demon's eyes, she knew he would tell her the truth. He had the answers, all she had to do was ask. Elidad sank to her knees before the demon, his smile widening as she came to kneel before him.

"The power can be yours, Elidad; give yourself to it."

She needed to know. She wanted it all to stop: the pain, fear, the deceit.

The demon, pleased with himself, began to purr again. "Yes, bow before me and all the power of knowing shall be yours."

Elidad's head hung with the weight of his voice.

"Good . . ." He was alluring. "Give yourself over."

Elidad leaned forward, her hands touching the ground, bowing her head. The demon's cackle rattled in his throat.

"Lord, who art light and wisdom, Thou knowest all our thoughts and deeds. Lead us by the right path of the fulfillment of life, and keep us away from all sin and evil," Elidad said.

The demon screamed, wriggling like a cat held over water. Kicking, he grabbed at her. She popped to her feet, creating distance between them.

"In the name of the Father, the Son, and the Holy Ghost, I command you, identify yourself!"

A shrill cry came from the hanging priest, his flesh rippling like water. His grey flesh split across his chest and his shoulder. The demon possessing his body began taking shape, using the priest's skin for his own. A small skull came out of the corpse's chest, pulling forward on a long neck. The ghoulish gargoyle had wicked bat wings, human skin pulled taut across jagged bone. He left the body hanging, totally exposed. Stretching his wings for the first time, they were wider than Elidad's arm span.

Rows of fanged teeth reminded Elidad of a shark's mouth, ready to devour its prey, unstoppable in its power. He sat back on his haunches, like a wild cat ready to strike, his front talons in the lower abdomen of the priest. His wings began to pump up and down with a rhythmic beat of his impending attack.

"Tell me your name. In the name of God, I command you!"

"I am Vetala."

"Come to me, all you who are weary and burdened, and I will give you rest," Elidad yelled. A glimmer of a blue light glowed from inside the corpse. The demon cried as he released the body and took flight with means to kill her.

Elidad held her footing, strong with faith. "In the name of God I condemn you to hell."

Angry screeches filled the barn as he swept the room, dive-bombing her head, his talons aiming for her neck and face.

"Fear of others will prove to be a snare, but whoever trusts in the Lord is kept safe. Vetala, I send you to hell," Elidad yelled. He turned in the air to attack again. He launched himself across the room with impressive speed, his body aimed to kill. Elidad made no attempt to shield herself, but whispered, "The Lord will rescue me from every evil attack and will bring me safely to his heavenly kingdom."

With the demon's talons at her face, Elidad closed her eyes. When his gruesome flesh came in contact with hers, his skin turned to dust, blowing past her on the wind.

The air fell still around her.

Elidad opened her eyes. Vetala demons were difficult to destroy; fear and doubt was what they thrived on. Where had it come from? No one had fought one for hundreds of years. What was this place? Why were all these demons gathered in one spot? Why would they be here, way out in the desert?

Elidad made her way back around the triangle to see who was lying on the floor.

She saw his face. The man she had known her whole life as father. Abraham lay still on the ground beneath the hanging bodies. How could he still be alive? What she could see of him was frail. Elidad fell to her knees at his side and cupped her hands around his face.

His eyes slowly opened.

"I thought I had lost you forever," Elidad whispered.

His lips attempted a smile. "Elidad, my dear, you must keep the faith. You should know, he would not leave me here. None are lost forever. Forever ends some time, child. There is an end to this earth, and our Savior will call everyone to Him when the time is right." He struggled to speak so many words. His hand went to his chest, driven by an invisible pain.

"What is it, Abraham?" Elidad pulled back the tattered robes covering his body. His collarbones protruded from his skin. It looked like he'd been here for the seven months he was missing; and someone had fed him just enough to keep him alive. He was so fragile.

She wasn't sure how to get him out of here. Moving him would be enough to kill him.

Under his skin, she could see movement like a snake rolling under his flesh. She stared at it. The animation under his skin, portraying hands, arms, and faces pushing from within, imprinting through his epidermis.

Tears began to fall from Elidad's eyes; he, too, was possessed.

"I couldn't leave you here until then. I needed to find you," she finally said.

His hand went to her knee. "My fear is for *you*, Elidad. I do not worry for myself. My only regret is, I was unable to save you from loss and heartache."

Elidad reached down for his hand, it was cold. She was afraid to squeeze too tightly for fear it would shatter.

"You were always the best student," he said. "Without fear. Your faith is pure. Don't let them change that in you, Elidad. Nothing in this life is as it seems. You will need your faith to carry you through what is to come."

"What is to come? Why haven't told me, or told me about my parents?" Her voice cracked at the word.

His eyes opened again. "All things come in due time. You weren't ready. I wasn't ready. Leucosia will show you the way." Weakly, his eyes closed again, lightly squeezing her hand. "The Lord thy God is the one who goes with you to fight for you against your enemies to give you victory. Trust in him, child, and you will find your strength." He struggled for breath. "I am tired. I will not last on this earth much longer."

"We have to get you out of here," Elidad said.

"You know I can't. I am prepared. The last time I saw Remiel, I asked him to read my Last Rights, and take my confession. I am ready to rest."

Tears streamed down Elidad's face. "But I'm not ready," she whispered, trying not to let him hear her cry.

"For as in Adam all die, even so in Christ all shall be made alive." His voice was barely audible.

Elidad smiled, still holding his hand. With her other hand she touched his face. "Through the holy mysteries of our redemption, may all mighty God release you from all punishments in this life, and in the life to come. May he open to you the gates of paradise and welcome you to everlasting joy, amen. I love you," she whispered. As his last breath slowly moved across his lips, his hand released hers.

CHAPTER FORTY-TWO

Heartbroken, Elidad placed her hand on Abraham's forehead, gently opening his mouth. Opening a vial of holy water, she poured it into his mouth, closing it again. The next vial she opened contained olive oil. She used the oil to make the symbol of a cross on his forehead. At this, Abraham's skin began to move violently, images of body parts from within began to emerge frequently. Unraveling a white cloth that bore a red cross, she placed it over his eyes, and tied it around his head like a blindfold.

"To blind you from the evils of the world," she whispered, kissing the blindfold. She turned his hands to the sky, pouring holy water in each palm. Pulling a dirty blanket off him, she poured holy water on his feet.

Elidad sat back, pulling another vial, dark and small, from her pocket. She pulled the top from it. "He said, This is the blood of the covenant, which is poured out for many for the forgiveness of sins." Her voice wavered as she recited the words. Tipping the vial, red wine splashed down on Abraham's stomach. It turned to blood when it came in contact with his body.

The old man's face began to change. The evil she knew was there began to reveal itself. To someone else, it might appear that Abraham was coming back to life, his breath being pushed back into him, now hard and raspy. Elidad knew the man she loved was gone and the life he had known would never return. The only hope she had left was to release his soul, that it might be free from the grips of evil.

Elidad had never seen this type of possession before, nor had she heard any description of it. Whatever it was, it was strong. Abraham's body began to seize and shake. Blood poured from his ears and from behind the blindfold she'd placed over his eyes. His chest rose and fell unnaturally. Elidad was sickened by the movement under his skin. The writhing arms and feet was more aggressive than before, clawing Abraham's body from the inside, their teeth and nails piercing his skin. The sound that came from this creature was more horrifying than the one the banshee had produced.

Abraham's mouth opened to release a deep laugh, though his lips did not move. "He cannot be saved, Elidad. He belongs to *us* now," the voices said.

Abraham's body, now controlled by the demon, moved effortlessly. Without notice, he clasped her throat with the same bony hand she not so shortly before considered frail. He scooped her up in a choking embrace before she knew what happened.

Elidad clawed at the tight fingers cutting into her skin, his evil face close to hers. She could see the demons inside him swimming like fish in a dark ocean. There were thousands of them, laughing as they lifted her up. As he rose to his feet, she felt the ground fall away from hers. The harder she fought, the less air she was able to take in. Perhaps this was her dream—a foretelling of a dark figure winning her over. No matter how hard she kicked, she was unable to free herself from his grasp.

Her surroundings began to grow dark. The shrill screams pulsing in her head began to subside. Relinquishing power, she tilted her head back to catch a glimpse of sky through a hole in the roof. Her eyes began to close as she choked out her words. "Though I walk in the midst of trouble, you preserve my life; you stretch out your hand against the anger of my foes, with your right hand you save me." Her voice was indistinguishable.

A light grew all around the room coming from nowhere, yet everywhere. The light illuminated every crack and hole in the barn. It was so intense, even with her eyes shut, Elidad felt like she was looking into the sun. She sensed a great relief washing over her, and for that one divine moment she had a chance to forget where she was. As suddenly as it began, it was over. Her body gasped for air as she found herself on her feet. The demon stood across the room.

He began to laugh. "Where is your god?" he taunted. "He has *already* left you? He may have saved you but he has only prolonged your death. He is not *with* you; he left you here to die. He could have destroyed me, yet he didn't. He doesn't care for you."

When he spoke, there was no sign of the man she loved. Abraham was gone and in his place was this evil being, whose voice sounded like a chorus of a hundred people.

"You will die here alone, without your god, Elidad." Still blindfolded, it was eerie when he looked at her.

"Though an army besiege me, my heart will not fear; though war break out against me, even then will I be confident," Elidad said.

He hissed. His mouth opened like a giant snake, opening large enough to devour her. Fangs dripping, he began screaming again.

The demon bolted toward her. She tried to push him away but hands and claws came out of Abraham's body almost encompassing her, attacking from all sides. They scratched and bit as she pushed hard against the demon. Reaching into her pocket she opened her last vial of holy water and splashed it across the morphed body.

His flesh bubbled and peeled back where the holy water landed. He let go of her. "Your efforts are insignificant. You cannot kill us. We are Legion."

She backed away, stumbling over. "Legion . . ." she repeated, her eyes fixed on the creature. "That's impossible."

"If thou therefore wilt worship me, all shall be thine," he hissed.

Elidad's eyes grew wide. "Get thee behind me Satan: for it is written, Thou shalt worship the Lord thy God, and Him only shalt thou serve!"

The Legion shrieked. Elidad pulled the sword from her hip. The blade sang as she held it horizontally in the air.

Legion laughed. "Stupid girl, no mortal weapon can cause us harm. We are Legion!" His voices trailed behind him as he advanced.

Elidad's eyes caught the inscription on the blade. "Destruction cometh; and they shall seek peace, and there shall be none." Elidad swung the sword with all the power and faith in her body. Her motion stopped the demon's advancement, leaving Elidad frozen in her stance at the end of her gruesome sweep. Abraham's head fell to the floor.

Abraham's body stood still beside her, terrible shrills coming from within. The demons rose from his body in a tornado of screeching. She watched the demons clinging to the body and each other. As the last of the demons left his corpse, the decapitated body came alight with a blue glowing light. The blue light rose up, dancing around her, and disappeared into the sky. Abraham's empty body slumped to the ground.

Elidad fell to her knees, sobbing, the sword across her lap. Covering her face with her hands, her body shook with the severity of the emotions that escaped her. With Abraham gone, she was alone.

With the sleeve of her coat, she wiped blood from the blade of the sword. "The Lord will rescue me from every evil attack and will bring me safely to his heavenly kingdom. To him be the glory forever and ever. Amen."

She pushed herself to her feet, made a sign of a cross in the air and turned to walk through the doorway. She couldn't find it in herself to look back at Abraham.

In the darkest corner of the room, a pair of green eyes watched her leave. Through the exorcisms they'd gone unnoticed, still and silent amongst the chaos. When the small door swung shut behind Elidad, the dark figure stepped back into the wall and disappeared without a sound.

Elidad paused in front of the door and put the sword back in its sheath. Reaching into her pocket, she pulled out a silver lighter. Pushing back the top, she struck the flint. The way the golden flame danced in the breeze was hypnotic. Numb, she watched its movement. "I have fought a good fight. I have finished my course. I have kept the faith." With her words, she dropped the lighter.

The lighter fell, cushioned by the hay when it landed. The dry straw burned like it'd been doused with gasoline. She watched as the flames danced like the single flame of the lighter. Spreading in every direction, they flowed with the breeze. Elidad stepped over the flames as they grew quickly around the barn. When she reached the other side of the open space, she could hear the roar behind her, growing steadily louder.

Pushing the door open, she stepped out into the open air, greeted by the sunset on the horizon. Black smoke rose up behind her, flames rolling out the windows. She walked towards the two priests waiting for her at the car.

Aiden ran to her, his steps slowing when he saw her face. "Are you okay?" Aiden asked, throwing his arms around her.

"I'm fine, thanks. You should see the other guys."

"I hope they look worse than you do." Aiden's voice was light.

Remiel's blue eyes were red, his face streaked more than when she'd left. He might have been crying the whole time she was in there. He rubbed his hands together, looking from the barn, now fully engulfed in flames, to her, and back to the barn.

"What of Abraham?" Remiel looked as if he expected Abraham to walk out of the barn behind her.

Aiden pulled away from Elidad to hear her response.

Elidad looked at the ground, pressing her lips firmly together, her eyes overflowing with heartbreak. She didn't bother to wipe away her tears.

"He said you would save him," Remiel demanded.

"I did," Elidad said.

"How? He's not here."

"His tormentors are gone; he can be at peace. His body was too far gone. He couldn't leave."

"Tormentors?" Remiel frowned. "Were there many?"

Looking back at the burning barn allowed her to avoid their eyes. "He was possessed by a Legion."

"Impossible," Remiel said.

Elidad looked at him. "That's what *I* said."

"There hasn't been a Legion demon since Christ," Remiel protested. For the first time since their encounter, Remiel seemed coherent.

"You're right. And to make matters worse, they quoted the Devil," Elidad said.

"What did they say?" Aiden asked.

Elidad wiped tears out of her eyes. "If thou therefore wilt worship me, all shall be thine."

The two men stared at her.

"Elidad . . ." Aiden's voice was soft. "That's what the Devil told Jesus on the mountain, the night before he was crucified. The Devil offered Jesus the world in trade for his soul."

Elidad slapped him on the shoulder with her good hand. "Oh good, Priest, you *do* read the Bible." Elidad winced at the pain charging through her body, a hint of a sarcastic smile creeping across her face. She put her arm around Aiden. "Now help me get to the car."

DOMINION
SWORD OF JUSTICE BOOK 2

CHAPTER ONE

Aiden woke to a knock on his door. Rolling to his side, he grabbed his phone from the night stand. One thirty-five.

"Father Aiden?" Father Joseph's voice was muffled.

"Yes?"

"I need your help, Father." Joseph's words had a strange tone, like worry was pushing them through the door.

"Just a minute." Aiden got out of bed and looked around the room for his t-shirt. He'd only been in the parish for a week. The lack of sleep kept him from gathering his clothes with ease. At Abraham's house, with Elidad, he knew right where he would've left his shirt. Rubbing the sleep out of his eyes, he caught a glimpse of it lying across the chair in the corner. When he opened the door Joseph's face was as white as the shirt he'd just pulled over his head. "What can I do for you, Joseph?"

"I need you to come with me, quickly. Please."

An elevated pitch emanated from under the fenders of Father Joseph's car when they came to a stop kitty-corner to an apartment building. Parking the car on the street, the priests walked down the block towards the entrance. It was an older building but its white paint was clean and the fire escape didn't look rickety. A green canvas, worn by weather, shaded the front doors from the street lights. It wasn't ripped or tattered, just slightly askew in color, hinting its age.

"So what are we doing here?" Aiden asked, hoping for an explanation.

Joseph's eyes shifted. "Last night I came to this apartment to visit a family from our church. Their daughter, Emily, has been ill. It was late when they called, but her parents asked if I would come over and pray with them. Emily's been sick for months. Her doctors are at a loss. None of them can figure out what's wrong with her. The mother was a disaster. I'm pretty sure they think Emily is in her final days.

"After the parents and I prayed together, they urged me to go in and see Emily. She was lying in her bed." Joseph rubbed his fingers against the palms of his hands at the memory. "She's pale and her body looks frail. Dark rings under her eyes make her look deathly. Honestly, I thought it looked like her parents have been starving her."

"Are they?" Aiden asked. The elevator they were waiting for opened. The two men entered.

Joseph pushed the button for the eighth floor. "I don't think so. They're good people. I've known them for years."

"Sometimes good people do bad things. Just because they're good to *you*, doesn't mean they can't abuse their child," Aiden said.

"They told me she refuses to eat. There was a tray of food in her room." Joseph's hand went through his hair like ruffling it would shake loose the answer to what was wrong with Emily. "But when I spoke to her, she hid her face from me like an abused child might. She was definitely acting strange. She wouldn't look at me. She's never been like that . . . she knows me, she's always talked to me."

Joseph was four years older than Aiden, making him thirty, but the concern weighing down his brow made him look older. In the first week of his new job Aiden found out he was close in age to Joseph, but hadn't found out where he was from. Aiden guessed Joseph was Italian, his Brooklyn accent and dark features gave him away.

Joseph continued his story. "Emily got out of bed and stood in the corner when I spoke to her. I told her I was going to pray with her and that praying would help. She appeared to understand, so I began to pray. She started screaming." Joseph's eyes looked empty, taken hostage by memory. "Her parents came bursting through the door like I was hurting her. Thank God I was standing on the opposite side of the room." Joseph turned, locking eyes with Aiden. "There's something *wrong* with her. Her parents are afraid to be in the same room as her. I could *feel* it. They asked me to keep praying . . . they insisted. They were so desperate I couldn't say no. I began again. Emily started screaming like she did before. She ran and grabbed my arm, pleading with me to stop. She acted like I was hurting her." Joseph pulled his long sleeve back to reveal a distinct bruise on his forearm.

The shadow of a tiny hand on Joseph's arm made Aiden realize a cold sweat had moistened his palms. He wiped them on his pressed black slacks. "This happened just before you came to get me?"

"Yes, just over an hour ago. I don't bruise easily," he added.

The doors of the elevator opened.

Joseph was acting like he knew something more, but wasn't offering it. Aiden couldn't put all the clues together. It didn't sound like Emily was being abused.

Stepping into the hall lined with apartment doors, Aiden felt a rash of goosebumps tidal wave across his skin, climb up his neck, and wash past his knees. Carpet lined the floor, muffling their footsteps. It harbored a faint hint of mildew mixed with pet dander. Sounds of TV shows and conversations were a light hum behind some of the closed doors when they passed. Aiden looked at his watch. Two forty-six. How were these people still up?

Joseph escorted Aiden to a door and lightly knocked on it. They could hear footsteps inside. Aiden wasn't sure why, but his heart began to pound, almost loud enough to knock on the door itself.

A man three inches shorter than Aiden with a receding hairline answered, the chain still attached.

"Hello, Father," the man said, closing the door. The drag of metal on metal was amplified in the quiet hallway as he removed the chain and opened the door again.

Joseph introduced him. "This is Father Aiden."

"Hello," Aiden said.

"Thank you for coming, Father." The man stretched out his hand to shake Aiden's. "My name is Seth."

"Of course," Aiden answered, not sure what else to say.

"This way." Seth led them past the living room where a woman sat over her Bible with a rosary in her hand. She didn't bother to lift her head as the priests walked to the back of the apartment.

Seth stopped in front of a door. His fingers paused on the handle. Taking a deep breath, he cracked it open slowly. "Emily," Seth said softly. With no response, Seth moved into the room. Aiden and Joseph followed.

A white lamp with a green shade, sparkly fringe, and the image of Tinkerbell lit the room. Aiden's eyes went to the bed where he expected the sick girl to be. Empty. The white furniture contrasted the purple Disney princess comforter that lay across the mattress. A stuffed unicorn sat on a nightstand next to an untouched glass of water.

A movement caught Aiden's eye. Turning his head, he saw Emily's frail body. She couldn't be much older than eight. She was standing in the corner staring at the wall. The same feeling that prickled Aiden's skin earlier, made him shiver as he watched her. There was something about the way she stared into the layers of white paint, her finger tracing an imaginary line that made his heart pound against his ribcage.

"Emily . . ." Seth spoke softly to his daughter. "The Father is back to see you and he brought a friend."

"I don't want to meet him." The little voice came from behind her long dark hair.

Aiden wondered how she knew he was a *he* without looking in his direction.

Seth looked over his shoulder, like he needed reassurance to speak to Emily. Rubbing his hands on his pants he tried again.

"Emily, these men can help you."

Joseph was right. Seth look terrified of Emily.

"I said, I don't want . . ." Her face turned toward them. Her eyes were yellow and her voice became deep and animalistic. ". . . to meet him. I don't need their help." Her breath was raspy as she panted. Anger shook her body.

Aiden suddenly knew why they were afraid of Emily. There was no question in his mind.

She was possessed.

"Excuse me a minute," Aiden said, turning to leave the room with his extremities shaking. He rounded the corner and was by the front door when he heard Joseph behind him.

"Wait," Joseph said, grabbing Aiden's arm. "You can't leave."

Aiden frowned. "I'm not leaving," he said, withdrawing his cell phone from his pocket. Adrenaline surged through his hands as he scrolled though his recent calls.

"Are you calling *her*?" Joseph asked.

Aiden wondered how Joseph knew who *she* was as he selected Elidad's name.

ACKNOWLEDGMENTS

I thank God that people find enjoyment in my work.

Thank you to all my friends and family who've seen me through this crazy dream. Jim Hulett, thanks for letting me dream big, no matter how crazy it sounds. I love that you let me run with my ideas, and don't expect me to look back.

Kathryn Mattingly, you are an inspiring writing coach, amazing author, and a beautiful believer in people. I wouldn't be here without you.

I'd like to thank Winter Goose Publishing for being passionate enough about my writing to put their name on my work. I'd like to acknowledge the Central Oregon Writer's Guild where I met people who impacted my writing career in amazing ways. Without their support, I'd still be in a dark room writing for myself. Liz Sample, I appreciate your editing skills and the hours of discussion that kept me pushing forward on this project.

Zac Tennant, I owe you big time for the amazing book trailer! It's unbelievable to see my art and yours come together to inspire excitement about this project. You did a fabulous job. Shantae Knorr, John Kish, Faith Jacobs, Keith Peterson, and Simeon Purkey, thank you for bringing the characters to life and making the trailer what it is. I love that I live in a town where authors and actors can collaborate with a video production guy to produce something so special. I am truly blessed.

ABOUT THE AUTHOR

Novelist Eva Hulett has always been enchanted by the great outdoors in the state of Oregon where she was born and raised, and currently lives with her husband, their daughter, and a feisty Labrador. When they are not enjoying hiking, camping, and hunting, she and her husband spend their time running their two businesses in Sunriver Resort. Eva is a member of the Central Oregon Writers Guild, and was included in their *2015 Harvest Writing Winners Collection.*

CPSIA information can be obtained
at www.ICGtesting.com
Printed in the USA
FFOW05n1556090117